FORCES OF CHANGE

FORCES OF CHANGE

An Unorthodox View of History

Henry Hobhouse

COUNTERPOINT
BERKELEY

Library of Congress Cataloging-in-Publication Data

Hobhouse, Henry.
    Forces of change : an unorthodox view of history / Henry Hobhouse.
    p. ; cm.
    Originally published: New York : Arcade Pub., 1990.
    Includes bibliographical references and index.
    ISBN (10) 1-59376-075-2
    ISBN (13) 978-1-59376-075-5
    1. History, Modern. 2. Population. 3. Food supply. 4. Diseases and history. I. Title.

D210.H66 2005
909.08—dc22   2005042598

Text design by Gopa & Ted2, Inc
Cartography by Mike Morgenfeld, Kat Smith & Suzanne Service
Printed in the United States of America

COUNTERPOINT
2560 Ninth Street, Suite 318
Berkeley, CA 94710

www.counterpointpress.com

To all those unfortunates affected by the factors described in this book. They travail under incompetent, venal, and corrupt governments who do nothing for their people but steal everything they can for themselves and for other political beneficiaries.

Contents

LIST OF MAPS

NOTE TO THE 2005 EDITION

THIS EDITION OF *Forces of Change* is modified from the original, which was written more than fifteen years ago. Despite changes in statistics, the original thesis remains valid: The triangle of force—population growth, food supply, and disease—relate to and control each other.

In the last half century, the world population has more than doubled, but all of the increase has been in the Third World. But for the scourge of AIDS, malaria, and tuberculosis the increase would have been much greater, even if food supply were not an issue.

As this note is being written, there is a pledge by European politicians, inspired by populism, to "Make Poverty History." Can there ever have been an idea so lacking in intellectual content? The poor, as Our Lord told us, are always with us. They must be, since the poor are defined as the least well-off members of any society. In the First World of today, the poor are far richer than all but a very few people were in Renaissance Europe. In the Third World, the poor are the victims of historically bad governments. Fifty years ago oil-rich Nigeria (then oil-poor) was richer than South Korea. Today, Nigeria's national income per head, despite the oil, is one-tenth that of South Korea. No prizes for noting which country is a byword for Corruption and the resulting poverty.

This apparently inevitable confluence of corruption and attempts to alleviate the consequences of poverty is a serious problem for any country that suffers from real poverty; political slogans, inspirational do-gooders, and pop concerts cannot solve genuine destitution. The task to alleviate suffering is long-term and far too complex a matter for evening news analysis or celebrity solutions.

Introduction

A̲ll species try to multiply; it is their primitive yet continuous purpose. Mankind is no exception; indeed, *Homo sapiens* has become almost unique in an ability to attempt reproduction at any time, any place, anywhere. This awesome capacity has been canalized by custom and history into either marriage or love or both. The urge should not be underrated or its effects discounted. The sublimation of this unique driving force may well have been responsible for much of mankind's artistic and intellectual achievement. Or so we are told.

The subject of this book is more fundamental, and its theme more brutal. Every modern writer on population has agreed that all species have the capacity to multiply beyond any available food supply. It is mankind's unique quality to be able to increase the supply of food. Thomas Malthus, the first great writer on population, was led by his lack of faith in that ability (correct at the time) to doubt, along with many others, mankind's demographic future. Most of the history of the past five hundred years would be wholly different if the ability to increase the food supply had not been developed. Those people who have this ability have an advantage that remains of vital importance, however sophisticated the world may appear to have become. After population growth, provision of food is the second great force in human history.

The third great force in human affairs has been disease, but disease is helpless in a desert. Any gardener or farmer knows that disease is a function of high populations. The solitary rose does not incur fungoid troubles as easily as an individual plant that is one of many; similarly, a sheep's worst enemy is another sheep; humans only begin to suffer significantly from disease when populations reach a certain density. That is why this book starts about five hundred years ago. At that date in, say, 1492, Europe and Asia had only just recovered from the effects of the plague, known in England as the Black Death. It was the last time that the population of the world declined. From a global total population of about 360 million in 1340, loss from the plague was immense—10–15 percent of the world population. Recovery in numbers did not take place until the middle of the fifteenth century. By 1492, the human population of the earth was just over 400 million. Today, it is over six billion, or nearly seventeen times as much. The population of Western Europe is only about six times as much; less than half the increase of the world as a whole, but Western Europe, a mere 2 percent of the world's land area, has been largely responsible for the increase in the rest of the world. There are three reasons why this is so.

First, many of the useful edible plants in the world are indigenous to Western Europe; so are the animals. Second, while ships, guns, and navigational instruments were all available to Chinese or Arab precursors, it was Renaissance Europeans who brought them together and made of the opportunity trade and dominion over both hemispheres. With their unconscious agents, plants, animals, and diseases, Western Europeans conquered first the Americas, then Oceania, then most of Africa and half of Asia. This was unprecedented.

It may be coming to an end since the most "successful" non-European powers in the Far East challenge not only Europe, but also the most successful neo-Europe—the United States of America.

Finally, it is Europe and the neo-Europes that have checked diseases, then "cured" some of them. One disease has been "abolished." Others, less susceptible to human cleverness, have changed their character; yet others have recently been transferred from animals or been generated in some way not wholly understood.

The first theme of this book is the Triangle of Forces formed by population growth, food supply, and disease. Excessive population growth used to be answered automatically by food shortage, starvation, or famine until mankind found out how to increase food supply. This option is not open to hunter-gatherers who have no more opportunity to find abundance than predatory lions who follow game; or curious, ingenious monkeys who seek fruit and nuts; or stately, gracious whales who have to loiter close to their food, ingesting krill. Modern man grows food and trades and exchanges it for other goods, and that makes him unique among animals.

Together with other differences, human attitudes to food make advanced *Homo sapiens* wholly distinct.

However sophisticated and remote from fuel food may have become in the Western world, it still represents by far the most important human activity. More time and effort are spent on growing, transporting, distributing, marketing, preparing, cooking, serving, and eating food than on any three other human activities put together, apart from sleeping. Sleeping, on the other hand, offers few opportunities for entrepreneurial activity, historical imperatives, or world-shaking trends.

Disease, which is the subject of the first chapter, operated for centuries as an automatic system, controlling populations of every sort of plant and animal; humans were no exception. Disease is a much more merciful control system than famine. Death from most diseases is far kinder than starvation.

Disease also has three other characteristics. The first is that disease trims, reduces, and selects populations. As a population control, disease has been far more significant than warfare, even as recently as World War II. Disease is a means of selection; in earlier times adults had to be survivors, not just of modern "childhood" diseases such as measles or chicken pox, but also of pandemic killers. Apart from anything else, this favored people who preferred to be solitary rather than gregarious. Other characteristics will occur to the reader.

The second point about disease was that it discouraged urban development. Even the best managed ancient and medieval cities consumed people, a real percentage of the population every decade. Until this century, the death rate in some cities was, at a minimum, double that of the surrounding countryside. In others, the death rate was five times higher. In addition, birthrates were lower. In effect the city was incapable of survival without continuous demographic reinforcement from the hinterland, and cities of any size were, therefore, rare. When pandemics appeared, populations declined dramatically. Those left behind were those the least likely to be able to move: the poor, the old, the halt, and the blind. Plagues, therefore, acted differentially upon urban populations. The mobile, rich, young, fit, and fancy-free escaped by leaving the seat of infection. This pattern existed in Roman times and was repeated as recently as the late nineteenth century in places subject to yellow fever, for example, a disease not only of cities, but also of human density.

Finally, disease was a magnificent agent of Imperialism. This effect started as soon as Columbus arrived in the Caribbean in 1492 and continued until white man's disease had conquered the Earth. Smallpox performed wonders for the *conquistadores*. Malaria invaded and weakened resistance throughout the Americas where smallpox had not subdued the population. Measles, influenza, and the enteric disorders weakened native peoples with whom white men came into contact. Diseases were transported by mankind both ways across oceans, almost all since 1492. Columbus took with him malaria, smallpox, and measles and brought back syphilis. The slave trade took yellow fever and *Falciparium* malaria from West Africa to the Americas and then to the rest of the world. Every conceivable white man's disease was taken to Australia, a continent far too empty of humans to support much indigenous disease. Both Australia and the Amazon Basin, an area only slightly smaller, were thinly populated, yet huge populations were killed by white man's diseases, until the number of native peoples probably fell to one-fifth of what they had been. This kind of loss—as much as 80 percent of a population, had never been experienced as a result of war or famine. It is arguable that, without disease in their armory, Europeans could never have conquered the world.

As a matter of fact it was Europe and the neo-Europes in the Americas as well as Africa and Oceania that provided the great increase in population during the period 1776–1890. This was for two reasons. One was trade and dominion, which lifted many non-European peoples out of subsistence agriculture. Second, Europeans spread improved methods of food production all over the world, improving European diets dramatically and the diets of non-Europeans by a significant potential. (Not all non-Europeans took advantage of these opportunities, but they still existed.) Finally, Europeans brought huge new areas of the world into cultivation, sometimes for the exclusive benefit of European crops, but also by necessity for the benefit of the natives.

The nineteenth century is, above all, a hundred years of improved food supply, better technology, improved transport of every kind, and the application of intellectual effort to what had been traditional processes. This metamorphosis is often called "scientific," but it was

frequently the case that Europeans missed the essentials of a successful local practice and had to reinvent a native procedure to make the
sowing of maize or the culture of bananas or the preparation of rice or
cassava possible in new situations.

The early twentieth century, when world population reached 1.6–
1.75 billion, was a time of intellectual optimism with boundless faith
in the beneficent possibilities of science. A hundred years ago, there
was no doubt that progress was possible, that intellectual effort was
continually making life better; there was no danger foreseen in the
growth of population. Malthus, so fashionable in the early years of the
nineteenth century, and proved correct at the time of the Irish famine
in 1845, was made foolish by the success of, for example, the Irish in the
Americas and in Australia where they were breeding (and surviving) at
double the rate of the highest population increase in Europe. This was
not in Ireland, which was unique in the Old World, perhaps, in having a
population reduced by nearly half between 1845 and 1890. Europe as
a whole was increasing its population by more than 1 percent a year,
and the neo-Europes by two or three times that figure. This was partly
because there was so much less disease than in the home continent.
More importantly, for the first time in history there was ample food of
a high quality. Because of a manpower shortage in the neo-Europes,
people were cherished in a way that made children welcome, nurtured
and brought up as the finest physical specimens the world had ever
seen. Physical fitness is commonplace today, but a hundred years ago
it was a revelation to Europeans how much fitter the neo- Europeans
were than their kin left at home. Neo-Europeans were not only fitter,
longer- lived, rearing more children, but they also provided Europe
with an increasing proportion of its food.

The restraints of disease and starvation have been largely eliminated; conventional warfare is a much overrated means of population
control. World Wars I and II were mere blips on the demographers'
charts; in both wars, disease and malnutrition were more significant
causes of death than enemy action. In the conventional war between
Iraq and Iran in 1980–88 one million were killed, but during the same
period the two countries together have enjoyed a population increase
of not less than five million net despite the war.

Nuclear, chemical, and biological warfare are different matters. In these cases, non-combatant death rates could make serious inroads into populations, but the consequences are so fearful that great powers shy away from using these weapons. The existence of nuclear weapons since 1945 has had the virtue of preventing great power conflicts of a violent nature. Nevertheless, great powers have seldom united to prevent lesser powers from fighting; indeed, many small wars are proxy wars between agents of the great powers.

Great powers have, by definition, retained the initiative as far as weapon technology is concerned so that the nastier means of killing remain in few hands. There is one present exception to this rule: An estimated 20–30 sovereign nations outside Europe and the neo-Europes are capable of making chemical weapons of a very unpleasant nature. With a worldwide increase in biological engineering, the same sort of dispersal will exist in biological weapons by, say, 2010. By that time, a very serious non-nuclear war could be possible, killing huge numbers of people by genetic means. It will also be possible to engage in what has loosely (and wrongly) been called "genocide" in the past.

"Genocide" has usually been practiced only unconsciously: guilty parties may have included actions with political motives, but disease, starvation, and changes in environment have also taken their toll, leading to significant losses. Three-quarters of the Amazon tribes have probably been eliminated; so have perhaps half of the Aborigine groups in Australia and many discrete tribal peoples in West Africa. Primitive peoples who carved out a survival niche for themselves as hunter-gatherers or Stone Age survivors or Iron Age farmers were not capable of resisting whites. Hundreds of individual species of plants and animals have also disappeared. This is an inevitable accompaniment of change; it may be a mistake to blame only Europeans for these losses. Perhaps they would have happened in any case, without record, in the absence of human presence.

The third strand in this book, after the Triangle of Forces and the notable success of Western European diseases, plants, animals, and men, is the question of challenge and response. Certain peoples have been significantly more successful than others in overcoming disease and the problem of food supplies. Far more than any other factor, land use has dictated the very nature of nations. Three specific examples are treated at some length: the United States, Russia, and Japan. The argument must be allowed to speak for itself, but without straining the logic it is clear that the forces of population growth, food supply, and disease have operated in quite a different fashion in each country, to produce three very specific cultures.

All through this book it is assumed that good food produces a long-term advantage for those people who have enjoyed a better diet than others. Primitive men settled often, for other reasons, on the seashore and on riverbanks. Unconsciously they found chemicals necessary for the development of brains together with high-quality proteins and polyunsaturated fat. Successful peoples have had significantly better diets than unsuccessful peoples ever since. There is a rather strong modern correlation between protein quality—often fish—and group progress, whether expressed in terms of economic growth, science, technology, management skills, or whatever.

This point has not been heavily stressed throughout this book, but is assumed; several kind people who have read the draft have suggested that more should be made of this argument. Unfortunately, as with the inefficiencies of food supply in feudal village communities, or the improvement in protein quality in Renaissance Europe, or the serious long-term chronic shortages of food in France of the *ancien régime*, there are no quantities to make the contention numerate. A dozen graduate researchers working a lifetime each could not help. People did not, in most of history, record what weight of what edible products they ate. Ingestion statistics have only been available in most countries very recently. Even then, no one ever knows what was wasted in cooking, left on the plate, given to pets, or thrown out as swill or rubbish. It is generally true that many other people could survive, if necessary, on what the modern rich discard; the better the cuisine, the greater the waste; the poorer the society, the lower quality the detritus and (usually) the thinner the rats.

It is the pollution of the modern world that will produce an alternative control to diseases that have been "cured," and to hunger, starvation, and famines that have been defeated. There are three important problems already threatening mankind that have become obvious only in the past decade. They are the greenhouse effect, the destruction of the ozone layer, and acid rain. It is possible that mankind will drown in his own ordure; this will be true if the causes of pollution are not arrested and reversed rather rapidly. There are not only too many people in many parts of the world, but they are consuming too much; less than 20 percent of the world's population probably live in a way that truly could be called sustainable. Such lives would be regarded by most "advanced" people as mind-bendingly boring, and thus unacceptable. On the other hand, increases in consumption at the rate of the last hundred years are wholly impossible to imagine for the next twenty years, let alone the next hundred. A century ago, there were just over one-quarter as many people alive as today. Each person in the world then used only one-tenth, on average, of the fuel we use today, so the same Earth consumes and has to recycle waste products forty times the tonnage of a hundred years ago. In some parts of the world there is no chance that ecosystems can deal with the present problems. It is inconceivable that there should be increases in consumption comparable to those of the last hundred years; these increases lead directly to pollution in what is perhaps an irreversible way.

This book, like my first book, *Seeds of Change*, is not written to persuade; it is not intended to be didactic; readers are invited to make up their own minds. The evidence is presented, and it would be foolish to ask people to agree with a thesis that would have to be serpentine to cover every aspect of history since 1492. For that reason, each chapter is freestanding, written to be an open window on its time. People can look through the window and appreciate the view—but they are not expected to share the perspective without question.

CHAPTER ONE

Ill Winds Across the Land and Sea

Disease has only been a recognized historical factor in recent years. Links between disease, population growth, and food supply have never been made plain: it is the purpose of this book so to do.

This chapter starts with the Black Death, which is considered here to be the most important single event between the fall of Rome and the Renaissance. It was not, of course, "a single event" like a great battle, but both cause and effect rumbled on for a century, having very wide implications for the whole of Western Europe in particular. The disease was like a pebble thrown into a pond, the circles of ripples becoming larger and larger before their force faded.

Disease is far more lethal than warfare. For example, if the Spaniards alone had solved the hygiene problem at sea, the outcome of the Armada would have been reversed. Disease has killed many more people, even if only measured during wars, than all the actions of mankind put together.

Disease was the means by which the Europeans conquered the New World. This began with Columbus's arrival in the Caribbean in 1492, and the process continues whenever whites meet a virgin tribe, in the rain forest of the Amazon or some other "undiscovered" place today.

Disease "cured" has upset an automatic system that not only trimmed and selected populations, but also kept in some kind of balance food supply and population growth. Disease cured has thrown great strains upon Third World food supplies.

Finally, there is the remarkable case of the incurable virus, which changes its very character. The common cold and influenza defeat the doctors. A more recent problem is HIV, which gives rise to AIDS. There is now more than a hint of a suggestion that "new" diseases might take the form of attacking the immune system itself, not the antibodies produced by the immune system. This would be a chilling reminder of the potential impotence of arrogant mankind on an overcrowded earth.

For a hundred years or more, two men have greatly influenced thinking about population growth and natural selection, if not disease. Since they are mentioned throughout this book, it is appropriate to add a note about them here.

THOMAS ROBERT MALTHUS *was born in Surrey, England, in 1766. His father was a country gentleman, a "progressive" of the day, and a friend (and executor) of Rousseau. Malthus the younger became a Ninth Wrangler at Cambridge and was elected Fellow of Jesus College in 1793; in 1797, he became curate of Albury, Surrey. The first edition of his* Essay on the Principle of Population *was published in 1798. There were six further editions during his lifetime, each being more restrained than the last. The impulse for the work was his father's absurd optimism about prospects for the human race. Roughly, father Malthus, like many "social" liberals since, believed that human beings could be made happy, useful, and productive by legislation. Malthus presented for the first time the perception that "progress" was unlikely because of the inherent limitations of the food supply. The tendency of mankind's progenitive capacity to outrun food supply was the basis of his argument. A kind, rather jolly man, happily married, Malthus would have been horrified if he could have known the use that would be made of his name in the word "Malthusian." His book on population, however, triggered off one essential clue in Darwin's mind (see below). Malthus, a benevolent and amiable man, survived until 1834, as a "Professor of Political Economy" at Haileybury College, an institution that prepared young men for service in the East India Company. As far as is known, he never met Darwin.*

CHARLES ROBERT DARWIN *lived from 1809 to 1882. Both the Darwin family, and his mother's family, the Wedgwoods, were intellectuals of power. He read medicine at Edinburgh, then natural history at Cambridge. On graduation he was appointed naturalist on the HMS Beagle. The trip took nearly three years, 1831–34, and included Tenerife, Cape Verde, Brazil, Buenos Aires, Monte Video, Tierra del Fuego, Valparaíso, the Galapagos, Tahiti, New Zealand, and Tasmania. In the Keeling Islands on the way home, Darwin enunciated his famous theory about coral that contains the germ of natural selection. Married to his cousin, Emma Wedgwood, Darwin was a country gentleman, FRS, and practical animal breeder; he did not rush into print. The embryo of his theory was formed in 1835–38, the first notes made in 1842–34, the first paper read before the Linnean Society in 1853. The great book*

On the Origin of Species by Means of Natural Selection *was published in November 1859. Malthus's theory of population led Darwin to believe that "Natural selection was the inevitable result of the rapid increase of all organic beings." Thus Malthus inspired Darwin, and their ideas march together through this book.*

The Black Death: The First European Experience

THE WILDLY SUCCESSFUL Black Death plague sent deep reverberations through Europe. The labor shortages caused by its effect on populations across the continent brought about some of the most fundamental changes in social organization since the fall of Rome. In about 1300 the ratio of food to population of Western Europe was at an (unknown) level of danger. There were local famines in most years between 1290 and 1350, and most of Europe was affected during the years 1314–17. Perhaps the whole of Western Europe was as badly off between 1300 and 1350 as Ireland was between 1800 and 1850; Eastern Europe was less affected, less densely occupied. The limits of technology and husbandry had been reached in the West. There was little hope for the people except for cycles of famine, death, population growth, famine, death, and so forth. It was the classic Malthusian situation, yet unrecognized.

Into this time of great misery came the Black Death, arriving in Kaffa in the Crimea in 1346 and reaching France, Italy, Spain, and the rest of the Mediterranean coastline during 1348, hitting Atlantic countries during the following year. Finally, the plague reached the Northeastern North Sea and the Baltic in 1349–50. In each country, the plague fanned inward from the ports. It took many months to reach the Volga-Don trade route in Russia. Some parts of Eastern Europe, modern Ukraine for example, escaped the worst effects. In most of Western Europe, the death rate was on the order of 40 percent; but the most densely populated places suffered the greatest loss. The carrier of the 1346 outbreak was the black rat, *Rattus rattus*. The black rat is not alone in being a plague carrier; there are other potential hosts. In Asia there are tarbagons, marmots, and susliks; in Africa, gerbils and mice; in North America, prairie dogs and ground squirrels. In the early fourteenth century, the reservoir of infection was in the Yunnan area of China; the plague was disturbed and distributed by the Mongols. The black rat, an animal that always lives close to mankind, became a host through the Mongols, living in the saddlebags of mounted nomads, in the ships of merchants and warlike sailors, in the cottagers' thatched roofs, in bales of merchandise, and in ricks of grain.

Pasteurella pestis, the Black Death, bubonic plague, is still with us. It is endemic in certain rodents, harmless to them like a childhood disease. For mankind it is a killer. It kills today as it did in 1346 when it first arrived in Europe. In the most recent outbreaks in 1947, just before the discovery of antibiotics, a higher percentage of the sick died than did in the original outbreaks in 1346–51.[1]

The Black Death was caused by what was recognized, in about 1900, as a complicated cycle. The disease does not depend upon any human as part of the cycle. It does depend upon certain sorts of rodents and certain sorts of fleas. From the point of view of the disease, the black rat (*Rattus rattus*) and the rat flea (*Xenopsylla cheopis*) are the ideal methods of propagation. What happens during infection was only really defined accurately in the period 1900–20.

The flea preferred as host lives on warm-blooded animals. It is small (about 3 mm long), wingless, can cling to all types of surfaces because of hooks on its six limbs, and feeds upon only its preferred host. Hence, the rat flea prefers rats; the cat flea, cats; the dog flea, dogs; and in only the most exceptional circumstances is it likely that a particular flea will abandon its host. Fleas, like aphids, are particular parasites. Is it ignorant hysteria for a modern mother to become upset about fleas on the family pet? Or is it some deep-seated tribal feeling about the Black Death?

There have been more than twenty generations since the Black Death. Before the middle of the fourteenth century, there was no flea-borne disease to compare in horror with *Pasteurella pestis*, although probably 90 percent of the population carried fleas and other parasites, such as lice. The rat flea and its habits probably changed human toleration toward the lice, fleas, and nits that humans have carried since time immemorial.

When a plague-infected rat or other rodent dies, the fleas leave the corpse as the body temperature falls. If temperature and humidity are suitable, fleas may remain without a host for at least fifteen days. During that time, they become hungrier and hungrier, and, if they are heavily infected, ravenous.

The peculiar effect of the bacillus on the infected mammal is to create massive, fulminating, overwhelming septicemia. This is true of an infected human or an infected rat, both of which often die. Septicemia in the flea, however, does not foreshorten the insect's life. The bacilli multiply in the stomach of the flea, and the stomach gradually becomes blocked. Because the stomach is blocked, it does not nourish the flea, so the insect becomes not only stuffed with a solid mass of bacteria, but also very hungry because it is deriving no nourishment from the blood it is sucking. Ravenous because the stomach is blocked by the mass of multiplying germs, fleas jump off the dying host, the rat, onto any convenient warm-blooded animal that happens to be about. Horses, cows, camels, donkeys, and dogs, all attract fleas in this "blocked" condition; the plague bacillus does no harm to these animals, but when the flea chooses a human as an alternative host, matters are very different.

Because the digestive system of the flea is "blocked" the flea is, as has been explained, very hungry. This makes it an active bloodsucker, taking up to ten times as much blood per day as is normal. None of the blood reaches the flea's stomach, or nourishes it in any way, however, and it continues to suck blood until its gullet is distended and full. At this point the flea disgorges the blood, now infected with the bacillus that is blocking the stomach of the flea, back into the wound. Finally, the flea automatically defecates as it eats the blood, and some of this detritus is deposited on the punctured skin of the mammal whose blood is being sucked. There cannot be a more elegant way of spreading a disease. If the bacillus *Yersinia pestis* were capable of designing a method of self-propagation, the habits of the flea would come high on the list of available means. Any designer bacillus would probably decide that no further work could improve on that which was already available.

As has been noted, the flea feeding on other mammals than man may or may not transmit the bacillus, but the bacillus does little harm to other animals. It does not kill even as many rodents as it does humans.[2] The bacillus does not seem to benefit from life on many kinds of rodents: Rabbits, hares, and gray squirrels are not useful hosts.

When a human is infected with plague, the incubation period is from two to eight days. The number of bacilli is initially small and attracted to the lymph glands that are concentrated in the armpit, neck, and groin. In the Middle Ages, groin swelling was the commonest symptom of Black Death, perhaps because fleabites were more likely to be on the legs. This manifestation of lymphatic swelling in the groin is what gave the Black Death its name, "bubonic plague," from "*Bubo*," the Greek word for groin. The lymphatic swellings become very large and very painful. If the patient survives, the swellings may discharge like boils, and if the patient survives as long as fourteen days, they may burst. Of course the patient may suffer from a more rapid buildup of the bacilli. In such cases, massive septicemia sets in, as occurs in the rat; and cases were known of men retiring at night feeling fit and being dead in the morning. Such a systemic attack by the organism is not unknown in other diseases, but it was the dramatic deaths of so many apparently healthy people that so impressed survivors of the Black Death and all the subsequent attacks of the plague.

There is one other curiosity. The flea can take in large numbers of bacilli and transmit the bacteria from man to man, although this hardly ever happens. The rat, specifically the black rat, is an almost essential vector, except when the bubonic plague takes the form of a kind of pneumonia. Coughs and sneezes spread disease, most notably this one.[3]

Ultimately it was established that the plague takes four forms, all from the same original bacillus.

The first form is an established infestation in the groin and other lymphatic areas such as around the neck and in the armpits.

In a second form, exactly the same bacteria produce a more rapid result and more rapid success (for the disease). This form takes the course of a violent septicemia that can kill some sufferers in a few hours at its worst, and within a few days at its best. In this form, the lymphatic glands are overwhelmed and unable to resist the onset of the infection effectively. Lymph glands characteristically swell when they are fighting invading organisms, just as the whole body exhibits a rise in temperature when it is fighting infection. In this way a disease that overwhelms a patient may do so without causing any notable swelling of the lymph glands.

The third form takes the course of a violent lung infection. This form, the pneumonic, has symptoms similar to other forms of lung infection. Unlike ordinary pneumonia, the expectation of death from pneumonic plague is 100 percent, and that within two days. The grim difference between bubonic plague and so-called pneumonic plague is that the disease in the lung produces a far quicker death, and the pneumonic form does not require the intervention of fleas or rats.

With the bubonic form, 10–20 percent of victims survive; those who are dying often have a period of up to fourteen days to face the future, and are not in any way infectious during the crisis. Anyone could nurse bubonic plague: It was neither infectious nor contagious. Pneumonic plague, however, was, during the Middle Ages, a death sentence to anyone within range of the patient's coughing, breathing, or spitting.

No one originally knew that the three forms described here were three manifestations of the same organism at work. There is also a fourth form, originally thought to be a different disease. The so-called pestis minor is, in fact, a simpler matter. This "disease" occurs when the body's resistance to the bubonic infection successfully defeats the bacillus. This happened in a minority of cases, and the proportion did not appear to change much in the six hundred years during which the plague was observed. Unlike measles or smallpox, the Black Death did not become milder during the time it was observed by increasingly skilled and better-equipped doctors, health workers, and pathologists. In technical language, the disease did not attenuate.

Between 1347 and the first use of antibiotics against the plague in 1947 there were over one hundred recorded outbreaks known to European history. There may have been several hundred others. Deaths in the first wave, before 1360, varied widely, but if modern experience[4] is anything to go by, the death rate would not have been less than 30–40 percent over the whole continent of Europe. This average includes those areas that the plague did not touch.

Massive work has been done on the subject of births and deaths at the time, but most of it has been in England, with a few scholars working in Northern France. In the Mediterranean countries, death rates could have been much higher than in England where they were about 35 percent. In much of Europe east of the Rhine and north of the Alps, no parish records have survived and no convincing estimates have been made of either birth or death rates. There were recurrences of the plague in every European country, and at least four more waves of infection everywhere in the century following the first wave of 1346–50.

The Black Death is important for a number of reasons. It is the first plague of which subsequent centuries have any clear idea of cause, effect, and numbers affected. It radically altered the nature of life for the survivors. The creation of a shortage of workers, particularly skilled urban workers, changed the relationship of people to money, gold, land, or any other store of value. (The same sort of process occurred in the third century AD in the Roman Empire, and with much the same effect. We have no data on the cause, which may have been a disease.)

Before the plague of 1346, the fashionable Christian religion was much in tune with the teachings of St. Thomas Aquinas. An easy man to love, Aquinas formed a synthesis of the principle of truth. He held that authority was revealed by the human senses and by experiment, and by experience as well as faith. He died in 1274 and was canonized a few years before the Black Death. How could the optimistic, rational system of Aquinas stand up to the huge death rate caused by an inexplicable organism that no one could see or attach in any way to fleas, rats, or ships? Fatalism, superstition, and fear replaced faith and reason; and the incipient Renaissance was delayed for at least a hundred years.

In the absence of any rational explanation for the plague and the horror of the inexplicable, reason itself went out of fashion. It was not a question of a "sleep of reason," but of a much more serious flight from the intellect. The inexplicable could only be made acceptable by means of fatalism, the will of God, and millennialism—the idea that the world is about to end and the Kingdom of Heaven is at hand.[5]

There was a considerable difference in the death rates of various classes. The Second Plague of 1362 and the Third Plague of 1369–70 killed more children, more priests, and more landed gentry than the First, which was noted for its effect upon the aristocracy. There were, of course, many more outbreaks of the plague. In England, where it is easiest to check the records, there were outbreaks in 1375, 1379, 1381–82, 1383, 1387, 1390, and 1399–1400. In the fifteenth century there were nearly as many local or regional epidemics. There were nineteen, including the outbreak of 1470–71, which rivaled the second and third plagues. In Southeast England mortality reached 20 percent in 1471.[6]

Superficially, life went on. The Hundred Years War with France (1337– 1453) was not significantly interrupted; the War of the Roses in England (1455–85) was fought against the plague background. In the Mediterranean the rivalries between Italian cities, between Latin and Greek, Guelph and Ghibbeline, Muslim and Christian, continued. The long-term change was under the surface.

Response to labor shortage was vital. In the West, depopulation of rural areas also depopulated the cities since it was the rural areas that made good the non-plague losses of the cities. Marginal grain areas ceased to be cultivated as arable and were often converted to timber, vines, and permanent pasture. In England the area devoted to sheep probably multiplied by three, thus dealing with the shortage of labor as well as the unprofitability of grain-growing on unsuitable land; in sandy Norfolk, new grassland produced a proverb—"Sheep's hooves turn sand to gold."[7]

In Western Europe, the more servile aspects of serfdom came to an end, and the manorial system, already sick, went into a terminal economic decline; rents, taxes, and wages all became more important than service to the feudal lord. The modern economic system, based on cash, began to be important in the Western rural economy. Wool provided work that became the northern equivalent to wine as a sophisticated trade.

In the East, the response to the shortage of laborers, the depopulation of rural areas, and the "disenchantment" of German scholars was quite different. Poland, Prussia, and Hungary became great grain-growing areas, exporting grain to the West via the river systems of the Oder, Vistula, and Danube. Serfdom was actually instituted in parts of Eastern Europe only after the Black Death. In some parts of the West, a hundred years of plague led to an increasingly free peasantry, as for Shakespeare's yeoman of England, for example. In the East, there were places where free peasants became tied to the soil, serfs until the French Revolution and after.[7]

In the South, in the Mediterranean, depopulation was in many ways a beneficial agent of change. Timber recovered as pressure on marginal land eased. Specialized profitable crops developed, yielding a higher return per worker: silkworms in mulberry trees, stone-fruit trees and olives under-planted with vegetables for adjacent town markets, increased areas of sugarcane in Southern Italy and Spain. Wine improved in quality, and trade in better food and drink became important.

For the first time in centuries agricultural emphasis was upon the output per man rather than output per acre, and this induced an increase in the size of individual holdings. Returns as a multiple of what was sown also increased as unsuitable land was no longer cultivated for grain. Yields per acre rose not because of improved husbandry, but because poorer fields were abandoned.

Technology became important as the means to multiply the effective labor of a smaller population: In England the capital value of mills, both water- and wind-driven, nearly doubled in the half-century after 1347. There was a net loss of thousands of skilled masons, a trade requiring a very long apprenticeship, and a conspicuous rise in wages. There was also a net gain of labor-saving devices—animal-driven appliances to multiply the power of diminishing mankind.

There is a point made by William McNeill, in his important book *Plagues and Peoples.*[8] The steppes of the Eurasian landmass became a great reservoir of plague, with the various rodents of the plains as foci of infection—China lost nearly half her population during the fourteenth century—but the plague also disconnected China from the West by destroying the old Silk Route. It was no longer safe for caravan travelers to cross the grasslands, since whenever they stopped they picked up the bacillus. The steppes themselves became denuded of people. The settlers at the edges, if they survived, became comparatively much stronger. There being no population pressure on the nomads, the invasions from Central Asia came to an end. Whether or not the Black Death was the cause, the Mongols were to be the last to invade Europe from the steppes.[9]

Flight from the Intellect after the Black Death was due not only to an excess of death amongst the higher clergy, but also to a lack of students.[10] In 1349 Europe had thirty universities; by 1400 twenty of them had closed. The pursuit of profit in this underpopulated continent became more popular (and more important?) than the pursuit of knowledge; there was a shortage of undergraduates as well as candidates for Holy Orders.

There were other equally serious shortages. To keep the universities going teachers were recruited from primary and secondary schools, so the general level of literacy fell. This had two effects. One was the obvious disconnection between ordinary people and the universities that became an important characteristic after the Renaissance. The other was more intriguing: People started to speak, write, and use the vernacular in preference to Latin; English became the official language of all law courts in 1363. In the same year the "Speech from the Throne" in parliament was given in English, not Latin. Norman French, like Latin, fell into disuse in England. French native languages superseded Latin in France and Teutonic tongues in Germany, Holland, and Scandinavia. Nationalism inevitably followed language; "aliens" like Jews were persecuted.

It was not only language that was liable to change. Hanseatic towns lost their supremacy to the Dutch and English; Bruges gave way to Antwerp. Transalpine trade became a preserve of Southern German towns like Augsburg, which developed as a great entrepôt. Only Venice, the richest city in the West, remained at the top, distancing herself in wisdom, wealth, and glory from any rival.

All over Europe the Black Death altered the tax base in this new materialist age of money. Land was no longer an absolute source of wealth. In the absence of manpower, land became worth relatively less. More than 10,000 villages disappeared in Western Europe. Some towns had lost half their people; in others more than half the houses were unoccupied. New taxes, like the English Poll Tax in 1381, produced violent, negative reactions not only in England, but also in France, Germany, and many Italian cities. The new values placed upon the worth of the individual were to point the way to a consultative, if not representative, government. This was certainly true of taxation in more than one country, and it was because of the substitution of money taxes for feudal dues that this became a truth.

No society readily accepts a change in the tax base.[11] The largest change in Western civilization was the substitution of money taxes for feudal service. In achieving this change, rulers of every Western country had to negotiate many kinds of accommodations with their people. The rider had to consult the horse. This anteceded by several centuries the idea that the horse should elect the rider. Throughout history, of course, horses have known which riders were best for them. In time, people of almost every Western country would achieve the same result by a variety of means. It was the Black Death that accelerated the process, initiated it, or planted the seeds of change among both rulers and their people.

It would be wrong to think of the Black Death as a discrete event occurring in 1346–50. The plague continued, on and off, for three hundred years, more in Continental Europe. The effects of the Black Death and its immediate epidemic, rather than pandemic, successors in many ways reinforced what was happening in any case: the emergence of the middle class, the end of serfdom in its more rigorous form, the laicization of society, the adoption of new methods of raising taxes that were more susceptible to the taxpayer's displeasure.

There were other effects that were unique to depopulation: the survivors better fed, the search for "labor-saving" devices, the silting up of rivers, the abandonment of marginal grain-growing land, and an ecological reversal—wild animals returning nearer to centers of population because of diminished densities of people in the countryside.[12]

The Black Death and its immediate successors were the most important causal agents in European history between the fall of Rome and the discovery of America. Nevertheless, however much influence can be ascribed to the huge death toll and its consequence, the alternative of famine must always be considered. The famine necessary to reduce the population to below its Malthusian ceiling of the early fourteenth century would have been a horror worse than any disease. Against such a famine, the plague was positively merciful.

After the plague had done its work, population densities were much lower. In terms of the population, Italy was still the most crowded at only 2.75 hectares (7 acres) per head. France, Germany, and the Low Countries were all placed between 5 and 5.5 hectares (12 and 13.5 acres) per head. Iberia, England, Austria, and Switzerland were less crowded, at about 6–7 hectares (15–17 acres) per head. Southern Scandinavia was emptier still at about 20 hectares (50 acres) per head.

These densities were much lower than today, but they restored populations to a sustainable degree of sustenance at the kind of output available from feudal husbandry. Grain yields returned to the levels of two hundred years before. The discomfort of excessive density was removed from huge areas. Famine no longer stalked the land one year in three, and hunger was no longer a familiar event every spring. Lent no longer needs literally to mean a very long fast. The clock, however, was not put back. Post-plague people were entirely different.

One change was in the distribution of the population.[13] The reasons for this were threefold. First, depopulation affected rural areas more drastically than it did the towns. Although the urban death rate was probably higher than in rural areas, there was always a post-plague surplus of rural adventurers ready to fill the vacancies in town. There was a continual migration into towns; thus fewer post-plague people were living in the country directly off the land. Meanwhile, a rising urban standard of life, not necessarily connected with lower populations, led to the demand for more economically attractive cash crops—commodities rather than plain bellyfill. There was a move away from subsistence agriculture and a conscious effort to meet the needs of the market, real or imagined. Wine, wool, flax, silk, hemp, sugar, fruit, and the vegetable dyes became important objects of trade. In the North, beer, made from hops and the newer sorts of barley, was substituted for ale, since beer, with hops acting as a preservative, is longer-lived and a better traveler.

Rural depopulation affected both man and the land. The serfs were no longer tied to the land in the way that dense populations had forced upon both common people and lords in pre-plague days. A man could command a money wage, and a lord could not hold a man without meeting those wages whatever the law might say. The medieval laws which sought to tie Western European men to the land were no more successful in the fourteenth and fifteenth centuries than the laws that Diocletian had sought to enforce in the third century AD.

Large landowners became rentiers, their rents expressed in money terms; thus they left subsistence and feudal dues far behind and counted their wealth in the same coin as the richer merchants. Despite nostalgic efforts to reestablish a bygone age with an excessive display of chivalry, tournaments, and the like, aristocrats and gentry adapted quickly to the new conditions; they had to or they sank, hardly nodding to the yeomen and merchants who were on their way up. Social conditions among landed classes in post-plague Europe were a great deal more mobile than in pre-plague times, when land, serfs, and produce were commoner indicators of wealth than gold.

The greatest change in this area was perhaps the most long-term and the least noticed at the time. In 1340, only the privileged eldest sons of the landed class obtained any part of the real property left by a deceased father; by 1500, most sons, and some daughters, were left a piece of land by inheritance. Thus did the plague work its long-term effects upon land tenure and the landed classes.

Pressure on the land itself had fallen dramatically since the pre-plague population crisis. Marginal areas fell out of cultivation. Mediterranean lands and the Central European Plain had been deforested before 1340 to grow subsistence crops. Huge tracts were allowed to fall back into scrub, then forest.[14] Surplus peasants from West Germany and the Netherlands were free to emigrate to Prussia, Poland, and the Baltic provinces. What had been thinly occupied by Teutonic knights warring against Slav chivalry became prosperous, a productive part of the European trading community. Western Europe was thinned out so much that wolves, which had been driven to the northern limits by heavy rural population density, returned to most of Germany, France, and Italy. They were reported in the suburbs of large towns like Paris, equivalent to modern urban foxes who rummage amongst the garbage.[15] The Black Death reversed the kind of population/density/excessive arable syndrome that impoverishes Africa today and beggared India before modern methods were adopted in the 1960s.[16] It is the paradoxical effect of a rise in real wages (making for a concentration on output per man) that produces a rise in output per acre. This is because poor land, requiring a disproportionate input of expensive manpower, is abandoned. This raises the yield per acre on what remains, and encouraged cultivation of fresh, new land.[17]

Above all, the survivors of six generations of plague, taking into account the effect of the selection process of the disease itself, produced by 1500 Europeans who were recognizably very different from those of pre-plague 1340. Novel devices began to be employed to save labor, with technology making up for the losses produced by depopulation. It was largely technology that made people richer, not only the fact that depopulation meant the abandonment of less profitable processes and means of production. Grinding mills of all kinds became much more valuable. Fish salted at sea by the Dutch after the plague made for cheaper, better fish and richer Dutchmen.[18] Increased demand for noble metals and precious gems at a time of declining manpower made technologically assisted mining essential. Pumps, gunpowder, and shaft-driving methods were all adopted, often just in time to transfer the techniques to the New World.

Literacy and numeracy became as essential in the business world of 1500 Europe as computer use is today. The art of printing came to Europe from China; eyeglasses were developed to help the weak of sight to read; arithmetic became a general discipline amongst merchants; the abacus was revived from its Greco-Roman, Arabic, or Chinese model and was in general use in countinghouses.[19] Paper halved in true cost between 1340 and 1500, and by the latter date had superseded vellum made from animal bellies, except for the most extravagant use.[20] Printing, paper, eyeglasses, the abacus, numeracy, and literacy were all necessary for the modern world. A sense of time became vital. The compass, the compass rose, and the astrolabe were essential; but clocks were still huge.[21]

The Black Death was as important in its effects on the intellect as it was in the material development of Western European mankind or in its side effects on the physical environment, particularly in the Atlantic countries. First of all, faced with catastrophe, humans reacted in at least two ways. One was to be stoical, resigned, or fatalistic; the other was to take precautions to avoid the worst effects of the plague. Inevitably, these were selfish; the development of a *sauve qui peut* mentality amongst all classes inevitably meant a parallel breakdown of the corporate, cooperative, community feeling of the early Middle Ages. Yet individualism, not always selfish or hedonistic, may also, at its finest, be wholly creative.

In Italy, post-plague individualism became humanism of a very high order and wholly necessary for the Renaissance. In the Netherlands, Flanders, and the Rhineland personal mysticism and individual piety developed long before the Reformation, and it is arguable that they were necessary for Luther's work to be done. Above all, perhaps, the decay of the old bonds, the weakening of much sense of collective responsibility, and the post-plague unreality of Church, Lord, and People prepared the Europeans for the modern age. In one sense, successful post-plague Europeans were selfish, pleasure seeking, infinitely materialistic, and pursued leisure through personal wealth. On the other hand, they sought to think for themselves, made curiosity a virtue, and questioned their contemporaries.[22]

What, during this terrible century of recurrent plague, was the Church doing? Was it promoting the freedom of mankind? Was it reacting, in an obscurantist way, to the works of Boccaccio or Chaucer?[23] Did the Church help or hinder the post-plague intellectual movement that became the Renaissance? What was the Church's intellectual contribution to post-plague society?

The earlier plagues of the Antonine era (AD 160–260) materially helped the Christian cause, since Christians were virtually the only people to offer charity and comfort to the sick and the dying. The mature Church in the fourteenth century signally failed to follow the example of the

Early Fathers. There was a high death rate among the monks and nuns in enclosed communities, and probably disproportionate casualties among the early plague villages where priests went about their visiting in the traditional way, spreading fleas, microbes, and death as they went. In the later outbreaks of that first plague year, in the north and east of England, priests and prelates sometimes cut and run; death rates at York, for example, were less than at Oxford a few months earlier. Many more left town in favor of the solitary life. Acquired wisdom dictated that being alone might be prudent; whether or not solitude was physically advantageous, it was devastating to the moral cause of the clergy. They had acquired merit from their courage in the Roman plagues. They were rightly thought to be cowards as a result of their prudence in the fourteenth century. Writers from William Langland to the village poet noticed the unworthiness of the higher clergy.[24]

Then there were the revenues of the Church. Overpopulation had meant famine, starvation, even cannibalism. Deaths after the 1350s led to a desperate hunt for tithes, for any kind of income from a stricken and impoverished population that would soon be visited by further plague epidemics. The Church, having failed its people, now sought to beggar them.

Finally, there was the question of medicine. Then, as now, the lay population was convinced that medical men should "cure" disease. This quaint notion rebounded upon the Church in a devastating way. By 1300 medical men were all licensed and taught by Church authorities, and there was little or no independence outside the creed of the "humours."[25] These beliefs were fixed, unquestioned, never subject to experiment. When up to half the population died in great pain and horrific squalor and no churchman or doctor of medicine could help, the intellectual reputation of the Church, its claim to omniscience, became risible. Already occasionally found to be without courage or charity, the Church now also lost its claim to wisdom, power, or knowledge.

Of course not every cleric was a coward, but the terrible inadvertent damage done by the plague to the Church was a necessary prerequisite to the Reformation. Without disrespect engendered by the post-plague behavior of the clergy, it is difficult to believe that the heirs of Hus or Wyclif would have proven to be Luther or Calvin.[26]

The bubonic plague, the Black Death, rumbled on and on. The most familiar late outbreak was in the Great Plague year of 1665 when London was struck for the last time. It was not unique in the world of the 1600s. There had been plagues in Europe of notable severity in 1603, 1609, 1625, 1636, and 1647. None of them, including the Great Plague of 1665, was as destructive as were the plagues in Lower Egypt in 1603, alleged to have killed a million people; there was an outbreak in Naples in 1656 that killed 300,000; a pandemic in parts of China in 1641 is said to have killed three million at the very least. These were more deadly than London's last attack, which killed only about 75,000.

Smallpox ultimately taught mankind the lessons of vaccination, although not before it had spread throughout Europe and Asia. Its most dramatic first effect, however, was as an unconscious weapon against the natives of the Americas. The Black Death was a visiting horror that appeared as an epidemic or as a pandemic; the Red Plague, however, was familiar, and occurred everywhere, all the time, throughout Eurasia. It was so familiar that almost everyone of, say, forty years of age had survived at least one attack. In some cities, it was comparable to a childhood disease like chicken pox, inoculating the survivors. It was the first disease for which Western man found an antidote, called "vaccination." It was the first disease that in 1981 the United Nations claimed was "abolished." It used to be called "smallpox," and like the Black Death, it changed history.

Identified in the ninth century by the Arab physician Rhazes in Baghdad, smallpox was confused with measles by Europeans at least as late as the Renaissance; so earlier outbreaks called Red Plague could be either smallpox or measles. In fact measles, which is related to rinderpest in cattle and to canine distemper, was just as lethal as smallpox in the early days, and for the same reason. Smallpox is, in turn, related to cowpox in cattle and several other diseases in other animals. Both measles and smallpox emigrated out of animals into people, as did most of the "successful" organisms in history.[27]

Smallpox and measles both produce rashes on the skin. Smallpox produces much larger pustules. Temperatures in smallpox cases can be as high as 40–41°C (104–105°F). The pulse is very quick; the fever is accompanied by heavy sweating; there is thirst, constipation, and a tendency to rigor. There can be convulsions. The disease is confirmed to be smallpox by the rashes in pocklike form on the face, trunk, and extremities. The pox marks on the face are often hideous and disfiguring. The pustules emit an offensive odor; the voice is hoarse, and there is often a copious and uncontrollable flow of saliva from the mouth. The fever abates when the pox appears, but a few days later it returns in a worse form. There is restlessness, delirium, and coma. If the patient survives to this point, there are other hazards. Septicemia may set in.

There is another form of the disease that involves septicemia at once, without pustules. It is of little comfort to the patient suffering from this form of the pox that death usually comes before disfigurement. Most people would prefer to live, even if disfigured for life.

It was the lack of disfigurement enjoyed by dairymaids who had caught cowpox from their charges that first alerted Edward Jenner to the possibilities of vaccination.[28] It was wrongly believed by Jenner that one vaccination would last for life instead of the six or seven years accepted by about 1900. Compulsory vaccination was adopted by Bavaria, Denmark, Sweden, and Massachusetts and five other States before the Battle of Waterloo (1815). By 1898 the whole of Europe and the United States required compulsory vaccination, although there were provisions for "conscientious objectors." In the smallpox outbreaks between 1900 and World War I, most of the casualties were among those who had conscientious objection to the vaccination process.[29]

Europeans took smallpox with them all over the world. In India and the Far East that made little difference, since there was just as much smallpox in Asia as in Europe. The disease is, of course, one of population density. The disease is virulently infectious, charging breath, saliva, blood, and clothing with the virus. Even a dead body remains infectious for weeks. It is, therefore, a disease of cities, ships, and armies; it was known in Mecca in AD 550, in South Europe by AD 590, and throughout Europe by 1250. It is likely, therefore, that it came from the more crowded parts of Asia, probably identified in China in AD 317. The recorded losses at that date from what may well have been smallpox in China amounted to about 30 percent of the population in thirty years.[30] Similar losses occurred in the first outbreaks in India, Arabia, and the Mediterranean. By 1492 the whole Eurasian landmass had an endemic of smallpox that was caught and survived by large numbers of children every year.

There were certain caveats. Dark-skinned people were said to be more susceptible than those who were fair. Once acquired, the disease was said to inoculate for life. Urban losses were far higher in cities that were untidy, badly drained, and so forth. The rich, of course, by reason of living in a less huddled situation, were less likely to catch the disease. Those who lived in warm countries were more susceptible to infection transmitted in higher, ambient temperatures. This was the reverse of the experience with the Black Death, where the inhabitants of Northern Europe were closer to the rats in the winter than in the summer. Smallpox, though, was much less devastating to the nomad than the Black Death, which lived in the rodent host. Smallpox, the Red Death, was dependent upon crowded, static mankind for its successful migration from host to host.

Smallpox was at its most effective when the virus was introduced to new, crowded communities innocent of any previous experience of the disease. The first epidemic in the Americas came in 1518 in Hispaniola, the island that is now divided into Haiti and the Dominican Republic. The inhabitants were said to number one million in 1498 when Columbus made permanent settlements, six years after his first voyage. No one, of course, knows who counted the Amerindians, but all the Spaniards agreed that they were feeble and simpleminded. In the absence of the sought-after gold, sugar was introduced in 1506; and one of the first shipments of African slaves in 1512. In 1520, the Spanish historian Bartolomé de Las Casas reported that only 1000 Indians had survived the Red Plague.

If so, then this would have explained to the Spanish how the victory in Mexico was achieved in the next few years. Smallpox landed with the relief expedition that sustained the Spanish *conquistadores* in 1521. Aztecs, bewildered by death as soon as they had contact with the Spaniards, and sharing with the Spaniards the belief that death from disease was an indicator of God's disapproval, surrendered to Hernando Cortés and about 600 Spaniards, plus a small number of Amerindian allies. In the case of Mexico City in the 1520s, it is clear that smallpox had found an ideal home. Mexico City had, perhaps, 60,000 homes in 1520, with a population of 300,000. Within a month of the siege, a third of the population was said to have smallpox, and another third were feeling unwell. In the end, Mexico probably lost 90 percent of its original population within a decade. Not all of these were victims of the Red Plague; there were losses from malaria, measles, and influenza. Yet as late as 1980, Spain was teaching in its schools that they had triumphed over the Amerindians because of a superior civilization, the use of horses and gunpowder, and the faith in victory that came from having God on their side. Even so, for 600 men to defeat an army of 100,000 and a nation of two to three million is carrying the superiority of the moral over the material a little far.

Smallpox had reached Guatemala by 1520 and the whole of the Spanish Main by 1526–30. Prepared for defeat by the arrival of Spanish pestilence before the actual invaders themselves, the Incas in Peru were no more of a match for Pizarro than the Aztecs had been in Mexico for Cortés.

The Spanish who arrived in Peru were virtually inoculated against the Red Plague by their previous experience. The Incas reacted to the smallpox plague as the Aztecs had—it was a visitation of God upon a wicked people. This was not just the reaction in Europe when a new disease appeared; until at least the nineteenth century it was the universal reaction of all people everywhere to new forms of disease.

There was a great deal of obscurantism about disease. For example, Napoleon I vaccinated his soldiers against smallpox by using the new methods of Jenner; his enemies did not. They suffered; the Grande Armée did not. Yet his nephew, Napoleon III, allowed his army *not* to be vaccinated. Twenty thousand French soldiers died in the Franco-Prussian War of 1870; the vaccinated Prussians lost very few, if any, to smallpox. The French Army, defending France, spread smallpox amongst French civilians; the vaccinated Prussians did not. In 1904–05, during the Russo-Japanese War, the Japanese army was vaccinated; the Russians were not. The Japanese deaths from smallpox were negligible; the Russians lost five times as many men from disease as they did from battle. They lost more men from smallpox alone than they did from enemy action.

The great wartime killer in 1904–05 and before was typhus. A contagious disease of the crowded, poor, and dirty, typhus deeply affected urban populations and armies. Its prevention in the early twentieth century was an essential prerequisite to crowding men together in the trenches of World War I.

Typhus was a new disease in 1492. It came to Western Europe from the Levant, the first cases appearing in Spain in 1490, and was then taken to Italy by Spanish soldiers. The first mass European outbreak was in 1494, and thereafter typhus was a most significant disease of armies, of the poor and crowded urban proletariat, and of jails. It killed more soldiers between 1500 and 1914 than any military action. In cities, more people died from typhus than from street accidents, crime, and starvation. In jails, typhus killed far more than ill treatment, torture, or execution: It became known as "jail fever." Judges feared contact with prisoners, and smelled their posies of herbs and flowers in an effort to ward off dreaded unknown ailments.[31]

The path and pattern of typhus were not known until just before World War I. In turn, ability to prevent typhus gave rise to the most lethal possible conditions in the trenches in France in 1914–18, conditions that would have been impossible if clever men had not "discovered" the typhus cycle. The clever men, of course, were acting from the best principles and the best motives, humanitarians all.

Some diseases are directly contagious or infectious; the pathogens pass from animal to animal by contact, by sharing breath, or by mouth. Some of the most important human diseases besides smallpox are TB, measles, scarlet fever, chicken pox, mumps, flu, and whooping cough. All in turn have been fatal, then serious, then endemic, then "childhood" diseases and relatively harmless. Occasionally, a new strain appears and becomes, successively, lethal, then endemic, and so forth. Drugs have been found to deal with some of these diseases, notably TB. There is a vaccine for whooping cough. Most of the rest have become successful as diseases go.[32]

There is another group of diseases that involve at least two hosts. The Black Death, *Pasteurella pestis,* "bubonic plague" needs fleas and rodents, as has been seen. Sleeping sickness needs the tsetse fly and cattle. Typhus is a third disease that moves between rats and humans and kills differentially. These double-parasite diseases were much more difficult to understand and "cure" because the pattern established by the successful organism was so sophisticated. In short, all these "successful" organisms established patterns difficult for humans to detect and interdict. Lateral thinking was required to trace the life of the parasites. Typhus was no exception. For four hundred years, the problem was thought to be the smell of the great unwashed. Indeed, the poor smelled because they could not afford to be clean. The poor also had typhus; they were probably twenty times as likely to have typhus as the rich. QED.

This proof by association was common enough until about 1900. Malaria was connected to swamps, not to mosquitoes and plasmodia. The Black Death was connected to crowded cities, not to *Pasteurella pestis* and rats. The Red Plague, smallpox, was connected specifically to dirt, litter, and unburned rubbish as late as 1890–1900, even though there was proof that vaccination prevented it. The secrets of typhus were unraveled only a few years before World War I.

Typhus, according to an up-to-date account before the mystery was solved, has four stages. The first is that of incubation. This lasts from seven to ten days. "Languor" is the only symptom. As languor can be caused by many other factors, from insufficient nutrition to depression, this clue is not exactly helpful.

Then there are the symptoms of the second stage: rigor, chilliness, prostration, sleeplessness, feverish headache, and a temperature of 39–40°C (103–104°F). The pulse is rapid; the patient is at first excited, and after a week may become as feeble as the pulse. The tongue is at first covered with white fur, then brown and dry; appetite is lost; constipation is characteristic; urine is diminished and highly colored.

The third stage is that of the rash, which is very dark, with mulberry-colored spots often accompanied by a subcutaneous hemorrhage. The patient lies with his eyes open, on his back, with a stupid expression on his face, apathetic, but with a wild and maniacal look in the worst cases. The patient may also mutter incomprehensibly.

The fourth stage, at fourteen days, is the crisis. There is an abrupt lowering of temperature, a return of normality to the alimentary system, and a recovery. Alternatively, the patient may die. Death rates from the disease came down from the high point when the disease was "new" to an average of about 18–20 percent, noted in scores of statistical studies at the turn of the nineteenth century. At this level, typhus would have made trench warfare in World War I impossible.

The discovery of the cycle was rapidly followed by prophylactic measures that were developed during the two Balkan Wars of 1912–13. The cycle involves rats and their fleas, as with the Black Death, but the rat flea and the rat live happily with typhus and recover from any attack. The flea transfers its own parasitic passengers to the human louse, which then sucks human blood and infects one human after another. Certain prerequisites exist.

The virus *Rickettsia prowazeki* kills the human louse, as well as infecting human beings, guinea pigs, and monkeys, which, unlike the rats and the rat flea, are killed. Before death, the human louse can not only infect its own human host, but also move from human to human. Thus, proximity is necessary to the success of the disease. The louse may live happily on an immune native, then jump to a stranger, who becomes infected.

Typhus needs cool climates, people in mass (especially strangers), the difficulties of hygiene associated with war and famine, and the retention on the body of foul clothing. Jails, of course, were ideally suited to the spread of the disease. Yet although the disease was rampant in the eighteenth century, and although ships were often filled with jailbirds, outbreaks on board ship were rarer than in the army. This was presumably because ships' officers did not tolerate a lack of hygiene. There was also an ample supply of sterile water for washing that came at ambient temperature from the sea. The lesser mortals in the army, however, had to suffer and die until the cure was discovered, largely by the American Typhus Commission in the Balkans just before World War I. Standard procedure was, first, to remove clothing and steam or boil same, then bathe soldier, spray him with petrol *(sic)*, examine soldier for lice and nits, and allow him to get dressed in sterile clothing.

Once the static warfare of the trenches had become normal, Western armies followed this procedure. Troops were deloused every time they left the trenches and before they returned, say every two to three weeks. On the Eastern Front—in Serbia, Russia, and Poland—typhus began to rage through the armies when effective resistance to the Germans began to break down, as early as the winter of 1914 in Serbia. In the period 1914–21 losses in Eastern Europe due to typhus were at least double the casualties from action in battle. It was only the prophylactic measures that made possible trench warfare.

Ironically, many of the good men who solved the problem, those hardworking doctors, nurses, and health workers of the American Typhus Commission, were Quakers. All of them believed in peace rather than war. Yet their efforts to prevent typhus enabled trench warfare to develop in a way impossible to conceive without delousing stations. Out of their efforts came the ritualized slaughter of World War I in France. Perhaps this irony, like so many other ironies, is grossly unfair. If the Allies had not been given the benison of the work of the Commission, perhaps the Germans, much more alive to health and hygiene than the French or Belgians, would have deloused their troops first. In that case, the Germans would have won the war in the West as they did in the East.

It is entirely possible that if Russian delousing had not broken down, the Russians would not have lost; in that case, no 1917 Revolution, no Communism, no Nazism, no World War II, perhaps. These are extreme hypotheses. There is no doubt, however, that from 1494 onward typhus was a more important factor for armies than strategy, tactics, weapons, courage, or leadership. Human beings, of course, do not like to think of such matters. How dull history would be if it always were due to some causative factor invisible to the naked eye.

Typhus, of course, was not only a disease of armies. It changed history first in Naples in 1494, where it made the continued siege impossible. The French king, Charles VIII, discharged his soldiers, who had survived the typhus-ridden investiture of the city, without the formality of terminal pay or transport home. Naturally, they lived off the country, and in doing so, spread typhus wherever they went. No one knows how many reached France, but it is certain that the attempt killed many more innocent Italian civilians than the actual warfare. It is possible that winter warfare in cold countries became even more difficult than it had been because of typhus. Soldiers, huddled together to keep warm, may well have produced a death rate too high to contemplate. Hence the safer summer "campaigning season." Typhus, of course, like other diseases, became milder, but as a killer it exceeded all human efforts, even in that most savage of all conflicts, the Thirty Years War. Typhus was particularly lethal in Germany in 1618–48. During that time, Germany suffered so much that advances made during the Renaissance were reversed, and parts of Germany became a cultural and intellectual desert. Typhus, of course, killed half of the army Napoleon took to Russia in 1812. Despite all the great man's efforts to vaccinate his troops against smallpox, no one could, at that date, have prevented typhus. The disease was selective, in the Darwinian sense, like all diseases. It killed more Northerners, more men, more gregarious people rather than individuals, and above all more poor people. The death rate in prisons made a penal policy hardly necessary.[33] Above all, perhaps, typhus destroyed the already weak, those who were ill-fed, half-starved, and already on the road to death from famine. In this case, was it more merciful? The disease may have been the proximate cause of death for one-half or more of those who died in the Irish Famine.

It followed, therefore, that individualism, cleanliness, sufficient food, and a sharp sense of the disagreeable nature of smellier people were protective instincts that were selected over the four hundred years during which typhus occurred in armies, slums, and prisons. "The great unwashed" became a group to be avoided, potential killers. It would be interesting to know whether the fever made more obvious class distinction, pity for the victim, or a useful desire to find a cure. Whatever anachronistic moderns may think, the evidence of the time does not suggest that typhus sufferers were regarded by the majority as anything more than people to be avoided. Those who avoided typhus were the selfish, the rural, the clean, the well-fed, and those who had no desire to commune too closely with others. The sharp distinction between countries with and without a long history of typhus will not escape the amateur of history.[34]

Two types of malaria have had profound effects on human history. European malaria served as an important (but unintended) tool of colonialism for the white man in the New World, while the deadly West African strain had far less beneficial consequences for everyone, especially were it spread in the Caribbean. If people could escape typhus by their own prudent behavior, no such possibility existed with malaria. This disease, like bubonic plague and typhus, depended upon a parasite invading another host. The host was, of course, the mosquito. Everyone knows this today, but until 1910 or thereabouts, few knew anything of the lifestyle of the vector, the mosquito; the internal meanderings of the parasite in the mosquito and in the human bloodstream were other mysteries. Malaria (bad air) is a disease ascribed in history to swamps, the night air, heat, and in the nineteenth century, the mosquito. So people sought hilly land and running water rather than stagnant lakes and ponds, were careful where they slept, went into the hills in the summer, and, latterly, used mosquito nets at night. Malaria is a disease that, almost uniquely, diminished in intensity, if it was not cured, before anything was known about its progress in the human body. The whole amazing story of quinine has been told. Its influence on history has been profound.

In this book, two particular aspects of the disease are unfolded. One is not widely known; the other is original. In 1492 malaria was endemic in the Mediterranean. It was also much commoner in Northwest Europe than anyone could imagine today. Holland, Denmark, Southern Sweden, and Norway were mildly infected all the time; in parts of undrained England, in the Fens in particular, malaria, if not a killer of many, was an annual occurrence. The last person to be found to have died of native "English" malaria was in Essex in 1924. Malaria was no respecter of persons. It could not be avoided by repulsing the poor, as with typhus, or avoiding bubonic plague cities, or refusing to get close to someone who might have been in contact with the Red Plague, smallpox. Nor was there any ameliorative agent before quinine; nor was quinine freely available to any but the rich before about 1860. Thousands of travelers, merchants, and people from low-lying areas all over Europe were sufferers and losers. The disease of malaria was, like typhus, highly selective, but in quite different ways. It operated against landlubbers—since North European mosquitoes could not survive at sea—against summer travelers, and against rural dwellers in low-lying locations. The disease is recurring, so that people become lethargic, insipid, and ineffective long before death appears over the horizon. Western Europeans transported it all over the world, like every other white man's disease.

How much of a killer was malaria in the Americas? While the mosquito could not fly far overseas, the insect could recycle in the ship's bilges in a warm enough climate. The southern route taken by Columbus in the summer of 1492, via the Canaries, could well have brought the disease to the Caribbean in that year. In contrast, John Cabot's voyage to the St. Lawrence in 1496 would not have made possible a continuous breeding program for the marine mosquito. Nor was the European mosquito necessary to the success of the disease in the Americas. There are four hundred sorts of mosquitoes, and sixty are vectors of malaria; of the sixty, thirteen are native to the Americas. Enough sailors carrying endemic malaria could have arrived in the Caribbean or in Canada and been bitten by native mosquitoes, starting the cycle even if the ship had been clear of any European insects. So, one way or another, malaria was one of the gifts Europeans donated to Americans besides smallpox and measles. While smallpox and measles killed, and killed swiftly with indiscriminate success, the European type of malaria existing in 1492 was spread throughout the Americas. The survivors of smallpox and measles were profoundly affected by it. The survivors of malaria were like other survivors before quinine; they were listless and anemic, with badly damaged livers—they probably had cancer of that organ—and a shortened lifespan. The Europeans (descendants of perhaps fifty generations of malaria survivors) survived rather better, even without quinine. Malaria, unlike smallpox and measles, was not a quick ally for the Europeans, but a long-term one, as they took malaria with them throughout the double continent. Resistance lowered slowly. It produced the death of cultures, rather than people. Vigor disappeared; passivity and debility became the order of the day; optimism fled. It is almost impossible for a malaria victim to be anything but fatalistic, a chattering weakling during the recurrent attacks, listless and fearing the next when apparently "normal."

How could a native civilization survive such an attack, even if smallpox and measles had selected the survivors? Malaria was a more insidious foe. The real irony, of course, was that the (South American) cure was generally only available to the whites, who doled it out in every country to their slaves, serfs, and workers. It was a form of Imperialism that a mad biotechnologist might have invented: An incurable disease is introduced; the ameliorative agent is "discovered"; control of the agent remains in the hands of the Imperial power. Why did Marx not include the malarial quinine story in his catalogue of European capitalist crimes? Simply because Marx, who died in 1883, never knew about malaria, its cycle, its parasites, or its "cure." More importantly, Marx, like lesser men, ascribed all human misfortunes to other human actions. What price willpower in the victims of malaria?

The other point of the malaria story has never been properly considered. It is known that the much more lethal form of malaria, *falciparium*, was unique to West Africa and taken to the Caribbean. It is also known that native West Africans are partially immune to *falciparium* malaria because of their recessive genes. Negroes[35] became the ideal workforce in the Caribbean into which the non-immune whites had inadvertently introduced West African malaria in company with the slaves they had brought over by ship. *Falciparium* is a much more lethal strain than the ordinary European type called, today, *Vivax*. *Vivax* malaria was endemic throughout the Old World, an acknowledged minor drag upon enterprise and effort throughout written history, called "swamp fever," "marsh miasma," or "palundine poison." Malaria was recognized as a problem in many areas long before the name was invented. Eurasians from China to Portugal learned to live with its debilitating effects, and the whole of the African shore of the Mediterranean and the Indian Ocean contained millions of people who had experienced and survived the disease. It was a nagging familiar. As with other endemic conditions, it produced a population largely resistant to the worst effects. In a competitive world, those who did not overcome the depressing effects did not thrive.

Plasmodia falciparium was quite another matter. Before the Portuguese voyages it was confined to the West African lowlands where the native Negro population had developed an in-built genetic resistance. Invading Arabs and other Muslims stayed in the highlands and did not survive the penetration of the rain forests, swamps, and deep river basins. Nor did the medieval Arab trade routes across the Sahara permit of any recycling of the mosquito. Few mosquitoes could survive for more than a day in the desert. Few men with *falciparium* malaria would survive much longer, walking north from Timbuktu.[36]

So Negro slaves, perhaps 1000 a year, brought north from West Africa by Arab slave dealers before 1400, did not bring with them *falciparium* malaria. After 1440, the story was different. At least 500,000 West African blacks were brought into Portugal in the 150 years after 1440. They were set to work in the South of the country and made agriculture possible in what had been the empty Alemtejo, once the granary of Portugal, but barren since the Moors had left. *Falciparium* malaria needs a mosquito, like other malaria, in which to develop. *Plasmodia falciparium* needs a temperature of at least 20°C (68°F) to spread. At that constant, it needs twenty-one days to evolve in the mosquito. At 25°C (77°F) the time is cut to seven days or less. In the summer Southern Portugal became a killing ground. The survival of the immune Africans made Portugal south of Lisbon a black colony. Did *falciparium* also spread to Southern Spain? Can it explain much of the decay in the Iberian spirit in the first century after 1492? No one has discussed this hypothesis.

The effects of *falciparium* malaria in the Americas were lethal to the whites, as the *Plasmodia vivax* was destructive of the Red Amerindian. The whites brought malaria from Europe in all of Columbus's voyages, and it spread all over the Caribbean. Every Spanish *conquistador*, every Portuguese settler, every French, British, or Dutch buccaneer brought malaria of the *vivax* type from Europe—along with the measles, small-pox, and influenza—to every part of North and South America. This is documented from Quebec to the River Plate. The Europeans, after 1517, brought Negro slaves from Spain and Portugal to the Americas. After 1530, there was a direct trade from West Africa that went on for nearly three hundred years. During that time, millions of slaves and billions of mosquitoes carrying *Plasmodia falciparium* were brought over. European death rates in the West Indies were sometimes twenty times as great as at home. Some were victims of *falciparium* malaria, others of yellow fever.

The other great killer of white populations, yellow fever first showed mankind the dangerous potential of "solving" a major disease. Yellow fever is carried by another sort of mosquito, and it was brought by ship from West Africa. The insect can survive only in a temperature range much narrower than the range needed by the *falciparium* mosquito; the fever is an elegant illustration of how Europeans have made disease international.

Yellow fever did not appear as early as malaria. If it had, there would be evidence since the "yellows" were regarded with an even greater and more justifiable horror than *falciparium* malaria, but yellow fever depends upon a mosquito even more particular in its requirements than the type responsible for *falciparium* malaria, a unique mosquito called *Aedes aegypti*. It loves mankind, but in its original home in Egypt it is only a minor irritant. It is a parasite of man. It cannot breed in "natural" water that is above mud or earth or sand, nor can it breed in running water; so it must find a quantity of stagnant water in order to perpetuate its species. The stagnant water in bilges or barrels in ships is ideal, so *Aedes aegypti* became a great traveler, but breeding depends on certain conditions. The mosquitoes have a very narrow range of temperature, and must always stay above 24°C (75°F). Unlike some mosquitoes, *Aedes aegypti* cannot survive even one night at a lower temperature. Death intervenes at a drop of only 1° below 24°C (75°F). This gives a new meaning to the phrase "one degree under." For *Aedes aegypti*, one degree under means death.

So this mosquito thrives only in the tropics. A ship carrying the insects and its eggs would not normally bring the yellow fever north to Europe or south to South Africa or east to India or China. Yellow fever, unlike *falciparium* malaria, was uniquely brought across the Atlantic, always within the temperature zone above 24°C (75°F). Blown north on a voyage to the Caribbean or south on a voyage to Brazil, the mosquito usually died. The fever was first noted in Bridgetown, Barbados, in 1647 and in Havana the next year.

"Yellow Jack," as sailors knew it, killed all the time the ship was in the tropics. Sometimes slavers were left with only a few white survivors, occasionally with none. When that happened, the immune black slaves starved to death. Ashore in tropical America it was the greatest killer known to the eighteenth century. Sometimes whole regiments of soldiers were wiped out. A ship on a trip in the Triangle England–West Africa–West Indies– England might lose half its crew from yellow fever trading round the islands of the Caribbean, even if the mosquito had not been picked up in West Africa. In very hot weather the fever went north as far as New Orleans, Florida, and Texas and was so feared that the towns along the Gulf Coast were emptied in a hot, bad year. It also went as far south as Rio de Janeiro in the Southern summer.

Exceptionally, yellow fever moved as far as 40° N in both hemispheres during the period 1793–1821. Did the nature of the mosquito change? Or were the then Northern summers exceptionally hot? The disease at times survived in Philadelphia and in Cádiz, Lisbon, Málaga, and Barcelona. There was a single outbreak in Lisbon in 1857 that killed 6000 in six weeks. There have been no recorded cases in the Eastern Mediterranean. Death rates have been greater than with any type of malaria, and the disease was quite early connected with mosquitoes (if the wrong ones), high temperatures, stagnant water, and dirt.[37]

The final blow to the white man's pride was the Panama Canal, which virtually had to be abandoned because yellow fever defeated the contractors. The death rate between 1890 and the end of the old company in 1901 was on the order of 50 percent of those involved. "Sanitation" became an essential prerequisite of the new company. The mosquito was defeated by drastic measures, and the Canal was built. Yellow fever is not only defeated by dealing with the mosquito, there is an inoculation that confers upon other races the immunity that made the black West African the essential laboring race of the West Indies. Ironically, if the whites had never traded slaves in West Africa, yellow fever would never have left the Bight of Benin. The disease was brought to the Americas by slavers: It was the disease that later made black slavery "essential."

Mosquitoes were defeated by U.S. doctors, engineers, and sanitary workers by drastic use of petroleum products. Bilges, stagnant water ashore, lakes, and ponds were all sprayed with kerosene. Before DDT, this was a standard procedure all over the Caribbean and much of the rest of the Americas. Wooden ships harbored the mosquito much more easily than modern steel vessels. New building construction did not permit nooks and crannies that allowed insects to cycle and recycle. Commercial management of land did not allow stagnant pools of water. But it was the Sanitary Commissions of various kinds that, in the days before DDT, made yellow fever and malaria much less of a problem. DDT itself transformed the situation.

The liberal use of DDT at the end of World War II destroyed the home life of the mosquito. DDT also destroyed many other insects, including the enemies of mosquitoes. Its lavish use has had two uncovenanted consequences. The first result was relief. Thereafter, population growth took over and relief sometimes disappeared. Greece was relieved of malaria for the first time in history: Only then could Greece become a tourist paradise.

In Bangladesh, one of the poorest countries in the world, tourism is unlikely. Population increases at a rate that doubles in twenty-five years, far beyond the possibility of enough food. The density of population in Bangladesh is over six people per hectare (fourteen people per acre) compared with four people per hectare (ten per acre) in the Netherlands or Southern England, or one and a half per hectare (four per acre) in New York State. By 2010 it is likely that Bangladesh's population will be ten people per hectare, an ecological disaster. This has been the effect of defeating disease in many parts of the world, and will be noted in due course.

The other problem revealed by the success of DDT is the polluting effect of wonder cures. DDT was found all over the world by 1955. Like strychnine, DDT can never be denatured; it cycles and recycles, poisonihng the environment. It is found in the bloodstreams of Antarctic penguins and in fish that are eaten by mankind whose detritus returns to the sea to pollute other fish or the very rain that falls on the other side of the world.

Pollution by substances that can never be broken down is creating anomalies. Some chemicals, unwanted any longer for their original purpose, cannot be denatured or broken down, so they spend from now until eternity as doomed travelers, like Coleridge's Ancient Mariner.

It creates a very real problem if complicated, beneficent substances have side effects that cannot be assessed before those substances are used over a number of years. To this logical conundrum there appears to be no answer. Not to use insecticides means that malaria and yellow fever will remain chronic, mosquito-borne diseases. On the other hand, to use an effective insecticide may condemn the world to pollution at rates that could become irreversible. Fortunately this paradox applies largely to insect-borne diseases. The effects of the alimentary diseases, aided by man's ignorance of their cause, have only recently been understood and brought under control. Three diseases that, like malaria and yellow fever, had to wait for the end of the nineteenth century for their suppression were alimentary. Of these, dysentery and typhoid fever probably date from the early years of the Christian era. Cholera burst out of India before the early 1820s and is, *par excellence*, an urban disease of the nineteenth century. All three diseases cycle from human to human via the drinking water and sewage systems or, more domestically, from unwashed hand to food to mouth. Typhoid and dysentery have different symptoms, yet historically, it is difficult to distinguish between the two. Typhoid results in diarrhea, fever, and general debility, but the organism affects all the organs, and may live on for years, especially in women.[38] Typhoid fever organisms survive in water, but do not multiply there. They live in warm air long enough to infect people downwind of the excreta of the diseased. The organism prefers acid conditions, typically of the pH of a normal stomach, so alkaline soils, water, and cold conditions deter mass infection. Typhoid was always known as a warm-weather or tropical disease. It took a long time for people to realize that the active organism was inhibited by cold, but multiplied in balmy weather. Typhoid was a great killer of people in cities and in armies. As late as the Boer War (1899–1902) the British lost twice as many men from typhoid as from all battle casualties, and ten times as many as were killed outright by the enemy. It was this loss of life that made warfare so expensive; rarely the enemy.

Dysentery was also a great killer. In the Crimean War (1854–57) British deaths from dysentery were ten times those killed by enemy action, but dysentery, unlike typhoid, is not carried by women.[39] It was originally known in England as "the bloody flux" since the stomach evacuates everything, then starts to discharge skin, flesh, and blood. Ultimately the unlucky patient dies, usually in great pain, of internal hemorrhage, passing stinking matter of a peculiarly nauseous and unique nature. Old-time doctors could smell the difference between typhoid and dysentery a hundred yards away from a sufferer.

Typhoid was prevented by the injection of dead organisms in a vaccine, the process adopted in most armies before 1939.[40] Dysentery is another matter, needing constant care to prevent the problem. Prevention is still the same sort of hygiene and sanitation that wise people have practiced for centuries. Dysentery is spread by flies, by contact with infected people or feces, and by birds and other animals. Of the two causative factors, the bacillus that causes one sort of dysentery can be killed by the sulfa drugs.

Amoebic dysentery, on the other hand, is a subacute, chronic, recurring form of the disease and may persist for years, like malaria; as with malaria, the parasite can cause serious liver problems if untreated. For years, the solution was a derivative of the Brazilian plant ipecacuahana. This contains the alkaloid *emetine* that, combined with opium, was made up as Dover's Powder, without which no Victorian traveler was properly prepared for the rigors of "abroad." It is specific against amoebic dysentery, but it was widely used for every kind of upset, from diarrhea, however caused, through Gippy tummy to Montezuma's revenge. Probably the mild dose of narcotic did as much to comfort the voyager as did ignorance of the true nature of the trouble.

Cholera was another matter, because it was a "new" disease for the European. Like typhoid and some sorts of dysentery, cholera gives rise to fever. Unlike any previous "civilized" disease, it sprang upon the world at a time when its symptoms were fully noted. It has had a short career in the Western World, as diseases go. Cholera, or some other fever answering the description given by later writers, had been cycling and recycling in the Far East for centuries. A particularly bad outbreak occurred in Bengal, India, in 1816–17. Cholera, unlike dysentery and typhoid, is very rapid. Very often the disease reached the acute stage within twenty-four hours, and it has been known to kill within another day.

Unlike typhoid, cholera prefers alkaline conditions, so a stomach of normal acidity can easily destroy the cholera bacillus. The use of purgative medicines, the eating of unripe fruit, or alcoholism may all predispose the stomach to accept, rather than reject, the organism. In a dramatic demonstration given in the 1880s, the great German pathologist Robert Koch consumed in front of his students a capsule of infected matter from a cholera victim. He made quite certain that the pH of his stomach was below the normal value before he risked his life. Cholera bacillus is also killed by a temperature of more than 60°C (140°F), so tea and coffee are always safe. The reservoir of infection is often drinking water, in rivers or in reservoirs. The bacillus is not killed by adding whisky to water, contrary to what old Indian hands may have told their children.[41]

There were six great global outbreaks in the nineteenth century. The first, in the years after 1817, reached China and Japan in the East and

Astrakhan in the North. The next epidemic started in 1826, reached Astrakhan in 1830, Moscow and Berlin in the following year, and Paris and London in 1832. Carried to Canada by emigrants the same year, it reached all the North American cities by 1838. The next outbreak reached Europe in 1847 and lasted until 1855. The next two outbreaks, in 1865–69 and 1884–88, were taken from India to Mecca by Muslim pilgrims, then from Mecca all over the Muslim world and, by contact, all over Southern and Northern Europe.[42]

The final cholera outbreak was so widespread as to be almost a pandemic rather than an epidemic. From 1892 to 1895 the disease raged all over the world. In Hamburg in 1892, 50 percent of those infected died, nearly 9000 people. The same sort of story came out of France, England, and most of Western Europe. The next year, it was prevalent in the Americas. By 1895, it covered Asia. The situation was so serious that stern efforts were made to "cure" the problem. These were much inhibited by the received wisdom of the day, which rejected the theory of germs causing disease. Pasteur had discovered the first bacillus (of anthrax) in 1876; Robert Koch found the tubercle bacillus in 1879 and the cholera bacillus in 1883. Yet the Establishment still claimed, as did the great Greek physician Hippocrates, that sudden epidemics appeared out of the soil, the miasma left there by dead bodies.

This was the perceived truth in medical schools in the 1880s and 1890s, despite the efforts of the followers of the Renaissance germ theory of the Italian Girolamo Fracastoro (1483–1553). Was it theories of contagion that instituted the practice of quarantine? Or was it observation? In Venice, quarantine was instituted before 1450, a century before Fracastoro. It became common in every port by 1800. Unbelievably, quarantine was repealed as a compulsory precaution in England, the world's then great-est trading nation in 1896. This was coincidental with early pathological work by Sir Almroth Wright, whose pupils later included the inventor of penicillin, Sir Alexander Fleming. It was not the last time in the world when an obstinate, almost invincible ignorance coincided with the begin-ning of enlightenment.[43]

Until the true nature of diseases was revealed by observation, micro-scope, logic, experiment, thesis, antithesis, and synthesis, the Establishment held sway in a bluff, no-nonsense kind of way. Unfortunately, however, there was plenty of nonsense.

As late as 1895, after the work of the French physician Alphonse Laveran in 1881, malaria was still often said to be caused by turning up virgin soil releasing the miasma. Dysentery, typhoid, and cholera organisms were present in the localities where the outbreaks occurred. Against all the evidence, smallpox, bubonic plague, and typhus were due to the "floating atmosphere" of the place, ship or city. Smallpox could be vaccinated against. Plague could be avoided. It was recognized, however, that building new jails and poorhouses reduced the incidence of typhus. This is now known to be because rats and fleas live with greater ease in old buildings rather than new, in old ships rather than new, and in old cities rather than new.

Nevertheless, most physicians of the last quarter of the nineteenth century refused to accept more than an ancient explanation for the prevalence of serious epidemics and pandemics, an explanation that dated back to the times of Hippocrates, who had died around 359 BC. Charles Creighton, a leading medical man of his time, actually wrote a huge, tendentious study, *History of Epidemics in Britain*, in order to disprove the new germ theories of the modern pathologists. This came out in 1891 and 1894, nearly 2000 pages in each volume. The book was highly recommended by the obscurantists of the day and by the Establishment. It did not last long at the top. Within twenty years the theories of Pasteur, Lister, Koch, and Ehrlich were as widely accepted as the old "truth" of Hippocrates was discredited. Within a generation every serious infection was at least traced in its course, and avoidance or prevention became routine. It was not until the advent of the sulfa drugs and antibiotics that true "cures" became possible.[44]

Unlike most of the diseases so far considered, syphilitic infection has always carried a sense of personal responsibility. Wholly connected with sexual intercourse, it has always been considered avoidable, and has been uniquely powerful in shifting human sexual mores.

Syphilis is likely to have been brought back from the Caribbean by Columbus's sailors on the first voyage. There is another, non-Columbian history of the disease that has always been unconvincing, and the evidence accumulates in favor of the traditional explanation. The disease first appeared in Europe in 1493 at Cádiz.[45]

Europeans took with them across the world more than a score of diseases, all of which were fatal in the first instance to the native populations whose bodies were invaded by invisible European aliens. Syphilis is the only American disease that has had any success, from the point of view of the disease, in the Old World. After 1493, Europeans in turn took the new import with them all over the world.[46]

Syphilis is spread by contact between people engaged in sexual activity. It is difficult to catch by other forms of contact, except in the tropics where the ambient temperature may well permit the *spirochetes* to survive long enough for non-venereal transmission. The disease appears to have been widespread in the Caribbean, and it is known to be passed on in the milk of infected women. Children borne or suckled by infected women are inoculated against more severe forms of the disease; in generations, a whole population could well have grown up with a mild, secondary form of syphilis. This could have been acquired in the womb or in the first few months of birth. At the same time, such a population could never increase its numbers enough to produce market agriculture, villages, towns, and so forth. Can it therefore be concluded that syphilis was present in those Caribbean islands with low, pre-Columbian, populations? It must have been absent in those, like San Domingo, that allegedly had a native population of one million when Columbus arrived. More convincingly, syphilis cannot have been present, except in a very attenuated form, in Mexico or Peru, which had substantial populations with considerable surpluses that could be (and were) used by high priests for human sacrifice.

Such a pattern does not fit what is known of populations that have had syphilis for many generations. It is needless to add that no experiment has been conducted since the true nature of syphilis has been known only since 1900 or thereabouts, when it was "cured." The timescale necessary to prove the mild, attenuated form of pre-Columbian Amerindian syphilis must be on the order of at least ten generations. There is no isolated community in the world today that has congenital syphilis, and that can be guaranteed not to have been reinfected for ten generations. Sailors of every nationality, of course, have spread syphilis for nearly five hundred years.[47]

But sailors were only the first wave of white invaders. They acquired the disease from Caribbean women in 1492, and infected whores or wives throughout Spain on their return the next year. Some of them returned with Columbus on the second voyage. These then infected other Caribbean women. By the time serious Iberian conquest was involved in the 1520s, Spanish and Portuguese sailors had probably infected women all over the shoreline of the Americas. There was enough infection to ensure disease in those populations that had previously been free from syphilis: Aztecs, Mayas, Incas, and certain populated islands in the Caribbean. They were all infected by Europeans.

To "clean" Amerindian populations, the effects of syphilis must have been as serious as they were on virgin European populations. The density of people catastrophically declined. The first instance of an epidemic is an alarming rise in miscarriages. The next is a huge increase in babies dying in the first six months of life, shriveled and wan. Perinatal syphilis has been studied as a statistical phenomenon, and infected infants who lived for three years number only about one-tenth the number of surviving infants born to healthy women. Syphilis produces a demographic disaster.

This point, about differential incidence of the disease in the Americas in 1492, has never been examined. It is impossible to prove either way, but syphilis would be a satisfactory explanation of why Amerindian populations were so small in certain areas and so dense in others. There were no other comparable Amerindian diseases. It is also possible that syphilitic syndromes that Europeans experienced after the summer of 1493 had all been part of the Amerindian folk memory in some areas.

It is important to remember that before syphilis attitudes to sex were very different. It is true that promiscuity was the luxury of the rich, but certain populations in Europe still offered sexual hospitality to the peaceful stranger, as did almost every "primitive" people, and as some Africans and many Eskimos do to this day.[48]

Premarital intercourse was no more prohibited in some European societies than it was in the Pacific. It is true that Europe certainly had other sexually transmitted diseases, gonorrhea in particular, but these problems never had the impact of syphilis in the public psyche. After syphilis appeared, sexual manners and morals were altered permanently, or at least until modern man thought he had "cured" the disease.

First, there was a profound decline in the ability of royal and noble families to breed. Henry VIII of England, the Valois of France, the Ottoman Sultans of Turkey, all had difficulties that were unprecedented. So did dozens of aristocratic families. Did the decline of aristocratic vigor precede the demand of the plebs for public power, or did it follow?[49]

Second, the kind of sexual ebullience that characterized the lifestyle of every Italian family of the day—Medici, Borgia, Sforza—came to a sober end. The first priest died of syphilitic symptoms in 1496, the first bishop in 1506, and the first Pope in 1516. The career of Lucrezia Borgia, overstated as it has been in fiction, could never, for example, have existed after syphilis.[50]

Third, and as a consequence of the experience of the thirty years 1493– 1523, both Northern "Protestants" and the Southern Counter-Reformation Catholics became "puritan." The killjoy streak in humans, never far below the surface, became an absolute necessity to preserve the family, the tribe, and the race. In this connection it is arguable that in the period 1460 to 1520 papal folly and excesses that were such a causative factor in the Reformation would have been impossible in the Age of Syphilis. It is impossible to imagine Renaissance papal behavior if Columbus had sailed a hundred years previously.

Fourth, women had another reason to fear men besides the loss of virginity. Syphilis ruined lives. Certain classes of men were more suspect than others. Aristocrats acquired a reputation for raffishness, sexual irresponsibility, and an inability to reproduce that may well have helped the development of the modern world. The effective aristocracies, which survived in some European countries in all their vigor, were renewed all the time by new blood. The middle classes, meanwhile, developed a strong sense of sexual ethic that would one day be called "Victorian," sometimes an adjective of contempt. (This contempt could only be expressed by those who ignored the fact that syphilis raged throughout Victorian England, except among those who were prissily careful.) Ever since Columbus's time sailors have had a special reputation, not always good.

Finally, there is a point never before made about this revolutionary disease. Syphilis was the first disease in human consciousness that was obviously the direct result of human action. In an era innocent of any knowledge of germ, bacterium, virus, or causative agent of any kind, syphilis taught every European a lesson within a century—cause and effect. Leave the unclean alone; do not engage in premarital intercourse or promiscuity; plan marriages with children in mind. What were called the bourgeois virtues were combined with the Sixth Commandment. Indulgences, even Papal Indulgences, could not cure syphilis.[51]

For four centuries, nothing cured syphilis. Then in the late nineteenth century, a long and painful course of mercury effected a cure. The cure, however, was often worse than the disease and gave rise to the sailors' saying: "Better the disease than the cure." In the period 1910–14 Ehrlich invented two complex combinations of arsenic that were widely used to limit the damage from syphilis during World War I. But the real "cure" came in the late 1940s with the discovery of antibiotics. Antibiotics promised to "wipe out" syphilis. So said optimistic pathologists, and the people believed them, as people do when they want to believe. The combination of a "cure" for venereal disease and a birth control pill that was nearly 99 percent effective led to the sexual revolution of the 1960s. This in turn lasted until AIDS (Acquired Immune Deficiency Syndrome) came along.

Like syphilis, AIDS/HIV appears to have had enough destructive power to effect significant change in human sexual behavior. AIDS will probably produce the same kind of result as syphilis did five hundred years ago. AIDS is being underplayed by Western governments, which, being "democratic," have to carry their voters with them. Matters are more strictly arranged in dictatorship.[52]

The facts are stark in the extreme. AIDS is a venereal disease, but it is also spread by any exchange of fluids such as saliva, blood, or vapor from breath. The hotter the climate, the more easily the virus is transmitted outside the human body. In the tropics, for example, breath remains AIDS-active for many times as long as in freezing conditions. AIDS cannot be avoided merely by "sensible sex." The wearing of contraceptive sheaths cannot prevent transmission by an exchange of saliva. An AIDS sufferer can pass on the disease on the operating table to someone never seen. A shared cup and a cracked lip may make contagion possible. Non-Roman churches may have to give up the communion cup as Roman Catholics did, for different reasons, before syphilis came along.[53]

Survival of the bourgeois virtues, the family, and the framework of gentle society will depend on the reassertion of values that used to exist before the subculture of the 1960s marginalized received behavior. The process is similar to what happened in Europe after 1530. Historians confused it with the puritan religion and the rise of capitalism and so forth. They have often been dismissive of disease in history. Today, living historians can see what happened in the sixteenth century repeated in their daily lives.

The final point made about syphilis is happening once again. In an ignorant age, syphilis was the first disease about which cause and effect became obvious. Sexual permissiveness caused disaster. It would be three hundred years before cause and effect ruled in any other disease. AIDS is in the same league. Sooner or later, personal responsibility, not true in the case of typhus, or bubonic plague, or cholera, or many other killer diseases, will be so connected with AIDS that social behavior will permanently alter.

The tragedy with AIDS, which will make the impact far worse than appears at the time of writing, is the long, long incubation period. This makes the situation far graver than anyone is prepared to admit in public. AIDS could, for example, destroy one-third of the population of sub-Saharan Africa or parts of Asia. As in the case of the bubonic plague in Europe six hundred years ago, this would have profound consequences. Because it is currently incurable, AIDS is the first disease since 1347 that is likely to have consequences similar to the Black Death.

Apart from the special consequences of the diseases described, there are four general effects of disease in history.

First, there was nothing that the individual could do about most diseases before about 1800 when smallpox inoculation became available. Then there was an interval. All the great advances in bacteriology and medicine have been virtually in the last century. The major diseases already described had general and important effects, of which the individual certainly was not aware at the time. Usually the nature of the disease was not known to contemporaries.

Disease trimmed and reduced populations. Chronic diseases were present in Eurasian populations most of the time. The more obvious were malaria and smallpox, which many survivors suffered more than once, but it is likely that more people died from alimentary disorders than from all other causes put together. These ranged from typhoid to dysentery to various local enteric fevers to salmonella. Stomach diseases do not need mosquitoes, or rats, or lice. Enteric disorders cycle and recycle among the human, his sewage, and his water supply. Local populations can become tolerant of a local set of organisms that will kill the visitor. In the days before piped water supplies, travelers were often in grave danger. Safe sewage and water systems were not in place in most of Western Europe much before 1900. Sometimes the water improvements cleared up the local trouble before the medical men had properly diagnosed the nature of the problem.

The second effect of disease followed from the first. Dense communities were not really self-supporting in statistical terms until recently. Large towns encouraged all sorts of infections, and often required many immigrants to supplement those who survived perinatal death. In London, before 1750, death rates ranged from 5 to 10 percent of a population then above half a million. This figure included all deaths, including those from diseases not noticed here, like TB, cancer, and influenza. Children of every age were included. The crude death rate of adults was double the number of baptisms, and probably three to four times the number of conceptions.

Between 15,000 and 20,000 immigrants a year (or more than 3 percent) were needed just to maintain numbers. Later, immigrants increased the total population. Other cities were in the same position. It is almost certain that great centers in the Third World are in the same position today, but no reliable statistics exist. Calcutta, for example, must bear some resemblance to eighteenth-century London or Paris.

The third effect was when Europeans followed Columbus all over the world. They took with them a massive armory of disease. This killed the natives at the point of contact, as described with Cortés and the Aztecs. This condition was repeated all over the world. Disease landed in the Americas and spread ahead of the Europeans; disease landed in New Zealand and Australia with the first Europeans. By the time that later

Europeans "discovered" the Maoris of the center of the North Island in New Zealand, or the Aborigines of the area north of what is now Adelaide, Australia, the natives were already suffering from syphilis, smallpox, influenza, measles, and so forth. The same process fanned ahead of the Russians in Siberia and Central Asia, an Asian empire nearly twice the size of the United States.

Every area of the world has been transformed by the ecology of European disease. In the tropics, the local populations have been wholly rearranged, usually for reasons not unconnected with disease. Blacks were imported into the Americas; East Indians replaced the natives in Africa, Fiji, or Malaya; Chinese coolies were taken all over the Pacific. Only in West Africa were the residual natives left alone after the slave trade was abolished. In temperate countries, native populations were largely destroyed and replaced by Europeans; the countries became neo-Europes. This process would have been impossible if the native populations had been resistant to European diseases. As it was, the European victory was won by invisible allies who were never given the credit they deserved. In fact, it was often the microbes who deserved the medals, not the "heroic" men.

Finally, there has been the dramatic effect of curing disease. Apart from hygiene and sanitation, which took place largely before 1914, advances in pathology have been most dramatic since 1945. Since that date world population has increased by a rate much greater than in the previous forty years. Between 1905 and 1945, world population increased by less than 50 percent. Between 1945 and 1985 it nearly doubled.

The great increase is due to an improvement in two areas—food supply and disease control. The dramatic increase in control over most of the diseases that have checked and trimmed populations since time began is the more obvious. Which is more important may appear to be evident later in this book. The combination has sometimes been ecologically lethal.

There is one other possibility in the realm of disease about which there can be no kind of proof. It is possible that disease, which has for century after century been fighting a war with man's ability to resist pathogens, has now changed its very nature. It is possible that, instead of attacking antibodies directly, and provoking a form of warfare in which millions of active pathogens are defeated by millions of active defenders in the animal or human body, diseases may have changed into organisms that attack the immune system itself. There are three human diseases, two in cattle, one in sheep, and one in cats, unknown a generation ago, that now threaten each species rather seriously. This is very important for mankind, if correct. Some of the animal diseases could well transfer to humans. Humans, in turn, could not defeat these diseases en masse. It is possible that, in the new century, pathologists and biotechnologists may have defeated AIDS's ability to destroy the immune system. But how could humans defeat twenty different diseases, each of them behaving like AIDS, none of them transferred sexually? Such a course would restore disease to its traditional role as one of the Forces of Change. Such a future might quite easily terrify the optimists. On the other hand, it would be a rather *elegant* cure for the population/pollution problems that now exist.[54] These are rendered all the more powerful because of the defeat of the conventional diseases that attack human antibodies.[55]

CHAPTER TWO

Bread to Make the Old World Strong

The steady rise in world population since the fifteenth century has only been made possible by an increased food supply. In Western Europe in 1492, there was absolutely more food available per head than ever before, and techniques were known that would increase this still further. No one knew at the time that the technology to feed the whole world five hundred years later already existed in Western Europe. The technology to produce the first increases in food supply were developed by unscientific men; much of the daily practice on farms during the Renaissance was similar to good husbandry in the days of Virgil. Some things were different: animals instead of men used for labor, mills driven by wind and water, and much more flesh eaten than in Roman days. These improvements to classical methods were sufficient until the ratio of humans to land changed dramatically during the fourteenth century. First there was an enormous increase in population in the century before the Black Death, then came the loss of more than a third of the people in most areas. The feudal system, based on a population present about AD 800, began to break up as the population shifted. The second great challenge to the methods of the time was before and during the Industrial Revolution. In the second half of the eighteenth century the English population had increased by more than half; in the next fifty years it more than doubled. In the hundred years 1750–1850, the population tripled, from 5.5 million to 16.5 million, and 2 million people emigrated. Nearly all this increase was made possible by the abundant production of English food, and every English human being was fed by the fruits of English soil by 1850. This was a massive achievement.

In some years there was hunger, even starvation, but during an age in which there was little surplus in the Northern Hemisphere and none at all in the Southern, the English were the first people to feed themselves from their own soil while supporting such a large increase in population. Improved agriculture made the Industrial Revolution possible by increasing output per acre.

The problem of using every possible acre advantageously was solved by the rough and ready method of enclosure. This was a cruel policy at the margin: Many benefited, but a few suffered. It was, however, a uniquely successful solution to a problem that was peculiar to Europe, and thus, at that time, in the world.

This chapter is not wholly about England or English husbandry, but Europe and England taught agricultural techniques to the world. It was population pressure that made English success essential: Failure would have resulted in a very different story without an Industrial Revolution, without the defeat of Napoleon, and without the survival of an unprecedented (and unrepeated) increase of population in an already densely populated land. Unlike every other European country, England avoided revolution: That, too, is thanks largely to agricultural husbandry. By 1492 Western Europeans had an understanding, based on their own experience and on communication with others, of three distinct systems of farming: the natural alluvial cycle of Egypt, the dry farming of the Mediterranean Basin, and the relatively advanced husbandry of Northwest Europe. It was the last of these that contained the techniques whose developments would encourage the huge population boom of the following centuries.

B Y 1492 Western Europeans had acquired from the East most of the techniques from which they were likely to benefit. After this date technological leadership, then scientific research and application, passed to the West. Some of the *technological drift* from China was of recent origin, occurring in 1492; some was yet to come. There were advances that applied to food production. The technique to produce cast iron did not come into use in the West until about 1250, so plows had been made of wood. The concave moldboard, used in China in the ninth century BC, took twenty-five centuries to reach the West. The first formulas for the correct dynamic angles of a turnover plow were not worked out until Thomas Jefferson calculated the mathematics in the 1790s, unaware of Chinese predecessors whose manuscripts were uncovered by Western scholars more than a century later.

Although humble wheelbarrows were invented in China and transferred to the West as late as AD 1200, the most important improvement to husbandry was the animal harness that the Chinese had invented nearly ten centuries earlier. The breast strap was not widely used in Western

Europe before the twelfth century, and the more efficient breast collar, which did not cut the horse's windpipe, until later. Both were an improvement on the Roman sling, which was a rope that passed around the neck, between the legs, and under the belly, and was then attached to the implement being pulled.

In some countries, notably Ireland and some of the Baltic provinces, horses were hitched to the plow by the tail, a practice that limited the draught to less than a tenth of that available using a modern harness. Oxen were preferred as draught animals before 1492 partly because of the harness, partly because horses were more expensive and uncommon, and partly because of disease. Teams of two were normal, although three were used as well; a four in hand was a sign of either heavy soil or affluence. Regardless of the number, oxen, who had the advantage of being able to work without shoes, walked at half the speed of horses. They had a longer working life, were not subject to as many health problems, and were less attractive as loot. They also provided more and better meat when slaughtered at the end of their lives. Before 1492, either they were yoked or the draught trace was fixed to their horns. Either way, the efficiency of using oxen was low.

In 1492, "Agriculture" within any European experience was limited to three areas. In Egypt there was a perfect system, more than 4000 years old, that utilized the Nile flood in combination with the water and alluvial mud from the Central African highlands. The flood was in August each year and produced enough plant food to grow a good crop of wheat or barley. The water not only provided enough moisture to grow the crop but, before planting, it also killed all the living weeds on the stubble of last year's corn. The crop was planted in late autumn, when the flood subsided, and harvested in late spring after about 180 days of growth. The stubble burnt in the summer sun, destroying microorganisms that in other climates would have prejudiced continuous corn production. When the reliable flood came again, the process was repeated.

The Egyptian system was a perfect example of a sustainable man-made pattern that cropped nature and did not exploit or threaten the balance. The ecosystem was not dependent upon science, industrial tools, or added power. It had existed since 2500 BC and was capable of feeding up to ten million Egyptians. In Roman times the Nile fed four million at home, and exported enough to feed the same number abroad. In 1492 the population of Egypt was much as it had been in Roman times, four million, held in check by a whole catalogue of diseases.

In countries such as China, India, Burma, and Siam there were alluvial, flood-irrigated, river-basin cultures, about which Europeans knew little. Single river cultures existed in what is now modern Iraq—the Tigris-Euphrates Basin—as well as in Greece, Italy, Spain, many areas of the Maghreb, and, unknown to Europeans, the Americas. The systems used in Holland, the Po Valley, and parts of England did not involve flooding. For obvious reasons, at the time irrigation was not an option to massively increase the food supply. After 1350 the use of windmills for drainage reached a plateau, and the technology was replaced by machines using steam for energy. Modern techniques that make water use far more efficient depend upon power to dig channels and build dams, pipes to prevent evaporation loss, and power to pump and distribute water, often by overhead irrigation. In 1492, it is entirely possible that irrigation had reached a limit dictated by the state of the art rather than by economics.

There were two other systems of agriculture with which the Western Europeans were familiar. The first was hot-climate, Mediterranean dry farming. The purpose of cultivation in these areas was to conserve moisture, kill weeds, and grow the best possible crop every second year, or at best two years out of three.

The techniques of Mediterranean farming, as described by Virgil in a passage from the *First Georgic,* had reached a plateau in the first century BC that could not have been improved upon before 1492. Virgil wrote as follows:

> First, learn the peculiarities of your soil and climate. Plow the fallow in the early spring; plow frequently, twice in winter, and twice in summer unless your land is poor, in which case a light plowing in September will suffice.
>
> Either let the land lie fallow every other year, or else let spelt [wheat] follow pulse, vetches, or lupins.

Repetition of one crop exhausts the ground; rotation will lighten
the strain; exhausted crops must be well dressed with manure or
ashes. It often does good to burn stubble.

Irrigation benefits a sandy soil; draining profits a marsh.

Geese and crane and other birds, mildew and weeds are all enemies
of the crop.

Careful annual selection of the seed by hand must be the only way
to prevent degeneration.

Virgil wrote these lines about 35 BC and read them to the Emperor
Augustus five years later. Like the advice given by Pliny, Varro, and all
the other writers on agriculture, the *Georgics* were written in verse and
intended for a society that did not know anything about printing or much
about reading.[1]

In Northwest Europe the food production problem was quite different. There was a much older tradition of flesh eating. As population
density rose, the hunter had to become a herdsman. Originally, there
cannot have been much difference.[2]

By the time of the stable Roman Empire with its boundaries on the
Rhine and the Danube, Germans were using plows in clearings in their
gloomy forests as well as living off herds of cattle. The plows they later
used were claimed to be unique, different from the Mediterranean
implements, an answer to the problem of cultivation in heavy soils.
Modern research suggests that claims about Germans or Slavs giving
Europe the true heavy plow in about AD 600 are romantic.

A plow differs from a handheld digging implement in that it utilizes
effective movement of the soil against the plow to do the work, and
does this continuously. Traction from the draught team is transmitted
through the beam and pole and to the stock; the stock has a leading
point that lies nearly horizontal and does the actual job. The stock
might well be formed from a tree branch and, in the simplest plows the
stock and pole might be one piece. The handle that was single on Greek
or Roman plows was attached to the tree branch of another wood,
usually oak. These were the plows that evolved all over the Western
world before Christ. In some favored places, iron was cheap enough
to clothe the wearing point of the plow; in others, flints or other hard

stones were inserted in holes in the wood. The iron "shoe" would, of course, be used again and again, the wooden parts of the plow having a much shorter life.

Plowing has always involved huge inputs of power. A hectare of land plowed to a depth of 10 cm (4 in) involves shifting 1000 tons of dirt; a depth of 15 cm (6 in), 1500 tons; a depth of 20 cm (8 in), 2000 tons. Today, this takes a man and a pair of carefully bred horses, working effectively at about two kph (one mph), about twenty hours. No pair of horses could do more than eight hours a day at this work, so that two hectares, or about five acres, was work for five days; one day's light work, and one rest day completed the week.[3]

There was at one time a great school of Anglo-Saxon revisionists who propagated a golden pre-Norman past that included a heavy wheeled plow, drawn by eight oxen. This is said to have been brought to England by Teutonic invaders soon after the Roman withdrawal. These early Anglo-Saxons changed the landscape, the myth continues, by bringing into cultivation the heavy clay lands of the Midlands. Yet these stories from some golden past stand up to analysis no more than does King Arthur. In fact, Camelot is probably easier to "prove."[4]

The habit the Saxons *did* bring to England was that of flesh eating. In the post-Roman centuries, with the density of population probably existing in the Midlands, much more food was produced per acre by grazing cattle or sheep on grass than by trying to grow wheat instead. On a Midland pasture of a low botanical composition (largely agrostis, not much clover) and without fertilizer, the annual yield could be at least 50 kg of beef per hectare (45 lb per acre), or twice as much lamb. This far exceeds the net yield of grain at the same date with the technology then available. It was only the density of human population, demanding high grain output per acre, that dictated the plowing of clay lands. It is unlikely that this took place much before the time of King Alfred (849–900). The population of England after the retirement of the Romans in the fifth century is unlikely to have exceeded 600,000. Population did not reach the high Roman figure of 800,000 before Alfred's reign. At the time of the Domesday survey (1086), it was about twice that of Alfred's time. Despite Danish invasion, or because of Viking vigor, the population doubled in less than two centuries, a high rate of increase at the time. If the clay lands had to be cultivated, it was not until the High Saxon Age during and after Alfred the Great.[5]

Once plowed, the soil must be harrowed to break down the clods or to make a tilth for the seeds so they can germinate. The rule is simple: The bigger the seed, the coarser the tilth; winter-sown grain requires a cloddier tilth than grain sown in the spring, so as to protect seedlings from the winter weather; in some soils, too fine a tilth produces too many weeds. Grain is at one end of the growing conditions; onion seed is at the other. Both were widely grown all over the Mediterranean after 2000 BC. Harrows of all types are used to prepare the ground and cover the seed; they have probably been used longer than plows. In suitable wooded country they can be made in an hour by cutting thorns from bushes. Man-made harrows, wood frames into which iron spikes were fitted, were used from Roman times; so were roller harrows made of tree trunks spiked with large iron nails. Horse draught came in to break down clods or cover the soil because the horse's speed enabled it to accommodate the changeable weather of the Atlantic countries. The square or triangular wooden or steel frame with spikes is still widely used, but there are other modern harrows, based on steel technology, that use discs or chains or springs. These were all developed in the nineteenth century. More recently the power available on oil-driven tractors has given birth to power-driven harrows that can produce the correct tilth at one "pass" of the tractor; these can change the nature of tilth while working to suit difficult fields with several soil types. As with modern plows, these implements move tons of earth in each hour of work.

Sowing seed is still most efficiently performed by hand. No implement can beat a good man walking at 5 kph (3 mph) with the seed in a sheet suspended from his shoulder. It is the cultural necessity of placing fertilizer in close proximity to seed that justifies the expensive and complicated seed drills now in use. Nor can men be found to walk the distances required to do a day's work as in Biblical times. Such a task for a day involved 40 km (25 miles) in nine hours of sowing, planting a total of 20 hectares (50 acres). Such a machine-beating output can be achieved only in a few industries and in very few operations, but men do not like such effort today, even in agriculture.

Harvesting is another matter altogether. The scythe man, served by two or more men or women tying up the sheaves, was known in the Middle Ages, and even in Roman times. Sickles of every shape and size were developed in the Middle Ages, but it was commoner to harvest in earlier times by merely cutting off the heads of grain. Pre-Roman British Celts used carts for this purpose, and very efficient they were, capable of harvesting 10 hectares (25 acres) a day with one or two men pushing the cart and another two emptying it at the end of a "bout." A gleaner was also needed, of course, to pick up short-strawed grain missed by the harvesting comb, described by Pliny as a device fixed to the front of the cart. In the Mediterranean these carts were pushed, by slaves, mules, or oxen, and in Britain, by one or two men, but never by horses. Grain was threshed by hand in a basket or with a handheld and operated winnowing fan or by the wind, which is free. The winnowing machine did not reach Western Europe from China until the seventeenth century. Less delicate means of threshing, or "disintegration" as engineers put it, included treading the grain with oxen, a method still used in Eastern Europe in the 1950s. The simple threshing stick gave way to the hinged flail about 100 BC, and is still in use. There was a special, and violent, sledge that was dragged across the cut corn to separate the grain from the chaff; this was widely used in Mediterranean countries. In many parts of Atlantic Europe, heads of grain were scorched or burnt to make them digestible for human beings or animals. In this way, grinding the grain could be avoided.[6]

Burnt grain could be turned into a porridge-like substance, pre-toasted by the fire. Perhaps this is why no Neolithic querns or threshing stones have been discovered in non-Roman Europe. Ireland, North Germany, and the Scandinavian countries all burnt grain at one time—burning grain to make it edible is a very simple method, cheap and effective. Sometimes, further disintegration took place after burning the grain to "thresh" it, and use of the pestle and mortar was widespread before winnowing techniques became widely available.[7]

At some point in every civilization in the thousand years before Christ, pounding the grain was split into two operations: The first separated the grain from the chaff; the second ground up the grain to make it more easy for man or beast to digest. If the grain was burnt, then only the second operation was required. In the Mediterranean countries the pestle and mortar gave way to grindstones or querns.

The pestle is not to be despised. It was the first hand tool that was not only mechanized, but automated. The pestle and mortar were operated by ropes, with the return spring induced by an adjacent growing tree. This "mechanized" the operation at low cost, and the tree required no daily food.

To automate the operation, some bright person living alongside a stream invented a device involving the pestle operated on a beam, the end of which was arranged with a bucket. The bucket was attached at such an angle that it filled in the stream, lifted the pestle, and then rose, emptying at the top and permitting the pestle to fall. Fully automated machines of this type were in use in mountainous districts as early as at least 500 BC. They were probably the first automated machines in the world.

Pounding was used for the staples of the ancient world: grain, oil, and wine. Ideally, olives and wine grapes were pounded so that the stones or pips did not disintegrate and spoil the oil or grape juice. At some point the three forms of pounding separated. Grain was ground rather than bashed. Olives were ultimately crushed in a *trapetum*, which was a rotary mill with a minimum clearance of 1.8 cm, or 1 Roman inch.[8] This prevented the stones from being ground and entering the attached oil barrel. Wine grapes were pressed by feet, by beam presses tightened by levers, pulleys and ropes, and ultimately screw presses that tightened the mass of pulp between two wooden plates the size of large, square tables. Two wooden screws were used to tighten them. Presses of this type for wine and cider survive into the present. They were developed about 100 BC and in use all over Western Europe. As well as a tradition of effective, if limited, agricultural techniques, fifteenth-century European farmers also had access to a wide range of cereal crops.

Unleavened "bread" or flatcakes, baps, scones, tortillas, biscuits, and wafers can be made of any cereal. Some sort of "flatbread" can be made of wheat, rye, barley, oats, rice, millet, teff, and sorghum, all of which are Old World cereals, and from buckwheat, which is a pseudo-cereal. True leavened bread can be made only of *wheat*. Over the past five hundred years, wheat has been transported all over the world, and it

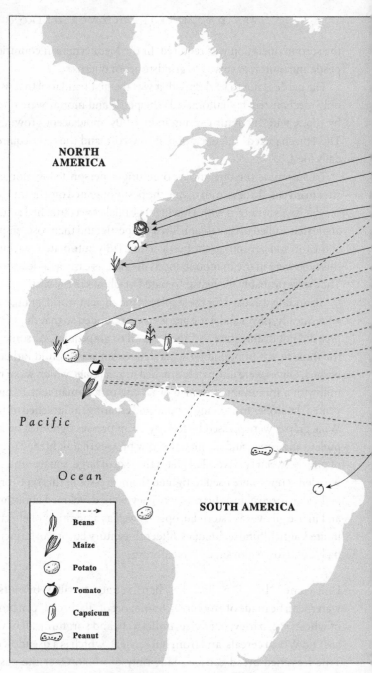

NORTH
AMERICA

Pacific

Ocean

SOUTH AMERICA

Beans	
Maize	
Potato	
Tomato	
Capsicum	
Peanut	

Post-Columbian Plant Transfers

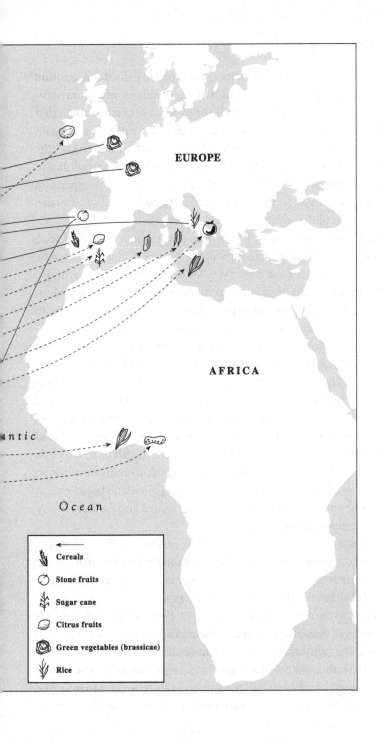

EUROPE

AFRICA

ntic

Ocean

Cereals

Stone fruits

Sugar cane

Citrus fruits

Green vegetables (brassicae)

Rice

has become the world's most important cereal. It gained this position only because of the unique bread-making quality of wheat, attributable to its gluten content. Gluten is the product of cereal protein that has been ground up and mixed with water. When further mixed with yeast, gluten expands to accommodate the gases produced by the yeast, mostly harmless carbon dioxide. Gluten has the extraordinary ability to expand to accommodate the gases, yet resist the expansion and contain the gas, so that risen bread is digestible and good to eat, except by the gluten-averse.[9]

Rye, the ancient cereal of northern countries, poor soils, and cool, moist climates, has protein that produces very weak gluten. Therefore, rye bread can be made, but it rises very little. The result is a dense, heavy, black, or dark brown product. Most modern rye breads contain wheat flour to enhance the poor gluten content of rye bread. Most rye is used in the developed world for hard bread, for crispbread, or for making spirituous liquor. As recently as 1956, Western Germany grew more rye than wheat, and the same was true of Eastern Germany until 1966.[10]

Rye bread is "slimming" because it contains a high proportion of pentosan compounds that swell in the stomach, absorb large quantities of water, and take a long time to digest, giving an impression of fullness. Rye is almost unknown in Southern Europe; it is typically the bread grain of the great European plain, running from the Rhine to the Urals because, until after World War II, it was difficult to cultivate wheat in these dry, sandy soils. Rye is now considered a poor man's bread, except for the fashionable crispbread that has been argued into the diet of every self-conscious slimmer.[11]

Barley was as important as wheat in the ancient world. Barley needs less time to grow and has adapted widely, from the Equator to the Arctic Circle. It needs less moisture than wheat and today is the preferred cereal for beer of all kinds. In the Middle Ages barley was the staple of the southern peasantry, as was rye in northern climes. Both rye and barley are less demanding of the soil and easier to grow than wheat. Barley is a grand animal feed. The cultivation of barley on some soils in England has extended beyond that thought possible a generation ago. One field in Somerset, England, grew continuous barley for thirty years, from 1952 to 1982. The average yield on a rolling five-year basis went up from 3150 kg/ha to 7750 kg/ha (2804 lb/a to 6898 lb/a) in the same period. No other cereal has such a continuous production record of increasing output.

Barley is still the staple crop of the Middle East, but is most important in the West for its ability to produce malt. Malt, in turn, is the product of barley grains that have been allowed to germinate in a controlled way. Malt contains the enzyme amylase, which turns starch into sugar, which in turn is converted into alcohol by yeast. Alternatively, malt can be used in baking, to make a mildly sweet, nutty range of cakes and breads.[12]

Greeks and Romans thought Oats were merely a diseased form of wheat. In Northern Europe, especially in Scotland, it became a crop that supported the people.[13] Today, only 5 percent of the crop is eaten directly by humans; it is allegedly good for fast horses. One of the cheapest balanced diets for Europeans a hundred years ago was milk, oats, and herrings, a diet that supported many a poor Scots undergraduate. Oats contain far more fat than wheat, together with an enzyme that digests the fat. The endosperm contains a natural antioxidant, furfural, that can be used as a benign preservative in foods like potato chips, nuts, instant coffee, and margarine. Some varieties of oats yield a narcotic, and this was the only use to which the Romans put the plant. An excessive dose of this infusion can be lethal. Is this how the Romans used the cereal, and was this why they thought the oat was a diseased, evil form of wheat?

Rice was unknown in the Ancient Mediterranean. It was brought west from India by the Muslims after Muhammad's death. The Moors grew large quantities in Spain, and it is possible that in 1492 it was a familiar cereal for Columbus and his crew. Long before the establishment of the familiar paddy fields, rice was a dryland crop in damp, hilly districts of India, China, and Siam.

The object of the paddy culture is not primarily to flood-irrigate the crop, but to drown out the competition for the weak young rice shoots. This is an excellent example of creating an environment that favors a crop that can survive flooding by prejudicing the weed competition that cannot resist the cultivated conditions. Today rice is the world's second most important crop, nudging wheat, which is still at the top. Rice is the principal food crop for the world's poorer half; wheat is manifestly the food of the rich, so rice is more vital. Wheat eaters can afford alternatives.

It is difficult to mill rice because the food is consumed as individual grains, not ground to flour and cooked into something unrecognizable. The hulls are removed, leaving the kernel covered by the bran; this is what is known in the West as "brown rice." Another process removes the bran and most of the endosperm, and this is called simply "unpolished rice." It is then polished in a vast wire-brush machine that removes most of the fat in the rice to prevent spoilage. Commercial polished rice looks nice, sometimes even nicer because it can be shined up with added sugar, but it is not a very good food. It has lost the bran that supplies the B complex vitamin thiamine necessary to prevent beriberi. Polishing also removes some of the protein and most of the essential amino acid lysine. Both problems have been avoided for 2000 years in India by parboiling before milling, a technique now known as "converting" rice. This process made rice in India both a food as valuable as raw rice and one that keeps much better than ordinary rice. This is because the heat of the parboiling kills the enzyme that causes rancidity in ordinary rice in hot climates.[14]

Millet, native to Asia and Africa, has a long history. Some millets have the lowest moisture requirement of any tropical food crop; some flourish in poor soils while others require regular rainfall, irrigation, and a high level of nutrient; some keep in store for years while others must be used within twelve months. The millets are of several families—Echinochloa, Eleusine, Papadum, Pennisetum, and Setaria—but the millet of history is probably *Panicum miliaceum,* the Common Millet. This was grown by lake dwellers in Switzerland before 500 BC and is said to have one of the lowest water requirements of any cereal. (Not a characteristic one would normally connect with lake dwellers.) It matures in two to three months and can be grown where climates are too hot, the rain too little, and the soil too poor for most other edible plants. The limit of its northern cultivation is a mean June temperature of 17°C (64°F), and in July, of 20°C (68°F). It is widely cultivated in Mongolia, Manchuria, North China, Japan, India, Asiatic Russia, and the Middle East. The Romans used millet bran mixed with unfermented wine, then dried, as a form of dried baker's yeast. The remains of the grain were used as slave food.

There is a huge genetic bank amongst the millets. No one has attempted to improve any of the many species. Millet has the greatest need for improvement, the greatest variability in protein level, and the lowest potential yield. It is also a very boring foodstuff. Yet it has the potential to be of the greatest.

Teff is a cereal unique to Ethiopia. Ethiopia was the original home of a wheat that has become essential in the two most important parts of the world; it was also the origin of the sorghum family of grains.[15] Both of these cereals have become commercially vital in many parts of the world. No one except the Ethiopians grows or eats teff. They have been devoted to this cereal for 5000 years.

Teff contains little gluten and cannot be made into bread. It is ground and mixed with water and allowed to ferment for one or two days; the fermented mixture is used to make a kind of pancake called "ingera." These are elastic, slightly sour in taste, and about the size of a pizza, but unlike the pizza, the cereal portion is not filled or garnished with meat, fish, or vegetables.

Teff used for grain normally has white seeds. Brown teff produces an excellent animal fodder—sweet and palatable, whether made into hay or cut green. This use of teff has made it an agricultural crop in South Africa and India. As with other cereals, there is a negative correlation between straw quality and grain quality. The better the grain, the lower the feeding value of the straw, and vice versa. Teff is a difficult crop to grow well. The seedlings are extremely sensitive to weed competition. The tiny seeds, about the size of onion seed, are easily washed away, so it is important to sow after rain, and not before. The crop is killed by frost and does best in temperatures of 15–20°C (59–68°F). Why, with all this difficulty, should teff form more than half of all the cereal grown in Ethiopia? Why should a virtual garden crop be preferred? Why should a sourmash pancake have been a unique food for thousands of years?

The Ethiopians could have tended the wheat that now dominates the Ukraine; brought from Russia by Volga Germans, it became "Turkey Red" when introduced into Kansas in the 1880s. Within twenty years, it had transformed the hard prairie sod and made the wheat lands possible. The Ethiopians, however, preferred teff to both wheat and sorghum. More difficult to grow, impossible to improve agronomically, boring to eat, teff is still preferred. There can be only one answer to the question why. Teff and the Ethiopians have formed a symbiotic relationship in which both are necessary to the other. This has been going on in a closed community for thousands of years. The closed nature of the community, breached occasionally, was nevertheless sufficiently intact to survive without major modification. Ethiopians, children of Judah, with the only indigenous native Christian community in Africa, also lived with a special cereal for at least 3000 years. Other parts of the world have been breached by botanical invaders from elsewhere. Ethiopia is unique, and worth mention on that account.

Sorghum has varied characteristics. The seed can be as big as barleycorn or only one-quarter that size. Some species make very good animal fodder, as grazed grass or as hay, and some have a considerable amount of sugar in the stems. The genus is extremely drought-resistant. After wheat, rice, and maize, sorghum is fourth in the list of grains that feed the most number of people. It is a staple food in the drier, frost-free parts of Africa, India, and China. In developed countries it is used as grain for livestock; it is grown in the United States, the Argentine, France, Hungary, Italy, Iran, Australia, and South Africa, as well as in the East Indies and Polynesia. The stems of some of the species are 10 percent sugar, and early in the Christian era these were used for sugar syrup production in areas of India and China. The genus came by sea to the Persian Gulf, probably about 500 BC, and arrived in the Mediterranean before 1492. It was useful in areas too dry for other grains or unsuitable for sugarcane. Benjamin Franklin is reputed to have been the first to plant it in the United States with seeds picked from an imported besom.[16]

Sorghum is a great tribute to genetic variation. Self-selected over centuries by the peculiar conditions of the African climate, relatively different populations survived particular environments. Over, say, five- hundred generations, such a process yielded segregated and distinct species. Wild selection favors small grains that disperse easily, or "shatter" as the farmer puts it. Human selection operates in an opposite direction, however, attempting to create large grains that remain attached to the plant for a long time, with chaff or glume that is easily threshed. No concentrated campaign has ever been mounted to make use of the great bank of available genes in the sorghum family. An effort comparable to that applied to the breeding of wheat or maize would yield even more results. For example, it could probably be induced to yield as much as ten times per acre of its present African average.

Sorghum, of course, cannot be made into risen bread, but it is consumed as unleavened flatbread, pancakes, or a kind of gruel or porridge. It can be made into what used to be called "small beer," which keeps only a few days because of its acetic acid content; such "beer" also contains valuable supplies of vitamin B. Sorghum "beer," containing 2 to 10 percent alcohol, is more interesting than the "mealie beer" made from maize. It is quite clear that the "Guinea Corn" to which the English referred was sorghum; they discovered it when they reached the Guinea Coast, an area that stretched for 5000 miles from the Senegal River to Angola. Besides "Guinea Corn" sorghum has been called "Kaffir Corn" (South Africa); milo (Europe); sorgo (United States); kaoliang (China); durra (Sudan); mtama (Kenya); and jola, jawa, or cholam (India and Pakistan).

There is one further interesting point. When young, sorghum leaves contain large quantities of dhurrin, a precursor to the lethal vegetable form of cyanide. Small plants and young shoots, compared to mature, adult leaves, have twenty times parts per million of dhurrin. The poison is destroyed when the leaves are made into hay or silage. Without this self-protection, sorghum could never have survived to become an important grain or forage plant. How many other useful cultivars have been lost because they did not survive casual grazing? How *elegant* a form of self-defense has sorghum produced, to protect itself from destruction! In turn, the same ecosystem produced a race of grazing animals that knew well enough to leave the immature sorghum plant alone and survived. Other animals foolishly grazed immature sorghum and did not survive to breed.

Buckwheat is neither a cereal nor a grass, but an herbaceous annual, a remote cousin of the geranium. The fruit has a dark brown, tough rind that encloses a kernel; the kernel is three-sided, like a beech mast, hence its German name, *Buchweizen* or beech wheat; the German word has become the English name.

Buckwheat arrived in Europe, significantly enough, in the late, hungry thirteenth century. It is a pioneer crop par excellence. Planted in June, it yields a crop before the autumn frosts. It was widely used in the Middle Ages in forest clearings and yielded another bonus—beloved of bees, buckwheat honey is a marvelous free gift. Today buckwheat is considered a food for wild pheasants or poultry in Western Europe, but in the past it was an essential crop for humans.

It was widely used in the Atlantic countries, just before the Black Death, to extend cultivation into forest clearings, up mountainsides, and in reclaimed bogs. Because of its short growing season, buckwheat can ripen where other food crops find life impossible, so it was taken to Russia by Germans, then by Russians all over their vast country and into parts of Central Asia and Siberia. Before the Russian Revolution, buckwheat groats were part of the ration for the ordinary Russian soldier in the Tsarist Army, cooked with butter, tallow, or vegetable oil.

Buckwheat was taken to the Americas by the Pilgrim Fathers, and it became associated with New England before the American Revolution. Buckwheat pancakes are popular in the United States; buckwheat crumpets are enjoyed in Holland; and buckwheat remains a staple in parts of Northern Russia. In Hindu countries buckwheat is permitted on fast days. (The relative absence of protein or fat in the flour renders buckwheat a relative penance.) It is a hard crop to find as a staple, yet it has kept thousands of pioneer people alive long enough to sow a proper cereal in the following year. It would be interesting to know how much of a part it played in the settlement of the United States before the railroads made such a pioneer crop unnecessary. However much potential the Northwest European system held, in 1300 the continent's population had expanded to the limits of its food supply. Although ideas that later proved to be extremely efficient were in place, feudal landownership and insufficient technology in traction, milling, irrigation, and transport restrained agricultural productivity before the Black Death.

By the time of Charlemagne's coronation on Christmas Day, AD 800, much of Western Europe was farmed on the manorial system. Five hundred years later, the system was beginning to break down under the stress of excessive population. In France, the country in which the feudal system lasted longest, the reverse was true. It had the lowest increase in population, by a factor of only just over three times in five hundred years, only five times in a thousand.

In the countries in which the manorial system failed at an early date, Flanders and England, the population increased by a multiple of five in five hundred years and by a multiple of ten in a thousand. This was double the rate of increase of that obtained in France. In Germany and Italy the increases between AD 800 and 1800 were of the same order as in France. In Iberia, the increases were smaller, with an increase under four times the base population. It would not be impossible to refine these crude figures and trace the survival of the feudal system plotted against increases in population. Conversely, they should be sufficient to accept the major thrust of the argument presented here.

The manorial system depended upon a manor, village, or township. Land was divided into five portions: The first was the best arable land. The second was the meadow that usually was mown for hay. The third was pasture that was grazed as common land, although individuals might be restricted as to the numbers of animals they could maintain. The fourth was waste ground on outlying areas of the village that normally was used only in summertime to graze geese, sheep, or goats during the day. The last portion was the woodland that was divided among the households so that each had some supply of coppice, timber, or windfall for fuel, building, and so forth.

The arable field was divided into strips, arranged so that most men had a mixture of both good and bad. One-third was sown with wheat in the autumn; one-third with spring corn, oats or barley; one-third was left to fallow. All the three were fenced in the growing season, as was the meadowland. Animals were encouraged to graze on the fallow one-third of the arable field and on the meadowland after the hay crop had been removed. Thus were animal residues recycled.

The yield of wheat on most land was less than 400 kg per hectare. An English acre, yielding six bushels of 60 lb weight, or 360 English pounds, was needed for each individual. There was rarely enough wheat for the cereal to enter commerce. Some Northern and Western manors never attempted to grow bread wheat, relying on rye, oats, and barley. Mixed grain, often more reliable, was also sown with or without beans.

The "cash crop" of the manor was often wool, traded all over Europe; the wool merchants of Flanders were already important by AD 800. The fairs of Champagne, Flanders, and Germany were the annual meeting places for the wool trades and traders. This is not to say that a money economy was widely at work; there were peasants who never saw a coin from one year's end to the next. Many European serfs did not know in what country they lived, only the name of their immediate lord.[17] Nor did villains or serfs have any more right to money, or access to the market with its wages and profits, than did slaves. The smallest holders of rented land were the cottiers, who held perhaps only a patch of land the size of a garden and owned no animals beyond the universal pigs and chickens; ironically, these cottagers often entered the market economy earlier than their larger neighbors, whose commitment to the lord for sizable landholdings made any cash nexus impossible. Cottiers, therefore, often became higglers, traders, and marketmen for their neighbors and themselves, buying and selling on commission. They might also very early become cash tenants, the lord not bothering with the few hours' service every month represented by a humble cottage and garden.

Institutions such as monasteries, nunneries, and cathedrals acquired lordships of manors by the death of the lord; so did the Crown, by default or crime of various kinds. During the thirteenth century, there arose in those countries whose population had substantially increased a tendency to commute labor rents for money. By 1300, five hundred years after Charlemagne and a generation before the Black Death, much of Western Europe had reached its Malthusian limit as far as food production was concerned. In those countries that made no change in the manorial system, output per acre did not rise. Indeed, no one today, observing the rules of the feudal system and using techniques available in 1300, could ever produce much more per acre.

It was the best guarantee of population control by hunger that could ever be devised. Nor could more acreage be brought into cultivation. The power, either of men or of animals, was simply not sufficient. The limits of cultivation were often dictated by the amount of power at hand. The only available addition to animal or human power was derived from wind or water and was of little assistance in cultivation.

Animal traction was limited, even in 1492, by certain inexorable facts. A horse can carry four times what a man can carry, a mule as much as a horse. A horse can pull twenty times what a man can pull, but in order to perform, a horse needs a proper harness, proper shoes, and a smooth road. Harness arrived later than shoes (about AD 900 in Western Europe), but roads deteriorated after the Roman Empire declined. Oxen are far slower than horses, but can exert traction for long periods on vehicles that are difficult to move. Carts that are bogged down in deep mud respond better to oxen than to horses. In Roman times, even with oxen a wagon-load of grain doubled in cost in the first 100 miles that it traveled, and this was along good Roman roads. Even then, efficiency was so low that each ox could only pull 70 kg (154 Ib) against 2000 (4410 lb) today. In areas where there were no roads, as in non-Roman Europe, the transport of grain by land was economically impossible, so local urban inhabitants, especially in large cities, adopted a carnivorous diet. Cattle, sheep, pigs, geese, even chickens can be walked to market.

Cities on rivers adopted water transport very early. Rivers used in the Middle Ages to transport grain long distances included the Elbe and the Vistula, which made Central European grain exportable via Hamburg and Danzig respectively. Almost every important town in Western Europe was close to some river, built upon a river, or limited by the deficiency. The exceptions were, of course, seaports, especially Venice, and cities that built their own transport canals, like Milan.

Water power also developed early. The great Vitruvius in *De Architectura* (before 27 BC) described the then state of the art. The simplest and earliest water wheels harnessed the flow and fall of a river to produce rotary power, usually to grind grain.[18] The simplest type of water wheel has been found in Scandinavia, Greece, Anatolia, Lebanon, and Central Asia, within living memory as well as in ancient times. It consisted of a horizontal water wheel on a vertical axle that drove the grindstones. These devices were limited to mountain regions with fast-flowing streams and were not efficient.

The Vitruvian mill was placed in a vertical mode with a horizontal axle. Gearing was required to link the horizontal rotary motion to the grinding stones. The Vitruvian mill was arranged to be what came to be called "undershot," meaning the stream of water pushes against the underside of the wheel, turning it so that the bottom of the wheel moves away from the force of the water. Undershot wheels are less efficient than overshot wheels. These water wheels utilize the combined force of the water flow and force of the water falling onto the top of the wheel. They can be usefully employed in a sluggish river, dammed to provide a millpond and a millrace. Aqueducts or canals also can bring the water to the mill.[19] Water transport and water power combined to produce flour at industrial mills at Venafro near Naples (about AD 50), and later at Arles in Provence.

The Neapolitan mills were undershot. They were destroyed by the Vesuvian eruption that buried Pompeii, but a model has been reconstructed from the impressions left in lava. The estimated power developed was about 3 hp and the output 1.5 tons a day, enough grain for about 4000 people. A much more substantial plant was built at Barbegal near Arles about AD 310. This drew water from an aqueduct, and it was arranged to pass at a slope of 30° through houses containing sixteen overshot wheels. The capacity of this series of mills was enough to grind 28 tons a day or enough for 80,000 people. Did the Romans export flour as well as grain from the river port of Arles, or was the flour used locally? If so, what was the density of population in Provence? At the time, Constantine the Great was living at Arles, so the addition of the court and the army to the indigenous population may have necessitated a huge milling complex. In all, it covered an area 200 meters (219 yards) long by 100 meters (109 yards) wide, or two hectares (five acres). Mills of this nature must have been the largest Roman industrial enterprises. There were, however, very serious intellectual limitations to the Greco-Roman use of power because there was no interplay between science and technology. This meant that most water power applications came long after Rome and were typical of the Middle Ages.[20]

By the time of the Domesday Book in 1087 there were about 4000 water mills in Domesday England, about one mill for every 250 people. Since this census was unique to England, no one knows whether or not this ratio was repeated elsewhere in Western Europe.

The floating mill was invented or developed by the soldier-genius Belisarius in AD 537. The Goths sought to starve Rome by cutting the aqueducts, but Belisarius set up a huge mill that was mounted on moored ships. Rome did not starve, and the Goths failed to take Rome. Such floating mills were used in Dover before the Norman Conquest, harnessing the tide. They were also found in the Tigris in the tenth century, in the Seine before 1200, in the Loire in 1330, and in the Yangtse Kiang before 1400. They were in use in the Persian Gulf, in the Po Valley, and near Venice. In seawater, tidal mills never really froze, nor did the sea dry up; but in the Low Countries, no sort of water mill could have served as well as the windmill did.

The windmill gave the flatlands of modern Belgium, Holland, and North Germany the same sort of advantage that countries with running water enjoyed, but the windmill has a more demanding technology than the water mill. The Eastern mill, originally turning horizontally, had a set of rotary sails like a Central Asian prayer wheel. This mill, in horizontal or vertical form, was found as far west as Southern Spain and wherever the later Muslims took the technique, but it was not present in Palestine during the Crusades, nor was the Eastern mill copied. For once, the Western Europeans invented something for themselves. The first post mill—wooden, with wooden sails—was found at the Abbey of St. Sauvère de Vicomte in Normandy in 1180.

By the Black Death, there were probably 1000 windmills in England, one-tenth the total number of water mills, most of them in Eastern England where river flow was too sluggish for water mills. In the Low Countries there were probably six times as many. In the Netherlands alone there were 10,000 in the seventeenth century, the era of Holland's greatness. Before steam there were probably a million water mills and windmills in the whole of Western Europe. There were probably as many or more in the states west of the Mississippi and Missouri Rivers in 1900, nearly all windmills. No farm could exist without one, but they were not very efficient. A rather large steel structure, weighing up to ten tons and having a wheel diameter of 7.5 meters (25 feet), could extract only 1.34 hp/h. It was enough, however. Without the ceaseless pumping on the prairie, settlement would not have been possible.[21]

The Romans (using gravity but no windmills) tried to drain both the English fens and the Dutch Rhine district. These efforts silted up in the Dark Ages, but were reborn in medieval times. The Po Valley improvements, completed before AD 50, were more robust and appear to have survived better, but without the windmill and the water wheel, there would have been no general drainage and irrigation of the sort carried out by the Dutch, or earlier by the Arabs in Southern Spain and Sicily. In Christian Europe, the religious houses became identified with wetland improvement, and irrigation and drainage were connected to canalizing rivers in turn. Some of these transport improvements were in place surprisingly early. Bruges, for example, was connected to the sea by canal in 1236; Haarlem, by 1315; and Amsterdam, by 1440. Milan's complex, using the flow from Lake Como and canals to the Po, was completed earlier, in the thirteenth century.

Population growth justified bringing marginal land into cultivation; drainage and reclamation of wetlands were responses to an increased population. In the absence of cheap and efficient land transport, water was the key. Access to water was necessary to trade because any serious trade in heavy goods had to be by river or sea. Canalizing rivers was expensive in both capital and revenue costs, so early cities tended to grow up where there was easy access to the sea, and by sea, to the world. Each town not on a river had a hard time just grinding the grain to make its daily bread. A town like Assisi, on top of a hill, used human or animal muscles to grind grain before the windmill came along. If it had used human power, it would have needed about one day's work to provide bread for every five people. This kind of proportion, that one man (or woman) only ground and baked enough for four other people, dominated the lives of ordinary people until steam came along to supplement animals, wind, and water. For a thousand years before steam, techniques very gradually improved. There was plenty of room for improvement.[22]

In 800, Western European agriculture was low in efficiency, but the population was so low in numbers that there was little incentive to improve. By 1300, five hundred years later, the germ of every possible husbandry improvement that would amaze and delight the world in the eighteenth century was already present.

In the years leading up to the Black Death in 1350, Western Europe pressed upon the Malthusian constraints. In 1850, the same constraints had been met and matched in Belgium, Holland, and England. The area of arable land available in 1850 in those countries was less than double what it had been five hundred years before. The population of the

Low Countries was nearly four times, and of England more than five times, the 1300 figure. This time, the constraints were defeated. It was a tremendous intellectual triumph for the people who had labored to grow enough food over the previous century; efficient agriculture was possible; it was also very profitable. Technical and legal constraints were gradually removed, both by slow structural improvements in communications, scientific knowledge, and the like and by innovative and perspicuous individual efforts.

In the 1780s there were eight separate improvements listed[23] as having been adopted by English landlords in the previous half-century in order to increase profits from land—either directly for the tenant or indirectly for the landlord by increasing rent. It was quite clear that the initiative was expected to come from the landlord and the improvements to be imposed by patrician and paternalist leadership upon the tenantry. The tenantry did not, of course, object provided their pockets gained as a result. Some of the tenants of larger farms became so much better off as a result of these improvements that they occupied themselves in hunting several times a week, leaving the actual supervision of the farms to their foremen. Alternative occupation was not entirely necessary, however, since not a single one of the improvements saved labor of any kind.

By these means England became the first country to survive a huge increase in population without massive social or political disruption. England's relative success with food supply in the century from 1750 to 1850 should be contrasted with that of the future United States during the same period. A country with virtually free land did not need improved agricultural systems.

Tillage improvements. Jethro Tull (1674–1741) was responsible for the great improvements in tillage. He advocated the drilling of seed in rows, and the movement of soil at frequent intervals during the growing season by hoes—either horse hoes or handheld hoes. He wrote, "By frequently turning over and pulverizing the soil, we not only destroy the weeds very effectively, but likewise also grubs, beetles, worms, and maggots of many kinds." Moving soil does not, of course, destroy either weeds or insects by itself. Weeds die because of lack of water—provided hoeing is carried out in dry weather. Insects are killed only if an attendant bird, following the implements, picks up and eats the insect. Nor did Tull or anyone else in the eighteenth century know that earthworms are beneficial; or that grubs, beetles, and maggots all have different life cycles; or the point at which insects are harmless; or the point at which the chrysalis is damaging, the fly dangerous, the grub a peril, or the maggot safely ignored. All these minute observations were to follow. Of Tull's theories in general it can be said that his advocacy did more good than harm, but no one subjected his theories to value for money analysis until at least a hundred years after his death. Then the seed drill became important, not to kill maggots, but to save seed and increase yield.

New Implements. The cost of cast iron came down by about half in England between 1700 and 1750 (later on the Continent), and this enabled its use to spread widely. Before 1700, most implements and hand tools, even shovels, were made of wood. After 1760, an increasing number were made by the village blacksmith using new cast iron; in the next century, the village blacksmith was gradually replaced by the agricultural machinery maker. Some of these were local, set up in business on a district basis by capitalists, or sometimes by customers.[24]

It is not easy to recollect, but in the same period the cobbler (roughly 1 per 250 souls), the blacksmith (roughly 1 per 500 souls), and the wheelwright (roughly 1 per 1000 souls) were as essential in the village as both the woman who delivered babies and the woman who laid out the dead. Gradually all the functions became centralized, and the jobs moved into towns, the manufacture into factories, and the midwife and the undertaker became professional specialists. Long before there were maternity hospitals or undertakers' parlors, the agricultural machinery makers had started to supersede the blacksmith. By 1850 rural blacksmiths had thinned out, and by 1900, just before the automobile replaced the horse, most blacksmiths were in urban areas, not the countryside. Today, the blacksmith is often mobile, traveling many miles to tend horses kept only for pleasure.[25]

Better ratio between seed sown and seed harvested. In the Middle Ages and in most of continental Europe in 1750, there was a time-honored belief that an increase in harvest of, say, 4:1 or 6:1 was all that any farmer could expect from his land. It was thought that to increase the harvest it was necessary to increase the seed rate, which would then be reflected in an automatic growth of 4:1 or 6:1, or whatever. Today this policy can be seen to be scientifically absurd, but it was challenged by the Dutch only generally in the late seventeenth century and by the English from 1750 onward. A parallel development was to arrive, by selection, at a cultivar that gave a better than average return, and a method of breeding that raised the long-term average over the years.

Wheat or barley seed runs from 12,000 to 30,000 per kilo, oats rather more. A pot-sown single grain seed, properly tended, multiplies by almost 100 if the right seed is chosen; wheat multiplies less readily than barley, maize by nearly 200 times in pot-culture. Best results in the field are achieved by selecting plump seed with ample food reserves for the tiny plant in the endosperm, and by sowing relatively few of them in well-tilled soil. Today, this means 150 kilos per hectare (133 lb per acre), or one-quarter of what was sown in England in 1750 and one-fifth of the quantity sown in France. Miraculously, it had occasionally been noted in *ancien régime* France that, after a long winter when some of the seed corn had been eaten perforce by hungry peasants, the subsequent harvest had been better than that of the previous year, and had yielded a return of 10:1 or 12:1. This benison was universally described as a gift of God.

No experimental work of sowing various rates of seed in otherwise identical conditions was performed in England until the 1790s or in France until the 1850s, and only in the 1960s did true experimenters carry such a test to its logical conclusion. In that decade, full crops were grown with seed rates of only three kilos per hectare, or 2 percent of normal. In order to achieve this result, all the other conditions had to be of a perfection almost impossible to achieve in the field. Nevertheless, it shows what can be done to multiply newly bred strains of seed when such a course is necessary.

Specialization. Suiting the crop to the nature of the soil, an obvious move, became possible only when communications improved. An entirely isolated community had to grow wheat for bread; rye for bread; oats for horses and bullocks—the sole form of non-manual power; barley for beer; all sorts of vegetables, suitable or not suitable for humans; trees for wood; and flax for linen. The district had to keep cows for milk, horses and bullocks for the plow, sheep for wool and meat, goats for milk and cheese, pigs as scavengers and for meat, animal skins for leatherwork of all kinds, poultry for eggs and meat, and dogs to be trained for the defense and herding of animals. An isolated community had no chance to grow and rear products most suitable to the environment, so specialization of crops and livestock depended on better roads, canals, and river transport.

It is not surprising, when one considers the situation carefully, that such improvements took place in the Po Valley and in the Netherlands and Flanders, countries crisscrossed by waterways earlier than anywhere else. Improvements up and down the Seine Valley were made earlier than in the Massif Central, and the lowlands of England were improved by specialization earlier than the Highlands of Scotland, parts of which had to wait for the internal combustion engine before they could safely stop growing barley for beer. Before railways, internal communications were usually less favorable than those for foreign trade. Although it is easier to export agricultural commodities from the specialist country and import them into the consuming country by river and sea than it is to grow the same commodities in every consuming country, it was not until late in the last century that some villages, such as the mountain villages in Greece, could safely give up growing consumables and import them from areas more suited to their growth.[26]

The biggest single beneficent change that specialization brought to individual communities was probably in discontinuing the need to grow bread grains in every parish. There was a long-held medieval practice, almost a law, that virtually every parish in Europe had an obligation to feed itself with wheat or some substitute. There are, in fact, millions of acres in Europe in huge areas that are wholly unprofitable for wheat. This was true for much of East Prussia in the eighteenth century where, because of the practice of growing one's own bread, Prussia ate rye bread, while its neighbor Poland exported wheat to Holland or Venice.

Rotation of crops. The old Mediterranean-medieval "rotation" (if it was a rotation) was either winter corn—spring corn—fallow or winter corn—fallow—spring corn—fallow. (The "fallow" was often a period during which the land tumbled down to temporary grass, mostly weed grasses, and the resulting mess was trodden and "grazed" by half-starved cattle and sheep.) By 1400 "improved" temporary grasses (Italian Ryegrass) had been developed in Lombardy, and by 1700 the turnip came out of the garden and into the field, as did the carrot. Longer leys (artificial grasses sown for more than one year) were also introduced by some "improvers" in the eighteenth century. The most productive (the "Noble") grasses— perennial ryegrass, cocksfoot, the meadow grasses, and timothy—are all indigenous to Europe, and by 1776 had been taken to North America and become native to that continent. It was the technique of their use in the rotation that was important—new management husbandry rather than new crops. Landlords imposed upon tenants the use of clovers— red, white, and alsike—which in some form or other are native to every Western European country; clover is much more sensitive than grass to acidity in the soil.

Dung, marl, and chalk. The practice of using dung and chalk (or lime) can be dated as early as 500 BC, but the application of both was very hard work. It was avoided by the inferior husbandman or when there was no immediate profit to be gained. Dung had a great chemical value as one of the few sources of nitrogen and phosphate, and urine was preserved for potash. Most of the chemical value of dung, if left in an uncovered heap, disappears in rain or, by nitrification, in heat, and the preservation of dung in covered pits or yards engaged "model" landlords and their agents from the sixteenth century. As with dung, so with chalk and marl. The landlord, having a longer-term perspective, again took the initiative. Landlords made their use a logical exercise, a necessity in long leases. Dung was to be preserved and used on the farm in rotation. Woe betide a tenant who used dung produced on the landlord's farm on his own land, if he owned any, or who sold it. This was an offense against every tenet of good husbandry, and almost a crime to boot.[27]

Apart from its chemical value, dung makes heavy soils lighter and gives lighter soils more "body." The actual effect on clay is to help flocculate the soil so that it crumbles and has an easier, blander characteristic. This makes the clay easier to till and produces a soil that can, aided by the influence of the weather, be worked with farm tools to produce a good structure and a good seedbed. The same is true of chalk and marl. Defoe, referring to Kent chalk applied to Essex clay, commented that chalk, added to heavy soils, "makes the strong clay rich and fruitful."[28]

Lighter land was always easier to cultivate, and it is no accident that the earliest true agriculture ("tilling of soil") took place in the sandy loams of the Mediterranean, or on alluvial bottoms in the Nile, Tigris, Euphrates, and Indus Valleys. Any form of calcium applied to the clay fraction in soil makes that soil "lighter" and easier to cultivate, since the action of calcium is to encourage earthworms and other fauna that break down organic matter into what we now call "humus."[29] The presence of lime in a soil is essential for nitrification, nitrogen fixation, and many other beneficial bacterial activities, including the fixing of nitrogen by the nodules on clover.[30]

At the other end of the scale, applying lime or chalk to very light or sandy soils is a waste of time and money. Since the sand does not have the necessary "body" to hold the calcium, the added chemical material washes through the sand to the drains, so marl is employed instead. Marl is clay mixed with animal residues rich in calcium. There are great stories in Elizabethan times of marl pits that were found to contain hundreds of horns of dead deer.[31] Over the centuries, the more soluble calcium in the bodies of animals, whether mammals or sea creatures (as in "sedimentary" limestone) or eggs (as in "oolite"), becomes mixed by natural action with the clay fraction. Marl is the end product, and it was dug all over Europe in the period following the Renaissance when various individual improvers were increasing the value of the land. The landlord's contribution was, again, to formalize the use of marl on the light land. It was an expensive business—a good dressing of marl cost double the rent of the land manured, and sometimes the tenant and landlord shared the cost by the remission of one year's rent.[32] Marling increased yield by a quarter, other factors being equal, and the landlord as well as the tenant benefited, since a good dressing of marl needed renewing only every twenty years or so, other acts of good husbandry being performed in the interval.[33]

New crops. The seventh great improvement was in the use of new crops, or of old crops put to new uses. Thus became possible the growing of cash crops in the countryside for other communities to eat in other places. This tied the farmer firmly into the cash nexus and ultimately into a capitalist system in which he was farming for the market. The list of crops grown for the first time in the century after 1700 reads like a table of contents of modern field husbandry. Sometimes "new" crops—turnips, for example—were not as new as people thought then or think today.

A distinction had to be drawn, not for the first time in modern history, between subsistence crops, grown for man or beast or for people within the localities, and crops for sale. Sometimes the same crop might be both a cash crop and a crop consumed at home. Wheat could be either used in the village for bread making or sold. Barley could be used to fatten cattle or pigs, to fuel oxen and horses, to brew beer locally, or sold to brewers several hundred miles away. Carrots, cabbages, swedes, parsnips, peas, and potatoes became field crops in the late eighteenth century and could be either sold as cash crops for human consumption or used on the home farm for animal feed. In that event, stock might be brought in to consume and "cash in" the crops. Cattle were purchased in the autumn to consume unsaleable roots of all kinds. Sheep were finished on field surpluses left in rows and "folded" with hurdles. Pigs could be profitably fattened on peas and potatoes, although these crops were usually intended for sale to humans. Poultry were used not only to cash in tail corn by means of selling eggs or meat, but by consuming all sorts and conditions of surplus (and boiled) vegetables. Sometimes the taste of parsnip or swede carried over into eggs or poultry meat.

The technological ideas that became much clearer in crop husbandry during the century after 1700 did not extend in the same force to the culture of animals, if only because animals are much more complicated forms of life than most plants. The aim was to shorten the time taken to produce an animal for market. In 1760, it was doubtful that most sheep or cattle could be grown to adulthood in under four years. Cattle types were indiscriminately mixed, often with unknown fathers. For centuries sheep had been selected for wool production, and there is a negative correlation between weight of fleece and quality of wool in most sheep; so as the English made efforts to increase the fleece weight, the fineness of the wool declined. Good lowland feed was found to produce coarser wool; the demand by English spinners and weavers for the finer merino-type fleeces from Spain or poor land fleeces from Ireland was embarrassing to a nation geared for a thousand years to the production of wool. In the generation after Bakewell's pioneer efforts in the 1790s, by means of selection, the English sheep breeds were catalogued, identified, and adopted for the first time. This process inevitably led to the widespread division of sheep into meat producers and wool producers.

There was a similar division of cattle into cattle for beef, cattle for milk, and, in some countries, cattle as draught animals. Economic efficiency ultimately led to the extinction of the dual-purpose or triple-purpose beast beloved of the peasantry. The twelve-year-old bullock, having drawn a plow for most of his life, was no longer the source and provision of beef as in old England. As horses and mules replaced slower, less efficient oxen, so cattle became more specialist providers of meat or milk. In this process the problem of winter was even more vital in cattle husbandry than in sheep production.

Cattle husbandry. This was cited in 1785 as the final great improvement in the following way: "the application of the foregoing to the rearing and fattening of cattle."[34] To understand the importance of winter feed it is necessary to take a quick dip into the natural processes of growth in Western Europe. In most temperate areas about 30 percent of all plant growth takes place in or about the month of May, with nearly 20 percent in June, and about 10–15 percent in April in favored districts. Altogether, in any area, the spring quarter of ninety days normally produces more than 60 percent of the annual growth of any plant. The summer quarter produces about 30 percent, leaving a mere 10 percent for the whole winter half-year. This is an average rule, and in a country like England with no apparent "average" weather, or in a country with no real winter like Southern and Western Ireland, or in a country like France big enough to have regional weather, these proportions may be modified, but the principle remains true.

Even in the warmest parts of the British Isles or in favored Atlantic provinces of France winter growth is much lower than in the warmer half of the year. So wintering is a major problem for all forms of animal husbandry. Without special provision for the winter, most grazing animals left to fend for themselves will survive, but lose weight that then must be replaced in the spring at some expense. This is as true of wild grass-eating species like deer, rabbits, and geese as it is of cattle or sheep. It was the adoption of all the principles of the new husbandry that made it possible for a meat-loving people to increase their meat production to keep pace with a rise in population of 300 percent in one century.

It is one of the minor ironies of history that, although the period up to 1760 saw the English working class (and no other) better fed than at any time in history, that well-being did not include much fresh meat, and none in winter. Outside a few "advanced" counties like Norfolk, there were few cattle available for fresh meat in the hungry months. By the time the techniques to fatten cattle had been developed—hay or straw, turnips or swedes, some crushed grain—only the rich could afford the end product. It has been said that the poorest quarter of the population of Britain fared worse in the period 1760–1940 than they had in the previous half-century. Whether or not this was true—and it is true that only government intervention brought some malnutrition to an end in World War II—it was certainly never true that the poor had daily fresh meat at any time in the same period. Even families living on farms in the late eighteenth and nineteenth centuries ultimately found meat a daily occurrence only when cheap imported beef and lamb came in from the new countries after 1880. On the other hand, only in Britain was the coincidence of meat and wealth so well connected. While there were plenty of affluent vegetarians in the Mediterranean Basin, no Briton was considered prosperous unless he was a carnivore. "Beef, beer, liberty, England, and St. George" went the toast.

"The new agriculture," then, was seen by the people of the time to be a matter of eight techniques. They are worth repeating again: better tillage, new implements, better ratio between seed sown and seed harvested, suiting the crop to the soil, rotations, manuring of soil, new sorts of crops, and the application of all the above to cattle husbandry. Very few of these techniques were "new" to anyone in Western Europe. They were brought together, interrelated, and properly managed, each affecting the other, in one country first, England. The honor fell to the English, not because of some great wisdom and nobility, but quite simply because the land/population equation that had been so favorable to the English in 1760, compared to the French or the Dutch, completely reversed itself when the population exploded. In 1760, the population was on the order of 6 million, and the improved agricultural sector (of 5 million hectares or 12 million acres) provided food for 140 percent of that population. In 1850, the population was three times that number (18 million), there were 7 million hectares (18 million acres) of "improved land," and the agricultural sector provided a much better diet for 125 percent of the population. In the period 1660–1860, 2.5 million hectares (6 million acres) were brought into better cultivation by enclosure from common land, scrubland, wasteland, poor timberland,

and so forth. This was the ultimate extent of cultivation possible by the technological means of the time.[35] This massive achievement was not matched in any other country in the world.[36]

But it was not only food for humans that the farmers grew. The figures of 140 percent of population in 1760 and 125 percent of population in 1850 include, of course, some export of grain, mostly wheat, for the first date and substantial *imports* of grain, mostly wheat, for the second. Far more important, though, was the non-human food that the land of Britain supplied. In 1750 there were probably more than half a million non-agricultural horses in use, or one non-agricultural horse to twelve people. Each horse required as much food to breed, rear, and maintain as ten men. Although a horse cost ten times the food of a working-man, at the very minimum level of feeding the man—30,000 K cal. against 3000—men cost more than just food and shelter. Even in very bad, hungry times, like the four great near-famines of 1795–96, 1800–01, 1809–12, and 1818–19, the bare keep of a workingman was at least as great as that of a horse. Two contrasts exist. In 1800, in a workhouse, a man could be kept much more cheaply than a horse. At the other end of the scale, a butler, in 1900, cost as much in food and perquisites as the very best hunter. The hunter did not have an added wage either.[37] Parallel to the technological constraints on food supply in the fourteenth century ran the sociopolitical conditions that perpetuated the inefficient open-field manorial system. Fields were enclosed as populations grew, but enclosure, in turn, had important reverberations on Europe's social arrangements.

Any modern farmer having to operate an open-field system considers himself lucky to produce a net harvest of one-half that of the same land operated by a set of rules known to anyone in Western Europe in, say, 1338, the date of the *Luttrell Psalter*.[38] In other words, land tenure in common made impossible sensible rotations, manuring, fallow, cultivations, and so forth. As will be shown, England's primacy in the eighteenth century grew from the (usually) adequate food. This was grown on land much improved agronomically by enclosure and by subsequent husbandry only possible on enclosed land.

Yet it was not hunger or population pressure that brought about the first enclosures, but the desire to create sheep walks. Wool was the first English crop to show a tremendous advantage as a cash crop. It was valued at many times the value of grain, which was sometimes in surplus, sometimes not. Wool was easily transported, and was the one product of England, a marginal wine-growing country capable only of roughish wine, to equate with the finest wines as an article of commerce. Long before the Black Death, merchants from Flanders and Italy were buying English wool. As the population declined after the Black Death, a kind of enclosure was taking place without any overt acts on the part of the lords, who often simply seized the deserted, empty villages and incorporated them into their own estates. The major sheep-walk enclosures came later, notably in Tudor times, when commerce had largely replaced subsistence as the characteristic motive in many agricultural areas.

Men of enterprise cleared out huge districts, sometimes including a dozen villages, and turned them into enclosed estates devoted to sheep. Inhabitants were compensated by means of a formula that was less than satisfactory for families who had never before handled money. In the end, many became landless peasants and, later, when the population pressure on the land became too heavy, the same people moved into towns and became the urban proletariat. This process was continuous from the time of the early Tudors, a hundred years before Shakespeare, until enclosure came to an abrupt end in 1869. Technological progressives like the Elizabethan writer Thomas Tusser (1520–80) were in favor of enclosure. He noted in the 1560s that Suffolk and Essex were benefiting from it, while Cambridgeshire and Leicestershire were still operating the old open-field system. In general, counties with ports and feeder rivers or counties near London, the big market, were enclosed earlier than distant, boggy, or dry counties. Transport was the key to the cash nexus in farming, even in terms of wool, a very easy commodity to handle. Enclosure in Tudor times was the driving force for improvement. Wool was the prime export until the end of the seventeenth century and ultimately paid for all the imported finery worn by the gentry depicted in the portraits of the time. It was wool that paid for the very pigment in the paint of the portraits, imported, as like or not, from Italy or France.[39]

There is a school of thought that says that it was population pressure that gave rise to politico-religious differences throughout Europe in the seventeenth century; in England, for example, it was the counties that had the highest population increases that appeared to have the sharpest divisions in the Civil War. It was the much smaller general increase in population (a drop in the rate of increase from nearly 40 percent per century to the equivalent of less than 5 percent per century) between 1700 and 1760 that made for the relative happiness of the English working class during that time; this resulted in an Augustan Age, not only in literature, but also in filling the bellies of the poor. The slackening of the increase in population pressure meant more food, more profit, and hardly any years of bread shortage in England. Pressure to enclose almost exactly followed the pressure upon the food supply. During the fifty years before 1760, there was an annual average of only eight Acts of Enclosure: This coincided with a population increase of only about 3 percent in the same period. After 1760, the increase in enclosure followed the increase in population: Between 1760 and 1815 there were nearly 1.3 million hectares (3.25 million acres) enclosed, more than half of all the enclosures. The population increased in the same period to more than double the 1760 figure. No contemporary, of course, knew of the population increase decade by decade, but the price of wheat was a nearly true correlation of the impulse to enclose. The change in the Bank Rate dictated the cost of the enterprise, as with all other commercial efforts involving the raising of capital. The relationship of grain price, cost of money, and rental income to be expected was a powerful instrument of calculation, and graphs have been prepared to define these relationships. The peace between 1802 and 1805 saw a decline in enclosures, and the peace after Waterloo in 1815, a temporary cessation. The drop in the price of grain can be plotted against these events.

We know the price of grain in England during the period; this increase in price was driven by population growth. What we do not know is what drove the population to increase by nearly 40 percent per century in 1600–1700, the rate of increase to fall to 5 percent per century in the sixty years before 1760, and the rate of increase to accelerate between 1760 and 1860 to 300 percent per century. It was this change that dictated the form that husbandry took in England, in sharp contrast to what happened in Ireland in the same period.

The process of enclosure displaced thousands of commoners. During the eighteenth century most of what was enclosed had been the old medieval arable strip fields: unfenced, cultivated in the summer, ranged across by every kind of animal in the winter, with the strongest male fathering the most animals of his species, making improvements in animal husbandry as difficult as were advances in the growing of crops. It is entirely probable that early enclosures more than doubled the production from any given area. The process was generally seen to be desirable, even by the displaced peasants who lost their rights in the field and became wage slaves. There were probably more jobs to be had in the new industries that arose in the period 1760–1800 than were lost in the process of enclosure. The new cotton mills and the older woolen industry were both booming during this period, as were the coal and iron twins. There was little hint of serious objection to enclosure as long as those displaced and their children found gainful employment elsewhere. It was a different matter in the new century.

Between 1800 and 1845, nearly 0.6 million hectares (1.5 million acres) were enclosed, and they were generally great tracts of moor and fenland. Though fewer people were displaced in a given area than by the enclosure of strip fields, there was also a much more difficult economic climate. In 1800, there were 50 percent more people in England than in 1760—nine million against six million. In the next forty-five years, the population of England doubled. Wages were held down by the high birthrate and by the continuous ability of employers to recruit unskilled labor at short notice from Ireland. In the same period John Bull's other island had a higher increase in her population by more than did England, and had no industrial revolution to absorb the surplus. The position of the new proletariat grew markedly worse in the years before the Repeal of the Corn Laws.[40] There were so many wholly unskilled men, women, and children that employers designed systems to employ people as virtual animals. Thus came about what we now regard as the scandals in the cotton, wool, and coal industries.

Two political developments became inevitable. First, pressure on food supplies led to a curious coalition of industrialists, who wanted cheap contented workers, and do-gooders and economists who together persuaded the Prime Minister, Peel, to repeal the remaining Corn Laws in 1845. Second, there were efforts to civilize the factories. Basically this meant designing systems that treated people as people rather than using children as pit ponies, cotton mill automatons, or (in a rare case) a live chimney brush. The Factory Acts, as is the way, came into force a generation after the abuses they were designed to correct had already peaked.

In the third period of enclosure, after 1845, there was no pressure on actual grain supplies since imports could come from Europe or the neo-European countries, notably the United States and Canada. From 1845 onward, and uniquely in Europe, the Irish population declined, not only from death during the Famine, but also from emigration and a declining birthrate. At the same time, the population of the United Kingdom as a whole increased at much the same rate as before 1845. English and Scots fecundity made good the losses in Ireland, but grain could be imported and, indeed, grown specially for the British market in any suitable place in the world, so in the second half of the nineteenth century, Britain became the greatest food-importing nation ever known.

The Enclosure Movement reflected these changes. Enclosure after 1845 was seen to be purely for profit, not for life-enhancing food. The enclosures after 1845 were largely of the primeval manorial common rights of all sorts of people, often near new towns or on the edge of old towns. The benefit to the Lord of the Manor was seen to be more personal, more socially questionable, than the improvements derived from earlier enclosures. At the same time, the philanthropic impulse of the age led to a decline in the automatic pursuit of economic efficiency. The idea of Malthus, that an excessive population would be automatically corrected by starvation, lost its appeal. Purity of vision was overtaken by the social movement to sanitize and purify that became known, in shorthand, as gas and water socialism. As part of that process, an increasingly polluted industrial society rediscovered the virtues of fresh air. Cheap food and fresh air put an end to any moral virtue in enclosure.

In 1869 the Enclosure Movement came to an end. This was not due to some great rural scandal that outraged public opinion. The movement came to an end in the towns, not ordinary towns, but in the metropolitan fastness of London. The twenty years after the Enclosure Act of 1845 saw more than 240,000 hectares (600,000 acres) enclosed, to add to more than 2.5 million hectares (6 million acres) enclosed since the Black Death. In 1865, an attempt was made to enclose Wimbledon and Clapham Commons and the Downs at Epsom where the Derby is raced every year. Reformers, suburban liberals, and horse-lovers joined to defeat such heinous proposals. They succeeded, and no further enclosure took place after 1869; enclosure, at least in urban and suburban areas, was seen to be a retrograde step. The debate will continue as to its value in the country as a whole. For those who believe that feeding the people was more important than people's "rights," enclosure was more important than Common Land.

For the mid-Victorian radical, with ample food available from anywhere in the world, the Common Lands were more important than the prosperity of English agriculture. Common Land was a place to walk, to observe nature, to breathe, and to enjoy birdsong. The repeal of the Corn Laws in the same year as the Enclosure Act of 1845 had, with all the obvious wisdom of hindsight, put paid to an era in the history of agriculture in Britain. Neo-Europeans initiated, at first for the British market, an equally important age of expansion in the United States, Canada, Australia, New Zealand, South Africa, Uruguay, the Argentine, and large parts of Southern Russia. All these became part of the European farm, neo-European feeders of Europeans thousands of miles away, participants in world trade.[41]

In the five years 1845–50, the population of the United Kingdom was still higher than that of the United States. The United States contained land parceled in thirty states amounting to more than two million square miles, more than fifteen times the area of the United Kingdom at that time. Only a few areas in the Northeast had a density of population approaching that of England, 350 people per square mile. In both England and Ireland there were districts more densely crowded than any place on earth, but no one knew this at the time. Certainly Britain was the most Malthusian problem to date, but no one knew that either. In England, enclosures met the problem for a time, then this policy was insufficient, and Free Trade and more consciously induced emigration followed. For a number of reasons such solutions were not possible in Ireland, and the Famine resulted with all its grave consequences.[42]

In both the United States and the United Kingdom, policies were dictated, not by politicians, but by territorial imperatives. The Jeffersonian dream was for a country of small farms, cultivated by noble farmers who would throw up local and national leaders conceived in the form of Cincinnatus.[43] Instead there was a nation divided into slave and free states, plantations and small farms, ranches and ranges, capitalists and settlers. The Jeffersonian dream existed for a short time in only a few areas before subsistence gave way to the market. Romantics in many countries have tried to create the same sort of conditions, with predictable failure. In some countries, notably Germany, the failure of the small farmer movement led directly to fascism. Today there are many people in many First World countries trying to re-create the same sort of dream out of its time.

In England, territorial imperatives demanded efficiency in the agricultural sector. Although hard on the commoners, enclosure guaranteed enough food, by and large, for a population grown by three times in a century. Enclosure also won three great struggles. The first, and most obvious, was the Napoleonic War that lasted, with intermission, for more than twenty years. Second, alone in Europe, England's revolution was industrial and economic, not political. Third, England, but not Ireland, went through a Malthusian experience that did not destroy the nature of the country. Enclosure helped defeat Napoleon, revolution, and Malthus. This record was unique, but by 1845, it was no longer enough.[44]

CHAPTER THREE

New Worlds, New Crops, New Beasts

The exploitation of the Eastern Atlantic Islands began before Columbus, and, as is well-known, Columbus victualed and repaired his ships in the Canaries, a new Spanish settlement, before he crossed the Atlantic. The Canaries are several hundred miles nearer the (then unknown) Caribbean than Spain itself.

When Columbus arrived in the New World, an immediately important exchange took place. As already related, diseases were given to the natives. This led straightaway to a weakening of any indigenous resistance to Europeans, a weakening that was repeated for more than four hundred years in all parts of the world. The next act of unconscious imperialism was European acquisition of American plants. These included cassava, yams, maize, the white and sweet potato, innumerable beans, tomatoes, squash, and capsicum. Europeans transferred these plants to Europe, to Africa, and even within the Americas. One plant that Columbus did not find was one he was looking for—pepper—but his discoveries were a more valuable alternative and an important side effect of the search for the Spice Islands.

The introduction of European plants into the Americas is a tale with uneven endings. Wheat found its niche long before any occupation of America north of the Rio Grande. It took nearly a century to cultivate wine fit to export, and then it came from Peru and Chile, not Mexico. The olive took longer to settle; it found a home in Chile after 1600 and in California much later. Since 1492 olive oil has been exported to the Americas, one of the few staple foods of which this is true. Citrus and stone fruits are another matter; they spread and bred and succeeded magnificently in the Americas. Animals—horses, cows, sheep, and pigs, unknown in the New World—not only prospered, but also mutated and went feral. They changed not only their own lifestyles and produced a cash crop for the Iberian settlers, but their arrival changed habits in animal predators and Amerindians alike. In the North in particular, the horse became a force of change in the lives of both the native buffalo and the native Indian who lived on the buffalo. Nowhere else in evolutionary history is there a development to match this extraordinary tale.

The horse in North America is a great example of Darwinian forces at work; it was not a story of which Charles Darwin knew anything although he visited other parts of the Americas, whose development triggered his whole corpus of writing about natural selection. The more that is known about the development of post-Columbian America, the more Darwinian the history of the continent becomes.

THE POWER OF EUROPEAN flora and fauna as tools of colonialism was given its first expression as the Spanish and Portuguese made their way across the Atlantic. The changes their imports wrought on the islands' local ecosystems, and the advantage that this often gave the colonists, were repeated with many species in many parts of the New World.

By 1492 the pattern had already been set. Long before Columbus's first voyage, an indication of effect that Europeans would have on the world was already available. The Americas, Australasia, and most of Africa were unknown to white men: Most of the world was "discovered" and conquered by European crops and animals.

The first Eastern Atlantic island to be settled was Madeira. The Pope granted a charter to Portugal in 1433. Earlier it was said to be uninhabited. From about 1420 onward Madeira and the smaller, lower, drier island of Porto Santo were colonized by the Portuguese. Porto Santo was almost completely ruined by one family of rabbits released in 1430; by 1455 the island was a desert. Whatever the Europeans did to contain the rabbits failed. They killed all the native vegetation, and the animals living on that vegetation have not survived. The island of Porto Santo, as an ecological entity, was killed by less than a dozen rabbits—one doe and her progeny that were born on the voyage from Lisbon. This happened more than a generation before 1492.

This kind of ecological disaster was repeated in Hierro, one of the Canaries, in Virginia, the Caribbean, and Australia. Christopher Columbus should have been warned. The man who released the rabbits, Bartholomeu Perestrello, was to become Columbus's father-in-law.

Men who inadvertently destroyed an island were matched by those who destroyed the ecology of almost every new Europe. In Madeira, the larger island of the group, the rabbits were not let loose. *Madeira* means "wood," and when the Europeans arrived "there was not a foot of ground without great trees."[1] Timber was the first export, but some of the settlers impatiently set fire to great patches of land to clear the forest to grow crops. They set a huge forest fire that lasted, some contemporaries said, for years. At the end of seven years, there was said to be not a native tree standing. The settlers introduced pigs and cattle that went feral; the pigs alone could have prevented reforestation. Honeybees were producing for export by 1460, but the colonists sought a crop to make them rich. It was *sugar*, they thought, a surefire crop with an unmeasured demand.

By 1432 the first crop of cane was being pulped. By 1470 the island was producing 70 tons a year and exporting sugar to Antwerp, Bristol, and Bordeaux, as well as to Lisbon. The Portuguese also introduced the grape from Crete, and wine was exported before 1492. This wine became a cult, a special "Malmsey"—quite different from any Mediterranean wine. Some Madeira wine is the oldest drinkable wine, as opposed to spirit, in the world. Some drinkable Madeira wine today dates back to the eighteenth century.

It was at one time believed that European men and animals had destroyed the unique flora and fauna of Madeira, but there are still survivors, an indication of what was destroyed by pigs or fire. There is a little wren among the birds that is unique; there are five species of birds also found in the Canaries; the only unique land reptile is a small lizard; there is a special sort of turtle also found in the Azores. The rest of the specialized fauna are lower animals, and mollusks such as snails and shellfish, divided into fresh- and saltwater examples. Over two hundred species of usually flightless beetles have been found; presumably, they survived the fire better than any larger animal. There are no unique butterflies, but more than twenty moths of a peculiar Madeiran kind.

Most of today's flora is of European origin, introduced by the Portuguese. Some indigenous plants are shared with the Canaries or the Azores and nowhere else. There are about a hundred plants that are peculiar to Madeira. Most of them are ferns, mosses, and heaths, but more interestingly, four are laurels that are found nowhere else. There are six ferns common to the Caribbean and Madeira, and two small trees or large shrubs that are otherwise wholly American. The unique Dragon tree, which survived the fire, is almost extinct. Some of the introduced species have become pests, such as the prickly pear.

Before 1492, Madeira was already a monocultural island, and the only cash crop was sugar. By 1492 Madeira was probably the biggest exporter of sugar in the world, and from the capital of Funchal the food (or drug) went to England, France, Flanders, Italy, and south Germany; one load even went to the Levant. At that date, sugar was worth about twelve times as much as honey, and, after the spices, it was the most valuable commodity in world trade. Madeira's 1470 export of 70 tons increased to just under 1000 tons. By 1518, the date of the first sugar grown in the Caribbean, Madeira was exporting 1600 tons a year. Since by nature there is hardly an area on the island large and flat enough for a pair of tennis courts, this was quite an achievement.

Madeira is a volcanic ridge, pushed up out of the sea so that the mountain chain averaging 1219 meters (4000 feet) lies roughly East-West. The highest peaks are at about 1829 meters (6000 feet). The main island, Madeira, is high enough to attract rain clouds, and the precipitation in the mountains is equivalent to about 1 meter (40 inches) per year. This is measured as snow (above 610 meters or 2000 feet), rain, or watery vapor. Frost is unknown in the inhabited towns and villages, the mean temperature at Funchal being 13°C (55°F) in winter, 21°C (70°F) in the summer. The other islands are too dry for any crop except barley, but Madeira's average humidity is about 75 percent. Conditions are ideal for sugar production; the moisture is in the soggy mountains and, unchecked, falls precipitately to the sea, and over the ages it has carved many near-vertical ravines. Sugar depends upon a massive redirection of this water. Hundreds of miles of channels were cut into the hillsides, redistributing the water with painstaking accuracy and backbreaking labor, to the terraces of some 10,000 of the original heriditaments. Today, there are still many miles of subsidiary conduits feeding individual patches of land.

Barley, a dryland crop, can be produced for less than 1000 tons of water per ton of grain. Wheat needs 50 percent more, and rice needs four times the water needed by barley. Sugar needs more water than rice. It also needs as much or more heat. Sugar grew on Madeira, but only after many man-years of labor had made irrigation possible. Only barley grew on Porto Santo.

The people who made sugar possible on Madeira were usually servile, if not always slaves. They were convicts, debtors, and delinquents who had sold themselves into slavery or transportation from Portugal. There were Guanches imported from the Canaries in chains; there were recalcitrant Jews and Muslims from Portugal and Spain who refused to abjure their faith; there were adventurers, some from Northern Europe, who won their land rights in exchange for so many years of labor. This disparate labor force numbered probably as many as 15,000 in 1492. Today there is a population of about a quarter of a million, supported by imported food and the tourist trade. Before any of that became possible, in say 1850, the population had not exceeded probably 70,000, mostly engaged in the wine trade and in victualing passing ships.[2]

Even then, and for two hundred years previously, not enough fresh fish were caught for the observance of Catholic fast days, so salt cod was imported from Boston and New York, pickled herring from Sweden, and kippers and smoked mackerel from England. The fish was a return cargo for the ships that carried first sugar, then wine, into Europe or America.[3]

Madeira is a signpost to what would happen if the Europeans found an "empty" island. The story in the Canaries was modified by the existence of indigenous people, the islands' closeness to Africa, and the much greater extent of potential farmland.

Like the islands of Madeira, those of the Canaries are volcanic; unlike Madeira, they are only from 60 to 250 miles from Africa. Madeira is 360 miles from Africa, nearly 500 from the nearest point in Europe, and 240 from Tenerife, the largest of the Canary Islands. At some point in the Stone Age the Canaries had been settled from Africa or Europe, and in historical times there has always been some sort of settlement on each of the Canary Islands, if not always a connection between them. The aboriginal Guanches, as the Europeans called the people they found on the Canaries, do not seem to have been able to use boats of any kind; nor were the Guanches of one island necessarily well disposed toward, or even aware of, the natives of another island. At the time of the European arrival the natives of the flatlands of Lanzarote and Fuerteventura seem not to have known of the inhabitants of the other islands. These two flatter, dry, eastern islands differ very much from the much higher and steeper Gran Canaria and Tenerife. The latter, indeed, rises to over 3658 meters (12,000 feet). The summit is the crater of an extinct volcano from which sulphurous steam still spews, imparting a whitish hue to the ground. This was falsely called "eternal snow" by those who had not bothered to walk up to see for themselves. In fact, snow lies for about 150 days each year, but moisture, in the form of mist or drizzle, heavier drops, or snow, occurs every day of the year.

Equipped with this kind of benefice, Tenerife, and to a lesser extent Gran Canaria, can grow almost any tropical, semitropical, or temperate crop. The native Guanches lived on grain, and at least one sort of pea was grown in a Stone Age manner; for protein and fat there were shellfish, which they plucked from the rocks, and meat from pigs and goats, which were feral when Europeans arrived. The aborigine people in Tenerife and Gran Canaria were peculiarly well adapted to their wild, mountainous life. They were surefooted, without shoes of course, and had developed a method of calling from one hill to another—like Swiss yodelers—to warn, to inform, and to reassure. In this respect, they were close to the African finches that had also arrived some hundreds of years previously and had developed a special method of survival in a peculiar place that was ecologically unique. Post-Darwin naturalists studied the finches. The finches of the Canaries were as interesting as the finches of the Galapagos; but the Guanches had died out three hundred years before Darwin.[4]

If the Guanches were fierce, good Stone Age fighters, capable of defending themselves when they sought and held the high ground, those on the flat islands succumbed much more quickly. Lanzarote[5] and Fuerteventura were Europeanized by 1450. A generation later, Guanches survived on only three islands: La Palma, Gran Canaria, and Tenerife. Guanches from the other islands had been killed, transported as slaves to Madeira or Portugal, or died of white man's diseases. In 1483, Gran Canaria surrendered to the Spanish after ten years of guerrilla war. Four years previously, the Treaty of Alcacava between Portugal and Castille had given the latter sovereignty over the Canaries, and that of Madeira to Portugal. When Christopher Columbus visited the islands in August of 1492, to revictual and refresh his sailors, there was food available only on Gomera, a flat, wooded island, green and fertile. This he had reached from Spain in only six days, a voyage apparently undertaken on one tack all the way from the River Tinto more than 800 miles away.

Though Guanches on Gran Canaria had only surrendered to the Spanish in 1483, there was a shipyard at Las Palmas where one of Columbus's ships was careened and her rudder repaired. The shipyard had been there since the Spanish expedition of 1475, which had taken all of eight years to kill or capture the last Guanche. The war of attrition in Tenerife took longer.

La Palma, a small island to the west of Gomera, was invaded by a tough Spanish adventurer called Lugo with about five hundred men. This was in the same month that Columbus set sail for the West. Lugo defeated the Guanches in less than six months using the same mixture that similar men, Cortés and Pizarro, used on the Amerindians—force, treachery, horses, gunpowder, and the nature of Christian belief. The Spaniards introduced sheep and cattle, donkeys, camels, rabbits, and honeybees into the Canaries. These all became wild from a very early date, even before Tenerife was subdued in 1495, three years after Columbus's first voyage. Did the Spaniards also introduce that great future ally, disease? If not, how did they triumph so quickly?

An estimated population of the Guanches in all the islands was between 60,000 and 100,000. This is not overpopulation by Stone Age farming standards. The islands have enough land to have allowed each Guanche a hectare (2.5 acres) to grow vegetables or grain. This occupied only 14 percent of the land area of the Canaries at the highest possible estimate. Today nearly 25 percent of the land area is covered by tarmac, concrete, buildings, airports, swimming pools, and other sterile areas, as well as cultivated ground. The current population is nearly two million at the height of the season, largely fed from imports. In 1900, the year of the first true census, the population was about 350,000. These people fed themselves from their own land and exported cash crops to Europe.

Before turning the Canaries into one of the first Spanish Atlantic colonies, did the Spaniards need to wipe out the Guanches? On the island

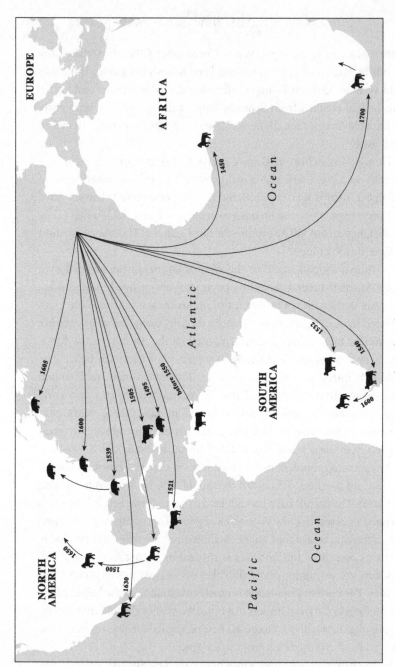

Animals on the Atlantic

of Hierro in the late 1580s, all living matter on the island was reduced to starving rabbits that lived on anything that grew. As a result, Hierro was almost denuded of plants of any kind. Nearly everything that now grows in that rabbit-induced desert has been imported. The island of Fuerteventura was ruined by the same date by feral donkeys and Bactrian camels. Over three-quarters of both species were hunted and killed in the 1590s and have been controlled ever since. The island of Gomera, a garden at the time of Columbus's first voyage, became a refuge for the other sort of camel, the dromedary. There were several thousand of them, eating their heads off, in 1640. No Stone Age people could resist a plague of rabbits; even a plague of camels or donkeys could wipe out Stone Age food supplies. Virgin areas free of natural enemies were so favorable to new species that European imports of animals flourished wherever they were introduced, causing a population explosion that may have starved indigenous humans.

Disease was far quicker than imports of rabbits or rats. There was said to be an epidemic, a *peste*, amongst the Guanches in the terrible winter of 1495, during which season the Spanish waited for victory on the low-lying ground of Tenerife. The Guanches who had been driven up the mountainside starved in consequence. The strategy worked. In the spring, so many unburied Guanche bodies lay in the ravines and on the hills that the fierce wild dogs who allegedly gave the Canaries their name were living on protein-rich carrion. Previously, the dogs had been vegetarian. Even the dogs' habits changed. No one knows the nature of the *peste*.[6]

The Canary Islands were notably healthy, to judge from remarks made by all early European arrivals. *La peste* was considered by the Spaniards, when it arrived (with the Spanish) more than a century after the first Europeans, to be a punishment for the Guanche practice of infanticide. No one could tell the Spaniards that a people without indigenous disease to control population have to practice birth control by some other method. No European Christians changed their perspective in four hundred years. In the nineteenth century, Anglican missionaries disapproved just as much of Australian Aboriginal infanticide as did Spanish friars in Tenerife.

Before 1500, the evidence was all there for anyone who wished to assemble it. An uninhabited island like Madeira could be exploited very quickly. The native plants and animals could be reduced to impotence by vigorous European imports, and they would not be defended by native humans. Introduced European crops could be grown profitably by known methods using human muscle in the form of easily managed, servile labor. Animal muscle, most highly developed in the Mediterranean, was from ox, buffalo, horse, donkey (to provide mules), or camel. Europeans had them all, the Atlantic islands none.

By 1500 Madeira was the world's largest sugar exporter. An island of only 15,000 acres of land (that could be cultivated easily) was producing enough food for 15,000 people in 1500 and exporting at least 1200 tons of sugar each year as well.[7] The relationship between the gold price and sugar price in 1500 was that the worth of 45 kg (100 lbs) of sugar was equal to 1 oz of gold, so 1200 tons of sugar exports from Madeira were worth as much as 24,000 oz of gold. The West African gold trade was only worth half as much as the Madeiran sugar trade. No wonder the Spanish tried to repeat the Portuguese success in the Canaries.[8]

The Canaries contained a human population that was killed, enslaved, or sold; but more died by disease. By 1525, a generation after the conquest of Tenerife, there were few pure-blooded Guanches left. Some had traveled in Spanish ships making for the Caribbean. Others had left, voluntarily or as slaves, for Europe and Madeira. The same pattern of conquest was repeated in every "new country" inhabited by indigenous, virgin populations. Having killed off the natives of most of the Caribbean islands, Europeans imported blacks who were slaves or whites who were criminals, debtors, or indigent. In some parts of the Caribbean, whites arrived to find paradise islands free from native humans. Then the problem was much easier. "Empty" islands offered facile solutions. "Empty" Madeira was in profit long before the populated Canaries.

East Atlantic islands were not always profitable paradises before the tourist boom induced by jet aircraft. The Azores are an example. They were apparently unpopulated at the time of the first Renaissance voyages. Situated more than a thousand miles from the Straits of Gibraltar, the islands appear to have been visited by the Carthaginians.[9] What did they do when they got there, in the absence of anyone with whom to deal? More importantly, the Carthaginians probably never returned.[10]

The Azores, named after the native hawks,[11] are volcanic in origin. They have a mild climate, less warm than either Madeira or the Canaries, but absolutely frost-free. They were fully occupied by the Portuguese by 1460, by about the same date as Madeira. They were "given" by the king of Portugal to his Flemish aunt in 1466. When they were first established in the Azores, the Portuguese attempted to grow wheat, in short supply at that date in Portugal.

After an attempt at growing wheat, an effort was made to grow sugar, that great magic drug of the Renaissance. Yields were far lower than in Madeira, perhaps because of the extremely stormy winds in the Azores, perhaps because not enough irrigation was available to supplement rainfall. After 1540 the growing of indigo was attempted and the making of dyes from a species of imported grass. *Indigofera*, a leguminous plant that was imported from Asia into many of the Atlantic islands, was the great origin of blue dyestuffs until the synthetic chemists discovered how to produce a more stable alternative from naphthalene. (Aniline dyes made redundant huge areas of plantations devoted to vegetable dyes.) Before this, India had been found to be a better source of vegetable dyes than either the Azores or the Caribbean. After indigo, colonists in the Azores attempted to grow pineapples, which became the favored nineteenth-century export. Over one million fruit were exported annually to Europe.

The Azores were never hungry, a thriving fishing industry, including whaling, having been established before 1700. Portuguese fishermen from the Azores also worked the Grand Banks, more than 1000 miles distant, but 1000 miles closer than Portugal to that once great source of cod. The Azores are in many ways too far north (and therefore too cool), too far from Europe, and too far from the United States to benefit as much from the tourist trade as the Canaries do. A third of the area of the Canaries, the nine islands in the Azores, have only one-sixth of the people. Perhaps their place in history was most important when their existence helped close the mid-Atlantic gap in the days of World War II. At a time when aircraft could not cross the Atlantic in one easy hop, the Azores were an essential refueling point.[12]

Columbus had taken six days to reach the Canaries about 800 miles from his departure port in Spain. He took thirty-six days to cross the

Atlantic from the Canaries to what is now Watling Island in the Bahamas, named San Salvador by the Spaniards. No one knows how far the three small ships traveled, but it is likely that the course taken amounted to more than 4000 miles. What they took with them was the hope of reaching Japan and the spices of the Indies. In fact, they had taken with them the cultivar of a plant that dominated the Caribbean for most of the next five hundred years. This was the noble cane—sugar. Among the crops imported into the New World, sugar deserves special mention for its far-reaching effects on the development of the Caribbeans, and because of its consequences for the people of Africa.

Sugarcanes were taken by many Renaissance travelers, by sea or land. The canes were cut into convenient pieces of thick cane, soft and easy to chew, high in energy, low in fiber. Columbus may have deliberately planted some of these on his first voyage. On the second voyage, in 1494, cane was planted in San Domingo, and settlers left to tend the plantation; both cane and settlers succumbed to natives, but within twenty years the sugar trade from the Caribbean had begun. It was not until 1550 that the West Indies rivaled the east Atlantic islands in production.

Sugar requires high temperatures, plenty of sunlight, and large quantities of water. Each ton of refined sugar requires enough soil nutrients to grow two tons of wheat, enough water to grow ten tons of rice, enough sunshine to grow a ton of cotton. Before 1800 a ton of sugar needed enough fuel in primitive refining techniques to produce a ton of iron; forced labor equated one ton of sugar with the life of a black slave. Sugar is often said, by botanists, to be "the cheapest form of energy-giving food with the lowest unit of land area per unit of energy produced." By what measure?

Sugar has never been as cheap as it should be in theory. Even today, when new breeding programs and growing techniques produce twenty times eighteenth-century levels, sugar is still nearly twice the cost of the same energy in wheat and much more than twice as much the same energy in potatoes or Indian corn. Nor is sugar a staple source of energy. No one who tried to use sugar in this way could survive for long. It is used as a confection, an attractive, unsatisfying addition to the diet, an addiction for some. For the Spaniards who were obsessed by the search for gold, Caribbean sugar was much less important than it was for others.

The sugar trade was the most important in the world until overtaken in tonnage by coal and in value by coffee. About 150,000 tons were exported to Europe from the Americas in the early 1800s; the figure a century later was twenty times as great. Sugar was the first massive transfer of energy from colonies to advanced countries since the Roman import of wheat and barley from Egypt, North Africa, Sicily, and Sardinia in the first centuries of our era.

More important than the transfer of energy was the waste of energy. In 1800 sugar cost seven times as much in economic terms as the same energy in flour from wheat, and twenty to fifty times the cost of the same energy in potatoes grown in the consumer's garden. It was, of course, a more attractive form of energy, but the waste involved must be noted in the huge naval resources required by the Triangular Trade, and in the provisions devoted to trade protection and to limit piracy. A huge number of people in Europe and the Americas engaged in the manufacture of sugar and in the African slave trade. It was a vast industry with great value added, except for the slave. An extreme modern economic parallel is good wine. This commands, in financial terms, from ten to a hundred times the cost of the same energy in fruit juice, but just as wine is more fun than fruit juice, so sugar was more fun than potatoes two hundred years ago; the idea that sugar could be addictive was wholly unimagined. Today the First World is divided between those who regard sugar as an addiction and those who have an interest in refusing to believe in such a possibility.

The sugar trade was never seen as a kind of energy transfer. Its importance was that it was the first modern trade in which a colonial people grew exclusively for the "home" consumer. In the process slaves, overseers, and even owners went hungry in the event of a blockade during one of the interminable wars of the eighteenth century. The colonial experience of a plantation product grown at the expense of native ability to subsist on native food has been repeated all over the Third World. One reason that Africa cannot feed itself is that it has lost the art of growing its own food, as has the Caribbean, because the land has been devoted to export crops. The sugar trade was the first to produce producer hunger because of devotion to export. It was not to be the last.

Sugar was grown in Southern Spain, all over the Mediterranean, and in the East Atlantic islands; metropolitan Spain had plenty of sugar because demand in Iberia never reached the levels of consumption attained by the French, Dutch, or English. There may have been fifty to a hundred plantations in the Caribbean by 1592, a hundred years after Columbus, but it was the Dutch, French, and English who made sugar a great international enterprise; they also made slavery an economic necessity and the slave trade a social shame. By 1650 the British colony of Barbados was the largest source of sugar, producing probably 50,000 tons of raw sugar, molasses, and rum; and exporting, perhaps, one-third of all sugar in world trade. Until the eighteenth century the statistics on sugar production and trade and reports of the numbers of slaves imported with or without the Spanish "*asiento*" (monopoly permission) were unreliable. There were, however, more plantations in English Barbados in 1650 than there were in all the Spanish colonies in 1600—and probably five times as much West Indian sugar in 1650 as fifty years earlier.

White man's demands for labor on the sugar plantations led to the death of most of the fierce Caribs, who would not be enslaved, as well as of the milder Arawaks, who pined away and could not adapt. Europeans then turned to Africa for their labor. For nearly 350 years Africans were regularly imported, until during the peak century, that of 1690–1790, 12 million black lives were involved in the production of 12 million tons of sugar. They were captured in Africa, sold, manacled, marched to the coast, sold again, chained on board ship, sold in the islands, and then "seasoned" to the prevailing Caribbean conditions. Africans became essential to the sugar enterprise, and slavery made Africans the dominant racial group in the Caribbean. In 1950 there were more people with West African blood in the Caribbean than there were in West Africa.[13] European agriculture benefited twice from the New World. Not only did sugar and other imports, discussed later in the chapter, find fertile ground in the Americas and thus help the white man to conquer them, but many of the native plants also served as valuable allies, either for the settlers abroad or for those left behind in the New World.

In fact, hunger in the midst of potential plenty occurred as early as the second voyage of Columbus. Finding that the stores brought over the Atlantic were spoiled or spoiling, largely because of humidity, the adventurers were driven to the only local supplies of human food—fish and cassava. *Cassava*, also called *manioc* or *tapioca*, is a shrub, the tubers of which were mashed and eaten throughout the Amerindian near-tropics from 25° N to 25° S. Sweet cassava has never been found in a wild state; therefore, it had been cultivated for generations before Columbus arrived.[14]

The sailors and buccaneers did not know how to eat the roots that derived from the annual plantings of this shrub. It can be either sweet or bitter. The bitter cassava often have a very high HCN content, one of the great problems of using the plant, which has many other advantages. HCN is the vegetable form of hydrocyanic acid and is liberated when the enzyme linease (contained in the living plant) acts upon the glucoside linamarin. In sweet cassava the HCN is usually found only in the outer layers of the root; in bitter cassava HCN is widely distributed and can be destroyed only by boiling, roasting, or fermentation. Stale tubers are more poisonous than fresh. One plant contains enough HCN to kill quite a large animal.

Amerindians did not have to cope with large animals in the Caribbean because there were none. At first, Columbus's sailors found the cassava almost uneatable although it was the staple starchy food of the Indians. Is it possible that the Indians did not let the invaders have the (cultivated) supplies of sweet cassava and permitted them to eat only the wild, bitter varieties? Or did the Spanish never have access to the methods that Amerindians found best to make cassava palatable?

Cassava is quite a good staple starchy food. There is normally over 90 percent starch and plenty of calcium and vitamin C in the dry matter. Nearly all the protein is in the leaves, which may contain HCN even in the "sweet" varieties. The boiled tubers are bland, tedious, not a food of which any cuisine can be made. Supplemented by beans or fish they become a balanced, if boring, staple.

Subsequent generations have found cassava interesting enough for a daily diet by fermenting the mashed, cooked roots. This is allowed to become what might be described as quarter-ale, then cooked in flat cakes. Like all fermented starchy products, these cakes are nutty and sweet, more interesting than the plain, boiled vegetable. Bananas and cassava can be improved by the same method.

Fermented, cassava is both a better food and a more interesting one. If allowed to ferment fully to become mild ale and drunk straight from the mash tub, it becomes a product even richer in vitamins, more easily digested, and far less boring. People actually enjoy fermented "mealie beer." It is significant that this technique was native to Africa and used for bananas, which are also native to Africa. These techniques owe nothing to the white man or any biochemists. Africans use the same techniques today on maize and cassava.

In all probability Columbus's sailors only boiled cassava, in which case they ate a pudding rather like the Victorian tapioca pudding fed to children every day. Columbus's sailors, however, did not eat it with milk or sugar, as was the custom for Victorian children. Alternatively, the Europeans may have eaten cassava raw, which is even more unpalatable; Columbus's sailors were hungry enough not to grumble. Cassava was a very early import into the tropical Old World.

The great virtue of cassava, perhaps a unique virtue, is that it is the only human food that is almost entirely pest-proof. Cassava is immune to the African locust, and bitter cassava can be planted in areas where monkey, ape, baboon, wild hog, porcupine, and even elephant are a problem. These animals do not eat cassava twice. Naturalists have been interested to see how quickly animal intelligence associates cassava with death. What probably happens is that an ester released by the leaves signals to predatory animals that HCN is present. Even when bitter and sweet cassava are planted at random, quite young animals know the difference. Humans find identification more difficult.

Cassava was taken to West Africa very early by the Portuguese. The plant was in São Tomé and the Bight of Benin before 1500, and in the Congo not much later. It was not much used elsewhere in Africa until the population explosion that occurred after European rule in the nineteenth and twentieth centuries. Cassava was planted as the great reserve crop of the tropics by white governments anxious to prevent starvation. It has one other great virtue: Certain cultivars can survive in the ground, unharvested, for several years. It is thus, literally, a food bank, untouchable by pests, in reserve until wanted. Grown at low cost, it spread all over the tropics. If it were still widely grown, people would not complain so much of starvation. Dry matter yields of over two tons per acre are not difficult to achieve.

The crop has acquired a more recent virtue or vice, according to one's perspective. Grown, dried, ground, and exported from Southeast Asia (mostly from Thailand) the crop is a cheap form of starchy animal feed available in Europe. The industry of manioc import has given rise to the ludicrous spectacle of European farmers substituting manioc for barley or wheat and selling the unwanted home-produced cereal to the European Community where it must be stored or sold, heavily subsidized, on the world market. Of course, this kind of folly is only made possible by excessive subsidy and Government action.

In a free market, manioc is used where it is cheaper. In a free market economy like that of Australia or Canada, European cereals are grown at a cost far lower than the effective cost of imported manioc. If European farmers cannot meet such prices in a free market, grain for animals will give way to imported manioc.

The true Spaniard could not eat without bread, and bread needs those Mediterranean essentials, oil and wine. Early Spanish *conquistadores* used cassava "bread" for poor people of all races. It was grown all over tropical America and in the West Indies; in other hot, wet areas it was a substitute for cereals. Spaniards unimaginatively sought in their first, golden century to impose the diet of Castile—wheat, oil, and wine—upon the New World. It was nearly a century before all three could be produced in quantity.

Columbus had not discovered a substitute for wheat, and cassava is notably low in fat. In addition, the native Amerindians had no wine of any sort.[15] On the second voyage, Columbus took over a thousand men and seeds and cuttings of a hundred different plants to Hispaniola. In the Caribbean, wheat and other grains failed, as did grapevines and olive seedlings, but about half of the Mediterranean imports flourished: cauliflowers (but not cabbages), warm-weather radishes, southern types of lettuce, melons (but not marrows), oranges, and lemons (but not apples). Figs did particularly well and could have become a staple, as they were at that time on some Greek islands, but figs did not provide a diet for full-blooded Spanish *conquistadores*.

The Spanish, to be fair, were not in the Americas to repeat the hard experience they had left at home. The idea that they should settle as colonists like pensioned Roman soldiers was not to their taste. Their aim was swifter wealth and glory: a quick profit. Quite modest settlers were given quite large land grants, plus, of course, the necessary Indian slaves to work the land. Unfortunately, the Amerindians continued to die of white man's diseases. Nor was the wealth of the Indies to be found cheaply in the earth. By 1556, when Philip II succeeded his father Charles as ruler, most easily worked and stolen gold had been discovered, and silver had become more important than gold. Because half the Mexican population or more had died of disease, a labor shortage was already in evidence there. Fortunately for Spain, technology came to the rescue. It was the introduction of the mercury treatment of ore in 1557–58 that raised potential in Potosí (in modern Bolivia), for example, to become the richest silver mine in the world. It produced more than three million ounces a year in the period 1560–1760.[16]

In the end, the deepest mine, the thickest lode, the most concentrated ore must be exhausted. The only true wealth is renewable, and America possessed renewable wealth in the form of two plants that would transform Europe.

Today Maize is the most widely distributed grain in the world; after wheat and rice it is the most important economically. It can produce more product per man-hour and more per acre than any energy crop in the tropics except sugarcane and, in colder zones, the potato. Maize is more adaptable, more widespread, and more easily handled than either sugarcane or potato. Maize was the staple crop for all the Americas from the River Plate to the St. Lawrence. Its use gave indigenous Amerindians more leisure than growers of wheat or rice: Less than two days of work a week suffices for maize against four to six days for other grains. There were seven main cultivars known to the Indians and the Spanish after 1520, and these are still the main non-hybridized ecotypes. Hybridization in the twentieth century has transformed grain and cob size. At the time of Columbus, grain size was like that of the modern lentil, about one-tenth the volume of modern grain.[17]

Europeans took maize seed grains with them all over the world, starting with Columbus's return to Iberia in 1493. Maize was an important food crop for both man and beast in the Mediterranean by 1550, and was certainly introduced into West Africa at some early time, although during the sixteenth century linguistic references in many languages to "Guinea Corn" almost certainly refer to sorghum rather than to maize.[18] Caution should be allied to the insights of husbandry. Maize cannot resist animal predators in the same way that sorghum, cassava, or millet can. In its original home maize had no natural enemies, such as there are in Africa,[19] and the lack of wild or domestic pigs, sheep, cattle, goats, and horses allowed for the growth, development, and spread of maize cultivars. Maize was certainly a major cash crop in West Africa by 1690, and during the next century it was used as provision for the slave trading forts and to victual ships for the Middle Passage from West Africa to the Americas. Today, maize has transformed Africa, directly feeding probably more than half the population in many places.

Maize flour, like cassava, cannot be made into raised bread, but scone-like flat "tortillas" were baked by Amerindians, and it was sufficient nutritionally that the native tribes avoided the pellagra that plagued whites who used maize as a staple human food. Pellagra, a deficiency disease, affected people all over the world, ten million in Southern Europe in the late nineteenth century, as many as 500,000 in the Southern United States as late as the 1920s, and more than five million during the depression of 1929–35. Pellagra is still an important condition in parts of Southern Africa.

In industrial countries, pellagra was cured by the addition of vitamin B4 (niacin), discovered in 1934. Amerindians had used three methods of processing maize that enabled them to avoid the disease,[20] but white men arrogantly ignored that part of maize culture when they arrived in the Americas. Although Europeans took maize seed all over the world, they failed to utilize the native processes that made the niacin nutritionally available.

The influence of maize throughout the world has been immense. Maize is now the staple food of millions, cooked as a thick mush or dough, as a gruel or porridge, as a mildly fermented beer, and as "bread" mixed with wheat flour. In the First World, immature cobs are eaten "sweet," the more mature cobs are roasted, and dry grain can be used to produce hominy grits, cornflakes, popcorn, and corn flour for thickening of all kinds.

After maize, the most valuable plant transferred from the Americas to Europe was the *potato*. The history of the potato is well documented. Brought by Europeans from the Andes, Peru, and Bolivia to various countries before 1600, it was of no great economic importance anywhere except Ireland before 1700. Although species of tuber-bearing solanum have been found as far north as modern Colorado, and wild tubers were, and are, eaten in parts of Mexico and the Southwestern United States, there were no "potatoes" cultivated except in the Andes, and no solanum species with edible tubers existed outside the Americas.[21]

Neither maize nor cassava (manioc, tapioca) will grow in the Andean highlands. It was the potato culture that permitted human settlement there at the end of the last Ice Age. At the end of the pre-Columbian period, the Inca culture evolved, and this necessitated, or was the outcome of, a centralized government. When the Spanish arrived in the 1520s, Inca potato agriculture involved irrigation, terracing, artificial reclamation of land, the use of guano brought from the coast, and the planned, directed colonization of mountain districts. The town of Cuzco, the center of Inca culture and wealth, lies at an elevation of nearly 3500 meters (over 11,000 feet). There is a mass of Inca artifacts relating to the potato, the only staple food that could have served the population. At the time of Pizarro's capture of the city in 1533, it is likely that the inhabitants of the valley numbered about 100,000, all of them basically dependent upon the potato or upon maize brought from lower elevations.

Protein was short in the diet, and potato-dependent Incas could not usually supplement starch with beans like the maize-eating Mexicans. There were few sources of animal protein except guinea pigs. Since the Inca dictatorship was not noted for cannibalism, it is possible that the potato was then of a higher protein content than the European varieties available today, or that guinea-pig culture was highly organized.[22]

The potato became of world importance in the peculiar circumstances of Ireland after 1650. The population of Ireland multiplied and multiplied, until there were nearly nine million people by 1844; and this despite twenty separate famines over twenty years of potato crop failure during which at least 15 percent of the population died.[23] Such horrifying failure of a staple food occurred because of six diseases that diminished the yield of potatoes from 10 percent to 50 percent in various parts of Ireland.

Before 1844, the potato crop had not failed throughout the whole island. In 1845, a new disease, Blight,[24] appeared and changed the course of history. Arriving from the United States by steamer in June 1845, the new plague killed every potato field in the United Kingdom and in vast areas throughout Europe. The disease was caused by a fungus, impossible to control until the 1920s, that killed the potatoes. The resulting famine killed more than a million Irishmen, prevented the birth of perhaps another million, induced four million to emigrate in the following half-century, and reduced the population of Ireland from nine million in 1841 to less than half that figure in 1941. In contrast, the rest of Western Europe had more than doubled its population during the same century despite considerable emigration.

On the European continent, the use of the potato was not normally monocultural. It took a very long time for the tuber to be accepted by the peasantry, and it was not really until after the Napoleonic Wars that the vegetable became a staple food for the poor. Ironically, it had been accepted as a curiosity by the rich a century previously. From 1820 onward, the cultivated acreage of potatoes increased throughout Western and Central Europe both absolutely and as a percentage of total arable and garden crops. In the last case, peasants were never driven to the Irish expedient of total reliance, but the potato as a source of human and animal energy was of great importance in all the major European continental countries. There were significant national differences. In Germany, potatoes were more important than wheat; rye and potatoes, grown on light sandy soils, were the essential German crops before the post-1950 agricultural revolution. In France, with better soils and a warmer climate, wheat was a more important staple, but potatoes were more widely grown than rye. In Italy maize was more widely grown than anything except wheat, but potatoes, at one-quarter the arable area of maize, were also widely grown in gardens and plots. Many authorities consider that Germany's nearly threefold increase in population in the century before 1914 was largely fuelled by the tonnage of potatoes grown, which rose from about 1 million metric tons to about 50 million in the same hundred years.[25]

Potatoes were of great importance in countries farther east, but statistics are not wholly reliable. It is obvious, however, that potatoes in Eastern Europe were of cardinal importance in saving life during both world wars and their aftermaths. Without this Columbian addition to the diet, so easily cultivated in a cottage garden, life in Germany, Russia, Eastern Europe, and the Balkans would have been even more savagely unpleasant than it was during the periods 1919–22 and 1945–50. The potato may have prevented 20 million deaths from starvation in these years. It remains a staple standby today in every kind of kitchen garden, allotment, or patch of ground in any troubled country with an incompetent government.

There is a certain amount of confusion about early references to potatoes. The name was given to the white potato, or *Solanum tuberosum*, which reached Europe only in the late 1570s. It did not reach North America until the white man brought it west. Indeed, it was known as the Irish potato in Virginia in the early 1620s. In turn, the white potato stole its name from the sweet potato, or *Ipomea batata*.

The Carib word *batata* was taken by Columbus when he took the sweet potato to Europe in 1493. From Europe, the Portuguese took it to West Africa. The Spanish took it from Mexico to the Philippines in about 1550, and the Chinese obtained it in 1590. It was seen growing in Japan in 1698. Meanwhile, it had been taken by the English from Europe (or the West Indies) to Virginia before 1650. This was later than the Irish potato, which by then had been harvested a score of times in the new colony.

Sweet potatoes have a nutritious tuber that can be baked or boiled. They are drier than white potatoes, with 90 percent carbohydrate in the dry matter, contain more protein at 6 percent, and are rich in vitamin C. As their name implies, they are, like most tropical vegetables, high in sugar. Like white potatoes, sweet potatoes must be ridged and are harvested as required. The tubers store poorly out of the soil. The crop is seventh in tonnage of world dry matter following wheat, rice, maize, barley, cassava, and white potatoes. It is ahead of oats, sorghum, sugarcane, and the millets. Since the sweet potato is easier to cultivate than yams, growing acreage is used at the expense of that vegetable, while cassava is easy to cultivate and can be stored with ease. Because the sweet potato is easy to grow but harder to store than cassava, it has been cultivated in almost every tropical and subtropical country. In one country outside the Americas, New Zealand, it was present when the whites arrived.

A New Zealand form of sweet potato, Kumara, was the staple food of the Maoris when the first Europeans arrived. They were the crew of the two ships commanded by Abel Tasman; some of the crew landed in what is now called Massacre Bay on the South Island on 18–20 December 1642. Four or five of the Dutch were murdered by the Maoris, and Tasman re-embarked, but not before he found the Maoris using sweet potatoes as a staple food. It was also found as a staple all over Polynesia. How had the cultivars reached New Zealand? This has puzzled botanists, geographers, and ecologists ever since.

To start with, mankind had to assume that *Ipomea batata* was taken by men from South America to the Southwest Pacific. This 6000-mile journey may or may not have been made. If so, it was the only voyage made to or from pre-Columbian South America. This link was posited by Thor Heyerdahl from the remains at Easter Island, and the superiority of the Polynesian voyagers led many white researchers to plot pre-Columbian voyages of great importance. The only problem with these theories is that, if the voyage was ever made, why was not much more than the sweet potato brought over? There are a hundred vegetables that would have been useful for settlers to take from South America to the Pacific, but the sweet potato is unique. To believe in the intervention of mankind, the searcher after truth has to believe that the sweet potato, either in tuber form or as seed, was brought, by itself, across the Pacific. There is an alternative theory.

Today the sweet potato is usually propagated by cuttings, not by seed. If they are allowed to become too dry, they die, as the early Spanish explorers observed while returning to Europe. Cuttings left soaking, even in salt-water, could live, so it is entirely possible that the sweet potato, like some of the coconuts, reached the Southwest Pacific on its own by sea.[26]

It is likely that the sweet potato was brought to New Zealand by the Maoris when they arrived in AD 1200–1300 from Polynesia. The Maoris also brought with them a small dog as their sole source of tame animal protein. The dogs were also seen in Tahiti, Fiji, and elsewhere in the Pacific at the first white contact. In addition, the Maoris were cannibals at the time Captain Cook arrived. This seems to indicate a protein shortage, as anyone would expect from a diet composed largely of sweet potato. The Maoris cultivated few vegetables high in protein.

Despite its boring nature, the sweet potato offers more return for less work than almost any other staple plant in any climatic zone. As a result, by 1800 it had spread to every part of the world where the white man was responsible for feeding people. It grows from 40° N to 32° S in the tropics, from sea level to 2200 meters (7000 feet), but it needs a temperature of about 23°C (75°F) and lots of sunshine. It needs an annual rainfall of at least 762 mm (30 in), and this should be well distributed, since sweet potatoes do not stand drought at all well. They are a short-day plant, and long days—of more than twelve hours of daylight—inhibit flowering. It is wrong to confuse the moist, jelly-like flesh of some of the varieties with yams, and modern Americans are apt to do so. The flowering members of the tribe are called "Morning Glory" by subtropical gardeners. The sweet potato does not travel well in commerce, and it has not entered world trade.

The Irish or white potato has undergone a profound and almost incredible mutation in the years between its "discovery" by Pizarro's ruffians and its adoption as a staple European food. In the Andes, it was a short-day plant grown almost on the Equator at a great height in relatively dry climatic conditions. In Ireland, it became a long-day plant in a notably high-humidity climate at low elevations.

Some of the best-quality potatoes in the world are now grown in the Arctic Circle—in Northern Norway, Sweden, Finland, and Russia. In the Americas, better potatoes are grown in the North of the United States or at high latitudes in Northern Ontario as well as in Southern Argentina and the Falkland Islands. Whatever has happened to potato cultivars, they remain divided, after thousands of years, into mealy types and waxy types. The mealy types contain more starch. The difference can be discovered without cooking. A brine solution of 10 percent (ten parts water, one part salt) can act as detective. Waxy potatoes float; those with mealy interiors sink. No potato buyer ought to be without a 10 percent brine solution. (The reaction of the average friendly shopkeeper may be imagined.) The Americas had no native domesticated animals of any agricultural consequence, but they had a great many available plants besides the four staples that have been discussed at length here. These other plants were used by the Iberians to create Latin American cookery. They were taken back to Mediterranean Europe, and from the Mediterranean they spread all over Europe, then all over the world. These food plants comprise a formidable list, but they include everyday vegetables that Europeans now regard as their birthright, as well as extraordinary exotica like vanilla and "allspice," which took many years to find its place in European cookery. The most important group, nutritionally, is the beans.

Beans, amazingly, were hardly known in Europe before Columbus. The broad bean (also known as the horse bean, field bean, tick bean, and Windsor bean) is the only European variety. In antiquity its reputation suffered because some Greeks and Romans thought that this then unique vegetable contained the souls of the dead. Certain Mediterranean people do evince a peculiar genetic sensitivity to the toxin, *vicine,* that occurs in broad beans. The toxin causes anemia called *Javism* (because the broad bean is also known as the *Java* bean). Did the Ancients know about the danger? Was the genetic condition commoner in Ancient Greeks and Romans, perhaps only 5 percent of the gene bank of the modern Mediterranean? Are there other peculiarities of this kind, now swamped by the genetic change in people?

The "French" bean was grown in Mexico for nearly 7000 years. Although it was brought to Spain, it grew best in France, hence its European name. Europeans in turn took it to North America where it became a staple legume together with peas and other beans. Grown in England before 1592, the French bean has spread all over the world. It is very old. Recognizable uncharred pods have been found in Mexican caves and carbon-dated at about 5000 BC.

The scarlet runner bean was grown by Amerindians in maize sections, and allowed to take over for a couple of years after the maize harvest. The ground was thus rested and restored. This is a long-day plant, killed by frosts, but specimens have been found from as long ago as 7000 BC. Has the scarlet runner changed since that date? As a garden cultivar, this bean is more successful in cool, moist Atlantic climates than the French bean.

The lima bean, also known as the butter, Madagascar, or Burma bean, is grown for its shelled seed like a broad bean. Some cultivars, like cassava, contain hydrocyanic acid; other cultivars, like manioc, are harmless. The more dangerous lima bean should be soaked or boiled before eating; to be safe, this means all varieties of lima bean.

Every other known garden bean has been developed from genetic material brought from the Americas, including the special bean grown in Michigan that is used for Boston baked beans. In Mexico, one plant biologist has identified over seventy varieties of beans in a variety of colors—white, black, red, green, and yellow. It is probable that, like maize, beans contain a huge bank of genetic material that even now has not yet been fully exploited.

Like maize and potatoes, beans became important in Europe as a "break" crop. Instead of fallow, crops that make different demands on the soil can be planted alternately, and so "rest" the soil because different nutrients are required. For example, the cabbage family—the brassicae—require certain qualities in a soil that potatoes do not; beans and peas are both legumes, so their growth not only demands different nutrients than cabbages or potatoes, but the action of the nodules on the roots of legumes makes nitrogen (from the air) available to soil and to subsequent plants. Of course, this process was not known in the Ancient or Middle Ages, but beans and peas were regarded, nonetheless, as restorative crops.

In Europe, potatoes, peas, and beans were not grown on a farm scale until the eighteenth century when the farms became more mechanized. By the eighteenth century the peasantry was using maize as an alternative to fallow in a broad swath through Portugal, Spain, Southern France, and Northern Italy to the modern Balkans. Arthur Young,[27] writing just before the French Revolution, said: "Where there is no maize, there are fallows; where there are fallows, the people starve for want."

To Arthur Young the cause and effect were quite clear. For the French landlord of the *ancien régime* cause and effect was less certain. For the peasant, as was true for the Russian peasant as late as 1913, agricultural methods came from above. In England in Arthur Young's day, this was also true, but in England there were landlords who imposed upon their tenants both land tenure and good farming methods that made profits for both landlord and tenant, and brought plenty to the people. The improvements in England described in Chapter Two were not in place anywhere else in Europe before about 1850, nor was the use of fallow crops systematized. If the French peasant grew maize in the 1780s, he was lucky and ate better than his neighbors.

Maize was the basis for many modern French meat dishes, including pâté de foie, the goose being overfattened by force-feeding it maize, and thus making a fatty liver.[28] Maize was known as *"bie d'Espagne"* in France, and similar names were in use in Italy, Greece, and Turkey. It was used almost universally in Northwest Europe as a feed for fattening animals, whether homegrown or imported from the Americas. Thus it has remained. Some efforts to use maize directly for human consumption were not successful.[29]

In Eastern Europe, matters were very different. Maize "bread" is a tradition in the Balkans, Hungary, and Romania. Hungary has become one of the great modern maize-growing countries; but right up until the eighteenth century, while most of the population were inert victims of conflict between Turk and Christian, maize may well have kept the Magyar peasantry alive. To a peasant, the crop has three advantages over wheat: It produces much more per unit area on a small, unscientific scale; it is easier to store in cob; it is in many ways easier to render palatable by cooking. In Romania a production pattern grew up in which the natives grew wheat and maize. Wheat was exported; maize supported the people. Wheat, a centuries-old staple, became a luxury. If maize helped Southern Europeans, then potatoes were slower to catch on in the North and in the mountains.

In places there was an almost religious objection to the potato because it is related to the poisonous belladonna or deadly nightshade. There was also an objection—semireligious, seminaturalistic—claiming that mankind should not eat any crop that grows beneath the earth. This prohibition was in force at a time when Jerusalem artichokes, turnips, swedes, and radishes were all new ideas for human food. It was sheer necessity that drove Europeans to eat the potato, led by the Irish in the seventeenth century.

Frederick the Great (1740–86) forced the tuber upon his subjects a century later with limited success. In pre-Revolutionary France almost no farmland was given over to potatoes. In contemporary Russia potatoes were considered weird, strange, evil, underground, and unnatural. In France, Germany, Poland, and Russia the potato became popular in the nineteenth century, and while it never became the staple it was in Ireland, it nevertheless became as important a primary source of energy as wheat or rye. Potatoes were seen as a staple accompaniment to meat at a later date, when meat was affordable. Since World War II, the standard diet has included "chips with everything," and some potato varieties are grown especially for chips or french fries.

A cousin of the potato was adopted in the Mediterranean much earlier. The tomato, now in every kind of Italian dish, was generally available but used widely only in Italy before 1600. Other Europeans were highly suspicious of it because the tomato was considered poisonous, like the potato. (Perhaps Europeans had had bad experiences with cooking and eating the foliage, which would have caused indigestion, serious poisoning, and even death.) One English herbalist called it a love apple; others thought it a form of mandrake. Like the white potato, the tomato was introduced into North America by Europeans some time after 1750, a century after the potato.

Tomatoes, squashes, the capsicums, and even potatoes all increased the amount of vitamin C available in Europe, thus assisting in the cure of scurvy, which was a recurrent problem.[30] Various beans greatly increased the protein level in the food of the poor, and indeed became known as "the poor man's meat." It is difficult to see how, without beans, a vegetarian could find enough protein of a high enough quality to raise a considerable family. The soybean was, of course, not available in Europe before the twentieth century, but other beans must have had a profound effect on European diets. The use of potatoes has been fairly well documented. The effect of the crop on Ireland was not beneficial in some ways, but the population rise in Middle and Eastern Europe in the nineteenth century was almost certainly helped largely by the potato. West German peasants had been exported to Pomerania after the Black Death to settle the sandy wastelands. Six hundred years later, Pomeranians were moved by the Ruhr coal and iron undertakings back to the West. This surplus peasant labor came from using the potato to augment the diet. There simply were not enough rye and wheat grown in the middle of the nineteenth century to account for the increased population.[31]

As for maize, it was primarily a Southern European crop for humans, but it was imported for animal feed from the 1850s in a steadily increasing tonnage. Maize became the fuel for the animal-protein explosion of the twentieth century, in Europe as well as in the Corn Belt. Today, grain maize is grown as far north as Northern France and Southern Germany. Whole maize for silage is grown over much of England, Northern Germany, and Southern Scandinavia. The line creeps northward every year. The effect upon animal nutrition of maize cut green for silage has been profound in post–World War II Europe, as grain maize was in the first half of the twentieth century.

There is another point. Maize is the only crop that can benefit from saturation application of animal manure upon the ground. In a winter, a cow can be fed by the ten tons of maize silage that can be grown upon a quarter hectare, if it is properly manured. The total detritus from the cow during the winter, all fifty tons of it, can be spread on the quarter hectare chosen for next year's maize crop. The cycle is beneficial in the sense that the cow has become a provider of plant nutrients. There is, of course, a great input of energy into the virtuous cycle in the form of horsepower, but there is far less need of pest control and no need at all for artificial fertilizers. The same process can be established with pigs or poultry and grain maize and has been in parts of West Germany, especially with pork pigs. Problems arise, though, when surplus organisms from the manure reach the water table.

It is entirely arguable that pre-Industrial European populations "took off" only because of the important additions to the diet that came from the Americas. There is one exception to this truth, if truth it be. In England, as opposed to Ireland, Scotland, or the maize-eating countries, agricultural husbandry and capitalism alone were sufficient. England was capable of feeding a huge increase in population without any important use of American cultivars. Everywhere else, the European increase in population, proportionally the highest in the world in the years 1500–1900, could not have taken place without Amerindian plants. In England, it was imports of staple European foods from neo-European countries that helped fuel the doubling of population between 1850 and 1914.

Finally, in examining the effects of New World crops upon the Old, it should be remembered that many New World crops were removed and grown elsewhere. These will be noted in due course. What happened to the condiment that started it all? Whatever happened to pepper? Did the Europeans forget pepper when all the lovely new plants were available? Far from it. There is no doubt that pepper, like sugar, is a habit that can easily become addictive, in the sense that the use of either becomes habitual, and the habit is difficult to give up.[32]

Pepper was only one of the "essential" Renaissance spices. The others were ginger, cinnamon, nutmeg, cloves, mace, and cardamom, in no particular order. All these spices and others were important in cookery and as constituents in Chinese, Indian, and Arab medicine. Before Columbus, pepper was first in importance and ten times as valuable in bulk as other spices in world trade. It is assumed, with considerable justification, that pepper formed about half the total Eastern spice trade in 1500. Today, it still forms a quarter of the spice trade.

It was also of universal application. Historically, water was of doubtful quality. Vegetables, by themselves, boiled, are boring in the extreme. The only preserved meat or fish in many areas was salted. Water to wash out this salt may not always have been available or clean enough to perform this duty or close enough to the cooking pot for the water to be changed frequently. Oatmeal, spirits of wine, and even throwaway vegetables were cooked with salt meat to reduce salinity, but often this was not enough. Pepper is a safe way of making oversalted meat or fish edible. Once used for this purpose, it became difficult to persuade the natives of Europe to return to pre-pepper cooking. It was also widely used to make less boring a mass (or mess) of boiled vegetables masquerading as stew.

Pepper was in use in antiquity, in Greece rather than Egypt. Pre-Muslim Arabs were not exactly in charge of the pepper trade since time began, but there were two ancient Arabian routes. One was from the Indian Southwest coast to the Gulf of Hormuz, then to Basra, Baghdad, and Syria, and, in Greek and Roman times, on to Antioch; after Alexandria was founded as a Greek city in 322 BC, there was an alternative route via the

Red Sea. Both routes later led, of course, to Rome, and Rome consumed an unimaginable tonnage of pepper and spices.

Prices to the Roman Empire were somewhat reduced by the Greco-Roman discovery of the Monsoon Route in the first century BC. It went from the Red Sea to India, outward in the Southwest winds from April to October, and back to Egypt in the Northeast airstream in the northern winter. In about 260 BC the Egyptians had founded Berenice, a port just north of the Tropic Line in the Red Sea. From Berenice, a road provided with watering holes led to a point near modern Aswan on the Nile. Trade was carried out for five hundred years on the Red Sea until the port silted up, and later Romans returned to the use of Suez. A land route via Attock in the Indus Valley joined the Silk Route from China in Central Asia at a later date.

Silk, spices, and pepper became unobtainable in Europe from the time of the Arab Muslim explosion into the world (632–732) until the Venetians and Genoese resumed East-West trade, the chief long-term result of the Crusades. During the pepper dark ages (to coin a phrase) meat was relished redder and redder, often hardly hung or seasoned as in some periods of Texan cowboy history. What happened in the winter, in the absence of both fresh meat and pepper, no one knows. It is possible, however, that pepperless barbarian Northern Europeans taught the Mediterraneans to smoke meat and fish instead of salting it. Certainly smoked viands of all types are more characteristic of the cuisine of the Northerner. Even Vikings preferred smoking and the smoked cure to salting—witness smoked herring, cod, and salmon. But who first smoked duck and other game?

It is always assumed that the pepper trade became very difficult only after the Turkish occupation of Constantinople in 1453, but this is not necessarily the case. After the failure of Byzantine traders in India in the sixth century AD, the pepper trade reverted to the Arabs, who were shortly to become Muslim. Demand picked up strongly as Europe returned to East-West intercourse after the Crusades; and Venice in particular grew rich on the pepper trade, which is largely responsible for the Venetian Golden Age.

It was not the Turks who destroyed the Venetian-Turkish-Arab-Indian pepper trade, but the Portuguese, rounding the Cape and finding their way to India. The Arab merchants on both sides of the Indian Ocean reacted in two ways. One was to plead with the Turks to fight the Portuguese at sea. This was partially successful; Aden was retaken by Muslim forces, but was successfully blockaded by the Portuguese. Hormuz (Ormuz, or Ormes) had become a Portuguese colony in 1514 after Albuquerque had established the Portuguese in Goa and Malacca. Ormuz, as the Portuguese called it, remained an entrepôt for the spice trade. Some cargoes went around the Cape to Lisbon. After 1560, some trade was allowed to return to the Arab-Venetian pattern and route, but only after the Portuguese had extracted a sizable "tax" upon every ton. This was a mistake. An easily levied toll or tax offers too much temptation to sticky local fingers, and little of the proceeds arrived in Lisbon. The Lisbon pepper trade dried up, and the tolls from Ormuz that were meant to replace it did not materialize in any substantial form. Venice was very much on the ascendant again in the second half of the sixteenth century.

The second reaction of the Arab and Muslim Indian merchants was to move the cultivation of pepper farther east to what is now Malaya and Indonesia. There was probably an oversupply since *Piper nigrum* is an easy plant to grow in the tropics. The Portuguese at Malacca were not successful in controlling this traffic, and their monopoly was broken.

From 1600 onward the Dutch drove the Portuguese out of the East Indies—the Spice Islands—and established a monopoly in nutmeg, mace, and cloves; later they controlled the world supply of cinnamon, but not of pepper. Pepper ceased to have the glamour of a commodity worth as much as any other edible, at times nearly as much as saffron in Europe, vanilla from Central America, or gold dust from the Sudan. An end to the European distribution monopoly revealed that there was nothing magic about pepper production, as its importers had suggested. Pepper went from being the European necessity that paid for, and even produced, the genius and glory of Venice to a dull, rather pedestrian commodity on a par with salt and vinegar, and not much more expensive.

Piper nigrum is one of over 1000 species of the genus pepper. They are nearly all climbers. Its original home was Travancore and Malabar, but it is now grown commercially in Indonesia, Malaya, Thailand, the Philippines, and the Caribbean. Black pepper is the dried fruit of *Piper nigrum*; white pepper is the dried fruit, further treated, with the outer black skin removed by chemical or physical means. In modern plantations in its original home, Malabar, yield is more than five tons of dried pepper per hectare (2.5 acres). In the Middle Ages this yield on 300 hectares (740 acres) could have supplied the probable annual import to Venice. Even if the yield was only a fifth of modern yields, a mere 1500 hectares (3700 acres) would have supplied Europe in, say, 1400. No wonder the Arab and Indian Muslim merchants pretended to a skill and hidden magic that never existed. No wonder there was a conspiracy of silence among Arabs, Turks, and Venetians. No wonder the morality of the pepper trade was no better, or worse, than that of the modern drug trade. Even in the 1790s, without any kind of "improved" European husbandry—without modern fungicide, insecticide, or fertilizer—dry yields were about 1 kg (21 lb) from each vine, 1000 plants per acre, nearly 2300 kg per hectare (2000 lb per acre). As a conspiracy against the consumer, pepper was treated by the merchants in much the way harmful drugs are treated today. Every outsider tried to break the monopoly.

One East Indian alternative to *Piper nigrum* was, and is, long pepper. It was known to Greeks and Romans and said by them to be better than black or white pepper. Rarely cultivated today, its roots are used in Indian medicine, and the fruit is appreciated in India for pickles and medicine. Little Long Pepper is exported from the East today.

The first true alternative, exploited by trans-Saharan traders in the thirteenth and fourteenth centuries, was the Ashanti pepper, *Piper clusii*. Arriving on the Muslim camel train at Tunis or Algiers, it was distributed by Genoese merchants all over the Mediterranean as a rival to the (largely) Venetian *Piper nigrum*. It reached France and England at some point after the Black Death in the 1360s, and for a short time a century later the Portuguese tried to break the Turkish-Venetian monopoly by following the Genoese and trading in *Piper clusii*. After the Portuguese installation in the black pepper trade, little was heard of Ashanti pepper, which was "hunted" in the wild rather than cultivated. It still is.

The other early, pre-Columbian substitute for the expensive true pepper used to be known as guinea grains or grains of paradise. These are the exceedingly pungent seeds of a member of the Melegueta family, a sort of ginger. It was carried by caravan overland to Tripoli as early as the thirteenth century. Queen Elizabeth I was very partial to its use in her cuisine; it was also used at the time for disguising poor wine and flat beer. Later it was prohibited as an additive to beer, and in the eighteenth century a brewer was subject to a fine of £200 if he had guinea grains in his possession. The seeds form part of the spices of North, Central, and West Africa because of their very great strength and, therefore, economy. It is a reed-like plant, and today is regarded as a substitute for cardamom rather than pepper. On the beach in Cuba on 4 November 1492, Columbus showed the natives a peppercorn that had come from Malabar, via the Arabs and the Venetians, to Seville, and with the explorer across the Atlantic. "Ah, yes," said the natives, "we have lots of those." Or words to that effect. What Columbus was then shown was *Pimento officinalis.*[33]

Pimento is indigenous to the Caribbean and was found wild by the Spaniards in 1494. After 1509 the fruits were "hunted" by Spanish settlers, like everything else. After they captured Jamaica in 1655, the British cultivated fields of the smallish, evergreen tree, exporting more than 200 tons in 1755 and a record of more than 10,000 tons in 1908. The Jamaican pimento, or allspice as it is known, is not a pepper and does not taste like a substitute, although it has been employed as such by the Spanish, the French, and the British. It really tastes like a mixture of cinnamon, clove, and nutmeg. Pimento has been a relatively unsuccessful transferred plant; nowhere has it done as well as in its original home. It is widely used in meat processing, canning, fruit preservation, jam and marmalade manufacture, pharmaceutical products, and male perfumery. World production today remains steady at about 10,000–12,000 tons.

Finally, there is cayenne pepper, which was also "discovered" by Columbus, who must rank as one of the most pepper-obsessed people in history. Cayenne pepper comes from an extremely hot member of the capsicum family. There are thirty of these, ranging from the hottest Mexican chile to the mild green, yellow, or red salad plants. Cayenne pepper, which comes from *Capsicum frutescens,* is more pungent than paprika, which comes from a European cultivar developed or "discovered" in Hungary in the seventeenth century. The paprika type of capsicum possibly came via Turkey, in which case the cultivar may have come around the world from Acapulco in Mexico to the Philippines, then to India, Persia, Syria, and Turkey. Capsicum plants were in cultivation in the Philippines in the 1570s, and there were seven species in India by the 1580s; they were found in the Eastern Mediterranean before 1600. The cultivars also traveled eastward with Columbus and later sailors. The seeds remain viable for a very long time, and the capsicum has a huge gene bank of potential cultivars, not all of them explored.

In Baroque Europe, flatulence from onions, cabbages, and beans was reduced by the use of capsicum; it also reduces hysteria. Today it is an essential ingredient in various curries, and India and Thailand export the hotter sorts of capsicum all over the Eurasian landmass. Curry powder, or something like it, is in use in every country east of Italy. It is difficult to see how curry (Indian *Kara*) could have reached its current power without capsicum. The powder may contain from three to thirty species of spices; few Eastern people eat anything without spice of one sort or another. The curry smell is permanent.[34]

Pepper today is a condiment taken for granted, cheap to produce, and medically less important than salt; the alternatives to *Piper nigrum* are mere addictions to the diet, luxuries, just options, however attractive. Pepper, however, influenced history in three fundamental ways. First, after a long, hard fight, Venice became rich and glorious in the late Middle Ages from its trade in pepper. Second, the whole history of the backing for Columbus's voyages depended upon the prospects for pepper profits. Third, two other countries, Portugal and the Netherlands, became rich and important because of the trade, which was as significant in the sixteenth century as the drug trade today. As an aside, it can be claimed that the Americas were discovered as they were and at that particular time as a by-product of the pepper trade.

There were no imports of American animals to compare with the transatlantic transfer of syphilis, maize, or the potato. No Spanish entrepreneur made much use of the llama, the vicuna, or the guinea pig. It was many years before the North American turkey became "useful" in Europe, and the American bison, the so-called buffalo, the moose, and the caribou have never been tamed or transferred, nor has the coyote.

Rich in wild game that could be caught easily and eaten, much of

Amerindian North America was well suited to support a relatively small human population without farming. Some of the North American Indians, however, lived as semi-farmers before the white man came, and they lived happily for centuries on maize, squash, and beans of many kinds supplemented by flesh from birds and fish. No animals north of the Rio Grande were domesticated, however, and there were few tamed animals on the American continents. Many thousands of years were needed to turn the American buffalo into a transatlantic version of the European ox.[35]

Very, very ancient America seems to have been a veritable park of wild horses, dogs, cattle, sheep, pigs, and so forth. They were apparently killed by the early human arrivals who walked across what is now the Bering Strait. Traveling south and east, early humans killed and ate much of what they found.[36]

These humans must have been extraordinarily successful as a species. They are said to have obliterated all trace of any of the animals that Europeans have since domesticated. Whether this is credible or not, the fact remains that there are plenty of fossil remains and absolutely no native American horses, oxen, asses, sheep, goats, or pigs.[37] More significantly, there are no native American species of grass or graminae out of which a true mixed farming pattern could evolve. The import of European plants and animals met with variable success in the Americas. In a few cases, species brought to the New World from the Old had as great a historical impact as those going the other direction.

Since European plants and animals came over concurrently, and since, by selection, grazing animals can "create" their own pasture, plants and animals must be examined together. Hay for shipboard horses and cattle contained seeds that spread; seeds that spread conquered the continent before Europeans. Animals, released by mistake on the Caribbean coast, reached Lower California before the Spanish; pigs escaped on some Caribbean islands, killed all the native flora and fauna, and made reforestation impossible, as rabbits did on the Madeiran island of Porto Santo.[38] So animals and plants, introduced by mistake, in the New World have to be examined together.

It all began very early. The Iberians, when they had to, survived on manioc and maize, but the preferred staple, the bread of life, was wheat. With wine and the olive, these were the traditional plants of Iberia, indeed of the Mediterranean. Iberians tried to grow wheat wherever they could. It failed in the hot, wet Caribbean, the ocean provinces of Brazil, and the Amazon, of course, but there were places where it succeeded, and succeeded before many years of Iberian occupation.

Wheat was successful, as can be imagined, in the drier lowlands and in the highlands, wherever a temperate climate could be found. In Mexico, it was grown in the highlands as early as 1525; ten years later, Mexico was exporting wheat to the Caribbean. By 1556 wheat flour in Mexico City was cheaper than in Madrid; by 1590 it was even suggested that wheat might be a good export to Spain during the fourth quarter of the century that saw so much hunger, misery, and local famine at home. Since the problems in the Spanish cities were due to landholding contradictions, agricultural husbandry incompetence, and almost incurable transport difficulties, imports of wheat from Mexico would not have solved many shortages except in areas immediately around Iberian ports.

In the sixteenth century, wheat became the staple energy food of the Spaniards, not the natives, in the valley of the Rio de la Plata in what are now Colombia and Ecuador, in Chile, and in the Central American highlands. Wheat was often grown by Amerindians as a tribute crop that replaced rent or service. By 1592 any of the 50,000 Iberians could obtain wheat flour and, therefore, bread unless they were both too poor and living in a non-wheat area. Some Amerindians were weaned to wheat from the staples of maize, potatoes, or manioc. Perhaps risen bread was also used, in larger volume than the wafers at Mass, for the conversion of the Indians. If so, wheat bread became a status symbol, but not universally. Even today, wheat is not the staple food of more than a third of the inhabitants of Latin America.

Nor was wine a substitute for maize "ale" among the Amerindians. To begin with, maize requires much less skill to ferment. When the Spanish started growing wine grapes for the households of the *conquistadores*, the Indians quite rightly pointed out larger, sweeter, and better grapes growing in many places. Although there are many native American grapes, there is no known American cultivar out of which wine can be properly made. Mexico is not good country for wine because European grapes do not ripen properly there. In Peru and Chile, it was a different matter. The first Peruvian vintage was produced in the 1550s and export commenced in the 1570s. The first good Chilean vintage was produced in the 1580s, the first export in the 1600s. The Mexican experience, however, became ecologically important more than three hundred years later.

Despite the fact that wine was no longer necessary for the lay mass because of the edits of the Council of Constance in 1415 and the Council of Trent in 1562, the Roman Catholic clergy are historically connected with viticulture in the Americas. The word "mission" used to be a great selling ploy. There was one great lay exception to this rule. Hernando Cortés (1485–1547) was the *conquistador* of Mexico. Among his more peaceful traits was his residual inherited interest in agriculture. His father was a minor landlord and a keen yeoman fruit and wine grower in the Estremadura.

Cortés Senior became the hero's agent for the transmission of hardwood cuttings of apples, pears, peaches, apricots, and so forth from Europe to Mexico. Vine cuttings sent from the Canaries and acclimatized to the no-real-winter, perpetual spring of those islands failed in Mexico. Cuttings from the continental uplands of the middle of Spain, with harsh winters and baking summers, succeeded.

In Mexico, the *conquistador* ordained that every land grant, the usual semi-feudal way of rewarding the adventurer and to which natives were attached as slaves or serfs, should be conditional upon a quota of vines being planted. Land grants were for about 50 hectares (124 acres) of land, depending upon the quality of the soil, aspect, drainage, irrigation, and so forth. One hundred slaves were allotted to work the land, and 1000 vines to be planted on each *repartimento,* or grant of land. Many of the slaves died of disease, perhaps up to 90 percent in places, but the vines flourished.

This was one of the few recorded Spanish cases of relating land, serfs, and crops. If there had been more husbandmen like Cortés, Spanish occupation of the Americas could not have resulted in hunger in the midst of plenty, as it sometimes did. Sometimes hunger was as bad as in Spain, not that the hunger, in Old or New Spain, was ever allowed to hurt the ruling classes.

The grape in the Americas went on spreading northward from Mexico and westward to California where it became indelibly connected with missions. North of modern Arizona and east of the Rockies grapevines from Europe never performed. It was not until 250 years later that phylloxera was diagnosed.[39]

The third element in the ancient diet—olive oil—was more difficult to produce than wheat or wine. How many transatlantic attempts were made to grow the olives before the first successful efforts in Chile in the 1560s? Olive seedlings require a Wardian case[40] for successful transfer and even then have difficulty acclimatizing. The olive, a native of Syria, loves a dry, Mediterranean climate with winter rain and summer drought. In the right places, typically the Levant, Greece, and Italy, trees of very great antiquity survive. Edward Gibbon (1737–94) was shown a tree near Rome allegedly planted at the time of Virgil (70–19 BC). Whether modern skepticism imitates that of Gibbon at the time, it is certainly true that trees of well over five hundred years of age are still yielding. Carefully pruned and tended, olives improve with age.

Olive oil was the regional alternative to butter and goose fat in the traditional tricorne cookery of France, long before cuisine became intellectualized. It was universally used inside and outside the body in Ancient, Medieval, and Renaissance civilizations from Afghanistan to Portugal. Long before Christ the olive became a symbol of peace, abundance, and goodwill among people, no accident that the olive is a metaphor for these qualities in the writings of Ancient Greece and Rome and in Hebrew and Muslim holy texts. Live olive trees are more than that today; they are an indicator of faithful husbandry over the ages. The first act of a barbarian conqueror, ignorant of the benevolence of the olive, was to cut down the tree for fuel. Survival, for the olive, indicates at minimum an invader with a savagery mollified by knowledge of the plant. Very old olive trees are an important indicator of a region's history.

The olive, however mystically regarded by the husbandman, is not happy to grow everywhere in the world. It was unsuccessful in the Canaries (insufficient frosts), and it died of new parasites in the Caribbean where it was also too hot and without a winter. The first ideal place found for olives in the Americas was in the dry valleys in the folds of the Andes in Chile, irrigated or watered by winter rain. In about 1600 it transferred successfully to Peru; much later, it found a home in California. Generally less successful transfers were made on the East Coast, after the founding of the United States, in Florida, South Carolina, and Mississippi. White men introduced the plant to China, and it is a feature of Queensland, South Australia, and the Cape of Good Hope. The Mediterranean remains its chief home, and despite all the efforts of those involved in plant transfer, over 95 percent of the acreage is still in the Mediterranean. Olive oil was exported from Southern Spain to most of Latin America at one time or another after 1492, and it still is.[41]

The stone fruits and the citrus trees planted in the Caribbean prospered with unaccustomed vigor. Not all of them became of economic importance in the area where they were first lodged; they were often more successful as feral escapes from men's orchards. Citrus and stone-fruit trees were to be found in suitable places all over tropical and temperate America within two hundred years.

Citrus fruits bred new "sports" for themselves in the Caribbean, including the ruby variety of grapefruit (eighteenth century), a genetic Texan "sport" of 1926, and the Ugli, which appeared in the West Indies in the 1950s. The lime of modern commerce is a natural hybrid of the European lime and the Chinese citron, both carried to the West Indies by Europeans. There are other hybrids: the "temple orange," which is a cross between the ordinary orange and the mandarin, the tangelo (mandarin/grapefruit), and numerous crosses and sub-crosses between various mandarin/tangerine/satsuma cultivars. It appears that citrus fruits have only to be loosed in the Caribbean to set up an intensive biological hybridization program. In this respect, citrus fruits do not differ from humans.

Stone fruits did not follow citrus fruits into commercially profitable hybridization. There are no peach/apricot hybrids or cherry/peaches, but cherry will cross with plum, and nectarines and peaches can hybridize with ease. Nectarines, fuzzless peaches, have become several times bigger since the Renaissance, although the hairy peach remains genetically dominant. Some peach sports are so hairy as to be unsaleable.

All the fruit tree members of the rose family—apples, pears, apricots, cherries, peaches, plums—were introduced into the Americas before 1500, as were citrus fruits. They wandered far and wide. They were found up the Orinoco, down the Mississippi, on islands on the Paraná River, and on the shores of the River Plate before white men settled any of these places as farmers or fruit growers. Feral fruit trees became a particular feature of South America. Areas covered by escaped and much modified citrus trees, stone fruits, or apples and pears were as large as an English county.[42]

The other members of the rose family, the creepers—the berries, the *Rubus* genus—are native on both sides of the Atlantic. Blackberries and raspberries are multiple fruits; the strawberry, a false fruit, an *achene*. Wild Chilean strawberries have had a distinguished role in improving bred strains of European strawberries.[43] The most interesting rubus "sport" is the loganberry, named after its discoverer, an Oregon medical doctor.[44]

The chief impact upon the Americas of the Iberian immigrants is not remembered as an invasion of microbes, still less of plants that were transferred or moved themselves; nor is European fauna considered important. Most history books tell us about gold and silver; most economic historians tell us of the impact of gold and silver upon Spain and Europe; most conventional historians ignore the natural world altogether. But gold and silver in great amounts could not have been mined without three animal products; without them, the ore would have remained underground.

The first was meat. Without meat, and plenty of it, the hardest of mine work would never have been done. There has never been a vegetarian mining community that achieved the output of carnivorous men before the advent of power tools. Modern attempts, in the Soviet Union and elsewhere, to use underfed humans as miners merely killed the miners. This may have been the Soviet intention; but despite Spanish brutality toward the Amerindian, they were always short of labor after the first few years; and the huge losses occasioned by disease made getting output per man out of the miners vitally important. It was not until the nineteenth and twentieth centuries, in Mexico, that there was a large enough population for the ruling class to be brutal in its demands upon labor. By that time, the ruling class was of Mexican stock.

The second mining commodity essential in a sixteenth-century mine was tallow. Millions of candles a year were in use in Latin America by 1600. There was no other form of lighting available underground. Perhaps by that date as many as 100,000 sheep or cattle a year were needed for tallow, up to thirty kilograms available in each beast.

The third piece in the jigsaw was the ox, used for transport and for plowing, as well as tallow. Where roads could be built, the oxcart was the only heavy transport available. Without roads, it was a question of using llamas, horses, mules, or donkeys as pack animals.

Most metal that reached the coast after 1557 was silver. In the first century after the Spanish management of the great silver mine of Potosí, production was over three million ounces a year—or 10,000 tons in the century. This required the mining and transport of a million tons of ore, the feeding of a total of nearly 100,000 people every day for a century, the transport of supplies inward to the mine, and the transport of silver, well-defended, to the coast in the Caribbean 1500 miles away. None of this could have been performed without the animals that the Spanish brought with them. Nor could Potosí have functioned until animals and plants had modified themselves to survive in the new land. Potosí was only half the production of the mines of Mexico in 1600, one-tenth the production of Mexico in 1800 on the eve of independence. How can animals be ignored or their existence be assumed?

There were huge cattle numbers in four places in Latin America. These places had been found by accident, or more properly, by the animals themselves. Cattle had been ranched in Spain for generations, the only part of western Europe of which this was true. The nearest non-Spanish ranches were in Poland, Hungary, and the Ukraine. Spanish cattle were fast and scraggy, fit to run or to defend themselves with their long horns. They were the relatives of the cattle bred for the bullfight. In 1520 they were raised in huge numbers in Hispaniola, Mexico, and their slaughter was forbidden in the next year; by 1540 they were in such quantity in Mexico City that beef was cheaper than anywhere in Europe. Cattle found their great home on the ranges south of the Rio Grande. By the end of the century they had expanded north and occupied what is now Texas. By 1592 over 200,000 head a year were being slaughtered in New Spain (Mexico) alone.

The second great place for cattle was in the so-called *llanos* of Venezuela. In the flatlands of this hot country, with a temperature far higher than in even the Spanish summer and with both drought and flood, it took some time for Iberian cattle to adapt. Production did not build up for at least fifty years after the first large-scale introduction in the early 1550s. As in Mexico, the cattle moved inland ahead of the human "owners," and a vast number of feral cattle filled the land. These longhorns were fierce and well able to defend themselves from jaguars and snakes.

The third and fourth great natural cattle regions were the hinterlands of two great modern cities. The first was the plain inland from Buenos Aires, first "discovered" in 1535. The second was in Portuguese territories inland from São Paulo and permanently settled in 1532. Buenos Aires, abandoned by the Spanish between 1540 and 1580, was so favorable an environment for cattle that by the time of permanent Spanish settlement there was a "crop" of nearly 100,000 a year to be taken from the descendants of the few hundred that had gone wild in 1535–40. These cattle bred every year for at least ten years, and the herds grew and grew. What was true in Buenos Aires was also true in São Paulo. In this great empty land, one day to be a giant coffee plantation, there were so many cattle that they could not all be eaten. Slaughtered for hides and the tallow derived from suet, the rest of the body was left to rot in the semitropical sun. How many parasites also had a population explosion to deal with the carcasses?

Cattle produced a "cash crop"—hides—that could be exported to Europe. In 1600, hides from Latin America were a more valuable export than anything else except gold, silver, and diamonds. Even in 1650, hides were more valuable than sugar, even in America. To our modern age, sated with plastics, rubber both natural and synthetic, and paper, the importance of leather is generally decorative. Before about 1900 it was essential for boots, clothing, harness, saddlery, buckets, washers, seals, pumps, bellows, belts, boxes, and a hundred and one other uses. In some areas of the Americas hides produced the best (and cheapest) ropes.

Sheep were brought over to produce wool. In the end, outside the area that became Chile and Mexico and in parts of Brazil, there were not enough people to shepherd the sheep. As a result, they ran wild and took their chances in areas where the native or introduced predators were not too thick on the ground.[45] In the areas where they did well, the superb merinos were valued more for tallows and hides than for wool or even meat. They also had a devastating effect upon the native wool-bearing, camel-like creatures—guanaco, alpaca, llama, and vicuna. These four species shared about twenty sheep diseases with the European intruders. As with humans, the native immune system was incapable of dealing with the novel parasites. As with humans, the new settlers, unconsciously or not, killed off the natives. As with humans, it all happened so quickly that it was over before the full story was recorded or quantified. As with humans, perhaps 90 percent of the natives were killed off by imported disease.[46]

If sheep were downgraded from being producers of wool to mere carcasses from which hides and tallows were removed, it explains why sheep meat has been considered only fit for the poor and shiftless in most of the Americas. American cattlemen inherited from the Spaniards their contempt for sheep raisers. This is entirely a Spanish-American experience and development. Pigs were also deflated in esteem by mere numbers. They were landed on every island. They preceded mankind across the Continent, arriving in Guatemala ahead of the whites, in Massachusetts before the Plymouth Brethren, in Virginia (complete with peach trees) before the English brought pigs from the home country. They also met the same sort of Englishman when he arrived in Barbados or Bermuda. The English found the islands "uninhabited" by humans and thought the wild pigs were native.[47]

Pigs were poor man's meat in the Latin American countries and remained so in the United States. Next came the sheep, still a poor man's meat, but slightly upmarket from pigs. Next came the beef animal, bigger, more expensive, but still one-tenth the price of the same animal in Europe. Because of the difficulty of transport in the days before refrigeration beef was relatively far cheaper in producing areas than it has been in the last one hundred years. In every future neo-Europe, meat was far cheaper than in the old Europe; it was one reason the new countries had a birthrate three times that of the old. The Americas set the pattern for animals. In Cuba cattle went wild; Mexican pigs arrived in Lower California before the white man, thus mightily confusing the contemporary naturalist; sheep were found in the Rocky Mountain foothills before any white shepherd had arrived; modified and evolved, cattle were settled in the Amazon Basin before the first whites settled there. Of all such developments, that of the horse is the most causative of evolutionary change in wholly unexpected directions. The evolution also goes full circle.

A small horse *(Equus equus)* was apparently native to the Americas, dying out about 6000 BC after the initial onslaught when men crossed over the Bering Strait and killed a large proportion of American fauna. The first Old World horses were brought to the Americas by the Spaniards in 1494. Both Iberian countries had had experience of the value of the horse used as a weapon of war against horseless warriors both in the Canaries and in West Africa. To have the use of the horse, even by the individual man at arms, was at the time believed to multiply the power of Europeans against horseless natives by a factor of eight or ten to one. This was the first time that Europeans had fought with a weapon of this order of advantage, and it was comparable to the effect of firearms against "natives" armed only with spears or bows and arrows. In the sixteenth century the horse was a greater asset than firearms, since firearms at that time were not much more efficient than most good bows and arrows. Both Cortés in Mexico and Pizarro in the Andes relied on the military effect of horses, which together with gunpowder and religion, were the contemporary explanation of Spanish success.

Cortés originally set forth from Spain in November 1518 with not many more than thirty horses. Until reinforced by the troops sent by Velázquez to "arrest" him, Cortés had fewer than a dozen horses by the time he reached Mexico City. In the end, in 1523, after the successful second siege of Mexico City in August 1521, Cortés had still fewer than a hundred horses. Two years later, five or six, necessarily including both genders, escaped. This flight (and others after 1530) produced the feral horses of the North American continent, and from these accidents were derived a complete change in the habits of the Plains Indians; these new habits in turn brought about the inevitable destruction of millions of American buffalo.

Horses multiplied in Mexico and Texas in numbers that can only be estimated. In most of the New World horses were without natural enemies; there were neither the macroparasites of wolves or lions nor the microparasites of the score or more diseases that afflicted horses in the Old World. If the experience of the human increase in the temperate New World is translated into an equine increase at the same time, then the five or six escaped horses of 1530 could have grown to several thousand by 1600. After that time geometrical increase showed up as significantly more powerful than mere arithmetic. If the wild horses of America increased in number twice as fast as the wild horses of the steppes of Eurasia, then there could easily have been several million horses in favored places on the Great Plains of North America, in the pampas of the Argentine, and in many discrete parts of Brazil, Uruguay, Mexico, and California.

Three Darwinian processes took place at the same time. First, the horses themselves were selected for the characteristics of survival in their new environment. "Mustangs" (anglicized from the Spanish *mesteno*) became a distinct type of range horse—hardy, capable of long distances without horseshoes, sure-footed, and with great courage of a frontier type. The wild horse of North America redefined, once again, the relationship of horse and rider, not necessarily to the rider's advantage. Often the horse knew the job better than the rider. Certainly a wild horse was often wiser than a "dude" rider.[48]

Second, the horse altered the ecology of the plains grasses. By the 1780s there were so many horses in Texas that the earth around watering holes was carrying European species of grass. The horses had killed the native grasses that had previously supported a much thinner population of buffalo or no herbivores at all. Horses made their own new pasture out of European seeds that had traveled either within the alimentary system of the imported horses, sustained on hay during the voyage, or as passengers clinging to their coats, contained in the horses' bedding on board ship. There are many stories of this kind of accidental import. What is not documented is how the original imports crossed the continent so quickly that Kentucky Blue Grass, for example, was found in Kentucky before the white man arrived there, but after the first feral horses and cattle. Before Kentucky, its more modest name in English was (and is) "smooth-stalked meadow grass."[49]

Third, the horse changed the habits of the Amerindians who were parasites of the American buffalo. How many buffalo were there at that time? Five million? Ten million? Nearly two million square miles were originally occupied by American bison in Canada and the United States. That makes 500 million hectares (over 1 billion acres). Ten million animals in the United States and Canada would have resulted in a density of one buffalo per 50 hectares (124 acres). In 1900, when the killing stopped, there were fewer than 1000 wild buffalo, with 1119 residing in parks and zoos.

Amerindians who had never seen a horse found the feral horses; many horses may have been eaten before the Indians learned to ride them. When first seen by whites, mounted Indians, like some of the Asian invaders into Europe at the end of the Roman period and like the Romans themselves, had no stirrups. They often had no bridles or saddles either. Amerindians never made horseshoes.

By 1800 most, but not all, Indians encountered by white trappers were equipped with horses, bridles, saddles, and stirrups. Then the Indians had to teach themselves to shoot arrows from horseback, often from moving horses; this was a key problem in Eurasia for hundreds of years. It is a difficult art and was much admired in Persians, Mongols, and, above all, Parthians. How did the Indians teach themselves to become so expert in such a short time—perhaps a hundred years at most?

On top of all this, there is a further Darwinian possibility. Did the arrival of the mustang increase the birthrate among what might be called the buffalo Indians, which are not quite the same thing as the Plains Indians? Horse ownership could have led non-Plains Indians to adapt to a dependence upon the buffalo. Logically, the possession of the horse—a multiplication of mobility on the order of between five and ten times—would increase the range of operation of a hunter-gatherer tribe by a significant amount and led to increased intertribal conflict, before any friction occurred with white neo-Europeans. The key to this friction was not land use, but water, wintering grounds, sites to grow the essential Indian corn, and the habits of the buffalo that had themselves become much modified by the Indians' possession of the horse. The buffalo, of course, evolved to respond; the animals were divided into the quick and the dead. None but the quick could survive the mounted Indian with bow and arrow. Many agricultural Amerindians became hunter-gatherers again because the horse made it possible and profitable.

The arrival of the horse and its explosion of numbers sealed the fate of both Indians and buffaloes. Without the horse the Indians would have been more settled than they became once mounted. It is entirely possible that because of the opportunities offered by the horse, the Indians reverted from farmers who had an annual buffalo kill to hunters who followed buffalo all the year round. Whether or not this is so, they became so identified with the buffalo that the animals were deliberately exterminated by whites to drive the Indians onto the reservations, making the range available to grazers and farmers. As a by-product, buffalo meat fed construction gangs on the railroads.

Without the horse, the argument runs, the Indians would not have become so dependent on the buffalo. Had they had the horse since time began, on the other hand, instead of from only about 1750, the Plains Indian, the buffalo, the horse, and (presumably) some sort of ox and sheep and goat would have worked out a self-renewing, sustainable ecology. As it was, the ecology of the mounted Indian was too fragile to survive the white man, the white man's diseases, and the white man's greed. In these years, the descendants of half a dozen Spanish riding horses escaped from Mexico City in 1523 had changed the habits of Amerindians in one-quarter of what would be the United States, and the change killed the culture.

At no point before the present did Europeans question the means of their victory over the world. This victory was won by the inhabitants of only 2 percent of the Earth's land surface. These inhabitants—diseases, plants, and animals—conquered most of the temperate and subtropical regions. Europeans transferred and improved the performance of plants from the Americas. The pattern of biological dominance is so markedly favorable to the European historical case that it has been largely ignored. Europeans have invented all sorts of political and intellectual theories to account for their success. In few cases can non-biological explanations for the Triumph of the West prove to be as convincing as the more earthy, the more visible, and the more palpable. Because every action in history provokes reaction, inhibits other actions, or can be examined only in relation to other events, there can be no certitude—but there can be recognition.

CHAPTER FOUR

Challenge and Response

This chapter treats the development of the United States in detail, both before and after Independence, accentuating the physical. The primacy of disease and food supply in an almost "empty" country and an important truth about the New World are contrasted with ideological explanations of American success. The important truth for the time was that this was the first country in the world in which it was unnecessary for a person to be hungry. The effect of this fact upon the future has never been properly measured, but there were still challenges in the young United States, and American responses have proved valuable in every other new country.

The story of the neo-Europes outside the earliest, in the Americas, is told mainly in the next chapter—most of the important relationships between the new countries and Western Europe have grown up in the last hundred years. However, the pattern followed in the United States has been an ambition of many other countries. Canada has developed economically in juxtaposition to her big neighbor; Australia has been conscious of the American example for a century; New Zealand, once so interlocked with England, is now more of a Pacific country, with the United States as an example.

In Russia, old challenges became almost insoluble problems because those in authority walked away from them without responses. This is as true today as in Tsarist times. An astonishing nineteenth-century birthrate produced no more food, nor has the last half-century. In Japan, the challenges have been accepted and triumphantly answered. A country with only 20 percent of its main island potentially agricultural, against 75 percent in England, maintained a glorious isolation for two hundred years with an increase of population during that time of only 28 percent—against 400 percent for England. During those two centuries, Japan was self-sufficient, much more crowded than England. She still is. This space challenge has produced a response that is unique in the world. It is not properly understood, but it is a prime cause for Japanese success.

THE SPANISH AND ENGLISH colonies fared very differently in the Americas. While the Spanish sought to replicate a centrally organized, Old World hierarchy, the English settlements were free to adapt to their situation, to create a new identity for themselves, and to improve their situation as best they could. The U.S. experience is so profoundly different from that of any other country that Americans today are apt to ascribe their history to special factors. Many speak with a tinge of sanctimony, a hint of holiness, of the unique nature of the United States of America. Freedom from the arbitrary rule of kings and nobles was obviously important; escape from the tyranny of some church or other was at least as significant; even the all-important change between the medieval meaning for the word "liberty" (privilege) and the modern meaning (natural rights) has been ascribed to the American Revolution. In fact, all three of these desirable elements were held by John Locke (1632–1704) to be essential in a modern free country and were nominally in place in England by 1715. Largely because the Founding Fathers had to appear to be anti-British, the credit for these vital ingredients in the Constitution was attributed to Greece or Rome rather than to England. To be fair to the men of two hundred years ago, it also appeared at the time that King George III was trying to abrogate what the Glorious Revolution of 1688 had done to the rule of kings. Eternal vigilance is the price of liberty. Many Englishmen supported the Americans, regarded as fellow citizens suffering for liberty and justice. The loss of the American colonies was the price that the English paid for their lack of vigilance about their king. There is another physical scenario about America, which is an alternative to "Man's arrogant insistence that he alone has been the principal player."[1]

Neither in Spain nor in England were there insupportable increases in population in the two hundred years before the American Revolution. Spain's population increase in the eighteenth century was less than that of the European average (44 percent instead of 50 percent). England's was more, 60 percent, but most of the increase was in the last third of the century by which time the troubles between London and the colonies were already important. There was not much British emigration into the thirteen colonies or states between 1770 and 1800. In fact, the total emigration from Spain and England across the Atlantic was about the same before 1800, one million from each country. What happened when they got there was what was important.[2]

In 1650 there were, perhaps, 50,000 Spaniards south of the Rio Grande. They were an elite. They did no manual work; even plantation managers were usually half-breeds.[3] There were huge losses from disease in the Spanish Caribbean colonies and some in other parts of South and Central America. Only in certain areas did the absence of disease coincide with massive food supplies. There were three principles about the Spanish Empire. First, all power centered in a provincial viceroy, usually a grandee from Old Spain, who went home, if he survived, at the end of his period in office. The "captaincies" or viceroyalties were, from north to south, New Spain (Mexico); Cuba (the Caribbean); Guatemala (Central America); Venezuela; New Granada (Colombia); Quito; Peru; Charcas (Bolivia); Chile; and Buenos Aires, which was huge, including modern Argentina, Uruguay, and Paraguay.

Second, it was the function of Spanish colonies to furnish the mother country with precious minerals and tropical products. The strictest mercantilism was implicit. There was little trade between colonies or between Spanish possessions and those of another country, and no approved trade with Europe other than between Spain and the colonies. Inevitably, the rules were honored in the breach, not the observance.

Third, since Spanish whites could not hope to occupy Central and South America, much less the three Guianas and Brazil, an area bigger than Europe, interbreeding was encouraged. Red and black should be made more Hispanic; the *conquistadores* should spread their seed throughout the continent. This philosophy was even approved by the priests. Was it before or after the connection between Spain and *machismo*? The result is that Latin America is an extraordinarily complex mixture of red, white, black, and, ultimately, yellow genes. The pure Spanish did not multiply very greatly.

The English, of course, had no "philosophy." The colonies just grew up, but they were of vigorous stock. They lived in an empty paradise compared with England. Shakespeare's England was no more, no less crowded than the Continental United States of today. England at the time of the French Revolution was as densely occupied as is the Eastern seaboard today, but without railroads, with less coal and water power, without any cheap steel, and without the internal combustion engine or electricity. The early English emigration during the eighteenth century was mostly to the Caribbean; this destination was even truer of seventeenth-century movements. Most of those who went to the Caribbean died of disease—yellow fever, *falciparium* malaria, enteric disorders. In 1700, there were about 250,000 people in the colonies running from Maine to South Carolina. In 1800 the same colonies, now States east of the mountains, contained nearly four million people; they were overwhelmingly white.

There have been great arguments among demographers and historians about how this increase came about. Was it all natural increase, in which case it would be about 3 percent per year, about the same as in Ireland at the latter end of the period? How much was immigration—400,000? More? Less? Politics are mixed up in this argument. If in 1800 the American population had increased by 60, 70, or 80 percent, derived from the 1700 stock, then the Americans of 1800—Washington, Jefferson, Madison, Adams, Hamilton, and the rest—were all special people, not just overseas Englishmen. And what about that quintessential American, Benjamin Franklin, signatory of the Declaration of Independence; born the seventeenth child of poor parents, self-educated, an FRS; the discoverer of the lightning conductor, the course of the Gulf Stream, and the heat-absorbing quality of different colors? He crossed the Atlantic on four missions, fought the English but retained their respect and made peace with them. No one could call such a man anything but an American. He was more uniquely American than Washington or Jefferson. He was one of the first poor children able to make good.

This, then, was the quality of America on which the hope of every subsequent revolution has, in part, been floated—from France (1789) and the Spanish colonies (1809–23) to Russia (1917) and even to the Iberian Revolutions of the day before yesterday (Portugal, Spain). Every free man or woman living today believes that he has the right to make the most of himself. The Parable of the Talents takes new form. It was previously the law, the inaccessibility of education, the unfairness of autocracy, the unbridled privileges of the nobility, and the corruption of the Establishment that prevented men from making good. Whether this was true of the England whence came the inhabitants of British North America, the important point was that people were able to believe it. This sort of freedom meant that people had to be allowed to forget the past as well as to look forward to a prosperous future.

If there is no structural reason for economic inefficiency, people get rich. Americans in 1775 were richer than the English. Poor Americans, even ex-convicts, were very much richer than poor Englishmen. If men believe there is no limit to the gross wealth of this world, they are more likely to increase that wealth rather than attempt to share it. If men believe that anything is possible, some part of that possibility may be realized. If economic freedom, without overmuch regulation, and true competition exist, there is more chance of efficiency. If the market is more important than politics, then there is less likelihood of corruption. There was an implicit belief in the Constitution that economic freedom was part and parcel of the total freedom of mankind, part of his birthright. It is an intriguing possibility in history that, if the Americans had not been there pointing the way in the 1790s, as in the 1950s, Europe would have reverted to the cozy restrictive practices that those in positions of power and privilege regard as "normal." Guilds, combinations, and cartels all have the function of reversing the word "liberty" from its modern meaning to its more ancient, an acceptable form of "privilege." Despite British mercantilism and attempts to replicate Old World authority in America, the colonies were too distant, too large, too prosperous, and growing too quickly to remain under strict royal control. Frontiersmen, New Englanders, and Quakers all responded to local conditions in a spirit of innovation and independence.

By 1592, a century after Columbus's first voyage, mercantilism had already been perceived by a few to be a fallacy. The received opinion is that it was Adam Smith who proved that mercantilism was damaging to everyone who traded. In fact, English Elizabethans had included men of sufficient vision who saw that the mere pursuit of gold was not as valuable as the creation of wealth. The earliest, truest creation of wealth was growing food in a hungry world. "That is the richest land that feeds the most men," said Sir Humphrey Gilbert, brother-in-law of Sir Walter Raleigh. Gilbert drowned in 1583, homeward bound on the Atlantic, having failed to find the fabled Northwest Passage, but having taken possession of Newfoundland for Queen Elizabeth. Raleigh died on the scaffold in 1618, having been in turn the quintessential Elizabethan: courtier, poet, wit, explorer, historian, soldier, and lady's man—a survivor into a subsequent, darker, ungenerous reign. It was Raleigh who had a vision of planting an "English nation" in North America that would be an outlet for England's surplus capital and people. In 1584 a full-scale expedition had planted people on Roanoke Island near Cape Hatteras. The 150 colonists did not survive; perhaps they were massacred. After Raleigh had spent most of his fortune on this and other expeditions, there was no result, except for the well-known introduction of the potato and tobacco plants to Ireland. Both had momentous, unforeseen consequences.[4]

Raleigh, broken in fortune as well as reputation, was succeeded by a chartered company. In 1620 the London Company became two, the Virginia Company and the Council for New England. The Virginia settlers were mostly wellborn and did not welcome toil; starvation was a familiar, friendly and supportive Indians notwithstanding. Like Spanish "aristocrats" the British gentry preferred to find gold; if gold was not forthcoming, others worked; after 1619 there was a slave trade to cure the shortage of labor.[5]

In 1623, after the massacre of 1622, there was an inquiry. Five thousand five hundred whites had arrived in Virginia; 300 had returned to England; 4000 had died; only 1200 had remained. The next year it was judged that the "democratical" colony had failed, and Virginia became a Royal Colony. By 1642, when Sir William Berkeley became the Governor, there was already a self-sustaining corn-based colony, with tobacco as a "cash crop." Gradually other crops were grown. Apart from maize, legumes, and tobacco, the plants were all introductions. Squash came from the Caribbean, brought by the Spanish; peanuts, brought from Brazil by the Portuguese to West Africa, came over with the slave ships; the Irish potato was brought over by Englishmen, went wild, and was adopted by the Amerindians. Onions had gone feral, having been introduced farther south by the Spanish and spread by the fauna, perhaps pigs, also left by the Spanish. Tomatoes, Jerusalem artichokes, capsicum (peppers), and sunflowers were introduced from the Caribbean. The stone fruits had been introduced by the Spanish missions farther south, had gone wild, and traveled north with the pigs. This was true of figs as well as peaches, both of which thrived in Virginia.

Native fruits and nuts prospered as distinct American cultivars and included grapes, whortleberries, cranberries, huckleberries, gooseberries, strawberries, certain apples, persimmons, and mulberries. The last excited exaggerated hopes for a significant silk industry that never materialized. Maple sugar was the standard sweetener of the Northeast and was extended south by the English. Indigenous nuts included pecans, butternuts, hickories, chinkapins, and chestnuts. Few fruits or nuts were domesticated, although their genes were used in improving European varieties. It is not clear whether anyone could survive without agriculture. The only form of native livestock discovered by the original settlers was turkeys, some sort of "peacock," and "guinea fowl." There may have been a domesticated hen, but the settlers' poultry crossed with the natives, so by 1650 no one could tell which poultry were indigenous. Pigs had migrated from the Southern tidal country before the establishment of Jamestown in 1607–08.

The cultivation of tobacco soon boomed. Under Charles II the colony became the monopoly supplier to the United Kingdom in exchange for which the colony's entire trade had to be with London. The brave vision of Raleigh did not survive the mercantile bureaucrats who took over his legacy. The Dutch had broken the mercantile system during the English Civil War and Interregnum, while Cromwell in turn broke the Dutch and introduced the Navigation Acts. These locked the English and their colonies and trading "factories" into a rigid system from 1655 until the 1840s. The British Empire prospered in spite of these Acts, not because of them, but they formed a point of grievance for every enterprising American from the very earliest days.

Tobacco is a very demanding crop. Three plantings in ten were sufficient for the poor land of coastal Virginia. By definition, small farms did not have enough land to fallow or to grow restorative, rotational alternatives, so tobacco exhausted small farms and impoverished the farmers. Poor men left the tidal water and went west. Joining them was an average annual crowd of 1500 "redemptioners" who had worked out their term of service. In 1676, a hundred years before Independence, a complicated, populist revolt was led by one Nathaniel Bacon (1647–76), who challenged the long, apparently wise rule of Sir William Berkeley. Charles II pardoned all the rebels except Bacon (who, fortunately for reconciliation, died of fever), and Berkeley was recalled. The latter refused to return to England until he had hanged a score of rebels and illegally sequestrated the property of those who opposed him. The consequences were important.

Poor whites identified with the frontier. From 1676 for at least two hundred years, the East became more and more Establishment, ruled by men who did not work with their hands. Jamestown, burned out in 1676, was replaced by grander, more urbane Williamsburg. The executive and the judiciary were under control of the Crown, but the Crown was at least a month away; sometimes three months were required for an answer. This meant that the governor, burgesses, and judges, drawn from the same educated classes or from England or educated there, represented the Eastern Establishment. On the frontier—a moving line—were the enterprising, the discoverers, the men of the future. On worn-out tidewater plantations, magnates employed black slaves, white criminals, or British indentured servants; the whites had to work seven to ten years to pay for their crimes or their sea passage.

The frontier was peopled by those who had to make good; the coast was controlled by those who already commanded wealth and position. One way to divide the growing colony would be to say that on the tidewater were the territorial settlers; in the Piedmont and in the mountains were the entrepreneurial men. That idea uses divisions that exist in the majority of European countries to this day. The important point to remember is that it was population density that brought it about in America.

However well farmed, the coastal regions from the Potomac to Key West could only support so many people in comfort before the Industrial Revolution. When life became too difficult, the poor whites moved west if free to do so. If there was Indian trouble as a result, so be it; there was "Indian trouble" as early as 1622 with 347 white deaths; no one thought twice about the causes, then or later, with whites and Indians competing for the same land. Because there was always more land to the west, Americans did not farm "well" from the first. The shortage was not of land, but of humans, so output per man became more important than output per farm. Even if labor was in the form of black slaves or white indentured servants, it still cost money; even if a free paid laborer was not to be found in Virginia in 1750 and the only workers were blacks, tradesmen, or indentured servants, there was still a labor shortage. In the end it would lead to an important sort of freedom. Its origin was confused with some special kind of intellectual or spiritual cause; but in truth, the agent that produced this form of freedom was a shortage of people compared with a bonanza of "empty" land.

The New England colonies had a different youth. There were vague traces of European fishermen and traders spending winters (before 1607) in what is now New England, perhaps with ships damaged in the Grand Banks fishery; there was an abortive "Popham Colony" near the mouth of the Kennebec in the winter of 1607–08. The *Mayflower* arrived near Cape Cod with 102 passengers in September 1620; they survived with Indian help. The Pilgrims undoubtedly took white man's diseases with them to the Americas, but they found in 1620 that other whites had already given the Amerindians of Massachusetts "a raging mortal disease." This was smallpox. The Indians kept their distance and did not mingle with the Puritans, who met little resistance. This they ascribed to Godliness, not bad Indian experience with the Red Plague. The death rate among Indians in New England appears to have been as high as the death rate a hundred years earlier in Mexico, and higher than in Virginia. This may well have been because smallpox is a disease of density. This would suggest that Indians were settled densely in Hispaniola, Mexico, Peru, and New England, less densely in Virginia and the Carolinas. Or had the Spanish already spread smallpox along the coasts of the South from Florida northward before the British arrived?

It is suspected that smallpox had been taken, by some infected person in a boat, to Florida before the Spanish arrived and up the Mississippi before either the Spanish or the French came. It was endemic when George Vancouver arrived in the 1790s on the island to be named after him,[6] so why should smallpox not have reached Chesapeake Bay previously? In any event, the existence of smallpox in New

England, brought farther north by Amerindians after being infected by the French, is virtually certain in 1620, and to that accident can be ascribed some of the Puritans' success. John Winthrop said of the Indians in 1634: "They are all neere dead of small pox, so as the Lord hathe cleared our title to what we possess." The Puritans benefited from the disease in two ways: It emptied the land for them to fill, and by striking the Indians, it proved that God was on their side.[7]

Of course smallpox hit European populations very hard at the same date, but it killed children, not adults. Survivors were inoculated for life against death from the disease. Attacks in later life, if any, were mild and innocuous except for disfiguring the face, but almost every living Englishman in the seventeenth century had been exposed to smallpox, as were most other Europeans. Death rates among children were very high; perhaps as many as 75 percent of the victims were under four years of age.

In the Americas, wherever the white man went smallpox killed indiscriminately. Instead of having to replace a baby, biologically and economically not too difficult, the Amerindians had to replace people of every age. This was impossible demographically. The Algonquin were hit in the middle 1620s;[8] and the smallpox slaughter went on—Cherokees, Catawbas, Hurons, Iroquois—culminating with perhaps half the population of Indians in the Mississippi-Missouri basin dead in the Great Plague of 1837–38.[9]

Assured of God's favor, the Puritans marched forward to the tune of success; success on this earth ensured heaven in the next. New England, ill suited to become a Plantation Province, became instead, and very early, a much more urban place than Virginia. Within a generation the South had acquired the characteristics that would still pertain in 1860. A broad, flat land of magnificent horizons, it was sparsely populated. Immigrants had arrived, not as complete "congregations," or even as families, but as individuals. In the South there were few Indians organized in tribes against whom whites had to huddle in self-protection. The rivers and sea inlets lent themselves to a direct trade with England. The English county was easily transferred as a unit of jurisdiction with a court established in each county, usually of eight justices. They made the rules, enforced them, and acted as the petty judiciary as they did in England until 1889. The Common Law obtained as far as serious crimes were concerned. Common Law was shared with England, as it is today, and decisions of the courts remained vital.[10] There was a governor, usually appointed by the Crown, and the Church of England was ultimately the established religion even in tolerant Maryland. Throughout the South, there was far more religious toleration than was possible in New England.

In New England the settlements were formed by the facts of population density, disease, and food supplies. Because of the Indian population, the unit of settlement was the town, laid out around a square common with a place for church, school, and town hall. The town gave protection from the Indians and easy access to church and school during the savage winters. Frontier towns acted as forts against the Indians, and before 1700 it was illegal for settlers to abandon their lands and move north or west. Because of the rigorous climate, broken terrain, poor communications, rocky soil, and a shortage of potential arable land, no system involving plantation crops grown for Europe would have provided a decent standard of living. Subsistence crops were grown, but wealth was generated in other ways.

Fish were a major export from the first—dried, smoked, or salted cod for Catholic Europe. Timber and timber products were obvious, and even as early as the 1650s and as late as the 1850s, New England built wooden ships cheaper than anyone in Europe. New England challenged the Baltic in the production of masts and planking, and Old England in the production of the ribs and knees of the wooden walls, and tan bark for the curing of the essential leather. Barrel staves, hoops, and whole barrels were exported to the South, to the West Indies, and to all of Europe. Timber was burnt in huge tonnages to make charcoal and potash. Fur remained important long after most fur-bearing animals had been driven from the other Atlantic colonies. Trade of every sort was essential for poor New England.

By 1700 New England had over 1000 trading vessels in a population of not much more than 100,000. A triangular trade grew up between Africa, the West Indies, and New England that involved slaves, rum, sugar, and the products manufactured in New England. New England developed manufactures earlier than any other colony of a white imperial power and became independent of the home country for its supply of wooden goods, ironwork, and pre-industrial craftwork of every kind. Earlier than any other colony of a European power, New England demonstrated an ability to live in comfort without depending directly or indirectly on the home country. New Englanders ascribed these characteristics to superior Puritan virtue.

In fact, they were the effects of geography, climate, disease, food supply, population density, and so forth; they were exactly mirrored by the absence of slavery, which was due to the same factors. In 1700, Massachusetts and Virginia probably had the same population of whites. Virginia, with eight times the total area, had more than twelve times as much agricultural land. Against those imperatives, what position can ideology hold?

It was chance that landed the Pilgrim Fathers on Cape Cod. It was the circumstances of their new life that made Puritans who they were. By 1700 there was as much urbanization in Salem, Boston, Newport, New Haven, and more than 200 other towns as there was in any comparable area in Europe at that time. Is it idle to speculate about what the Puritans would have been like three generations later if they had landed on Long Island or near Cape Hatteras instead of Cape Cod?

The Middle Atlantic colonies had a much more varied history before 1700. In 1609 Henry Hudson, an Englishman in the Dutch service, arrived in his ship, the *Half-Moon*, in what would become New York Harbor. His crew offered Dutch gin to the local Indians of the Delaware tribe, and the island on which this historic exchange took place was henceforth known as Manhattan, or "the island-where-we-all-got-drunk." The Dutch very quickly established trading posts, not settlements, at New Amsterdam (New York), Fort Orange (Albany), Fort Nassau on the Delaware River, and Fort Good Hope on the Connecticut River. The island of Manhattan was purchased in 1642 for a few dollars.

The region was not much cherished. Furs and wheat (established by the Dutch in 1625) were less desirable commodities than tea from China, the huge trade in spices from the East Indies, gold stolen from the Spanish, or the slave trade between Africa and the Caribbean. Even the salt trade from the island of Aruba in the Caribbean was considered more valuable than the products of New Netherlands, as the Dutch settlements were called. When the Dutch were defeated in North America in the 1660s and title passed to the English, there were probably only 8000 people in New Netherlands, not many Dutch among them. For a generation there had been an autocratic, corrupt Dutch rule ill-supervised from Amsterdam, ill-supported by the directors of the West India Company, and ill-regarded by the native Netherlanders.

New Sweden was an interlude allowed by the Dutch who were temporarily in alliance with Queen Christina. From 1638 to 1655 a Swedish settlement was permitted at "Fort Christina" on the site of present-day Wilmington, Delaware. In the latter year it surrendered to Peter Stuyvesant, the authoritarian, peg-legged "director" of New Netherlands. Nine years later, Stuyvesant surrendered it to the English.[11]

As is well-known, the Quaker William Penn acquired title to what is now known as Pennsylvania in 1681. The feu-rent payable was two beaver skins. An aristocrat by birth, Quaker democrat by conviction, Penn drew up a form of government that gave franchises to all landowners and taxpayers, allowed freedom of worship, and named treason and murder as the only capital offenses. The Penn family remained in a quasi-landlord position for nearly a hundred years. Meanwhile, the City of Brotherly Love had developed into the most American city, larger than any other in 1700; the next most populous city was Boston, although its rival, New York, always had a more commercial and cosmopolitan air. The Middle Atlantic colonies prospered exceedingly, growing grain and producing butter and cheese, beef and pork, and exporting these all over the Caribbean and to many parts of Europe. In 1700 there were British colonies all the way from Maine to South Carolina, and inland to the "fall line."[12]

Inland from the fall line and as far west as the mountains was the Piedmont, a gradually rising plain. Below the Piedmont, land was easily brought into cultivation, easily approached by ship, and useful for the primary production of cereals and tobacco. Although unable to withstand the improvidence of plantation monoculture, the tidewater lands below the fall line were never a limitation in those areas that were farmed so badly as to cause exhaustion or erosion.[13] The feckless just moved on. In those areas of New England to which the early settlers could not emigrate, the population either earned its living from non-agricultural pursuits or treated the land with the same sort of respect they would have shown at home in England. Emigration from New England to the West was not a general option before Independence.

In Virginia, westward movement was popular with those who had worn out the land of the tidewater and with indentured servants who were free of obligation after their redemption. In the South, redemptioners received fifty acres of land plus the usual tools, clothing, and livestock. The land tended, of course, to be in the West.

In Pennsylvania and New Jersey there were opportunities in the Piedmont. It is narrower than in the South, but a rolling countryside of higher than average fertility. West of the Blue Ridge and its northern extensions lies the "great" Appalachian Valley, the Kittatinny Valley in northern New Jersey, the Allentown-Lebanon-Cumberland Valley in Pennsylvania and Maryland, and the Shenandoah in Virginia. These areas are the most fertile, the most moderate in climate, and the best watered in the eastern United States. Because pre-railroad transport, except by water, was so expensive and difficult, the parts of these valleys nearest the rivers became influential in eighteenth-century America. They were more than that. They were the main reason that Americans ate, on average, twice as well as Europeans of the same class. These valleys not only fed Americans, they also provided food exports of great economic value to the Caribbean and Europe. These exports, according to figures published at the time, were far less than recorded imports, except in the South. However, researchers do not have quite the faith in colonial statistics as they once did. For example, over the fifty years before 1776, New England statistics reveal a deficit larger than either New York or Pennsylvania. Common sense suggests that exports were either undervalued or underrecorded. How could the coast be watched by a body of officials with whom the population had scant sympathy?

There was an independence bred in most Americans that derived not from politics or religion, but from the effects of the natural world. The sheer scale of the landscape in North America, dwarfing in 1600, 1700, 1800, and even today, the works of man on the same continent, rendered most men conscious of their humble gratitude. To this was added the tendency of Europeans to eat far better in America than at home, to rear more children, to lose far fewer neighbors to disease, to live longer themselves, and to surprise each other. This was true not only of the English; Scots came as families or small congregations and became prominent in America as merchants, lawyers, schoolmasters, and ministers of religion. Their influence on America before Independence was profound. It could never have happened if these men and women had had only the opportunities available to them at home.

The same is true of the Scots-Irish, or Ulstermen, who came over in large numbers when the English, after only a century of settlement in Ireland, restricted their woolen and linen industries. A people planted by James I in the middle of largely Roman Catholic natives, the Ulstermen were of pioneer stock at home. They imported these qualities to America, and they settled in the Susquehanna Valley and in the Carolinas. The flood of Ulstermen coincided with large numbers of peasant Germans who settled in the so-called "Dutch" counties of Pennsylvania.

These Pennsylvania Dutch were encouraged to settle by William Penn himself, and he attracted many settlers from Switzerland and the Rhineland. By 1776 there were probably more than 150,000 of these peasants, immensely hardworking, thorough, thrifty, patient, industrious, and with large families. They had a mystical love of the soil (and of real estate) combined with an intellectual and intelligent application of new methods of husbandry. What is so notable about these Germans, Ulstermen, and Scots is that each group developed positive characteristics that were obvious in only a minority in their own homes. The full potential of all these people occurred only in the new Europe that they called, in time, the United States of America. At the bottom of the success of the new country was a simple fact, often ignored. The plentiful food supply and low population density in the New World had three important effects: It served as a magnet to the poor and hungry in Europe; it allowed their rapid multiplication once they arrived; and it drove the early market upon which the United States has built its strength.

At the bottom of the success of the new country was a simple fact, often ignored. For the first time in history the poorest person in America had enough to eat. That could never be said of the poor in Europe, still less of Asia or Africa, before 1776. It has only been possible to claim that there is enough food of enough quality for every Western European for the last generation and a half. This boon is not yet in place in Eastern Europe, Africa, or Asia.

The effect of such circumstances upon mankind in the seventeenth and eighteenth centuries was to unleash the full physical potential of human beings. Europeans were "restricted" by religion, constitution, politics, or feudal custom. In fact, is it not time that an alternative be considered? Is it not more important to eat properly; to rear most children born, instead of a minority, to live ten years longer, to see large numbers of grandchildren at a time when descendants looked after the old? Is it any wonder that Americans, even before Independence, were regarded with ill-concealed envy, tinged by the kind of patronizing superiority exhibited even today?

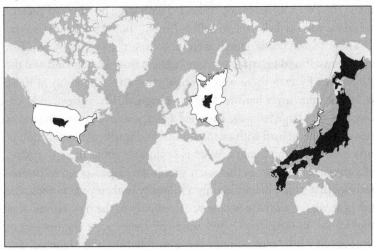

Three Superpowers, Redrawn to Show Density of People in Cultivated Area.
The larger the area, the more dense the population.

The key tools to make market agriculture possible were the children of steam power: the railway and the steamship. It is true that there had been a market agriculture in the United States operating by water. The land serving the trade necessarily had to be beside a river or the sea. At the time of Independence, such a system existed in the river valleys east of the Alleghenies. The Connecticut, Hudson, Delaware, Susquehanna, and Potomac Rivers all gave easy access to the sea, and small ships had sailed almost directly from the wharves on these rivers, and those of the South, for a hundred years before Independence.[14] Northern farms found markets in the Caribbean, the South, and in the growing American cities long before the first railroad was built.[15]

The loss of the British West Indies as a preferential area after Independence led to a change in a market that had taken over 20 percent of all Northern farm production in 1776. When the young United States became (for the British) a foreign nation, the British navigation laws excluded American ships from the trade of the British West Indies. Trade between the United States and the West Indies did not cease. American merchants were hampered; English merchants helped. Fortunately for the United States, the war between England and France that occupied most of the years from 1792 to 1815 led to a relaxation of the Navigation Acts; but the war, waged with increased success except for one short interval by the Royal Navy, led in turn to a short war between the United States and the former mother country. Through all these alarms and excursions, American food production and the American food trade expanded at a rate whose volume meant a doubling of trade every twenty years. In the years between 1783 and the Wars between the States (1861–65), U.S. food trade increased by more than eight times. The population, meanwhile, increased by only three times in the same period.

Most of the reasons why the food trade grew so greatly were domestic, not foreign. First, the South was a deficit food area, partly because the more suitable Southern grain crops were not bread grains. The South grew more than half of all Indian corn (maize) in the Union, even as late as 1860, but less than a third of the wheat, a fifth of the oats and rye, and a twentieth of the barley and buckwheat.

Second, the South grew a great many cash crops for direct export, or export to the North—cotton, tobacco, rice, indigo, and sugar. Of these crops, only the unexported portion of the sugar and rice crops directly increased food supplies.

Third, labor organization in the South, dependent as it was upon slavery, did not assist in the economical use of food. Slaves were given land to feed themselves or so many bushels of corn per family per week. There was little incentive to use either land or labor properly.

Finally, the urbanization of the North was an important factor in the food trade long before railroads. The urban element in the whole U.S. population increased between 1790 and 1860 by three times the national average, or nine times altogether. In the North, the increase of urban population was the order on fifteen times the 1790 figure. By 1850 urban growth in the whole of New England and the Mid-Atlantic States, except for Vermont, was greater than the rural increase. In that year, urbanization was greater in Massachusetts, Connecticut, Rhode Island, and New York than in Old England. Before the railroads, foreign trade, usually meaning trade with England or the English colonies (still 80 percent of the whole), was the chief function of all cities; after railroads, cities had a primary function outside of foreign trade, and they were often only able to practice that function because of the railroad.[16]

In 1790, 80 percent of all gainfully employed workers were in the countryside. In 1860, more than half were outside agriculture. In 1790, 95 percent of Northern farm production was consumed in the Northern countryside. In 1860, the figure had fallen to 50 percent. Only 4 percent of farm production was exported in both years; the difference was the greater proportion eaten in Northern cities and in the South. The United States had become one of the world's first market-driven agricultural economies.

There had been, of course, many colonies in the past that grew food for the Home Country, the Greek city-states, for example. There had been empires such as Rome that had taken tribute from colonies in grain. There had been, and were in the nineteenth century, many places where peasants paid their lords in kind, who then sold the produce on the national or European economy. This was true, for example, of Russia, Poland, Prussia, parts of Italy, and France, but the United States was the first *free* agricultural economy. By 1914 she was followed by Australia, Canada, New Zealand, and to a certain extent, the Argentine and South Africa. These neo-Europes became part of the European economy.

There are two favorite "truths" about the American population. If immigration had ceased in 1776, the population of the United States would probably have been at least as great in quantity as it is today. Second, in that case, half of all Americans would be descended from those who had been transported as criminals, debtors, or indentured servants.

Even as early as 1700, some non-Establishment people like Quakers supported transportation over imprisonment at home, seeing in the New World the possibility of a fresh chance for "misfits" in return for the provision of labor for an area that was almost "empty." Humane people increasingly tended to regret the death penalty for the theft of objects worth about a month's wages; in the absence not only of detective methods but also of almost any effective policing, transportation was, therefore, to be favored.

The original impulse for transportation was the need for an alternative to the death penalty; Elizabeth I's Vagrancy Act empowered magistrates at Quarter Sessions to banish vagrants to some place overseas, as should be directed by the Privy Council. This was extended by acts in each of the next reigns, so that by 1666 perhaps two-thirds of those sentenced to prison or death had their sentences commuted to transportation "for life." These people, rescued from jail or the gallows, were not treated with any degree of gentleness. There were also "vagrants," or those shipped out as surplus by their lord, and those who volunteered to work as indentured servants for so many years in exchange for passage. Today no one knows the sum total of those "transported," nor do figures exist for the total of criminals, vagrants, or volunteers who crossed the Atlantic for many and complicated reasons, some with great hopes. Such cargoes included eighty-one "maids" sent from Liverpool to Virginia in 1683.

Transportation meant that thousands were sent out to the Caribbean Islands, to the mainland colonies, to Bermuda, and at least one cargo-load to Newfoundland, from about 1620 onward; and more than 1000 were sent out to Barbados after Monmouth's rebellion in 1685–87, a shipment exceptional, and thus recorded for posterity, only because of the circumstances.

Between 1493 and 1846, probably fewer than seven million people had traveled the long haul from Europe. Some went across the North Atlantic; some went on down the South Atlantic, across the Indian Ocean, and finally, all over the Pacific. Of the seven million, at least two million died prematurely; did a million return to Europe, leaving barely four million to settle long enough to produce progeny? In 1846, those progeny amounted to more than 50 million, 25 million in the United

States alone. That was the result of three and a half centuries of emigration and "transportation" from Europe.[17]

Between the repeal of the British Corn Laws in 1846 and the outbreak of World War I in 1914, Europe increased its population by 100 percent. Of that increase, a quarter emigrated to the "new" countries, including the United States, then in the prime of life. In those sixty-eight years, in other words, probably five million went abroad and settled permanently.

These new emigrants were the more enterprising of their kind— or the more desperate, opportunistic, or fickle, or they were the more entrepreneurial, or those with fewer territorial ties at home. There were always more men emigrating than women, more poor than rich, more unskilled than qualified; but despite the apparent shortage of social virtue among them, they nearly all did far better in the new countries than anyone, including themselves, could have imagined when they arrived as poor huddled masses on Ellis Island or wherever. Even the surviving convicts in Australia surpassed and surprised themselves.[18] The health of the immigrants was improved on landing. Quarantine was carefully enforced in most ports in the United States from about 1819. There was a by-product of this sanitary prudence. Because ships had to be less crowded, in order to avoid the disapproval of the Health Inspectorate, transatlantic fares rose. Because they rose, the quality of immigrant, or the wealth of those paying for the passage, rose. But fares came down rapidly in the last quarter of the nineteenth century, from $50 to $10; neither figure included food, which the immigrant usually carried and cooked on board. Once arrived in the United States, the immigrant enjoyed better food, cleaner air and water, and less disease than in most European cities. Ordinary workers in the United States ate far better than Europeans of the same income group. American cities usually had little smog, and supplies of clean air and water were expected. It was not until after 1865 that places like Pittsburgh or Birmingham, Alabama, or the mining towns in the East, or the manufacturing cities, would have serious pollution problems. Those of Los Angeles and other places had to wait for the motorcar.

Immigrants were attracted by brokers who were acting for railroad companies, or for New England mill owners, or for companies running coal mines or steelworks. So German peasants, overburdened by fees and rents due to feudal landlords and often in debt, sent part of their family to the Midwest; this happened both before and after the 1848 revolutions. Almost everyone knows about The Irish: 100,000 emigrants a year for fifteen years after the Famine. Scottish mill girls were imported, sometimes for only a few years, to work in the textile industry of New England. Welsh coal miners came to Pennsylvania, Ohio, and Western Virginia; Slavs from every point of the compass staffed the steel and metal-bashing industries; Greeks formed colonies all down the Eastern seaboard; Italians flocked into the large cities; Sweden sent one million people—a quarter of the population—because of insufficient food at home. Finns, fearing a repetition of famine,[19] left in nearly as large a proportion as the Swedes. Jews, especially later in the 1800s, left Eastern Europe in droves, and by 1914 formed a quarter of the population of New York City.

Of the 25 million Europeans who came to the United States in the years 1846–1914, more than a third came across the Atlantic in steerage. The contrast with the luxury of the first-class section in the same ship made the conditions even more startling.

Arrived ashore, the immigrant was still at risk. Did the ignorant immigrant speak English? More than half did not. Did European ignorance lead immigrants into grave trouble? Well, there was always Tammany Hall or equivalent organizations in other cities to bail them out. Ignorance, misconceptions, and romantic views of available opportunities undoubtedly existed, but conditions were so much better than those left behind that most immigrants prospered. About one-quarter went to work on the land between 1846 and 1914; three-quarters went into the cities. An unsuccessful European farmer could sell up, buy passage for himself and his family, and still have enough left to establish himself in the new states close to the frontier. The United States had a different spirit than the feudal society still present in parts of Europe. There were no kings or nobles; no extortionate taxes, rents, or tithes; and no master acknowledge. Farmworkers sat at table with their masters; there were no large estates with a "ruling class"; there was no danger that the arm would be worn out doffing the cap or touching the forelock. Rural America was often unbelievable to a European farmer. The extraordinarily efficient agricultural techniques fostered by the

American market system were the product of four factors: cheap and plentiful land, a low population density, climatic conditions that necessitated quick work, and sophisticated human technology, most notably the railroad.

For any European the most incredible feature was the cheapness of land. For most of the century, land could be bought for $1.25 an acre. A section (260 hectares or 640 acres) therefore cost $800. Each section, half-section, or quarter-section required water, usually pumped by windmill costing at most about $500, and a house. Houses were made from a variety of materials, from a sod cabin, to a log cabin, to a wood-framed house, and cost anywhere from a few dollars to around $800 for materials to build a frame house with four rooms. Every house had to have a stove, costing from $12 to $50. The requirements for an arable farm, in the period after the Civil War and after the railroads were in place, would include horses, cultivating equipment, harvesters, and so forth. These might come to between $500 and $2000 for a farm of a section size, depending on the quality of the land, soil aspect, whether fencing was required, and the nature of the neighbors. The first three harvests of grain off prairie soil broken for the first time might average $20 per acre.[20] If the immigrant spent $800 on a section; $2000 on windmill, house, and furnishings; and $2000 on livestock and deadstock on the farm (all outside figures), he would have invested less than $5000. One harvest would come to over $10,000, allowing for a proportion in fallow each year. The balance was represented by hard work; on the debit side was the cost of keeping farmer and family for a year between harvests. The whole equation depended upon cheap land, healthy demand for grain, and cheap transportation.

If the putative farmer had to buy from the railroad rather than from the Federal Government, he paid more for his land. If there was no water on the section the land would have been useless or water would have been bought from next door at great expense. If he had "bad luck," was incompetent, broke a leg, or contracted some lethal sickness on his way west, or if he was cheated, the immigrant would fail; there were not a few who did. It was often said that those responsible for the farmers' "bad luck" were the railroads.

Unregulated before the end of the century, the railroad track mileage increased by four times between the end of the Civil War (1865) and 1900. The railroad companies were led by buccaneers of whom their victims said: "When they speak, they lie; when they are silent, they are stealing; while they sleep, they sin."[21] The "sinners" included Dillon and Sage, who were operating before the Civil War, and their younger colleague, Gould, who was the most spectacularly successful and outrageous. This is not to say that the actions of Morgan, Vanderbilt, Rockefeller, Huntington, Stanford, Cooke, Villard, or Harriman would prove to be legal at a later date, but for their times, they acted within the law. Government help to the railroads west of the Mississippi was given to provide an impetus to open up and populate the West. Nearly 210,000 square miles—an area almost exactly the same size as France—was given to help get the railroads built. It included wasteland, mountains, deserts, unfarmable areas, and range unfit for grazing, but cheap or free land had been the only way to make sure that the railroads were built.

It was, in fact, the railroads that gave the land any value. Land and railroads formed an elegant syndrome. The lands in Minnesota, with 40 percent of the state area granted to railways, were originally sold for $3–$5 an acre in the 1890s; in the 1910s they were worth perhaps $25 an acre in big blocks of arable land. By the 1920s the wheat price had risen (through World War I), then fallen, so that Minnesota became much more a land of mixed farms. The land was then worth more than wheat farmers could afford to pay. Farmers, or the original farmers' sons, either changed their husbandry or new people moved in.

The process was more rapid in Iowa. By nature it has some of the richest soils in the world, comparable to those of the Ukraine and with a better climate. Iowa had the highest percentage of "improved land" as defined by the Department of Agriculture. Even in 1900 the proportion was nearly 60 percent. In that year Iowa's agricultural production was greater than that of any other state. Iowa was a child of post–Civil War railroad construction. In 1860 there were only 655 miles; in 1900, more than 9000 miles. The state became a network of railroads. Fifty percent of all farms were within 5 miles of a railroad station before 1900, and after 1900 only 10 percent were said to be more than 10 miles from a railroad. In this respect, Iowan farmers were better off than their equiv-alents in Europe. In 1900 the agricultural production of Iowa was worth about $20 per acre and nearly $1000 per man-year. The first figure was below the equivalent mixed-farming area of Europe, the productivity per worker far higher. The Iowa farmer was, of course, a beneficiary not only of good soil and an unsurpassed railroad network, but also of the most efficient agricultural implement industry in the world.

Before 1914 and before any internal combustion engine had been applied to agriculture, this industry alone had produced the potential for a grain-growing system. In essence, this machinery was identical to that which every child in the Western world can watch with awe in the field today. The system included high-speed plowing, high-speed cultivating and sowing in the spring, and high-speed harvesting. The speed was an answer partly to climatic conditions and partly to the cost problem. It was practiced in the wheat belt of the United States, on the Canadian prairies, in California, and in parts of Australia. The system was described at length in many publications before World War I, and would have been the answer to grain growing in Russia, France, and South America. It depended not only upon cheap land that was flat and lent itself to mechanization, but also upon the necessary infrastructure. The railroad was vital, of course, but so was what the railroad brought—all the necessities of modern agriculture. The railroad, of course, was also essential for cheap marketing of the main product—grain, ani-mals, or whatever.

By 1900 the spring wheat "Scotch-Fife" had begun to rival the win-ter variety "Turkey Red," and 40 percent of the bread-making wheat in the United States was of this ecotype. Hard spring wheat was sown throughout the Northern prairies, in the Dakotas, and in Minnesota, and the total product in Minnesota in 1900 was more than two million tons, more than the United Kingdom produced (of wheat of all sorts) and twice as much as Australia produced. The wheat could only be produced in such profusion because of the low cost. The low cost, in turn, was due to an effective system.

First, in August, the straw of the previous crop was burnt—a great labor and unrewarding, but one that limited plant disease. Then began the plowing. At these latitudes there are only about eight

weeks in September, October, and November when the year's plowing can be done.[22] This was managed at the time by putting in teams
of plows, each to cover 100 hectares (250 acres) in 50 days, or 2 hectares (5 acres) a day, five times the contemporary English rate. A team
of five horses drew two furrows of 41 cm (16 in) each. This compared
with a pair of contemporary European oxen or horses each pulling one
furrow of 19–20 cm (7–8 in). The American team was also required to
move faster. An hour with the American plow produced nearly an acre
plowed, while the European plow of 20 cm (8 in) turn-furrow would
have to pass through nearly 12.4 miles to plow an acre. There was more
waste in the European field since the fields were smaller, and the plow
was not as productive as it was in a long field. One "field" in Saskatchewan at this date, alongside a railroad line, was so long that plowing
outwardly took all morning, and plowing back to the starting point
took all afternoon. Such fields were exceptional, but gangs of eight to
ten plows, moving in echelon, shifted a great tonnage of soil. That is
the function of plowing.

After plowing, the land was left in furrow for the frost and snow to
act upon the soil; this was wholly beneficial. Less beneficial at this time
was the habit of dismissing most of the men, casual workers, who went
home for the winter. When they worked, they were paid a quarter as
much as Henry Ford paid men for similar work in 1914—$25 a month,
instead of $100. The plowmen also received their board and lodging
just like cowboys. In those days, board and lodging cost farmers about
50 cents per head per day, but were of great importance.[23]

Much of the year's moisture on the prairies and in the Midwest falls as
snow in the winter, and the snow must not only melt, but also sink into the
earth as water before spring cultivation can begin. That depends upon latitude and season, but it is usually April before the plowed land is dry enough.
Ground that has been set up in furrow can be very quickly "knocked down,"
ready for sowing after the winter frosts. In the early 1900s, chain harrows
had already grown huge: 7.5 meters (25 feet) or even 9 meters (30 feet) wide,
drawn by four to five horses, capable of working down 24–30 hectares (60–
75 acres) a day, with one man walking behind.

Throughout the world, the seed drill has always traditionally followed the harrows. This was to conserve moisture and to prevent one

part of the field from being harrowed, but not sown, while another part was sown and not harrowed. A good manager of any farm, regardless of size, would arrange the "bout" for the day—harrow once, drill the corn, and harrow again to cover the seed to the correct depth. Harrowing is no problem. Drills require more time than harrowing, being narrower, and because the farmer has to stop to refill them with corn. At that date, fertilizer was not sown with the seed. Thirty acres would be a good day's work for a drill, involving a walk of nearly as many miles for horses and men.

The spring sowing was carefully tailored to an elegant equation. Time involved, say, 25–30 days, dictated the number of workers in ratio to the acreage sown. If the sowing took only 15 days, too many seasonal workers had been hired. If the sowing took 35–40 days, too few had been found. After the spring sowing, the workers were "let go" again. Too much social indignation should not be developed about this practice since seasonal workers, who valued their independence and freedom, often returned year after year to the same farm.

While spring warmth encouraged the young wheat, the permanent staff of such a farm would be sowing oats for horses, Indian corn for man and beast, and millet or barley as a failsafe measure; there was little work for horses in high summer, and they were left out in a grazing paddock. By the end of June the earliest grain, sown only 90 days before, was ready for cutting.

By about 1900 the reaper-binder, invented by Cyrus McCormick (as the reaper) in 1837, had developed into a reliable machine used the world over and built by hundreds of makers. In Europe, machines with a cutting-bar of 1.5 meters (five feet) would be typical in the small fields, often as small as two hectares (five acres). These machines cut, assembled into sheaves, and dropped off the corn in groups of sheaves, usually five or six. One man drove the two-horse team and another man sat on the back of the machine watching to be sure that everything was working properly, the twine moving smoothly and so on.

Such a relaxed and bucolic picture did not obtain in the new countries. Teams of six to ten horses would draw a huge reaper-binder, with a cut of five meters (16 feet). In a good crop, the sheaves would pop out of the carrier-deck, which held them after they were tied, like chocolate bars popping off a conveyor belt. These large machines, each with a team of horses far more difficult to drive than a coach-in-hand, were tended by two men, just like the European example whose output would be no more than 20 percent of the American, Canadian, or Australian equivalent. In California, Canada, and Australia, combine-harvesters that cut and threshed the grain were already in use, with as many as twenty-four horses pulling a machine whose whole rumbling interior was driven by the forward motion of the vehicle. In Australia, there were combine-harvesters drawn by as many as thirty-two mules. This must have been one of the most demanding tasks in the age before internal combustion, and a fit challenge for the young men of the young nation.[24]

The reaper-binder/thresher combination was more general than the combine-harvester. Both cleared fields with great rapidity, but the advantage of the combine was not only in the actual harvesting. Straw came out of the back of the machine, as it does today, in a continuous stream, which made it much easier to burn than when it was left in huge heaps next to the stationary threshing machine.

However threshed, the grain was carried in bulk from the machine in the field to the silo, which was characteristically by the side of a railroad siding. Tipping box-wagons were as close to the modern truck or trailer as can be imagined, except that they were horse-drawn, usually by three horses. The grain was lifted to the top of the tower-silo, confusingly called an elevator. From the elevator, grain was shipped in bulk all over the world, without involving any manual labor. All this bulk-handling was common in most of the wheat states by 1910 at the latest.[25]

The bottom line around 1910 was of vital interest. Assuming a land value of less than $25, including all buildings and improvements, the cost per acre, allowing 10 percent interest on the capital employed, was about $9. If the yield per acre was 20 bushels (544 kg, 1200 lb), the cost per bushel was 45 cents. The average price at the railhead in the fifteen years before World War I was between 56 and 60 cents, allowing a modest profit of between 11 cents and 15 cents a bushel. This does not sound like much, but 10,000 acres of wheat at 20 bushels to the acre would yield a profit of between $22,000 and $30,000, clear of all expenses, land taxes, and interest. This was equivalent to twenty times those figures in today's situation, and a respectable yield from a middling-sized business in 1910. By such industrial methods did the new countries compete with the old, assisted by cheap steamship transport.

Not everyone could make this kind of money. Yield in the Northwest wheat belt averaged 18 bushels, not 20, in the period 1899–1913.[26] Planting could be less than timely; insufficient labor at harvest might risk the early autumn rains. Incompetent selling might not achieve the optimum price. Each and any of these and other aberrations might well destroy not only the "profit" of 15 cents a bushel, but also the ability to pay interest on the money employed.

The selection process applied to farmers was as harsh as any applied to plants or animals. Failure in times of excessive production was common enough; farmworkers, often without wives or children, might arrive with little and move on, usually to the West, with less. Failures in times of scarcity proved to be more incompetent. Iowa and the older settled states east of the Mississippi-Missouri were not as subject to climatic changes as those in the shadow of the Rockies. Drought was rarely an excuse in the true Midwest. Failure was always cushioned by the rise in land values. Bought from the railroad at less than $5 per acre, perhaps, in 1880, the farm might well be worth ten times as much a generation later. In the absence of progeny, such a capital sum could provide capital for retirement in a warmer state in an age without federal pensions.

The corn kings, wheat viscounts, and barley barons, producers all, were not, of course, true farmers. They were primary producers, very efficient primary producers, but they were monoculturists. It is, of course, one of the minor ironies of all environmental arguments that the term "monoculture" is used pejoratively about growing cotton, grain, or tobacco; there is a long history of the dangers and tribulations of soil erosion and self-induced poverty as a result of such practices. No one ever complains about the "monoculture" of indigenous timber or grassland. These are the crops that shield the land. In the case of the United States, it was more than three centuries before any efforts were made to encourage the nationwide use of restorative crops like legumes and grasses. By then, much damage had been done.

It has been reckoned that in 1492 only 7 percent of the United States was wholly useless by reason of soil condition (i.e., desert). By 1910 half of the natural forest of the United States had already been destroyed, and between a quarter and a half of the topsoil of the Missouri-Mississippi Basin had been shoveled into the rivers and washed downstream. Vast areas of the Eastern states had been abandoned by early farmers who had moved west.

Throughout the nineteenth century, agricultural prices tended to fall over a long period, and it was often commercially possible for the farmers in only the new countries to skim the cream from the situation and pass on. The "cream," of course, was the topsoil, a precious commodity made by man in the old countries and by God in the new. When it was destroyed, blown away in the wind, or eroded into the rivers, the farmer moved on. One old man, surviving into his seventies in Nebraska, is said to have claimed that he had worn out as many farms as he had had wives: four of each. He was proud of his manhood.

The farms of post–Civil War America were also made possible by one further factor: cheap, efficient machinery produced by the ancillary industry that had replaced the local blacksmith. John Deere, McCormick, Massey-Harris—all these names are now connected with tractors involving internal combustion engines. In the period 1900–14, there were virtually no tractors on any farms. The motive power was the horse on the farm and the steam locomotive on the railroad. The technology consisted of plows from Iowa, harrows from Indiana, harvesters from Illinois, seed-drills from Pennsylvania, barbed wire from Ohio, horseshoe nails from Delaware, horseshoes from New Jersey, harness from New York, and human shoes from New England; and when these objects were worn beyond the ability of the farm staff to repair them, there was no point in seeking any other solution but to replace them. Farms were littered with the dumped, scrapped hardware from industrial America. Anything that would not burn would be left to rot in the field.[27]

Slightly modified by patterns of trade, climate, and communications, exactly the same symbiotic relationship, between industry in the town and industry in the countryside, had grown up in parts of Canada, California, Australia, the Plate Basin, and Southern Russia at the same time. By 1914 the only way to compete for grains in the world market was to industrialize the growth of the crop. The mixed farmer, the trustee of the soil, the true husbandman could never compete with the economy of scale. It is a mistake to imagine that grain monoculture is a modern phenomenon.

The Eastern United States, the small farms of old Canada, and the traditional holdings of Europe were all turned into something quite different. They might still rather grow than buy feeding stuffs, but their most profitable enterprises were those based on animal husbandry. Milk was becoming desirable to consume as hygiene and transport improved. Meat became cheaper, more of an everyday occurrence, not reserved for Sundays. Chickens came down in price and continued, all through the century, to cheapen in relation to red meat.[28] The conversion of grain into the more appetizing and higher-protein meat, milk, and eggs became, in the end, just as specialized as the monoculture of grain. It would not be rare to find a European farm "importing" far more energy value in the form of cheap feeding stuffs than it "exported" in the form of human food.

Nor were the underdeveloped nations as bad off in 1910 as such a waste of resources suggests. There were less than a third as many people in the whole world alive then as there are now and one-sixth as many in Africa. There were fewer than 300 million in the Indian subcontinent, against three times as many now; in China, fewer than 500 million against more than 1 billion; in hungry Africa, there were 110 million at most in 1910, against six times as many today. It is arguable that in the world of 1910 a peasant in a village was better off than a poor person in today's cities of Calcutta, Cairo, and Mexico City. One of the great, lost virtues of villages is the possibility of being poor with dignity; that, too, is a part of husbandry. With the United States and other neo-Europes producing cereal crops in quantities and at prices with which their former colonial masters could not compete, other agricultural economies had to adapt. In Western Europe, most countries did so fairly well, adding layers of productivity, diversification, and luxury to their produce.

Between 1846 and 1914, the population of Western Europe doubled. The rate of increase was uneven and depended, as always, upon disease and food supply. In the sixty-eight years to 1914, 40 million people left Western Europe, many times the number who had emigrated in the previous four centuries. Most of the whole world population increase, from about 130 million to 260 million, was due to better food supplies. These in turn were the result of better technology in the field, on roads and railways, and at sea. There was very little scientific biology or chemistry applied to agricultural problems, and little physical science involved in transport, the design of farm implements, or the application of power to field husbandry. Practical men using what came to hand did much to make money and educate their competitors. "High Farming," limited at first to England and Scotland, involved farmers and landlords. Peruvian guano, Chilean nitrate, and superphosphate were all available from the 1840s as the result of a shortage of bone-based fertilizers. Plant breeding was not in the heads of geneticists and biologists but, in a pre-Mendel age, in the hands of practical farmers, as were animal improvements.[29]

Drainage was improved by the use of steam-drawn mole plows, and British Government subsidies encouraged tile drains from 1846 onward. Steam was used in the form of "stationary" engines to draw plows, cultivators, and even harvesters; truly stationary engines drove stationary threshing machines, and this last activity went on until after World War II in parts of Europe. Science was unable to relieve numerous severe animal and human diseases. Then there was a succession of wet summers before and after the disastrous year of 1879.

In the succeeding twenty years, the urban consumer suffered little. Grain, meat, and animal foodstuffs were available from all over the world. Cultivation in Europe declined, and pastureland increased proportionately. Liquid milk became a "cash crop" taken by fast, cheap trains to the large cities. By 1900 European agricultural systems were much modified. Cereal growing had been reduced. Meat, milk, and eggs were produced to exploit grassland and cheap imported feeding stuffs. New crops included the mass field production of potatoes, green vegetables, and root crops that were formerly grown in the townsman's own allotment or garden. Farmers who adapted survived.[30]

In Germany, the best English practices were introduced by up-to-date landlords, and German biochemistry under Liebig and Hoffmann and their pupils was ahead of the British.[31] Fallow as a proportion of total arable fell as new crops came in. Tile drainage systems were imported from England, including, at first, the tiles themselves. Chalk, marl, and artificial fertilizers were applied to the poor soils of the German plain. The tonnage of potatoes grown increased by eight times between 1846 and 1914, while that of rye increased by six, and wheat by four. Germany was much better fed in 1914 than in 1846, even if there was more than twice as many Germans, and much of the potato crop was used for industrial purposes. The German population had grown from 33 million in 1846 to nearly 70 million, while that of France increased from 35 million to only 40 million, a mere 12 percent against more than 108 percent. More Germans had emigrated too.

The very low population pressure in France compared with Germany combined with better land, better climate, and twice the area per head to produce a curious circumstance. Urban intellectuals were interested in improving agriculture, but drainage was so expensive relative to increased output that it did not appeal to peasants. Early plant breeders found their barley more appreciated in England, and their sugar-beet seed sold better in Belgium and Germany than at home. After 1880, animal breeds were established in herd books on the English pattern; but this was the action of the same sort of gentleman-fanciers as bred racehorses. Seed-drills, mowers, and reaping machines replaced hand labor on the bigger farms, but much of France was so subdivided by the Code Napoleon that it was not always possible to apply modern techniques to small areas. Potential output per hectare increased, but the gross national production of wheat did not alter, nor did that of rye, while potato production only doubled. In one area, that of wine production, France remained supreme, surviving losses engendered by phylloxera. These were reckoned to be three times greater than the cost of the Franco-Prussian War.[32]

The Low Countries were still farmed as well as anywhere in Europe. Although their population increased by less than it did in England or Germany, the primacy of rotations, root crops, and heavy horses and cattle was still notable. Dairying became more important in Holland than in Belgium. In the Netherlands, too, an increased demand for foodstuffs could always be met by land reclamation and polderization.[33] Drainage throughout the Low Countries was vital and essential, even for ordinary, non-agricultural purposes, as army generals discovered in Flanders after 1914. Grain was imported from overseas to maintain the average townsman's standard of life, while farmers were encouraged to adapt.

In Italy, the sixty-eight years provoked the least positive reaction. With an increase from 22 to 36 million, population pressure at first glance would seem not to be critical, but the political changes involved in the Risorgimento (Unification) from 1860 to 1870 did nothing for the post-feudal system of landholding. This was usually a form of share-cropping, onerous to the peasant.

There was a general decline in the productivity of most commodities except for liquid milk for towns and sheep for wool and meat. Peasant poverty led to large-scale emigration, not only to North America, but also to the Argentine. The challenge in Italy was not only unanswered, but in many cases unrecognized. The only product whose quality really improved from manufacturing methods was wine, which benefited from the post-phylloxera revolution. The rest of agriculture was in a poor way to meet the conditions of the modern world. Agricultural stagnation remained largely true until after World War II despite an occasional flashy improvement such as the drainage of the Pontine Marshes.[34]

The management of food between producer and consumer in the sixty-eight years affected everything eaten. Stone mills gave way to roller-milling; bread making became an automated, industrial process; the curing of fish, bacon, and ham was transformed; milk was "pasteurized"; butter was standardized by centrifuge cream separators, whey removers, and, above all, refrigeration; cheese became a factory product from neo-European countries; Borden invented evaporated milk (1853); vacuum drying of milk followed; canning and refrigeration were applied to meat of all kinds; vegetables and fruit were bottled and canned. Refrigeration before 1914 was not generally applied or even widely available in the home, so daily shopping was still often a necessity in towns. European governments became anxious to ensure a higher standard of hygiene and purity in food supplies. This was often difficult in the absence of modern packaging, whose influence has been at least as great as refrigeration in the urban environment. Only since 1914 have the many subacute forms of enteric disorder been reduced so that stomach trouble is an occasional misfortune worth noticing rather than a common occurrence. In the same area, attention should be drawn to improvements in dentistry. No longer did "civilized" man, teeth made rotten by diet, have to suffer from unchewed food.

Extraordinary, luxurious vegetables and fruit that are taken for granted in every First World supermarket today had to wait, in general, for further technological improvements to make their everyday consumption possible. In 1914 there was probably no one person who had eaten litchis, kiwi- fruit, avocado, mangoes, and kumquat. Certainly, no living European could have eaten all these fruits of the earth if the European had not been a great traveler.

These exotica had to wait for packaging and transport even faster than refrigerated steamers. Improvements to diet due to the import of tropical and semi-tropical products were limited to what could be called "bulk staples." Sugar was one-fifth the price it had been in 1846, resulting in medical problems. Imported edible oils of various kinds were challenging butter in the United States and Europe, margarine having been widely introduced about 1880. Market penetration depended upon the political clout of the butter lobby. Sweden and Switzerland were notable opponents of margarine before 1914. In the United States, the Federal Government refused to buy it for the armed forces, and it was illegal, bootlegged in the state of Wisconsin before 1965. Today, three times as much vegetable margarine as butter is consumed in the United States and twice as much in Europe. Ice cream, another (largely fat) product, was an important semi-luxury in 1914, reaching its peak about 1950; it is now in decline, for obvious reasons.

Meat became much cheaper in Europe in real terms by 1914, but consumption per head was still only one-third that of the United States and one-fifth that of New Zealand or Australia. Today meat is under the same sort of lifestyle cloud as other fatty products. Fish was a considerable social cut below meat in 1914, even the most expensive fish being one-third the price of the most expensive meat. Today, fish is dearer, with a higher retail price than most meat. Bread was white in most countries in 1914, having been wholemeal almost everywhere in 1846. Again, fashion has reverted to the former practice.[35]

Railways made possible rapid transport of perishables on land—broccoli from Cornwall to London, winter vegetables from California to the East Coast, fresh saltwater fish all over Europe—but between continents the improvements between 1846 and 1914 were much less significant than future developments. The combination of air freight, deep-freezing, and hygienic packaging proved to have an even more dramatic effect after 1945 than any improvements after 1846. None of these would have been possible without the transformation of the neo-European countries in the nineteenth century. Russia has historically faced different challenges than those in the New World, most notably a much harsher climate, but with no tradition of good husbandry and little pressure on either land or population, Russians have made scant effort to improve their agriculture and have suffered greatly as a result.

The great French historian, Alexis de Tocqueville, drew attention to the resemblance between the United States of America and the then wholly feudal Russia. His great work, the first reasoned book about American democracy, came out in 1835. Neither he nor his readers gave enough thought to the physical problems of Russia. These physical problems still dominate the country. Most people today believe that man controls the environment in which he lives. People who can be halfway around the world tomorrow in person, or see it all on simultaneous television, or eat food from anywhere, anyplace, and anytime, are impatient about physical geography. In Russia, facts about climate, geology, and botany are paramount. The environment represents a serious challenge to settlement. Russian response to this challenge cannot be ascribed to political or doctrinal lapses in the recent past. Russian leaders are changed with normal, human frequency according to power ratings and operational effectiveness. The ecology remains and changes, if it does at all, very slowly.

Russian answers to the challenges of climate are very different from the responses of Americans to the challenge of living in North America. It is essential to try to distinguish between cause and effect. European Russia extends from the Arctic to the Black Sea, in a north-south line, and from the Urals westward as far as Muscovite power has been able to extend. The Russians are Eastern Slavs and have been living in the Moscow area since only just before the Norman Conquest of England. The tribes settled in this now sacred heartland about the same time that Christianity was accepted in Kiev, in about AD 988.

The climatic zones are very important because they break the rules of the rest of the world. In the extreme north there is tundra that can only support lichens and mosses. The reindeer are supported upon these unpromising materials, and with the reindeer there are Lapps, living an existence originally nomadic. The tundra gives way to the forest, irregularly, but a timberline is clearly visible from the air. The northern timber is almost exclusively spruce and pine; farther south, and in the milder pockets, needle-leaved trees give way to mixed woodlands, broad leaves predominating in areas of better soil or climate. South of the forest, which is the largest wooded area in the world, lies the Steppe, a sort of savannah. The Steppe runs from Hungary to Mongolia, south of the Urals. It was the pathway for all the Eastern invaders, the commercial route in the Middle Ages before the Black Death, and the parade ground for the Mongol Golden Horde itself. The Steppe also has a more agricultural function.

The largest area of the Steppe is composed of Black Earth. The soil contains up to 15 percent humus, the age-old product of decayed grass, bushes, and scrub trees. In Russia, the Black Earth is in a layer up to two meters deep. Handled properly, the Black Earth of Ukraine, as of Iowa, is one of the most valuable agricultural soils in the world. North of the Black Earth is the podzol of Russia proper. In the podzol grows the forest, mixed around Moscow, boreal or "taiga" farther north. This forest runs from between 45° and 50° N to the tundra at the Arctic Circle. The forest is a zone of sand and clay in patches with no pattern; there are many bogs and marshes, and streams and rivers run slowly without much fall, since no part of European Russia is more than 400 meters (1313 feet) above the sea. Rivers start in swamps and lakes and run mostly in a north-south direction. The main rivers in European Russia are the Volga and the Dnieper. Together with their many tributaries they formed a network, with easy portages for trade at an early date. Frozen far longer than rivers in North America, they were perhaps an even more convenient passage in winter when sledges were used instead of boats.

The secondary fact of life in Russia was, is, and will remain the climate.

Leningrad, formerly Petrograd, now again St. Petersburg, lies on about 60° N, the same latitude as Stockholm or Bergen, the southernmost tip of Greenland, and the northern border of the Canadian provinces—Manitoba, Saskatchewan, Alberta, and British Columbia. The far north of the Canadian provinces is more unsuitable for agriculture than the area round Leningrad, and today no Canadian would think of growing grain in those latitudes.[36] The southern tip of Greenland, with its Atlantic climate, and Bergen, washed by the Gulf Stream, were sites for Viking farming that lasted in Greenland for nearly five hundred years and that has survived in Bergen. No one in modern times could grow wheat or rye economically in either location. Stockholm is more moderate in climate than Leningrad. Although the Baltic exercises an influence smaller than the Gulf Stream, Stockholm is warmer in winter and cooler in summer than Leningrad.

The peculiarity of the Russian climate is that lines of constant temperature, isotherms, lie not east and west, as in the American landmass, but north and south. The winter gets colder the farther away the land is from the warm air of the Gulf Stream; the Gulf Stream warms Western Europe, losing heat as it moves east, and is no longer much of a moderating influence by the time it gets to the longitude of Minsk, let alone that of Moscow. These are important and interesting considerations. From these derive the short Russian summer.

In the north on the podzol, in the taiga, and around Novgorod or Leningrad, the frost-free farming season is less than 120 days; around Moscow it is less than 150 days; in the Black Earth it is 180 days. In Sweden around Stockholm the season is longer than it is in Ukraine; in Bergen and the Shetlands it is longer again. The winter breaks suddenly in Russia. The thick snow that has lain on the ground for up to 180 days melts; the ice in the rivers breaks up. There is a sudden flush, a sharp rise in temperature, and spring is soon over. For the peasant, spring and summer were and are a period of backbreaking toil. The short, hot summer involved another risk, rainfall.

The warm westerly winds that encompass the earth bring much rain to Northwest Russia, to the Baltic Provinces, and to the taiga around Leningrad. Inland, the rain falls at the wrong time of year. In Moscow, the precipitation—snow, sleet, and rain—is about 550 mm (22 in) a year. This is a little less than London or San Francisco, but good crops are still possible. Unfortunately, July and August are the wettest months of the year, with 23 percent of rain falling in those two months. A drought in May and June can prejudice both winter and spring grain crops. Too much rain in the next two months makes harvesting very difficult, but another structural problem remains. The rain in Russia falls mainly on the poorer soils. In Leningrad, precipitation is a quarter more than in Moscow. In the Black Earth region, it is often below 400 mm (16 in) per year, too little for a good crop of grain. This would not matter if there were any great tradition of good husbandry.[37]

If there is too little rain in any one year to grow a decent grain crop, there is a solution that the Greeks used when they farmed in this area of Southern Russia more than 2500 years ago. The method is to let the fields lie fallow one year every two or three and "use" the "saved" moisture to grow a good grain crop in the year or years of planting. This is especially apt in the Black Earth area, which is so high in humus that it retains moisture from one year to the next. There has never been a tradition of good farming in Russia, however; husbandry was an unknown art among all classes and no one was interested in it. There are good historic reasons for this, but it has affected the whole history of Russia right up to the present.

The Slavs who took over the area round Moscow about a thousand years ago were originally a pastoral and nomadic people with no knowledge of how to cultivate the soil properly. By that date some Russians had proper harness from China, but certainly did not have a proper plow. The usual medieval Russian plow, or *sokha*, was a scratch-plow without a moldboard. This type of plow was in use on Tolstoy's lands as late as 1870. In the Russian heartland the usual crop was rye. When the productivity of Russian grain fell below a minimum of three to one, the peasant broke in new land. The slash-and-burn technique—applied to the forest—yielded a decent series of crops for a short period, then the peasant passed on. This was fine if the population did not increase too fast.

When measured, the Russian peasant birthrate in the nineteenth century was running at a rate of more than 5 percent per annum. Allowing for life patterns of a century ago, this meant that one in ten of every adult couple was producing a child, and one woman in five of childbearing age was either pregnant or suckling an infant. If the death rate of children under five was more than 50 percent, population growth did not follow birthrate; in the absence of disease this birthrate could result in the grave danger of starvation, famine, or worse. Russia was saved from this fate by two forces.

One was low density of population. Using the boundaries of today, yet excluding land in what used to be Poland, Romania, Czechoslovakia, Finland, Estonia, Latvia, Lithuania, and East Prussia, European Russia encompassed an area of Black Earth greater than the whole of France, at least 270,000 square miles, as big as the entire state of Texas, and nearly twice the size of Iowa. This gives European Russia about 270,000 square miles of the best grain-growing soil in the world, quite separate from the podzol farther north. Russians always moved south and east to the Black Earth because it was easier to cultivate and produced a better return in a shorter period of time than forest soil.[38]

There was a struggle that went on for several hundred years between the Russians and the Turkic pastoral nomads who occupied the Black Earth Steppe. When the Russians won a battle or a campaign, they took over an area. When the Turks from the khanates of Kazan or Astrakhan won a battle or a campaign, they destroyed the Russian settlements, made the Russians prisoners, and sold them into slavery. Farther west there was another solution to Russian progenitive capacity. For a thousand years, roaming bands of Cossacks and Tartars made the hinterland of the Black Sea a recruiting ground for fair-skinned slaves for sale in Constantinople or Cairo. It was the huge Russian birthrate that made this possible, and Russian slaves were a feature of Muslim life for 1000 years. Slavery ultimately ended, but the surplus population remained. The problem of population growth could not be solved except in the most brutal modern fashion.[39]

Towns certainly never offered a solution. Peasants could not immigrate into towns or grow grain for urban consumption. Surplus grain was never worth growing since here was no growth of towns to encourage any kind of trade. Most European towns were established in the four centuries before 1600. During the same time period, three Russian efforts had been destroyed. Between 800 and 1200 there was a string of Viking settlements between the Baltic and the Black Sea that followed the rivers and formed a useful "back door" to Constantinople. This string of settlements was cut off in the south when Asian nomads severed the route to Constantinople.

Before and after the Black Death, Novgorod had been a member of the Hanseatic League, and Western European merchants traded furs and metalwork in that town. Jealous, inward-looking Moscow destroyed first the trade, then the city itself. Finally, Ivan the Terrible sacked the city in 1570, killing, it is said, 60,000 people and enslaving 10,000. If so, he was less terrible than the Black Death, the true cause of the earlier decline. In 1467, 1508, and 1533 more than 100,000 are said to have died of pestilence.

There was one final post-Renaissance effort at Russian urbanization. The Renaissance was not, of course, engendered by Russians, but by Dutch and English adventurers who set up trading posts on the river line from the Baltic to Moscow. This lasted from about 1540 until 1580 when the Russian government bowed to its own merchants, who were jealous of Western success. After that, there were no towns in Russia other than military or government centers. Even in 1846 the urban population of this huge country of 65 million people did not exceed 6 percent. By the beginning of World War I, the total population had increased to 170 million. Only 17 percent were dwellers in towns and cities. The urban population had increased from about 4 million to less than 30 million. Some would be hungry very often.

The Russian population increase of over 160 percent between 1846 and 1914 was not matched by technological advancement, and emigration was of minor importance. In 1783 the Russians had annexed the Crimea and tamed the Tartars as well as the Cossacks. Three million are reckoned to have migrated into the Black Earth region before 1846; nearly ten million between 1846 and 1914. In the same period, four million went to Southern (Black Earth) Siberia, and two million to the less favored Central Asian Steppe.[40] Only four million went to the New World.

After Emancipation in 1861, the peasant serfs who moved became free. They were deliberately assisted by the government, and the Russians established neo-Europes the same way that Western Europeans had unconsciously established neo-Europes.[41] The colonial expansion of

Russia, which had begun in the time of Tsar Ivan the Terrible in 1552, was initially of unfree serfs attached to their migrant masters. Siberian immigration also included political exiles, entrepreneurs amongst the aristocracy, and foreign concessionaires interested in mining or timber.

There were two reasons why the Russian peasant was a poor farmer. Both derived from the availability of ample land. Like the American, the Russian could always bring virgin land into cultivation. This was worth much more than trying to improve the home farm. When all the virgin land had been cultivated within the technological abilities of the time, trouble ensued, but that time did not come until the nineteenth century. The influences that made the Russian serf such a poor farmer, however, were in place long before.

There was no gainful winter occupation and little outlet for surplus grain, so three consequences ensued. Much surplus grain and potatoes was turned into spirits, and there was a serious peasant drinking problem after every successful harvest. During the long, long winters when no work could be done, drinking became a relaxation, a solace, but it also made a grain shortage worse. The Russian weather made outdoor work possible for only half the year; the rest of the year had to be endured in a very cold climate. Being huddled on top of a communal stove may have been one way to spend the winter. Drink could have helped. Livestock enterprise was apparently never considered. The number of farm animals in relation to the population fell throughout the nineteenth century. Between 1867 and 1913 the number of horses, cows, and pigs increased by only 50 percent while the people increased by more than 100 percent. Sheep numbers actually fell.

The second point is the communal nature of the peasants' work. When was this kind of communality established? It was long before any idea of socialism. It probably derived from the very earliest pioneer days under Ivan the Terrible. This organization of the extended family, so characteristic of historic Russia, probably descended from the primeval Slav tribal organization consisting of a group of about fifty to one hundred related people. This broke down into the communal organization. In turn, the commune was the legal tenant in many settled places. This did not mean that the Tsarist *mir* bore any relation to the Soviet collective.[42]

Miserably low returns in Russian agriculture are nothing new. They are, today, between 30 and 40 percent of what a Western farmer would get in the same conditions—they always were. In 1846 when a good English or Dutch farmer could get a yield of over one ton per hectare, the average Russian yields were 350 kg (772 lb). In Russia in 1913, the average yield for wheat over the previous five years was 0.7 ton per hectare; this was twice the 1846 yield per hectare, but still only one-third of the English yield. No attempt was made to solve the problem. Russians emigrated away from the difficulties. They still do.[43]

Virgin land, as has been seen, was one answer. Another was to find other employment. Instead of sitting on the stove all winter drinking vodka, another option was to trap furs; the forests were very rich in animals in early times, and Russians became great exporters of furs. Another winter possibility was to cut timber in the forest zone. The Baltic became the great source of timber for the West, and Russia is still a great supplier. Another answer was mining. Russia, like India, became a country noted for precious jewels and metals, even if it was also very poor. Another choice was home manufacture of craft products in the village. These activities were communally carried out, requiring neither great brains nor much capital.

Russia was unique in the world in that she had no shortage of land or people. If neither the problem of productivity per hectare nor of productivity per man exists, how do you manage? By solving neither. In the absence of capitalism and the profit motive, how can there be efficiency?

Before any competent practical farmer answers the question, it would be well to remember that nineteenth-century Russia was the only country in the world in which this was a problem. If they had been short of land, Russians would have learned how to manage husbandry properly; if they had been short of humans, they would have learned how to grow food and use early labor-saving devices. As it was, Russians neither learned to be good farmers like the English nor learned to be efficient ranchers or monoculturists like the contemporary Americans. A visitor from almost anywhere was appalled by what he saw.

A structural problem was the nature of the emancipation of the serfs in 1861. It had left them so badly indebted that the debt grew instead of being paid off. In 1907, forty-six years after emancipation, more than

85 percent of the peasants were still in debt, most of them for a sum twice that of the original computation. In 1907, Stolypin abolished the debts of the ex-serfs, but in the ensuing six harvests of peace, grain yields per hectare did not decrease or increase significantly. Apologists have always deplored the Russian climate with its uncertain rainfall, but hardly any irrigation or drainage was practiced, even in areas close to rivers that obviously would have benefited. Introducing new crops was an intellectual burden comparable to the labors of Sisyphus.[44]

Potatoes were introduced in 1833 and coincided with an outbreak of cholera. By 1913 potato production was still less than that of Germany, which had half the population. Sugar beets took twenty-five years to reach half a million hectares (over one million acres). In 1913 sugar production was less than that of France, with one-quarter the population. Maize was not really grown, however well suited to the Black Earth, until the four hundredth anniversary of Columbus's voyage, in 1892. In 1913 Russian maize production had not reached that of Italy, whose population was less than one-quarter that of Russia.

In 1920 an expatriate Russian figured out the available grain per head in exporting countries in 1910–14 as follows: Canada 1696 kg (3740 lb), United States 1151 kg (2536 lb), Argentine 1322 kg (2915 lb), Romania 875 kg (1929 lb), Russia 445 kg (980 lb). Contemporary importing countries had the following amounts available: United Kingdom 680 kg (1500 lb), Germany 497 kg (1100 lb), France 480 kg (1060 lb), Italy 442 kg (974 lb). Russia, with 445 kg (980 lb) available, exported 60–70 kg (132–154 lb) per head, leaving the Russian people with the lowest amount of grain per head in Europe—381 kg (840 lb). This was 1 kg (2 lb) less of grain per head than available in Spain, a much warmer country.[45]

The Russian Revolutions of 1905 and 1917 were ascribed by contemporaries to political injustice, a marked distaste for the autocracy, and an overwhelming desire for liberty, equality, fraternity, and so forth. Has enough been said to suggest that a much simpler cause existed? Faced from very early days with no imperative to farm efficiently by any measure, the Russian peasant, leaderless, was left to look after himself. When help was forthcoming, it took a political form. The commune gave way to the collective. Soviet dictators after 1917 bent all their efforts on improving the armed forces, industry, and communications. The same has been true of subsequent Russian rulers.

In fact, did not population pressure plus masses of virgin land operate in such a way as to stultify all the responses with which contemporaries in other countries were answering the challenge? In the United States, a relatively small population increased production and food supply per head to heights never before achieved. In the other neo-Europes, the same sort of pattern also emerged. New Zealand, Australia, Canada, South Africa, and the Argentine, all became increasingly able to produce foodstuffs at such a low cost that they could export produce all over the world and leave their own populations far better fed than their relatives in Europe.

In Europe itself, production per hectare became of increasing importance as land rents rose. Even when they fell after the crucial year of 1879, the profitable way to farm was still to select a product that the farm or the farmer produced with efficiency, and then optimize output per unit area of land.

Russians never attempted solutions to these problems by government action or intellectual discussion at the university, college, or with the landlord. As a result, Russians were often hungry. In some years, they were hungrier than anyone in Europe, Spain included, which suffered two real famines in the 1870s. There is no better recipe for revolution than insufficient food. It was, in all probability, one true cause of the French Revolution, idealistic talk notwithstanding. The statistics, however, do not exist to prove or disprove the thesis in relation to that event in 1789.

In relation to both 1905 and 1917, the figures are available. Do they prove beyond all reasonable doubt that the reason for the revolutions was hunger? Population growth was pushing against some force. It was not pushing against the supply of land, which was still plentiful in Russia, but against the lack of capital, technical advances, applied intelligence, curiosity, rules of good husbandry, and a real love of the land that is essential to good farming.

These qualities are still absent in Russian agriculture. Every intelligent young person wishes to leave agriculture, and parents encourage children to abandon collective drudgery in the field to become desk workers. The truth is never told, *glasnost* notwithstanding. Practices that any good

Western farmer would call wrong, bad husbandry, and even immoral are common. There is no honest criterion for success, only reports to and from a corrupt bureaucracy.

European Russia, allowing for the use of fertilizers, pest control, and machinery, produces less today than in the five years 1909–13. During that period, Russians were the worst fed in Europe. They still are. But for the secret police, there would have been several revolutions since 1917, and there still might be. Well-wishers in 1913 waited for improvement. They still do.[46]

Japan demonstrated great wisdom in the face of an extremely difficult agricultural situation, adopting changes where necessary and maintaining successful traditions. This prudence has provided the basis for a remarkable history and a formidable present-day economy.

Far more devastated from World War II than Russia, Japan had far fewer resources than any European state, very little indigenous fuel or arable land, none of the animals and machinery needed to cultivate the soil, no merchant marine for essential imports, a minimum of help from former enemies, and a worse international image than usual for a defeated nation. In 1945 the country would have been considered a candidate for long-term convalescence, not triumph. No one could have imagined that Japan would be a wealthy country within forty years, as wealthy as any country in the world. Nor would anyone have believed that in just over a generation Japan would produce 50 percent of the world's ships, 25 percent of its cars, 90 percent of its videos, and 40 percent of its integrated circuits.

If farsighted Westerners had studied Japan's history and culture, instead of being sidetracked by aberrations from the 1920s to the 1940s, they would have been wise enough to perceive the possibility of a Japanese miracle. The signs were there. With the wisdom of hindsight, it is possible to explain how it happened.

The name *Japan* derives, via "Cipangu," from an East Indian corruption of the Japanese word "Nippon" or "Nihon," which is what the Japanese call their own country. "Cipangu" was what the Mediterranean world called Japan in 1492. It was many years before a European traveled as far as the main southerly island, Kyushu, and even then, trade and intercourse between various foreigners and the Japanese lasted for only a century. It was not until the late nineteenth century that Europeans came to know the full extent of the Japanese islands.

There are over 4000 islands, and the number is always increasing, since the geology of the archipelago is volcanic and new islands appear from time to time. More land area is added because of the efforts of the Japanese themselves. They have reclaimed more land than all Europeans put together—they have "created" nearly half their coastline; the whole of the center of modern Tokyo, for example, was reclaimed in the seventeenth century. Land is in permanent shortage in the Japanese psyche. There are nearly 143,000 square miles of land in the islands, which extend from the sub-arctic Hokkaido— frozen for 150 days in the year—to the subtropical paradise of Okinawa. The north-south stretch is almost as great as that of the mainland United States at 20° latitude.

Okinawa, with its crops of oranges, sugarcane, pineapples, and bananas, is a contrast to Hokkaido in the far north, legendary home of the primeval, "tree-living" *Ainu*. Hokkaido lies entirely south of the forty-sixth parallel, about the level of Lyons, France, or Portland, Maine. Hokkaido and the west coast of the main island, Honshu, have cold, wet winters. By contrast, the twenty-sixth parallel, which runs just south of Okinawa, is far south of anything in Europe, on the same parallel as the Sargasso Sea, the Bahamas, and much of Florida. Okinawa is cooler than the Bahamas in winter; the west coast is cooler than the east since the winter weather comes from Siberia in the northwest, with bitterly cold wet winds full of snow. Tokyo Bay, in the middle of the archipelago and on the east coast, is more moderate with temperatures ranging from a January average of 5°C (40°F) to 25°C (78°F) in July. Japan hosts a current analogous to the Gulf Stream, but it affects Japan less than the Gulf Stream affects Britain.

A hundred years ago Japan was often compared to the British Isles, but seasons in Japan are much more regular. There is a special regularity about the renewal of spring with the cherries trees blossoming in a regular pattern and the front advancing one degree of latitude in each couple of days, taking forty days to travel from south to north. The climate is regular, but the weather is not.

The Japanese islands are subject to the vagaries of two major seismic fault lines. The islands are volcanic in origin. Some of the consequences of this are the appearance of new islands every ten years or so and the forty active volcanoes. Japan experiences at least twenty minor earthquakes a year—10 percent of all those recorded in the whole world. This seismic activity gives rise to avalanches, tidal waves, and inland floods. The last great earthquake was in 1923 and caused far more destruction than did the San Francisco earthquake in 1906. The death toll from the 1923 earthquake was over 100,000 with the loss of perhaps 70 percent of the flats and houses in the Tokyo conurbation. The earthquakes are said to occur in a 69–70 year cycle, so the next one was expected in 1992, but it did not happen in the Tokyo area. Today, twenty-five times as many people live in the area as did in 1923.This figure illustrates Japan's problem.

The population as a whole has only increased by about two and one-half times since 1923, but they are crowded into flat land, of which there is a grave shortage. The density of population on Honshu, where 75 percent of the population lives, is slightly more than that of England, which has a rather higher percentage of the UK population. However, while there are 380 people per square mile in Honshu and 360 in England, there is far less flat land per head in Honshu. There is, in fact, only about one-fifth of the land fit to cultivate or pasture, against more than three-quarters in England, so the density of the Japanese population becomes an obsession. Four-fifths of their country is fit only for forest, if that. The slopes of most of the extinct volcanoes, Fujiyama being the most famous, are bare, sulphurous, and sterile.

The *Lebensraum* problem of the Japanese is central to the history of the last five hundred years, so it is worth stating the problem another way: Each Englishman has a potential 0.28 hectare (0.68 acre) for all purposes; each inhabitant of Honshu has 0.25 (0.63). However, each Englishman has more than a half acre fit to carry buildings while each inhabitant of Honshu has only one-sixteenth of an acre fit for buildings. Put in square meters, each Honshusan has 300 square meters (250 square yards) for all building purposes; each Englishman more than nine times as much, 3000 square meters (2500 square yards). No wonder that real estate has entered the Japanese soul. Even 150 years ago when they grew all their own food, each inhabitant of Honshu had only three times as much land as today, for all purposes. On the original islands of Japan as a whole before the annexation of Formosa or Korea, there was just about a half acre per head for all purposes, not including the forest. That was all the land available to grow essential rice and to produce fruits, vegetables, tea, silk, chicken and eggs, oxen, the squat brown Japanese ponies, and everything else demanded by a pre-industrial country in 1860. The Japanese had lived liked this for four centuries.

Values for Japanese real estate have always been ridiculously high. Today, the gross value of all the land in Japan, plus the infrastructure, has been valued at twice the value of the whole landmass of the forty-eight mainland United States. The continental United States, without Alaska or Hawaii, is more than twenty times the size of Japan. On a per capita basis the land, buildings, and infrastructure of Japan are valued at thirty-five times as much as Americans value the same assets in the most expensive of the forty-eight states. This is ridiculous. So is the fact that two tennis courts in the center of Tokyo made $500 million or $400,000 per square meter, when sold for building purposes in 1987. People who regard London or Manhattan real estate as inflated should recognize that similar land and buildings in Tokyo cost at least one hundred times as much. A million pounds or dollars outside the city of London or Wall Street buys a respectably sized office or a fairly luxurious house or flat. Japanese real estate is more expensive—even more expensive than that of Hong Kong or Singapore whose island-states have, respectively, 5000 and 4000 people per square kilometer against 3800 per "safe" square kilometer in Honshu. Allowing for land unfit to build upon, Singapore and Hong Kong have more than double the density of Honshu's population, yet land values in Honshu are about five times those of Singapore and three times those of Hong Kong. This is not surprising since only the Japanese, of all people, refuse to build anywhere except on flat land.

Five hundred years ago it is probable that no European had ever been to Japan.[47] It is true that Columbus's first voyage was known to be aiming for "Cipangu," but Columbus never defined the products of this fabled country, nor was the position of the islands very accurately charted. They were thought to be in the same latitude as the Bahamas, but the distance was seriously underestimated. The earth was known to be a sphere—the longitude of the Canary Islands, for example, was known to be about one hour, 15° W of Barcelona; more elegantly, the nearest point of the Azores was also about 15° W, one hour from Lisbon. Cipangu, however, was placed in quite the wrong position, and the earth thereby made to look smaller by nearly 40 percent. This logic was never pursued so that the longitude from Barcelona to the mouth of the Ganges was known to be about 90° or six hours eastward. Cipangu, however, was held to be only about five hours west, so what happened to the rest of the twenty-four hours? According to this calculation, there were thirteen hours, 195° between the mouth of the Ganges and Japan. In fact, there are only about three hours, or 45°. One of the major causes of the "loss" of nearly 10,000 miles or 195° at the latitude of Japan was the fatal dictum, widely believed five hundred years ago, that five-sixths of the world was terrestrial and only one-sixth water. In fact, the surface of the earth is less than one-third land and more than two-thirds water. Even so, one of the great mysteries about the events of 1492 remains how much knowledge Columbus had and how much in ignorance he was of the positions of the places to which he was sailing. Whatever else happened in 1492, no one reached Japan that year.[48]

The first categorically known European arrivals in Japan were three Portuguese passengers on a junk traveling from Macao to Thailand who were blown off course by 1500 miles and made landfall on Tangeshima Island, one of the string connecting Kyushu Island with Okinawa. This was in 1542 or 1543. The Japanese were reported to have been curious and hospitable. The Portuguese, eager to trade, gave them many Western artifacts and were in turn most impressed by the quality of Japanese steel swords—then, as now, the finest in the world—which were being exported in large numbers to China and Korea. The Japanese were more impressed by the three personal firearms, crude arquebuses, possessed by the Portuguese. Characteristically, the Japanese copied these weapons within a month of the Portuguese arrival. Equally typically, the Portuguese weapons, having been stripped of their secrets and laid bare, were returned to their owners. The Portuguese trio, nameless pioneers, was followed by many more like them.

In the next few years, Portuguese merchants arrived in force. They traded between Japan and Goa, and among Japan, Macao, the Philip-pines, and other East Indian islands. All would have been well except for the confusion between trade and dominion. The dominion sought by the Portuguese was not temporal, but in 1547 the King of Portugal deliberately encouraged Francis Xavier, the Jesuit friend of Loyola and fellow founder of the Society of Jesus. King John III had sent Xavier to Goa in 1542 as the "Apostle of the Indies," and Xavier, having made thousands of converts in Goa, went on to Malacca, the Banda Islands, Amboyna, the Moluccas, and Ceylon. Concentrating upon converting rulers and nobles in feudal societies, Xavier found that this policy mul-tiplied the efficacy of his work many times over.[49] The feudal rulers' followers were converted by the native nobles without any further intervention by Xavier. Whether the simple peasants understood Chris-tianity in the many separate languages of the Indies is another matter. Francis Xavier started his work in Japan in 1548, and it led directly to the success of modern Japan, not noted for its Christian ethic. Xavier's efforts were almost wholly counterproductive.

Francis Xavier himself visited Kagoshima, Hirado, and Kyoto, the last a huge city with 96,000 houses according to a Portuguese estimate of the time, and thus bigger than Lisbon. Xavier stayed twenty-seven months in Japan, and during that time he made several hundred converts. He left in 1552 for Goa and died on the voyage. He never attempted a mission in China.

No language is more difficult for Europeans to learn than Japanese because the construction of the language does not lend itself to alien philosophical concepts; nor was Xavier a good linguist—in fact, he was a very bad one—but the Portuguese traders quite clearly linked the possibility of trade to the degree of toleration for the Christian religion shown by the Japanese. The Japanese, who imported small foreign consumables to make their lives more pleasant, as well as the oriental spices controlled by the Portuguese and occidental weapons, were usually willing to swallow their philosophic doubt and pride and accept Christianity as the price of trade. To the great detriment of Jap-anese national unity there were at that date massive and expensive feudal wars between various sections of the country.

Two examples of this process are sufficient. In about 1555 on the island of Amakusa, the chieftain became a Christian and forcibly converted his followers. The chieftain quite clearly associated conversion with trade, but no Portuguese ship appeared, so the chieftain smartly converted himself and his followers back to Buddhism and expelled the European Christian missionaries. In Nagasaki, then a little fishing village, a more positive development took place. A church was built there in 1567, and Sumitada, the feudatory, encouraged the development of the port. Five years later in 1572, the inhabitants numbered 30,000, and there was an annual visit of at least half a dozen Portuguese ships. By the 1580s most of the island of Kyushu had some kind of Christian presence, balanced by the annual visit of at least one Portuguese ship. In 1581 there were said to be over 125,000 converts in Kyushu out of a Japanese total of 150,000 adherents. At this point, Christianity was confused not only with the positive virtues of Portuguese trade, but also with the negative virtues of not being Buddhist. Many of the Buddhist monasteries were hives of feudal industry; they were often defended camps, supporting local feudal lords against the centralizing influence of the great trio of Shogun overlords: Oda Nobunga, Toyotomi Hideyoshi, and Tokugawa Iyeyasu. Hideyoshi, in particular, used Christians as a counterweight to the Buddhists. He allowed a church to be built in Osaka, then the capital, and a year later he changed his mind. The pretext for the change was that Christians ate useful animals like oxen and ponies, then no part of the Japanese diet.

Hideyoshi's mood reversal may have been due to the Christians' intolerance when they were in a majority, as was the case in parts of Kyushu where converts had been compulsorily turned to destroy Buddhist temples and other holy places. In 1587 the Christians were expelled; the next year, this order was rescinded. The Portuguese made clear once more that without tolerance for Christianity, there would be no foreign trade. The Japanese judged foreign trade too important to enable them to dispense with Christianity.

This tolerance lasted for ten years and was broken by rivalry between Spain and Portugal. Although the Iberian countries were united in a joint crown from 1580 to 1640, there had been a demarcation agreement between the two countries and a Papal bull that gave Portugal the monopoly of trade with Japan. The Spanish Dominicans and Franciscans in Manila, having largely converted the (not very many) natives of the Philippines at the point of the sword, sought fresh fields to conquer and landed in Japan in 1593.[50] There was also the singular incident of the *San Felipe*, a galleon, loaded with wealth from the Spanish Indies on track for Acapulco in Mexico. It was blown off course by a hurricane and landed in Tosa. The ship's pilot showed all the wealth on board—worth $50 million in today's money—and a map of the Spanish and Portuguese kings' dominions in the world, including most of the earth after 1580, to the Japanese and told them: "Our king begins by sending into the countries he wishes to conquer, missionaries who induce the people to embrace our religion, and when they have made considerable progress, troops are sent who combine with the new Christians, and then our kings have not much trouble in accomplishing the rest."[51]

On learning of this speech, Hideyoshi reacted with fury; the Franciscans were mutilated alive, then crucified at Nagasaki, the Christian epicenter in Japan. One hundred and thirty-seven churches were demolished in Kyushu, and the Jesuits were sent back to Goa. The Japanese penalties of the period were merciful. Only the lobe of one ear was cut off, and crucifixion consisted of tying the victim to a cross and driving a spear through the heart. Death was instantaneous, as it was for the Christian Samurai who had to commit suicide. Hideyoshi died the following year. Though his policy was initially reversed, his successor, Tokugawa Iyeyasu, ultimately arrived at the same philosophic position.

Japanese statesmen were wedded to toleration; they also believed in a national consensus. Both aims were challenged in feudal Japan. Philosophy was confused with party interest; consensus was sacrificed to the internecine feudal warfare. The foreigners brought in more dissent. Spanish friars quarreled with the Portuguese-dependent Jesuits; Portuguese traders fought with the Spanish who followed the priests from Manila. Spanish government emissaries demanded the expulsion of the Dutch, who had arrived in 1602; and the Dutch, although they traded without the imposition of missionary Christianity, sought to fight the English, who arrived in 1613. The Japanese sought to separate the European enemies by allocating a different port to each nationality, but there was also the problem of the Japanese Christian converts. They took up positions in the feudal battles then going on in Japan, ultimately in the nearly successful Shimabarra rebellion in 1638. The Spanish had been expelled in 1624 and the Portuguese in 1638 because the latter were thought to be conspiring with the rebels. These were not the first anti-European edicts, just the most effective. Between 1600 and 1640 there were many anti-Christian incidents often encouraged by one faction or another. There was also the question of firearms. Perhaps, in the end, gunpowder was more important than an alien religion.

In the seventeenth century Japan was far ahead in iron and steel technique. Japanese pig iron, smelted by cottage industry methods, was far cheaper than European, and Japanese steel was acknowledged to be the best in the world. Japanese swords had a unique quality. The blades were formed by being beaten and hammered for weeks on end, giving them a characteristic that few sword-makers have ever been able to achieve since. Blades could sheer a fairly thick nail without damage to the sword. One sweep of the samurai's two-handed sword, correctly used, could remove a man's head clean at one blow. A sixteenth-century Japanese sword could cut through any sword ever made in Europe. The Japanese had mastered the supremely difficult art of making the edge of the blade a series of thin laminates, each forged until the edge was sharper than anything made anywhere in the world, as sharp as a modern razor blade, but to avoid brittleness and prevent shattering, the body of the sword had to be soft. The edge was highly tensile and unbelievably sharp, and the body low-tempered so that it might accept shock without damage. The Japanese sword of quality was far superior to the best Damascene products of the Muslim world, until then the swords most admired by Western nations.[52]

Each sword also had a personality, a life of its own. A great sword was passed down from one feudal warlord to another, from one swordsman to another, from one soldier to another. It was no disadvantage that the sword had been used by a samurai to commit suicide. The sword was not buried with the corpse, as in some Western funerals. The sword went on and on. Indeed, since a great sword might take several years of a great steelmaster's life to make, it was just as well. In all probability, steelmasters were less common than samurai.[53]

There was a ritual about fighting with swords. It was icily polite, had important gracious preliminaries to bloodshed, and was sincerely courteous in its formality. No such ritual could exist among large numbers of men drawn up with muskets or arquebuses; they just fired the guns.[54] There was also the class problem. Gunpowder had destroyed the validity of the feudal European castle, and brought to an end the host of mercenary soldiers who rampaged through late medieval Europe. Only a nobleman could use a sword; anyone could shoot a gun. The knight was no longer a match for an infantryman, so technology democratized warfare. No one would express this sentiment until the 1800s, but it was true. These fears were mouthed by Japanese noblemen as they had been by Frenchmen after poor British yeoman archers at Agincourt unhorsed the flower of chivalry. So the gun threatened the Japanese way of life, and the gun could only be banned from Japan if the foreigners were also banned. Perhaps too much has been made of the disruptive nature of Western Christianity on the Japanese reaction to Europeans. Perhaps the vile nature of the gun was more important. Perhaps there was a third reason.

The extraordinary and very advanced nature of Japanese society at the time of first European contact was not properly recognized, then or now. They were a highly educated people with a far greater degree of literacy than in any European country, higher, even, than in Florence in 1598.[55] Tokyo, a city of half a million in 1610, built largely on reclaimed land, opened an aqueduct that year that brought pure water to a city center for the first time since the Romans accomplished that feat in the first century in the Mediterranean. The carnivorous Europeans did not understand the nature of Japanese diet; before 1870 the Japanese did not eat meat or kill domestic animals for flesh.[56] Their consumption of fish, then as now, was at least ten times the European level; perhaps this helped with the intelligence of the race as a whole.

Above all, in 1600, Japan had a very large population. It was home to 22 million people compared with about 10 million Iberians (then under one crown), about 16 million Frenchmen, and just over half as many Germans or Italians. The great trading people, the Dutch, numbered only 1.5 million, and the English a mere 4 million. In 1600, as in 1900 and 2000, the Japanese were the best educated people in the world.

The Japanese did not know these comparative facts or figures, but they knew there were 22 million of their own countrymen long before any European country had done an accurate census. The Japanese also knew the size and power of their two neighbors.

China was immense, disorganized, and self-contained, and since 1521 had been greatly reluctant to engage in any kind of foreign intercourse. Copper was the only material China seriously lacked, and this the Japanese supplied. The Koreans, with whom the Japanese had conducted a war in 1592 that was successful until the Chinese intervened, much as they did in 1950,[57] had a much smaller population than Japan. The Japanese considered neither China nor Korea to be a threat. Even without gunfire, the Japanese argued, they were inviolate. Japan was too difficult a country to invade, too tricky to move around in, and almost impossible to occupy. The war-like temperament of her people made the success of a foreign adventurer unlikely. The Japanese too had a great sense of superiority, equal to their sense of harmony with importance given, then as now, to consensus. This contradiction arose because of the peculiar circumstances of the Japanese triumph over adversity.

What had a hundred years of foreign intercourse produced? A new philosophy or religion, Christianity, that preached the alien and subversive creed that the loyalty offered to God was greater and far more important than loyalty to one's feudal master. This directly threatened the status quo, and the Japanese decided that Christianity should be banned. It was. The Europeans had also brought in various vegetables, some of which proved either useful or beautiful. Tobacco was banned, as were other drugs such as opium, but legumes of various sorts were welcomed by thrifty Japanese gardeners and farmers. New sorts of rice may have been introduced in that century, as was maize for use in the dry lands and different millets, sorghums, barley, and capsicums, or sweet peppers from South America via Manila. Some other Columbian plants, such as yams and sweet potatoes, failed to challenge the native giant radish, nor did the white potato appeal to the Japanese palate. It is possible that the natural insecticide pyrethrum reached Japan from the Arab world at the same time, but not derris root. The Japanese gained a great deal from their hundred-year intercourse with Europeans, including a belief that they were better off isolated. It was this conviction that saved the Japanese from the sub-European colonial status that every other country in the world (Thailand excepted) has suffered.

Since 1950 the yen has appreciated nearly eleven times against the pound sterling and nearly three times against the U.S. dollar, yet in none of the years since 1950 has Japan had a trading surplus of more than 1 percent of gross domestic product. In seven years there has been a deficit, supported by the United States; in most years there has been a surplus of about 0.55 percent of GDP. The economic virtues of Japan are less obvious than the consumerism of others. Against the Swiss franc, for example, the yen has maintained a parity limited to a movement of about 5 percent. At the moment of writing, it is within 5 percent of its 1950 rate. This may merely mean that the Swiss and Japanese economies are successful and those of the United States and the United Kingdom less successful.[58] Even the currency of the most successful EEC economy, that of West Germany, had declined before the advent of the euro by over 20 percent against the yen since 1950. Against almost every other currency, the Deutschmark has appreciated. For the West Germans, this was a challenge. Possessing the hardest currency in the EEC, they had to export their goods with the handicap of an automatic and rising Deutschmark in relation to the devaluation or depreciation of the currency of their competitors and customers. This the Germans have succeeded in doing; but the Germans have been only 80 percent as successful as the Japanese, who now export more cars than the next three exporters combined. It started with ships in the 1960s. Today the Japanese cannot compete with the South Koreans in either shipbuilding or steelmaking. By the time that Korea, Taiwan, or Brazil can undercut Japanese cars, other products will have been invented that other people will take a long while to copy or surpass, for this nation of onetime "imitators" now originates a great many products.[59]

The Japanese are a people nurtured in an earthquake zone, yet they prosper. There were so many people living in paper houses that tobacco had to be banned, not on health grounds, but because of the fire danger. This was a people of 22 million with a density of settlement unknown in Europe. Today, the Japanese have a people/flat land ratio eight times as dense as the English. In 1660, the same ratio was four times as unfavorable. Today, flat land has to include buildings, roads, factories, railways, airports, and so forth. In 1600 flat land had to produce enough food to feed five times as many Japanese as there were Englishmen. To do this, there was only one-quarter as much land as in England per head of population. (Hokkaido, with more than one-fifth of the land area, was not occupied until the nineteenth century.) Japan, more so even than China, had a marvelously developed pre-industrial economy, with perhaps the most efficient agriculture in the world. No European, of course, knew the facts. In seventeenth-century England the best fed people in Europe had four times the land per head of the Japanese, yet Japan was the best fed country in Asia. She still is. The extraordinarily efficient agriculture of Japan made possible its splendid isolation during the two centuries from 1640 until the white man returned. In turn, the splendid isolation made efficient agriculture continuous and essential. The magnificence of the Edo period, which lasted until the Meiji restoration in 1868, depended upon sufficient food, an end to feudal warfare, an absence of foreign intercourse, and consensus being allowed to play its part. This period of isolation was an essential precursor to the extraordinary story of modern Japan.[60]

CHAPTER FIVE

Malthus Defeated?

In the last century, world population has multiplied by four times. In other words, it has doubled twice. This simple arithmetical truth is a causative factor more important than any action of mankind. Procreation has become more important than politics, increases more than economics, population pressure more than political belief.

The taming of disease has been a prime reason for this increase. Perinatal mortality at one end is matched throughout childhood and adolescence, while at the other, lives are extended far beyond their former span. This may prove to be admirable in rich countries able to feed themselves or to buy food from others. Not so happy for the poor.

Yet food supply has advanced in this century to meet and match population increases in western Europe and in the neo-Europes. Shortages of food are limited to second and Third World countries. Inappropriate management policies are the main problem. In Soviet eastern Europe, a 25 percent increase in fertilizer usage between the 1970s and 1980s produced only 2 percent more grain. In North America, in the same period, 11 percent more fertilizer produced 23 percent more grain. In Africa, state control does even worse. In some countries, not only in Africa, "planning" has been directly responsible for starvation.

Intellectually poor countries do not have the distribution systems to use First World surpluses properly. Technology transfer may be the best policy. In some countries, peasants have even forgotten how to use basic manual tools, bemused as they are by pretentious agricultural policies propagated by ill-adapted urban civil servants. In other countries, the Green Revolution—sensibly organized—meets human needs without difficulty. In India, Mexico, China, and Indonesia productivity increases have been important. The world as a whole has every reason to believe itself capable of feeding its people—at a price.

The price is that no demographer can seriously see a future in which the world population stabilizes at less than double today's number. With natural control measures defeated, the world stares at several "options"—war, new sorts of incurable disease, famine on a wide scale, or the world drowning in its own ordure, wrecking the fragile ecosystem of One Earth. The only alternative is to work for some improvement in every process to prevent the kind of breakdown that otherwise will assuredly happen before populations level off. A number of improvements related to the prevention and cure of disease largely explain the massive growth in world population over the past one hundred years, to a point where food supply was at times considered to be growing too slowly.

IN THE SECOND HALF of this century, the rate of change in every kind of human activity has speeded up and continues to do so. In some areas, the acceleration has even become a mental health problem. In some others, the process threatens the environment. In yet others, the whole moral base of human life, the sacred nature of creation, is jeopardized. We live in an age when anything appears to be possible. Anything goes, as the song says.

These truths are self-evident however much they may baffle priests, elude the philosophers, and render anxious ordinary men and women. What is not obviously clear is the cause of these changes. It is the purpose of this chapter to examine the driving forces in our own times. Not surprisingly, these turn out to be the same three that have formed a triangle throughout history. Population growth is the engine of change. Population growth in turn is much modified by disease and food supplies.

In the twentieth century, world population doubled nearly twice. The 1900 figure was 1.625 billion. The first doubling occurred at some time in 1964. The second doubling took place before 2000. The first doubling in the twentieth century took sixty-four years: the second took, perhaps, thirty-six years; logically, the third doubling should take place in about 2015. This is logical, but unlikely. The one certitude about population projections is that they are nearly always wrong.[1]

This is both a comfort and a cause for anxiety. The comfort is that such uncertainties create jobs for many professional people: actuaries, economists, and demographers. The cause for anxiety is that what they have to say in terms of the future is often worthless. There is one absolute certainty: It is that population growth is a profound cause of our present condition. Things would be very different but for sustained population growth. Without the pressure of population, the world would not be as it is. With the same population as in 1945, about 2.2 billion, the rate of change would be slowed down; there would be an almost continual First World agricultural slump, not surpluses; inflation would not have to be resisted; pressure on resources such as oil would be so much reduced as to render oil producers unimportant; the Third World would be a backwater—quaint, visited for its ethnic qualities—and not a cockpit for the ambitious. Few animal species would be endangered. The sea would not be an area of deep anxiety, polluted by man's activities, short of fish and devoid of whales. There would be no acid rain, no greenhouse effect, no threat from aerosols, no hydrocarbon-related smog even in Los Angeles, which, incidentally, would probably have a population one-third what it is now. This fantasy has only to be stated to be ridiculed.

Population growth is a fact of life. It has been much accelerated by mankind's activities—even more in the last half-century. It has been modified by the retreat of disease in the recent past. The twentieth century was also notable for personal cleanliness.

Cleanliness declined after 1492 for at least 350 years. First of all, bathing became suspect because of syphilis. The daily, weekly, and monthly public bath taken by both genders in Renaissance cities in Europe disappeared from the ritual of life. To the fear of syphilis and to the connection between the bathhouse ("*bagnio*") and prostitution was added the high cost of heating water as wood became unobtainable and coal had to be mined, moved, and burnt in low-efficiency devices.

Cleanliness implies drains, which were one of the great pathways for disease. There were no main sewerage drains on a citywide scale until the nineteenth century. Londoners, proud occupants of the then largest city in the West, used so-called cesspools, which were, literally, pools of polluted effluent, soaking away into the surrounding earth. From the local earth these cesspools drained into the local wells that supplied the local population with water and their own (and other people's) enteric organisms. It was the connection between wells and cesspools that killed people as eminent as Prince Albert (died in 1861 from typhoid fever) and many, many more and humbler inhabitants of large English cities. During the mid-Victorian period, in very hot, unfavorable years it was probable that 10 percent of the population of all ages in poor districts would die of some sort of enteric disorder. In London in 1862 there were nearly 400,000 cesspools draining into 100,000 drinking-water wells. The bacterial connection was not made for another generation.

There was, however, a view, identified in particular with northwest Europe and the United States, that cleanliness was connected to Godliness. This implied that there was a connection between dirt and disease. From this partial truth emerged the great clean water movement.

New York City was the first in the modern West to divide water and sewage. This was done by reaching farther and farther out for freshwater. By 1900, water was piped from the Catskills to Manhattan, from Wales to Liverpool and Birmingham, and from the Pennines to Manchester, Leeds, Bradford, and Sheffield. The inhabitants of the Thames Valley, from Oxford to Greenwich, had to rely on the river, which acted as both water supply and sewer, and still does. In between these two functions are a number of purification plants, much chemical activity, and more than 20 million people. This treatment removed a fundamental restraint upon population growth, probably reducing mortality more than many medical efforts.

After pure water, a second important contribution to health from the United States was anesthesia. The Chinese had used acupuncture for at least a thousand years. Hypnotism was employed in India and Persia and by some Arabs. Ether was suggested by the English polymath Michael Faraday, who also experimented at length with nitrous oxide (laughing gas). The heroes of early operations, however, were American dentists, not doctors. Dr. Horace Wells of Hartford, Connecticut, removed his own tooth while under nitrous oxide sedation in 1844. Dr. Morton of Boston used ether as a general anesthetic (on others) for tooth extraction and general surgery. Mr. Robinson of London worked with Liston, the great surgeon, on several operations before the end of 1846. Sir James Simpson applied ether to midwifery the next year. By the time of the Crimean War, 1854–57, and even more, by the time of the War between the States, 1861–65, anesthesia was in general use. Antisepsis was another matter.

Survival from surgery was originally considered so unlikely, and so unknown were the actions of microorganisms, that surgeons never even changed their bloody clothes or washed their hands before the work of Lister, Pasteur, and Koch. Lister, an English surgeon son of an inventor and developer of microscopes, was intellectually well placed to combine the two disciplines and use antiseptics to increase survival rates after surgery. Previously, the operations had been successful, but more than three-quarters of the patients died from shock, loss of blood, or, more usually, septicemia. Anesthesia overcame shock. Lister's work on ligatures stopped internal bleeding, and his use of carbolic acid stopped sepsis.[2]

The Frenchman Pasteur was the son of a tanner and trained as a chemist; he worked on ferments and set out the rules for preventing putrefaction in processes such as winemaking, milk handling, and brewing. The word "pasteurization" derives from his discoveries. Although milk can be made safe by pasteurization, humans cannot survive such treatment, so antiseptics that kill germs, but not human flesh and bone, were substituted. Robert Koch, the third (German) hero, was an early Nobel Prize winner who specialized in bacteriology, and worked on tuberculosis, cholera, rinderpest, and other diseases.[3]

A hundred years ago surgery was still daring, if no longer as painful for the patient. Before World War I the appendectomy was the fashionable new operation, first performed in 1886, then on Edward VII in 1902. Operations on diseased kidneys, lungs, and ulcers were all performed before 1900. Surgery was improved just in time for the carnage of World War I and the annual increase in road accidents in every country in the world during the twentieth century. Outside Europe and the neo-Europes, surgery was insignificant in affecting population growth.

Drugs, pharmaceuticals, and more sensible habits were of greater importance than surgery in most countries. In the 1870s both morphine and cocaine were in use, and proper needles were widely available for injection. As a local anesthetic, cocaine was compounded with various other substances and even used at one time as a dental painkiller in medicated chewing gum. The great drug of all the malarial areas was quinine, which became freely available in the 1880s and cheap enough, at one farthing (one-half cent) a dose for wide use. Quinine probably had more effect upon population growth than all the efforts of all the doctors ever born. Later, it was preventive measures, like drainage, that did as much as quinine in combating malaria.[4]

Preventive medicine, vaccines, and drugs have made light of what had once been killer diseases. Scarlet fever, measles, diphtheria, whooping cough, German measles, and tuberculosis have all been rendered relatively harmless in the First World. The common cold defies defeat. Influenza, with its ability to change its very nature, a characteristic it shares with AIDS, is always capable of pandemic. The flu outbreak in 1918–20 killed more people in Western Europe than did the battles of World War I. Before 1970 in most advanced countries, antibiotics and the sulfa drugs cleared up all sorts of local and generalized infections, often undiagnosed and treated before they were identified. A new generation of doctors is less certain about the merits of the blanket use of antibiotics. The habit of the 1960s—"Here are some pills; come back if you're not cured"—is no longer regarded as good medicine. Careless medical men have bred all sorts of new, antibiotic-resistant organisms. Some hospital walls are covered with drug-resistant organisms of great power. So far, the drug companies have kept ahead of the germs. This has been reversed in the case of MRSA[5] in hospitals.

Simple, cheap drugs are now widely used on a daily basis by millions of people at home. Aspirin (1898) was often compounded with Phenacetin (1887), and both are widely used today. Chloral hydrate, the first (stinking) hypnotic, was followed by others, less smelly: Paraldehyde (1868), Sulphonal (1880), and Barbiton (1898).[6] From these came a long sequence of barbiturates, all synthetic, that held sway before Librium (1945) and Valium (1947). Iodine, which occurs naturally in seaweed, was synthesized in 1885, and became a household antiseptic until superseded after World War II.

Two massive developments required no hardware, no technology, and no modern industrial base. Both required a change of attitude, one of the hardest objectives to accomplish.

The first was the general view of mental illness. Greco-Roman attitudes were more humane than those of the Middle Ages. In extreme cases the mad were regarded by Christians as being possessed by the

Devil. In an age of Conformity it was comfortable for the Establishment to consider dissent disorder. In London, lunatics were housed in
institutions like the Bethlehem Hospital (1247), hence Bedlam. There
were similar institutions in other cities. In villages, the local idiot was
treated more tolerantly.

Renaissance attitudes were more easygoing, less dogmatic. The first
inkling of a modern approach was to split the "mad" into what remains
a modern starting point: Neuroses are natural disorders; psychoses
are unnatural fantasies; the latter may or may not be accompanied
by organic changes in the body, the former never. Gradually, people
recognized that mental health was a problem associated with the
environment. "Madness is a disease of civilization" became a common
comment, and the observation was often made that the talented were
not far removed from the demented.

By 1900, some sort of organized "science" had supplemented philosophy. There was a physical school that sought to treat the insane with
aural or electric shocks, or by drugs. The school of thought associated
with Freud passed from hypnosis to "free association" to the interpre-
tation of dreams. The "Oedipus" complex is the overwhelming desire
of the infant to have exclusive possession of the parent of the opposite gender; this is suppressed by the ego, the awareness of self. The
id, the unconscious, is the home of repression, and is responsible for
the content of dreams. The libido, the third element in the mind, is
responsible for the emotional energy applied to work, sexual activity,
or creative living. The superego is the conscience that develops later
and controls the ego.

Freud's disciples and followers have accepted most of his postu-
lates, as have many workers in the field since. Two famous disciples
were Adler, who invented the "inferiority complex" and thought that
desire for triumph was a most important driving force; and Jung, who
believed that the key to the psyche was the motive driving the libido.
Was it psychic energy, religion, myths, or the collective unconscious,
perhaps?

Of all three—Freud, Adler, and Jung—and of all modern practitioners, it would be fair to say that they were men of their time.

Nearly everything they postulated was known to the Greeks and to artist-genius figures ever since, in literature, painting, and music.

To a post-Christian society, nominally liberal, this whole industry can often be a prop, an alternative to personal morality, brutally misused in Stalinist Russia and Hitler's Germany. Its impact has been increased greatly by the use of drugs in every sort of society. The profession, divided into psychologists, psychoanalysts, and psychiatrists, is thickest on the ground where lifestyle is furthest removed from nature—Los Angeles and Manhattan. To be without a shrink among the smarter classes is equivalent to a humbler sort of person being without a car.

In the Counter-Reformation, Freud, Adler, and Jung would have been burned at the stake. Their crime would have been the relief of mankind from the consequences of belief or disbelief. What would the Inquisition have made of modern nurses?

The answer is that nursing was an old, gentle activity performed by patrician Roman ladies from the fourth century onward. Throughout the Middle Ages nursing was associated with nuns, and the order with the largest number of graduates is still that of St. Vincent de Paul, founded in 1633. It was in northern countries after the Reformation that the connection between nursing and domestic duties was first made.

Gradually, the patrician, almost professional competence of the nursing sister gave way to the deplorable old soak, the gin-sodden Sarah Gamp of Charles Dickens's imagination.[7] It was, in turn, Florence Nightingale who rescued the profession and made of nursing a modern skill. She grasped the principles of hygiene, long before most doctors; the essential nature of the educated girl, properly trained to be a sick-nurse; and the subsequent lifelong status of the professional woman. Florence Nightingale did more for women than reform and rebuild an ancient semi-charitable sisterhood fallen into decay. She gave girls from good families an opportunity outside marriage for a worthwhile career; better in many ways to be a nurse than a governess of the period. Florence Nightingale stamped upon the whole of hospital life the type of inspired common sense that she called "scientific cleanliness." No longer was the old-style muddle and dirt permitted to survive. She also believed in the virtues of Christian love and fresh air. The success of these measures in increasing life expectancy is indisputable. What goes unquestioned, however, is the underlying assumption that life must be preserved at all costs.

From this mid-Victorian beginning has grown what is the largest economic sector in every advanced country. In the First World, the health industry is huge. The British National Health Service, an unmanageable monolith, is the largest employer in the World after the Chinese Army. More is spent on health care in the United States than on any other sector of human activity except eating. These two items are not unconnected. Most health care expenditure in the First World puts right what results from expenditure on unsuitable food, alcohol, tobacco, or other follies.

Hospitals have developed a momentum of their own. The young are nearly all born in them; the old nearly all die in them. They are a natural dockyard to repair all the casualties of modern life: victims of street violence, bodies dead on arrival, the wounded from car accidents, even people who need a stitch or two because of a hand that went through a pane of glass. But should the hospital dominate society as it does? No baby has been born in a northern English or Scottish city on a holiday weekend for the past ten years because births are induced for the convenience of the staff. The chronically old and sick are kept alive, sometimes beyond their natural term.[8]

The very nature of those born is altered by the absence of perinatal failure. High-tech operations of every kind—to brain, to heart, to kidney—are regarded as professional challenges without thought of whether or not they should ever happen. The health industry, so magnificently served by so many, and occupying more than one in ten people in every First World country, contributes much to the survival of so many at both ends of life. Does it know where it is going?

There are two basic problems with modern health care. They appear to be social, political, and economic, but they go to the root of public morality. Needless to say, the problems are rarely articulated. If touched upon, the questions are fudged.

The first point is that high-tech medicine costs serious money. In England a patient with an acute heart attack who is brought into an emergency ward attracts an expenditure of not less than £10,000 and an average of £17,000 for drugs and intensive care. Organ transplant operations with "new" organs taken from a dying, but not dead, person involve several fudges. The cost may be as high as £100,000. The chances of success may be as low as 15–20 percent. "Successful" operations may prolong life for only a few years, and the survivor rarely can live more than an invalid's existence. Questions are never asked: Should organs be taken from biologically alive people? Should such huge resources be employed on high-tech operations to keep medical men happy? Are the lucky patients the right people to operate upon, or are they just guinea pigs? Who is to decide who the beneficiaries of all this high-tech attention should be? In some countries it is the market. In the Soviet bloc it was the rule that favored party members got all the care and attention available. Ordinary people over fifty were not carried by ambulance in some Second World countries, and before 1990 no one in Poland over sixty was allowed in a hospital unless an *apparatchik*. Like the market, this system is logical. In Western Europe, there is an uneasy feeling that any method of selection is wrong, that everyone should be able to benefit, but obviously this is impossible. A service free at the point of delivery can never work.

The effect of such contradiction at one end of life is matched at the other. Old people are sometimes kept alive as cabbages; young people are born who have no chance of a normal life. Before every birth took place in the hospital, general practitioners or midwives, especially in rural areas, did not officiously strive to keep every child alive. If a child was the product of incest, spastic, malformed, or born blind or diseased, it did not always survive. Today such conduct performed in public amounts to murder. A hundred years ago perinatal mortality took 20 percentof all births in the slums of London and 50 percent in rural Russia, so no one noticed the natural process that favored the fit. Today in Western Europe, perinatal mortality is down to such a low figure that many ask why any should die. In some hospitals in Scandinavia, perinatal mortality is felt to be a disgrace to the institution, yet those who are kept alive are often a burden on the state for the rest of their lives. The care of the unfit that took literally a fraction of 1 percent of the gross national product a century ago—because there were not many wholly unfit—will increase every year in the First World. It could well be as much as half of all "health" care and as much as 5 percent of national income in some countries. These questions make people feel uncomfortable. The decision not to keep a child alive at birth, so simple a hundred years ago when there was no one present at the birth except a faithful colleague and the mother, is today complex. Who makes the decisions? Who has the right to do so? It is not surprising that these matters should be fudged. Who, in all conscience, would wish to rule in such cases? Who would dare to judge the matter?

There is, of course, a sea change involved in the population of so-called "caring" countries. An increasing proportion of the population can be categorized as "disabled." The disabled population is said to be 18–20 percent in every Western European country. In the sense of not being able to run a four-minute mile, *and* understand the difference between the Baroque and the Rococo, *and* between fission and fusion, *and* to articulate the theory of relativity, everyone can be virtually disabled. That is, only a tiny minority can perform in every department as a dedicated, discrete specialist. The "disabled," however, all have some strength that makes them outstanding; if they are labeled "disabled," and if society sees itself as responsible for them, two dependencies are created. One is that of the "disabled"; the second is that of the "caring professions" that have a vested interest in the existence of the "disabled." This is another burden that has been imposed upon society without conscious thought.[9]

The problem is accentuated, perhaps created in its present acute form, by another sea change in the world. Christianity has abandoned the primacy of the hereafter; conduct in this world importantly obscures belief in the next. Few sophisticated Muslims are strong enough in their faith to put heaven before the mundane. Even in Israel, Jews are probably just as secular. Most countries in the world follow the example of many countries and profess a constitutional laicism. This officially makes death a difficult business to be avoided at all cost. Health care is devoted to prolonging life; proponents even talk about "saving life" as if such an action were possible. For those who do not understand the immense effects of not believing in the hereafter, a visit to a hospice might be convincing. To be in an institution whose purpose is dignified (even cheerful) death is far removed from the ultimately hopeless task of prolonging life. If people accept the hereafter, the whole health care business becomes much easier to manage.

The wisdom of extending all lives as a matter of course is further called into question in those countries, particularly African countries, where population growth cannot be matched by food supply, and where Malthus looks likely to be proved right.

Obviously, ample provision for the young and unproductive and the old and unproductive implies an unequal burden on different economies. The "compassionate society" cannot harm a country where each farmer feeds a hundred other people, and enough houses, factories, cars, washing machines, and electronic goods are made by modern means to meet demand at a low price. To establish lavish standards as "normal" and "civilized," however, is grotesque when they are transferred to poor countries. To replace family responsibilities for the old with institutions for them is a luxury that some Third World countries cannot afford. Time may tell whether or not the First World has been wise so to do.

To remove ultimate responsibility for the care of their young from parents, which is what the First World has also done, may save a minority of children from discomfort, even danger, but a society in which about half of all marriages end in divorce is more likely to neglect its children than one that has no alternative to the family. Indeed, the existence of an alternative may make unsatisfactory parents easier in their consciences and neighbors less critical. It is possible that easy divorce combines naturally with the removal of parental responsibility for children.

As to the young, African experience is valid. Sub-Saharan Africa increased its population by 25 percent in the first quarter of the last century, by 45 percent in the second, by 100 percent in the third, and as much again in the fourth, except where HIV/AIDS was prevalent. Nearly all this increase has been because of children surviving who previously would have died. Some of this medical success was because of vaccination and inoculation; some was by the apparent, and local, elimination of malaria, bilharzia, and sleeping sickness; some was much simpler, obvious, and known to every non-medical person in the West: Use only clean water, wash the hands before a meal, encourage clean clothes, wash vegetables, avoid parasites. By such simple means the survival rate of infants was increased many times. (See Notes—Chapter Five, Note 14.)

All very admirable, but there is little food for the increased African population—300 million of them under fifteen years of age. There is plenty of land.[10] There is enough water—at a cost, but to grow food requires capital—simple capital, tools, seeds, and animals. This might cost no more or less than $500 per head. The capital does not exist in Africa, and others must provide $150 billion for this purpose. Put another way, each sub-Saharan born requires a matching $500 of investment in order that the child becomes a useful adult. This is far more difficult than keeping the child alive. Unfortunately, none of the aid agencies can ever think in a long enough timescale to address the long-term problem. Far easier to be compassionate today and lay up trouble for the future. This is a respectable form of improvidence. It is practiced by a veritable army of the good.

Nor is this a problem that will go away. Rural "congestion" or extreme density of population existed in Europe for generations in Southern Italy, parts of Ireland, and the Balkans. Such local overpopulation was solved by emigration or by industrialization,[11] but the emigration of poor, unskilled, illiterate people is no longer a possibility. The industrialization of most of Africa is an intensive capital exercise that has only to be mentioned to be dismissed. The African case, therefore, will continue to haunt those who think of it.

African overpopulation is not solved by pop concerts. A single concert may raise funds to keep alive a proportion of the population for a year. What then? Another concert? Each year nearly 30 million sub-Saharan babies are born. This means that each year someone, somewhere, in Africa should invest $15 billion, or more than the surplus product of half the United Nations. To state the figure is to realize that it is unlikely to happen. Yet, to keep each of those babies alive over and beyond the efforts of the mother may cost only $10. Three hundred million dollars to keep alive one year's crop of African babies is much easier. It may well be within the abilities of the aid agencies, if not a pop concert. The problem, never faced, is what happens next year, and the year after, and so on.

We live in a squeamish age. To state the African problem of population is to invite the use of birth control. Disease and hunger, perinatal mortality, and the loss of two-thirds of the children born before they reached the age of ten used to be the means of population control in Africa. No African educated at the London School of Economics or at Harvard is impressed when told that these were once the methods of population control in Europe too. If Africa can be visited by jet, then all the latest, high-tech methods of birth control should also be available.

Overpopulation cannot be gainsaid. If it is not solved in one way, it has always been solved in another. There is no avoiding this truth. In

Africa, population control will be famine, disease, or interfering with reproduction. There are other, even less acceptable, alternatives.[12]

Famine is a comparative term. It is entirely possible that tropical and subtropical Africans could survive for years on a diet half that of Europeans, say 1500 calories.[13] Disease has returned as a great controller of infant numbers, especially where there is any kind of social breakdown.[14] The problem with physical birth control methods is the same as it is in India, and likely to be much worse.[15]

Most countries in Africa, South Africa included, are probably beyond any comfortable ability to feed their increase. Even in South Africa the task is daunting. In the Republic, there are nearly 30 million Bantu. The Bantu birthrate is over one million a year. No one, of course, invests $500 per head, $500 million in all, each year in Bantu agriculture. This is far more important than the current "absence" of apartheid. Elsewhere in successful neo-Europe, in the Americas and Antipodes, and in parts of the developing world, local conditions have been met with Anglo-American agricultural techniques to make further population growth apparently unproblematic.

Bantu, like perhaps half of all Africans, use maize as a staple source of starch. This Amerindian plant has been raised to its high current potential by Anglo-American methods. The British ambition has been transferred all over the world: output per acre within a renewable system, a "rotation of crops." The American aim, originally with the target of output per man, was transformed by the vastly increased use of machinery, fertilizers, and plant breeding techniques into a much wider philosophy. When the two ambitions—of output per unit area and output per man-hour—coalesce, as in the more successful neo-Europes, the results are dramatic. This has been true of Canada, Australia, New Zealand, parts of South America, and Southern Africa. These neo-Europes all derived their systems from both Britain and the United States. The English legacy was rotation of crops and the essential involvement of livestock to make best use of the necessary grassland within the rotation. This spread wherever the British settled in the neo-Europes.

The same kind of philosophy, modified to circumstance, came to dominate advanced Western European countries. Scandinavia and Holland joined English husbandry methods with good transport and supplies of electricity to turn from butter, cheese, and beef production to the provision of liquid milk. By World War II liquid milk production had become the most important agricultural activity in Scandinavia, Holland, Switzerland, and the United Kingdom, in that order. Milk not drunk "fresh" was converted into the traditional butter and cheese and into the new condensed and dried product; milk was put into chocolate, into canned soup, into prepared foods of every kind, even into bread. Great play was made of milk in "health" terms.

In the United States milk became healthy in direct proportion to the number of dairy farmers and their influence on state legislatures. Thus, milk was healthier in New York State or Wisconsin than in South Dakota or Louisiana. In Europe milk was much healthier in Switzerland than in any of the Latin countries. In France milk was healthier in Normandy than in the Midi. Electricity and good transport made liquid milk a possibility all through the Alpine regions; and farmers in Austria, Bavaria, and northern Italy were offered the same opportunities as in Switzerland. In Switzerland in the 1930s, milk became so profitable as to be taxed to subsidize the Federal Railways.

Liquid milk became identified with the care of children, nursing mothers, and the frail of all ages. Milk ultimately became a symbolic product of the Welfare State, a prop to agriculture in times of depression, wholesome, non-carnal. The drinking of milk became a "good thing." After World War II, welfare milk in England became much more than a symbol, a shibboleth. When Mrs. Thatcher, as Minister of Education, removed the subsidy from schoolchildren's milk in 1971–72, she was labeled "Thatcher the milk-snatcher" by interested parties. In some countries milk was already suspect. It was accused of making children fat, liable to adult cholesterol problems, and even prone to acne. As a fashionable commodity, milk peaked sometime in the 1970s.[16]

In the United States the same process of Depression, plus refrigeration and good transport, drove northern and eastern dairy states into milk. Because the railroads between the Atlantic and the Great Lakes opened the "bonanza" states to the growth of wheat, millions of acres in the East went out of cultivation. In Kansas, Nebraska, and the Dakotas there was a restless search for inherent fertility, a "mining" of the soil, and a tendency to move on. There were dry seasons, big blows when crops had too little root growth, plagues of insect pests, no fertilizers; neither rotations nor good husbandry involved leaving bare fallow as the only alternative to grain cropping. This unsympathetic treatment of the soil ruined not only millions of acres west of the Mississippi, but millions of acres unable to compete in the East or in Europe as well. Between 1879 and 1939, enough land went out of arable cultivation in Europe and the old United States to give an annual bread ration to 500 million people. By the time the need for such huge increases in supply became obvious, other crops used the "old lands" of Europe and neo-Europe more profitably. Only in the 1960s would grain production widen to cover almost any flat field in temperate climates, if such use was economically appropriate.

The wide prairie was also to be found north of the forty-ninth Parallel. Between 49° N and some point in the middle 50°s, Canada west of the Great Lakes was another strip of bonanza wheat land on either side of the railroads, stretching for mile after mile. From 1879 onward there were three sorts of wheat crop. There was the virgin prairie, plowed twice and sown first in August; then the portion that had been summer fallowed; then that which had been plowed in the previous winter and harvested in the current year. Harvest in the following year was, there-fore, prolonged and easier to carry out before the advent of internal combustion engines.[17]

The internal combustion engine arrived on the scene just in time for World War I. Ex-London and -Paris buses gave troops what was often their last ride into the trenches; trucks of all kinds hauled food and ammu-nition, and specially built tractors hauled guns; combat aircraft and tanks became possible. The long-term effect of the internal combustion engine was greatest, however, in transport and agriculture. The tractor solved both the British and the American problem. Cultivation became more professional, more timely, and more efficient; rotation of crops and the proper exploitation of grassland other than by grazing or haymaking became much easier, so proper husbandry of the soil was more capably achieved. By using bred strains of both cereals and herbage crops, fertilizers, and pest control, output per acre potentially increased between 1920, when tractors first became "serious" and available, and, say, 1970, by at least four times in cereals and by six to eight times in grassland. Output per man rose to such a level that in 1970 it was possible to grow a four-ton crop of wheat in England with one man-day per acre. In America, half the input of labor was applied to each acre, but the acre did not produce four tons of wheat. On the other hand, state-of-the-art techniques produced more maize-corn per man-hour in Iowa than anywhere else on earth, if that were wanted—even if Americans, New Zealanders, Australians, and Englishmen were all using the same machinery.[18]

Canadian cereals have been important since the 1870s. If world markets were open, Canadian barley, at one-third the cost of production in Europe, would be as important as "hard" bread-wheat or American maize. As it is, Western Europe, comprising the biggest market before World War II by its imports of one-third of all grain requirements in an average year, is now a net exporter. Canadian farming has had to adapt to the same crops as Old and New England—fruit production; vegetables; grain turned into meat, eggs, milk, butter, and cheese—and much more concern for the herbage crops than existed a hundred years ago.

Australia and New Zealand were countries whose formative years before 1939 were influenced by technology that, in turn, made them both part of the English economy. Australia, now settled for more than two centuries, originally starved when the convicts tried to feed themselves. Indeed, it would be twenty years before the raw colony of the land around Sydney would simply feed itself, let alone have a surplus for visiting ships or new arrivals. The state of the Aboriginal inhabitants is worthy of note. They were hunter-gatherers and would remain so despite the white invasion because there are few native plants and no edible native animals that can be domesticated. The Aboriginal people of the southeast corner of Australia may or may not have known other Aborigines. The individual Abo tribes may or may not have been similar people; they may or may not have had the same sort of habits. It is unlikely that indigenous people in lush New South Wales had the same patterns of behavior as people who survived round Alice Springs. The likely answer is that each group of Aborigines, perhaps an extended family or a small tribe, had a huge area of land to support them. There are berries, roots, and meat from marsupials (two-thirds of all native Australian mammals), fish, and birds. There are no ruminants of any kind, and no apes, monkeys, or baboons. There are few animals resembling any European species, the most obvious being the wild dog called the dingo. There are two interesting great birds—a black swan and a white eagle. There are few carrion birds—no vultures—but sixty sorts of parrot. There are many edible birds—pigeon, duck, geese, plover, quail—all unique to Australia. There is the emu, equivalent to the ostrich of Africa and the rhea of South America. The finest freshwater fish is the Murray cod, sometimes as much as 45 kg (100 lb) in weight. There are many saltwater fish and at least two turtles that humans can find useful as food. There are also crocodiles in the north, some having swum across the Tasman Sea from the East Indies. There are two other peculiarities. There are koala bears that live on eucalyptus leaves so tainted that koala flesh is unattractive to all predators, including humans. Second, there is no native method of recycling dung from ruminants; the dung beetle (scarab) had to be imported from Africa to deal with mountains of ancient, unrotted, fibrous dung from imported ruminant animals.[19]

The native, indigenous, ancient Aborigine had a thin life, but it was his own. He developed, as is known, special spiritual qualities to deal with the feast-famine syndrome; a special response to the challenge of a tummy first full, then empty; a special enzyme preventing aches during long periods of low intake, a condition that would produce much pain for a white man. The Aboriginal attitudes to birth control and the survival of the old were severely practical. There were few unfit in an indigenous tribe, but they suffered from the white invasion. The first agents of destruction were not, as ever, white men themselves, but the parasites they brought with them.[20]

Within months of the arrival of the First Fleet there was an outbreak of a severe disease among the native people. Was it smallpox? If so, it produced the same result as it did in Mexico and Peru. There was little further competition from the Aborigines in the area of Sydney. The next invaders, which moved more visibly than microbes, were pigs. They were released near Sydney in 1789 and ranged over the whole eastern third of Australia and much of South Australia. Regardless of breed, feral pigs are selected by nature to survive if they are thin, long-legged, with snouts adapted to burrowing, and with huge tusks in the male. This process of selection takes about ten generations, and is quicker than the reverse, which can produce a good bacon pig out of a modern wild boar. Wild pigs in both America and Australia have the same nickname—"razorback."[21] They were fierce, successful as a species, and capable of killing a cow, a horse, or a man with their saber tusks. Despite all the modern efforts at killing swine with gun and lance and poison, wild boar still figures in the Australian landscape as a semi-parasite, semi-independent animal, like the rat. Unlike the rat, razorbacks make for good eating.

Cattle became feral earlier than pigs. The first Australian cattle were loosed from those brought over on board HMS *Sirius*. They were not English, but South African. No one now knows what their bloodlines were, but they were great survivors. In 1789 eight animals strayed off, and by 1804, fifteen years later, the herds ("mobs" in convict Australian) numbered nearly 10,000. They were untamable, a resource of wild food for anyone in the bush and for any escaped convict or "bush-ranger." By 1830, despite an effort to kill African feral cattle and substitute European alternatives, there were still nearly 400,000; by 1850 there were said to be a million. Who counted? The introduction of the rabbit and its destruction of Australian sheep grazing is well-known. Less well-known, less damaging but bad enough, was the import of the European rat.[22]

Sheep made Australia. Wool was the first crop to be a commercial success. There are native grazing plants in Australia, grasses and sedges, but no legumes. These were introduced and largely spread by sheep. The merino, introduced in the early days, produced an average of less than 1.5 kg (3 lb) per fleece in 1850. By 1900 this figure had doubled, by careful selection and adaptation of Merino-type sheep and by introducing European herbage seeds. Wool remained the largest export by value until the 1960s. In the bicentennial year of 1988, appropriately enough, wool overtook coal as the greatest single Australian export. Its position in the future depends on the merino wool price, which has ranged between A$2 and A$15 per kilogram in the last twenty-five years, based on the strength of other currencies, international prosperity, and, to a lesser extent, fashion. Initially, merino wool from Australia was only of value because of English technology in spinning and weaving and finishing. Today, every advanced country buys and uses Australian wool.

Wheat production in Australia followed the curve of the Australian (white) population. Initially only the surplus was exported. In the ferocious drought year of 1902, wheat was actually imported. (Modern Australians would find this hard to believe.)

Breaking land in the absence of modern tractors was more difficult in Australia than in America, Canada, or New Zealand. Soil often lay in pits and troughs, and tree stumps proved impossible to handle economically before the native invention of the stump-jump plow. Arable land might take ten years to become fertile. In Australia, even more than in America, the shortage of manpower was always more serious than the shortage of land, a problem that has never existed. Before the introduction of superphosphate in the 1880s, yields were lower than in medieval England, as low as ten to twelve bushels per acre, less than one ton per hectare. To be fair to Australia, this was about the same as contemporary yields in Southern Russia where there was much better soil. Together with superphosphate, better management of the soil helped defeat drought, and yields rose in those areas with more than 20 in (500 mm) of annual rainfall. Wheat was pushed out of the higher-rainfall areas, however, and became rotational.

Cattle, largely feral until 1900, were important as a source of hides, tallow, and salted meat before 1880. Refrigeration made the export of butter, cheese, and frozen or chilled beef, mutton, and lamb possible. Great efforts were made to round up the wild cattle or make better use with imported beef or dairy bulls. By 1914 there was an important refrigerated trade, with at least one ship a week leaving each of the main ports. Successful as this development was, Australian beef did not compete in quality or price with beef from Argentina. Argentina was 7000 miles nearer Europe and the grazing was better. There may have been significant differences in the feral cattle stock: Longhorn Spanish of the sixteenth century, Anglo-African of the nineteenth. Did this factor make for higher-quality beef from the River Plate?

Dairying in Australia started in Victoria, then spread to New South Wales and Tasmania. Ryegrass, cocksfoot, and clover were sown on partly cleared land. Pastures took as long as arable land to come into full production. Sometimes it seems that European grasses had to turn into something uniquely Antipodean in order to thrive. This is true of clover and ryegrass in both Australia and New Zealand, and even of agrostis in Western Australia.

New Zealand had a much more favorable climate than Australia for the successful invasion of European flora and fauna. The European human was less favored. The Maoris were more numerous, more advanced, and more warlike than the Australian Aborigines. They were also more crowded by a factor of over 100 to 1 on the North Island in 1850. The only land mammals before the white man arrived were the two brought in by the Maoris—an edible dog and a black rat; both are now extinct or very rare. The early Europeans imported ferrets, cats, stoats, and weasels, which did so much damage so quickly that three islands had to be established as sanctuaries for native fauna. Acclimatization has been the name of the game for settlement in New Zealand.

Pheasants, five kinds of deer, ducks, and brown and rainbow trout all colonized with ease. So did grain of every kind, rich grasses, fruit trees, vines, and, long before any of these, white man's diseases. The one great failure was the salmon. More than a hundred efforts to colonize it failed, regardless of whether the salmon was from the Atlantic or Pacific.

The Maoris were debilitated by syphilis acquired from white sailors off whalers and sealing ships, and spread by the Maori practice of polygamy and sexual hospitality. Within a generation of Captain Cook's first arrival in 1769–70, venereal disease had joined Maori infanticide as a population control. The Maori population plummeted. Within another generation Maoris were also dying of "consumption." By 1830 there were thousands of muskets on the islands, acquired by Maoris in exchange for European crops grown under European direction, for visiting Europeans in European ships. In 1830–31, there were fewer than 800 whites in all of New Zealand. Inside fourteen months, Australia alone exported 8000 muskets to New Zealand; and three times that number came from Europe. In 1835 Charles Darwin arrived on a visit and found hundreds of acres of white man's crops, pigs, horses, and cattle—wild and in profusion—as well as rats everywhere.

There does not seem to have been an outbreak of smallpox in New Zealand comparable to those in the Americas or Australia, but measles acted as powerfully as smallpox in Australia. Missionaries were very active in the 1830s and 1840s, and they tried to introduce Maoris to examples of white culture other than alcohol, tobacco, gunpowder, muskets and barley, wheat, potatoes, clover, apples, pears, apricots, and peaches. By 1840, when the resident white population in New Zealand was less than 2000, the Maori population had been reduced to 60,000 by disease. By 1860, when the Maori Wars started, the Maori race was half what it had been only fifty years previously. By the end of the wars the Maori population was only about 40,000, that of the whites over 250,000. The wars did not make much difference to numbers, as always. Disease killed more Maoris than muskets did. It was the gold rush of the 1860s that brought whites to New Zealand. As in California and Australia, the chief long-term effect of the gold rush was the permanent increase of the white population. Gold rushes after a generation leave so many people per million ounces extracted. This is an important and very interesting ratio yet to be established.

No one thinks of New Zealand today as a gold mine, unless the gold is butter. It is the pastoral products of the country that matter. Lamb, butter, cheese, and, to a lesser extent, beef are the products of this most efficient grazing country. Almost no nitrogen is used in fertilizer form. Almost every grazing field is supported by an abundance of clover that draws nitrogen from the air and enriches the soil, along with the companion grasses and the clover itself. The clover seed originally came from England. Kent, Suffolk, Devon, and the Midland counties are represented in the genes of New Zealand clover. New Zealand White is a definite type, more prolific than its ancestors, and encouraged by the magnificent climate, the most suitable for clover in the world. For twenty years clover did not thrive in New Zealand because there were no bees to work their fertility-giving magic upon the flowers. Bees were imported in 1839, and since that date, clover and bees have been part of the essential fabric of New Zealand life. Clover makes New Zealand pasture the most efficient in the world. Bees made the conqueror of Everest.[23]

Clover, in an Atlantic context, produces its own herbage, and "subscribes" up to the equivalent of over 100 "units" of nitrogen.[24] In some parts of Europe, nitrogen gain from clover is so small as to make its culture uneconomic. In Holland, West Germany, Scandinavia, some parts of Eastern England, and on specialist farms devoted to silage making all over Western Europe, grassland may contain no clover at all. For nitrogen, the farmer depends upon the chemical company. In some systems, 300 "units" of bag nitrogen are used, three to five times what clover could provide. There is a straight-line payoff between nitrogen usage on suitable grassland and yield, and this line does not change on suitable soil, species of grass, and climate until the 500 "units" level is reached. In New Zealand, no one has ever made any money using bag nitrogen.

Phosphates are another matter. The use of superphosphate manures came into fashion only after their success in Australia.[25] They were not in general use on New Zealand pastures until after World War I. Used together with tractors, milking machines, and herd-testing to improve butterfat, the pastures of New Zealand started to support a considerable secondary industry. Milk was turned into butter and packed for shipment in cooperatives; lambs were slaughtered and frozen or chilled for transport over 13,000 miles to England; wool was sorted and graded and sold by a Wool Board. Beef, wheat, and sisal, which had been important in the early part of the century, gave way almost entirely to the processing of clover. Modern New Zealand was formed by exploiting clover for fifty years, from 1920 to 1970. It is fair to say that if the clover had not proved to be the boon it was, New Zealanders would have found something else to exploit as they have more recently—fine wines, deer-farming, tourism, and "kiwi fruit."[26] It is also fair to say that New Zealand might never have prospered without clover. It is a country built on clover. All over the islands there is not one statue, amongst many other statues, to the humble Wild White Clover.

The Argentine and part of Uruguay became involved with European food for a shorter period. Beef was not important as an export from the Plate until after 1900. The beef came from the pampas, and it had been there since before 1580 when the first permanent successful Spanish settlements were made. Cattle, not native to any of the Americas, had presumably been left somewhere by former (failed) settlers. The pampas of the Plate were virtually free of any indigenous competition for the cattle, nor were there many predators. Indeed, the pampas were originally virtually empty. There was nothing for the jaguar and puma to eat on the plains until horses and cattle arrived. The predators came down from the mountains when the food appeared. So did the Amerindians. The longhorn cattle resembled those of Texas, having descended from the same Iberian stock. Between, say, 1550 and 1850, they developed over more than 120 generations into fierce tribal animals, roaming in herds like the North American bison. Long of horn, speedy in reaction, sure of foot, they had been selected by their environment into two groups, the quick and the dead. As elsewhere only the fit survived.

The multiplication process was sure, producing an estimated 50 million by 1750. (Who counted them?) Thousands were killed every year for the hides. (There was not much tallow in them.) They were mean, thin, rangy cattle, more dangerous, more difficult to tame than the accompanying wild horses. Living with them and off them, having changed their habits, were Plains Indians, who became carnivorous as a consequence of an ample supply of feral Iberian animals.

When the Anglos arrived in Texas, the Argentine, or Uruguay, they sought to improve the wild cattle. Herefords (called "hurfords" in Texas), Shorthorns, Devons, and Aberdeen-Angus were all brought in to improve the native stock. In the Argentine, agriculture was neglected in the Spanish way; this led to a wheat shortage in the 1870s in a country capable, even then, of exporting several million tons a year. In that same decade, the last of the Indian Wars cleared the Plate pampas, and huge areas were sold, feral cattle and horses included, to largely English and American settlers for £80 per square "league" of 6669 acres. This amounted to less than 3 pence per acre, 15 shillings per hectare.

The second son of a Gloucestershire landlord bought £10,000 worth of this land in 1882. This amounted to over 323,760 hectares (800,000 acres), or over 1250 square miles. On this land were an estimated 6000 cattle and 10,000 horses with neither a fence nor hedge in sight, and more than 400 Indian families living off the cattle and horses. The "native" grasses, of course, were Iberian. The introduction of alfalfa (lucerne), British grasses, European cereals, and bred strains of maize brought in from the United States transformed the situation. The Indians became agricultural workers and cowboys; the cattle were thinned and improved; the horses were transformed by the careful choice of stallions; and a railway was built to a central wheat silo. Wheat, beef, and live horses were exported. By 1910 the property contained five towns, railways, electric generators, and hundreds of miles of roads. The estate was sold to a meatpacking company on the death of the childless pioneer. The incomparable Eva Perón was born in one of the towns.

It was Eva's husband who brought the export trade of the Argentine to an end. In 1930 the country was the sixth richest in the world. A combination of low primary food prices, war, and, above all, bad government made the Argentine twentieth in order in 1960. In 1985 the country was deep in debt, and Perón had greatly assisted the process. Beef was eaten at home rather than exported. Urbanization and secondary industries were much encouraged. Voters were bribed by competitive political parties, and brutal regimes stifled enterprise as well as inhibiting freedom. The social stability that existed in Australia and New Zealand was absent in the Argentine. Many English have no doubt that the absence of a fair legal system was the cause. In essential English Common Law, the Anzac countries follow the United States; they have their own ways of dealing with other matters. Argentines were said to be 95 percent excitable, carnivorous, and un-English. Peronista law was arbitrary, corrupt, and commercially difficult.[27]

There is another non-racial reason. The population density of Australia is two people per square kilometer, while that of the Argentine is ten. The agricultural production of the Argentine is far less per unit area than the Australian. Australia, the lucky country, is far richer in natural resources and has minerals beyond the dreams of the Argentine. Argentine urbanization is expensive—unconvincing in economic terms. Although "new Australians" come from every country in Southern Europe, the population is much more homogenous than in Argentina, and Australia does not have indigenous people resentful of a much richer Europe-oriented class. When the European dominance, especially English dominance, of Argentine agriculture was brought to an end in the late 1940s, progress ceased. There have been no advances since comparable to those in Europe, the United States, Australia, and New Zealand. The agriculture of the Argentine is now backward. Concentration on the urban proletariat and its perceived needs is as damaging as the same policy in Third World countries, and with the same results.

The failure of the Argentine, the most populous Southern Hemisphere neo-Europe,[28] should be compared with New Zealand, the most homogenous neo-European country. The population of New Zealand is only 3.5 million, with a density of 12 per square kilometer, compared with over 5000 for Hong Kong, 30 for the continental United States, and 360 for England.[29] The prognosis for New Zealand is good. Low population density combines with unpolluted, fragrant, productive countryside and efficient industry. Even the restrictive practices of twenty years ago have been curbed. Racial problems are less onerous than those of Australia, much less onerous than those of the United States; few whites or Maoris really resent intermarriage, which is one key to racial harmony.

Only a hundred years old in 1940, New Zealand became the richest nation in the world because of a secure agricultural base. Since then, other countries have become richer, as evaluated by the United Nations. The change in the world agricultural scene since 1960 has been a challenge which New Zealanders have met. The challenge has been turned into an opportunity.

The mild, equality-conscious, social security–minded New Zealanders surprised themselves. Like other countries that survived the Forces of Change, the New Zealanders proved that when the going gets tough, the tough get going. Like that of Australia, the New Zealand Labor Party abolished its belief in planning, embraced the free market, and welcomed "Thatcherite" reforms. Such a turnaround indicates, at the very minimum, a vigorous political culture. It may also represent the renewal of the Left, conscious of the failure of socialism, as with Blairism in the United Kingdom.

In one other neo-European Southern Hemisphere country, socialism has never entered the equation. South Africa, unlike Canada, the Argentine,

Australia, and New Zealand, has never produced any form of socialism in any party. It has a long and complicated history. In 1910 the Union of South Africa was part of the British Empire. This lasted fifty years until 1960 when Harold Macmillan made his "wind of change" speech in Cape Town. A few months later, South Africa left the Commonwealth.

For two centuries after its "discovery" by the Portuguese in 1487, South Africa was little more than a barren shoreline with a few natural harbors, an inconvenient land to be rounded. In 1654, occupied by forty-nine Dutchmen, Cape Town slowly became a stop for water, then for food and refreshment. By 1700 there were about 1500 Dutch and French Huguenots in the Cape. At that time, there were only about 50,000 Bushmen and Hottentots west of what is now the Fish River. Eastward, in modern Natal, the Orange Free State, and Transvaal, there were as many as perhaps a million settled, cattle-raising Bantu living on both slopes of the Drakensburg.

As is known, the Dutch were pushed north by the British, and then defeated by them. In 1902, when "peace" arrived, there were probably 1.2 million whites, outnumbered by nearly 4 million Bantu and half a million Cape Colored and Indians.

South Africa is a country tormented by hatred, racism, and the force of population growth. The tragedy of its history is not only in its wickedness, but must also include the forces inherent in human population increase. In the middle of all the sharp political debate it is worth noting that South Africa is at the limit of all but the best possible agricultural husbandry. Like its black-ruled neighbors, it needs only a little "bad luck" to go hungry.

By the time of the Union in 1910, the white population was about 1.2 million. Today it is rather less than five times the 1910 figure. In 1910, the non-white population was about 4.6 million; today it is about eight times the 1910 figure. By 2020 it is likely that there will be 5.5 million whites and as many as 50–60 million non-whites, perhaps more. The absolute and relative increase is significant enough and does much to explain the "laager" mentality of the stubborn whites.

Political concentration upon the evils of apartheid has obscured the very real demographic problems. The white population increase is about 1 percent, while that of the non-white population is at least twice as great. Non-white birthrates have fallen from a high of over

4.5 percent in the 1950s to the present level of about 3.5 percent, with non-white infant mortality higher than that of white infants. However, an increase of 2 percent a year, unmatched by agricultural increase and investment, is likely to cause serious trouble by 2020, if not before.

Two percent a year means a doubling of population every thirty years. It is unlikely that South Africa can double her agricultural production at present-day relative prices, or perform any comparable miracle. As for providing the capital for jobs for between 500,000 and 750,000 who come onto the job market each year, that is another challenge. South Africa's mineral wealth depends heavily on cheap coal without which many gold mines would be unprofitable. In turn, all the minerals—coal, gold, copper, uranium, and diamond—depend on cheap food. South African yields of maize and European cereals are up to world standards on white farms that use tractors, modern implements, hybrid or pedigree seed, fertilizers, pest control, irrigation, and so forth. On the overcrowded little patches of land in Bantu husbandry, "yield" is another matter altogether. Output is not properly measured, since grain is grown for subsistence only. The homelands, of course, do not feed many "workers," only men, women, and children not working in South Africa proper. The homelands have a population density many times greater than the white areas. It is this lesser-known fact that is at least as important as the segregation of black workers in places like Soweto.

Although apartheid was abolished practically overnight and there was an attempt to establish an earthly paradise, the same danger exists as it does in other Third World countries: overconcentration on the town, promotion of uneconomic industries, low prices for farm products, agricultural underproduction, and lots of rural "bad luck." This has led to poor performance in every African country, including South Africa. In each of the others, of course, there are special factors much cited by apologists. The truth remains that in any foreseeable political future, South Africa has to depend upon an industrial base founded on mineral wealth. Both are dependent in turn upon food supplies increasing faster than population. This is unlikely to happen unless Government attitudes change. There is also a burgeoning HIV/AIDS problem, fuelled by sexual energy.

One of the features of the colonial phase of many Third World countries was that subsistence was left to the natives to work out for themselves while the expertise of Europeans was applied to export crops. This argument has been much deployed by anti-Imperialists in the United States of America. They are not always conscious, of course, that the same criteria existed in Latin America, operating for the benefit of American consumers. Among all the developing nations one great country has probably done more than most to lift itself by its own bootstraps. That country is India.

There was, of course, a long way to go. India is less fortunate than most countries in its climate, in its huge area of land unsuitable for cultivation, in the high proportion of suitable land already in arable, and in the tendency of the main Indian cultures to be fatalistic. India's population density is the same as the whole of the United Kingdom, 250 per square kilometer (97 square miles). Unlike the United Kingdom, Indian population, and therefore density, were increasing at more than 2 percent per annum. Before Independence, population growth was only about 1.3 percent, but food production was growing at less than this figure. Indian nationalists claim that this was because of concentration upon the export sector. As the chief exports of India before independence in 1947 were inedible—jute, raw and manufactured cotton, tea, and, until 1908, opium—this argument is unconvincing. The chief agricultural exports since independence in 1947 have been—surprise, surprise—the same, but of course inedible products still occupy land.[30]

Early Indian plans for reinvigorating the country after several centuries of European dominance were based on an industrial sector, especially a heavy industrial sector. This plan poured capital into capital-intensive plants at the expense of less capital-intensive consumer goods and favored a static farm sector. In years of bad luck/ weather—1958, 1967, 1973—India had to rely on foreign aid merely to maintain basic food levels in the villages that had failed to grow enough to subsist, as in the European Middle Ages. In good years—1950, 1955, 1962, 1965, 1971—the situation looked much more optimistic; the talk both inside and outside India was of surpluses (even exports), and the world food situation was viewed in a more favorable hue. This rosy perspective lasted until the next bad year. The swings between good and bad years were beyond the ability of storage to cope, being as much as 25 percent on average. Losses during storage and distribution, from India's host of rodent and insect pests, were rather high, perhaps as much as 30 percent. Not enough care, attention, and imagination were being applied to agriculture. This was all characteristically socialist, and the same faults have occurred in the last century in every "planned" economy of whatever type. The universal mistake has been a failure of recognition. A strategy that encourages the industrial sector is only valid if the agricultural area produces a sufficient surplus to feed the industrial worker. In the event of crop failure or food shortage, the industrial sector may fare worse than the peasants. If this is reversed by the planners, the peasants object to food that they have grown being taken away from them and their families. This has happened all over the socialist world. The forecasts that university economists make regarding planned economies are not always foolproof; in fact, they are often the reverse.

India's increase in food production has gone through several stages. The first, immediately after Independence, was to increase traditional irrigation and apply more fertilizer. There was a huge program of drilling wells all over India to irrigate land to increase rice production. Rice increased in total yield by about one-quarter in the first decade of independence, wheat by rather less. Much emphasis was placed upon a so-called "Community Development Program." This produced far less yield increase than better irrigation, more fertilizer, and more labor applied to more land in cultivation.

The only social or political change whose benefit could be measured was the abolition of the zamindari system of tax collection. The zamindar was a traditional, pre-British tax farmer, operating in Bengal. For reasons of administrative convenience, the British made these tax farmers virtual landlords. They also became a hereditary class, and the zamindari system was imposed on other areas of India. To the British, who nominally arranged the theoretical level of tax assessment, the system seemed just. To the Indian peasant, subjected to pressure from the zamindar, who might combine money lending with tax collection, the whole system was corrupt and crudely unfair. The zamindars often became a privileged group of virtual landlords of large estates. The peasants, meanwhile, were in debt servitude. More important than any political or economic "planning" was the arrival of the so-called Green Revolution. This was based on new varieties of cereals capable of benefiting from more moisture and fertilizer and making better use of both. This technology had been developed in countries outside Europe and the neo-Europes such as Japan. In the 1960s, it became a "revolution" in others. In India, the first harvest after the drought of 1968 showed an increase in grain production of nearly 30 percent. Because rice is more difficult to hybridize than wheat, new varieties have had less of an impact in the irrigated portion of Indian arable agriculture. Irrigation, always a strong point in India, today approaches one hectare for every three planted with food grains, usually rice. The other grains, in order of tonnage, are sorghum, millet, and wheat. The most impressive increases in productivity have been made with wheat, as in the First World. Indian wheat yields per hectare are now ahead of those in the ex–Soviet Union, and about a third of those in Western Europe. In most years there is a wheat surplus in India available for export. Many opportunities exist to double-crop in India, the limitations being fertilizer for each crop and fuel for the irrigation pumps. Nonetheless, however well the economy appears to be managed, there is one time bomb ticking away, as in all Third World countries.

Peasants can be satisfied with about 220 kg (500 lb) of grain per head per year. Of this, 80 percent (176 kg/400 lb) is eaten as cereal products. The rest, a modest 20 percent, is eaten as the product of domesticated animals, such as milk, butter, eggs, and meat. In India, as in every other country, the rich eat as well as rich people in the First World. Such people eat more than a ton of grain a year—10 percent as cereals and cereal products such as pasta and bread, and 90 percent as the products of animals. The difference in food consumption between the rich person in Bombay and the average European or neo-European is not great. The difference between the film director in Bombay and his fellow countryman, the peasant on the plains, is very great. The peasant eats much less.

The modern history of eating has always been that the rich prefer meat, eggs, milk, and so forth, and as soon as they have more money, all people have eaten more grain, not as grain, but as converted by domestic animals. The trick is to prevent the majority of peasants in poor countries from eating like the majority of farmers in Europe or neo-Europes. This rationing by price means that, of India's 1 billion people, today 900 million poor each consume about 0.25 ton per head per year. The 100 million richer Indians consume about a ton per head per year. This means a total requirement of 325 million tons a year. If even half the "poor" consumed at the rate of the "rich," the requirement would rise from 325 million tons a year to 675 million tons. If, more reasonably, only 1 percent of the "poor" switched from being "poor" at 0.25 ton per year to being "rich" at 1 ton per year, it would mean an extra 7.25 million tons a year. This is more than the extra grain, 5 million tons, needed each year to deal with the extra population. The extra population ratio is well understood. If, as in India, there are about 2.1 percent extra people each year and 2.8 percent extra grain each year, happiness results. If the two figures are reversed, there is hunger, starvation, and an occasional famine.

India and a hundred other countries, including the ex-USSR, depend upon the population not changing its habits too much. That means not allowing the peasant sector too much money to buy goodies like milk, meat, and eggs. On the other hand, if the peasants are not given enough money, they do not produce, and deliveries fall. This has happened throughout the ex–Eastern bloc and in most of Africa. In China, the rulers have realized, since 1979, that peasants have got to be energized by the market. Since that date the Chinese peasant has had the highest sustained increase in productivity in the world, said to be as much as 12 percent per year; Chinese food increases per annum now comfortably exceed the Indian, having lagged for thirty years after 1948 because of civil war, revolution, and other political problems.

This time bomb apart, India seems well set to emulate Western Europe and the neo-Europes, where the "Green Revolution" (so-called) has been going on for the last generation and a half, since the turnaround in the world food situation that started in the 1950s. It has been an evolutionary process, not a revolution. The momentum of evolutions can be maintained better than that of revolutions. There is no reason to believe that India should not be able to improve its position by a significant proportion each year. There remains plenty of room for improvement, especially in low-level control measures, village pest control, and interdiction against field ruminants, small birds, and insects. Pests still take more than 30 percent of the potential crop, far more than in China. It has always been hard to persuade farmers that controlling pests is the easiest way to increase production; Indians are no exception.

America and Europe were completely different agriculturally a century ago; the inexorable Forces of Change have made the pattern of development on the two continents much more similar. A century ago American agriculture was characterized by four virtues.

First, inputs to farms were cheap, far cheaper than in Europe; land, of course, was far less expensive, but so were farm implements, animals, and even taxes. Ultimately this arose from the very low density of population in the United States compared with Western Europe.

Second, output prices were necessarily much higher than in Europe in relation to input prices. Put another way, because of the low cost of inputs, value added (however measured) was much higher in America than in Europe.

Third, land tenure, usually ownership-plus-mortgage, allowed farmers to adopt technologically advanced methods. In areas where there were sharecropping agreements, British-style tenancies, or other forms of long lease, innovation was much less likely to be pursued. Until recently, landlords in Europe determined farming methods in a way that Americans generally would regard as backward.

Finally, the American system of freedom of information was virtually unique in the agricultural world in 1876. "Cow" colleges, financed by the land grants in the Morrill Act of 1862, widely advertised genuine research; there were also magicians and medicine men not much better than snake-oil salesmen. From this system grew the tradition, now universal in the First World, whereby farmers, alone of all producers, exchange information in a way unknown in mining or transport or manufacture. Most farmers today do not resent other farmers knowing the secret of their success.[31]

There were financial crises throughout the period before the 1940s. The cause of the crisis is always the same, whether it occurs in 1873, 1893, 1907, or the 1920s. Agricultural production is elastic. Demand for food is not. This means that if food output increases by X percent, food prices decline by more than X percent. In order to offset a loss in total income, farmers who can afford to do so increase total output. This has the effect of increasing total production of food, and the price inexorably declines further. During the 1920s, food prices declined in real terms by more than any farmer's ability to cope. By 1933, farm gate prices were only 20 percent of what they had been in 1920. Whether the Great Depression was partially caused by the previous dozen years of low agricultural prices will be debated for years.

Before the 1920s and 1930s, in the then less developed countries such as France, Italy, and Germany, lower prices at the farm gate were not as devastating as in the neo-Europes. Peasants did not have to buy many inputs. Capital inputs such as machinery could be deferred. Animals were bred on the farm; food for the family was grown at home; workers were paid in kind or dismissed; fertilizer was generated in the course of the ordinary rotations and by the preservation of animal residues. Peasants used cash for luxuries, not necessities. If there was no cash, retrenchment was in order. This happened in Continental Europe whenever the growth in agricultural output exceeded the growth of population. After the railroads, the steamships, and the refrigerated vessels, it was not only local agricultural output that affected prices in Europe; the output of every neo-Europe fed into the worldwide system. Whatever countries tried to do to insulate themselves against price changes in other places, in the end, economics could not be defeated. Nevertheless, European peasant communities were often much better able to sustain a slump than the industrial workers in the towns. At minimum, unless incompetent, they fed themselves. Many European peasants went without tea or coffee when times were hard, but they were far better nourished than townspeople.

In the United States in the 1930s, such an outcome was impossible. Every farm was part of a much wider network that a later generation would call "agri-business." This involved farm machinery, motor vehicles, electricity in all its forms, fertilizers and chemicals, petroleum, water, gas, textiles, metal, rubber, glass, wood, and paper and plastic products. A huge and rising service element was involved with the complex business of getting the food to the consumer's mouth. These trades, obviously, could not be allowed to go bankrupt. The farmer was saved in the United States because he was part of a much wider network. In much of Europe and most of the rest of the world, the self-sufficient peasant retrenched. Such an outcome was unlikely in the United States where a kind of provision wasneeded for agricultural support.

Whatever it was called, the pattern set up compensatory devices. These devices gave the farmer more compensation for his product than he would have received from the market. Whether called "guarantees" or "subsidies" or "controls," the devices worked in the same way in the United States, Canada, Australia, New Zealand, South Africa, and some other countries. In Britain, the devices were not properly in place until World War II. In Latin America, their absence did much to destroy the viability of commercial agriculture in countries like the Argentine, Chile, Mexico, and Brazil.

In the United States, farmers were paid to reduce the area planted with specific products. Storage facilities were built and loan programs instituted to regulate the rate at which products came to market. Sometimes the methods were bizarre: little pigs destroyed, grain burnt in industrial boilers, cotton piled up to rot. Meanwhile, other people, even in the United States, were hungry, suffered from malnutrition, or could not clothe themselves properly. By the end of the 1930s the U.S. agricultural support programs had reached a generally acceptable level of activity that raised compensation for the farmer while controlling output at a level that neither forced up prices too much nor meant that a great deal of surplus production had to be destroyed.[32]

World War II changed the agricultural scene throughout the world. A combination of shortages and fragmented transport made discrete areas of Western Europe very hungry by VE Day; left to themselves, the inhabitants would have been even hungrier for the next five years. In Eastern Europe, the combination of mindless Nazi brutality and calculated Communist social engineering made for the extremes of starvation and famine. In Eastern Europe between 1941 and 1948, more people died from shortage of food and the consequence diseases than were killed in battle. Some, of course, were meant to die. These were Jews, some of the middle classes, and any non-Communist who could not escape or make peace with the new rulers. No one will ever know the full tally, nor will anyone ever know which of the two totalitarian regimes killed more people.[33]

Outside Europe, disruption of transport and other infrastructures made for hunger and famine throughout Asia. India was badly affected because there was both a shortage of shipping and a shortage of rail transport within India. China went into a long period of darkness resulting from the Japanese War, followed by the Civil War, and later by the confusion of the Great Leap Forward (1937–72). None of these disruptions, or the nationalization of farms, helped the hungry or starving. In Japan itself, rations for the natives in 1945–48 were down to about two-thirds of what they had been in the 1930s. There were surpluses due to poor transport—Australia and New Zealand could not export all they produced. In the Argentine, meat consumption was double that of 1938. Farms only a few score miles from big towns in France were flush with food that could not be distributed. In Germany all civilian railways and roads into Berlin were impassable in the summer of 1945 and deficit areas in the big towns in occupied Western Germany were as hungry as Holland had been a year before. Some farmers in Bavaria, however, were living as well as ever, conducting barter deals with the occupying Allies. There was some effort in democratic Europe to honor a relatively fair rationing system. Only in Communist countries was food used as an overt political weapon. The commissar fed well, as did the army and the secret police. "Heavy" workers and the "productive" were reasonably well fed, if bored. Those the regime regarded as unnecessary were half-starved. In some countries, a thriving parallel existed— the "free" or black market. There were strange currencies that citizens preferred to the often worthless paper money: cigarettes in Germany, petrol coupons in France, olive oil in Italy. The prudent neither smoked, nor used a car, nor cooked with oil. Very surprising fortunes were made by the abstemious. At the end of World War II, some advanced economies faced difficulties with their food supply, but these were soon overcome by three agricultural advances that laid the groundwork for the huge yields possible today.

The political masters of the Western World at the end of World War II saw food shortage as one of the great failings. Such a belief was justified. There were great dislocations of normal channels of distribution and supply in almost every country in Europe and in much of Africa and Asia. The food supply of perhaps as many as half the humans alive in 1945 had been adversely affected by the War. There was a serious shortage of shipping, especially specialized ships such as refrigerated cargo liners. Furthermore, areas of surplus had been prejudiced by the long slump in demand that had existed for many years before 1940. Even the United States, for the first time in history, had a marginal deficit between domestic food available and optimum food requirements. This was only between 1935 and 1940, and was due primarily to New Deal restrictions on farm output. As soon as the administration knew what was happening, the fault was corrected. The deficit was largely expressed by malnutrition among the poor and unemployed, rather than by any propensity to import food from other countries. None of the efforts of the politicians would have had any serious effect upon the world food shortage without advances in three areas of science and technology. All of these, in the end, derived from work done in other areas, often in pursuit of success in war. Almost literally, swords were beaten into better plowshares.

These advances derived directly from engineering, chemistry, and biology. In engineering, the greatly improved metallurgy, machine-tool technology, and batch production methods that had made possible tanks, aircraft, and guns in huge numbers also produced cheap, effective, and widely available tractors and implements. Internal combustion tractors had been used for nearly fifty years before 1950, but they were quite literally tractors. That is, they towed implements, mostly horse-type implements. Following the work of Harry Ferguson and others, the word "tractor" became a misnomer. After 1950, "tractors" generally carried implements, not towed them. The designs of the new implements were novel; so was the ability to control them by limiting draft, depth of work, wheel-slip, horsepower applied, or a combination. The power takeoff made possible new implements driven directly from the tractor. These technical improvements were massive, far greater in effect than the substitution of the tractor-that-towed for the horse-that-towed. Such advances were made possible only because of cheap and effective hydraulics derived from the wartime aircraft industry; new, cheaper, and better steel mixtures originally brewed for war purposes; and the mass production of thousands of parts for tractors and implements. These were built more precisely than cars, and with the same advantages of meticulous assembly needed for rifles, guns, and armored vehicles. Even nuts and bolts in 1955 were cheaper in real terms and far better than the same nuts and bolts manufactured in 1935.

The second great improvement was chemical and also derived from war. Fertilizer manufacture, in particular nitrogen manufacture, was a direct derivative from wartime explosives. Phosphate and potash became cheap and widely available because of mass handling techniques that derived from the same elements that gave post-war tractors their competence: hydraulics, high-grade machine parts, and the use of special metals to deal with difficult materials. The end-user product was no longer a simple chemical ground into a powder, with varying effects upon the long-term nature of the soil. Post-war fertilizers were often available as compounds of all three major chemicals or with "trace elements" added; straight nitrogen became available to fit particular needs. There were quick-acting, or long-term, slow-release forms of nitrogen; particular care was taken with the effect upon soil acidity, almost an unregarded after-effect in the 1930s. Fertilizers became notably easier to handle.

Derived directly from the war gases were the early "miraculous" selective weed killers. These attacked, for example, broad-leaved weeds without harming the crop. The crop might be wheat, barley, or grass, all of which were not susceptible to the weed killer that liberated the European farmer from the red poppy and the yellow charlock. Once upon a time these had been inevitable in any field of winter or spring grain respectively. Other weed killers for pests all over the world quickly followed.[34]

Following weed killers came fungicides to prevent the inevitable effects of excessive damp weather, of drought, or of too much nitrogen. Then came the more controversial insecticides that killed the beneficial ladybird as well as the aphid, or the beautiful, harmless butterfly as well as the bugs and beetles in the soil or on the plant.[35]

The combination of high nitrogen usage with the parallel advantages of pest control raised yields in the First World countries from a base in 1945– 46 that was lower than pre-War to three or four times the output of the 1930s by 1970. Since the techniques have become widely known, an annual increase in yield has become possible; this is currently in the range of 2 to 3 percent per annum over long rolling periods. None of this would have been possible without the further skills of plant breeding.

The integrated possibilities of new varieties capable of high growth rates had to await the presence of optimum water, plant food, and pesticides. These were developed only recently. Before the other elements were in place, the breeding of dwarf wheats or dense rice did not meet any of the local requirements, which were the same as they had been for centuries. A genotype, as in Neolithic times, was selected by local conditions, and less critically by mankind, in each generation and preserved for the next sowing. This process, carried out over 5000 years or more, has produced, for example, about 30,000 kinds of rice. Recently these have been collected by geneticists and used as a bank of source material for scientific analysis and propagation.

The rules of inheritance were first formulated by a yeoman farmer's son, then monk, then Abbot of Brunn, Gregor Mendel. Mendel, working with sweet peas, had first arrived at the correct answers in the 1860s. The rules were rediscovered in the early 1900s. A shy, modest man, Mendel did not trumpet abroad what would one day be common currency. The work he did on the mode of inheritance of single pairs of alternative characteristics gave the world what is basically known about hybrids, dominant and recessive characteristics, and much of the science of genetics. If Mendel had not been an Austrian Augustinian monk, but a less humble man, he would have achieved in his lifetime the same kind of fame that was Darwin's. Their discoveries bind them together in a seamless robe.[36]

By 1945, the principles of hybridization and hybrid vigor were well-known, and much work had been done in the United States on maize, and in various European countries on other grains. The hybrid methods of breeding require great resources, a huge data bank of original material, and much time. The original material derived from natural selection in a particular place that favors the development of certain characteristics. In most "native" situations, nitrogen is in short supply, and in tropical soils, nitrogen is in more severe shortage than in temperate climates. In tropical heat, nitrogen leaches or vaporizes and is used up more quickly than in cooler climates, so an increase in the rice or wheat crop in hot climates requires more nitrogen than the traditional ecotypes can use without the straw becoming weak and "lodging." Therefore, beginning in the 1950s the solution to the Third World food shortage was sought by hybridizing tropical rice and wheats.

Ultimately, this effort becomes a matter of numbers. The more lines hybridized, the more crosses made, the more chance there is of finding an outstanding answer to the problem. The first great result was in rice, and was the result of eight years' work. This was a rice called, without fanfare, IR8. It was created by crossing Peta, a tall Indonesian rice with vigorous growth, with a Taiwanese dwarf variety. To achieve IR8, 10,000 other hybrids were rejected. Obviously the numbers game is important. The International Rice Institute now has a gene bank of 30,000 wild or cultivated, but unbred, ecotypes. From these can be bred, in theory, new hybrids that can use water more efficiently, take up nitrogen, resist lodging, or contend successfully with disease or parasites. The yield of IR8, for example, using 100 kg of nitrogen per hectare, is double that of one parent and three times that of the other. Some "Green Revolution" hybrid grains can yield four times the original native ecotype. This is only because they can usefully use up to 150 kg per hectare of nitrogen. Such a fertility level would never occur in nature and causes many problems in "native" races of grain: lodging, excessive vegetative growth, huge leaf areas, fungus attack, and other disease problems. What is true for better rice is true for wheat, barley, oats, rye, maize, and any other grain.

Obviously, the addition of "artificial" nitrogen to the available plant food upsets the whole balance of soil nutrients; any additional nitrogen has to be accompanied by the necessary phosphate, potash, and trace elements to balance the equation. Susceptibility to disease and parasites can be reduced by plant breeding programs. It may be cheaper to use fungicides and insecticides as a routine measure and to concentrate plant breeding efforts on those genes that produce the highest yield, but the use of a given variety of wheat or barley in the First World is also subject to another restraint.

For more than two generations, Mendel's method of hybrid plant breeding has been used. In the United States, the maize program begun in the 1920s was followed by cereal programs in Europe during the next decade. The work of the Rockefeller Foundation in Mexico began in 1943 and proved that First World agricultural technology was transferable. In all these areas, it has been found that hybrids lose their vigor after a few years. With wheat in Europe, the time can be as short as two years or as long as ten. In barley, lifespans in Europe have been longer, up to twelve years before a breakdown occurs. In maize, the time can be longer again; in grasses, longer still. There is opportunity for "reselection," but the true hybrid cannot be guaranteed without recourse to a plant breeding institute. Left to a mere farmer, without the infrastructure provided by the men in white coats, most modern varieties would revert, relapse, or suffer from gene decay. In fact, one of the most salutary lessons ever dealt out to plant breeders was the discovery that certain "resistant" varieties became susceptible to "new" races of fungoid disease. No one but a fungologist could tell whether the disease was really "new" or just previously unrecognized.

Mendelian breeding may, in turn, be approaching its useful limits, although the problem has been overcome by scientific knowledge that could exponentially expand productivity yet further. The same general Mendelian rules applied to cereals and grasses are now used in animal breeding. Many animals are too slow, at a maximum of one generation a year, to produce results, but chicken and pigs have offered the same opportunities to the geneticist as do plants. Commercial chickens and pigs in the advanced countries are now tailored hybrids, and the original basic stocks from which the hybrids were derived are now "endangered species."[37] Sheep, to some extent, have been improved by establishing new, stabilized hybrids to act as dams or sires, comparable to long-term successes such as half-breeds.[38] In cattle, the generation span stretches out to at least twenty-four to thirty months, too long-term for the establishment of hybrids. Advance in this area is limited to the use of semen instead of a live bull, and to upgrading the whole national herd in most countries of Europe and neo-Europes. The use of artificial insemination has done more for milk and beef production in the United Kingdom, for

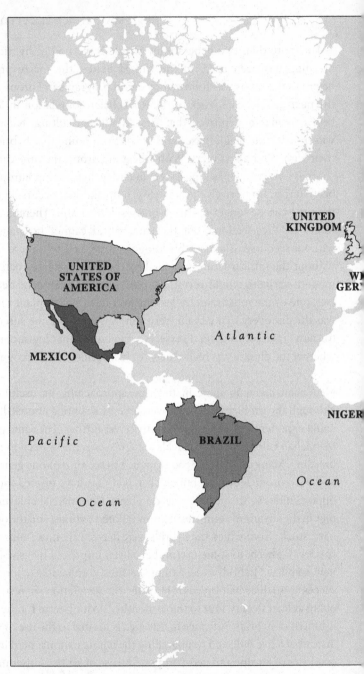

The World, Showing Slow- and Rapid-Growth Countries

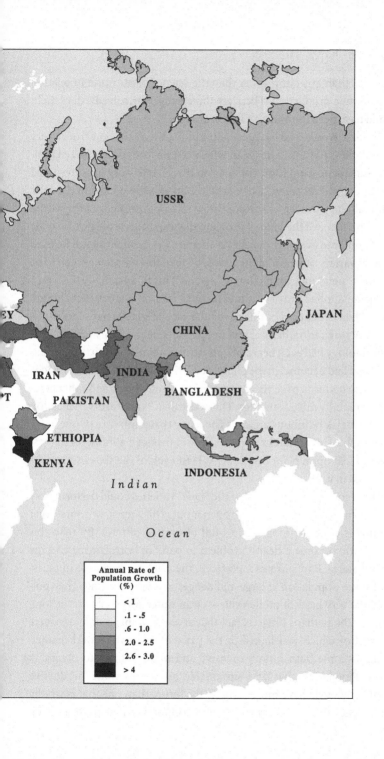

example, than any effort other than the science of nutrition in relation to economic production. There are three dangers involved. All of them would have been unthinkable fifty years ago.

The first problem is that successful cultivars tend to come from a very few families: Western European wheats come from only a dozen families, sugarcane from four, coffee from three. A new cry has developed for "biological diversity" as an antidote to excessive kinship. Genetic vulnerability was seen as a major threat to crops throughout the world. The experience of the kind of problem that might arise on a world scale was familiar to every "progressive" modern Western farmer. If he used a "new" variety of wheat in the 1960s, by 1970 this wheat was seen to be host to a "new" race of the fungus *septoria*. This fungus made the use of fungicide, applied five or six times in the season, obligatory even though no one had ever heard of this particular race of *septoria* ten years previously. A generation before, few people outside the charmed circle of microbiology had even heard of *septoria* of any kind. By 1970 the particular wheat had become, in the plant breeder's term, "outclassed." By 1975 elaborate patterns were recommended to plant wheats and other cereals in varietally mixed sowings. This was called "Varietal diversification to reduce risk of fungus attack." The irony that a mixture of one grain from each of six different varieties would produce a mongrel harvest was not lost upon plant breeders. At least each of the six varieties was well bred in itself.

The second problem was that the "new" varieties could perform only with the use of considerable nitrogen input. This meant, of course, that the drains could be more or less full of unused nitrates. By 1980 this had clearly become a health problem in parts of both Europe and the United States. Raw nitrates ingested in the drinking water are unpleasant for the population at large and dangerous for the young. They polluted the very basis of modern life—clean water. More vital in the long run was the perhaps obvious fact that at some point in time nitrogen, the cost of which was linked to the price of oil in the world market, would become both more expensive and more difficult to obtain. A Green Revolution that was sustainable as well as more productive would obviously have more value in the future than one that is wholly dependent upon infinite supplies of a commodity that most authorities expect to be in very short supply within fifty years. This shortage of nitrogen will coincide with what looks, at the moment, like a further doubling of the world population.

The third problem is consequent upon the development of bred strains of grain or grass that need high levels of fertilizers as well as other chemical inputs. More than half the cost of growing a crop may now be in seeds, fertilizers, other chemicals, and application. While the relationship between the cost of inputs and harvest value remains constant, no problem exists, but if commodity prices fall, as they tend to do if productivity increases, then the farmer or peasant is squeezed. The cost of inputs remains constant or rises; the value of the harvest falls. The farmer or peasant may find that work is in vain. The crop makes a loss and does not, in some cases, even cover the cost of the farmer's labor. All the farmer has done, in that immortal phrase, is "work for the bank."

There are strong reasons why this state of affairs should not continue. The opportunities offered by genetic engineering are rather great. Working on the principles of Mendelian mathematics and enlightened by the chemistry of the Double Helix, the biotechnicians can now see many alterations in the whole nature of crop husbandry. At the beginning of the twenty-first century, even more became possible.[39]

The world is only a few years away from the commercial exploitation of DNA transfer. This would mean "designing" a plant that would provide its own nitrogen as clover does. A wheat plant that had the ability to produce four tons per acre/ten tons per hectare of grain without any added nitrogen would solve many problems. Suppose the men in white coats added the ability to resist fungi so the plant needed no fungicide; while they were about it, they could add a repellent brought in from some other plant and add it to the DNA/RNA of the wheat so that aphids are discouraged. The farmer now has a plant that needs no nitrogen, no fungicide, and no insecticide. What about weeds? Well, some plants have the capacity to discourage all but their own species near them. It is the method provided by nature so that slow-growing seedlings can survive in the shadow of their parent. This characteristic could be provided so that nothing but wheat would grow near the wheat plant. What other pests are there? Rodents, for one. Could they be as deterred as the insects are?

Probably. What about weather, which is as great an imponderable as exists anywhere? Suppose the biological engineers attacked the Russian weather problem, which is that there is too little rain in May and early June, too much in July and August. How about one of two potential courses?

A grain could be developed for planting in May that needs fewer growing days than most wheat. If this putative wheat needed no more days than the average Western European spring barley, it could be bred to be ripe in 120 days, or sown on 10 May and harvested on or after 10 September, after the worst of the summer rains. Alternatively, the plant could be designed to need only a little moisture until it was "fully jointed," as the expression is, with the ear formed, and the grain ready to swell in July. This could be combined with an ability to stand a great deal of rain when the straw is at its full height and at its weakest. Are these ideas fanciful or "impossible"? Not to anyone who realizes that the first wheat bred to the prescriptions laid down by Mendel was not commercially available much before 1913. The first European spring bread-wheat to challenge winter wheats was not available before 1945. The first European winter barley to yield significantly more than spring barleys was not available before 1960. Within a generation most of the advances described as "possible" today will be commonplace, but there may be a high cost.

In the industries that are going to be superseded—bulk petrochemicals; fertilizer manufacture, transport, and distribution; pest controls; machines to spread fertilizer and chemicals on fields and the fuel needed to power them—all these resources will be unemployed, the workers needing new jobs. It is hard to believe that all this effort will be contained in the genes of the seed that the farmer buys and sows properly, according to prescription, and then very largely neglects. Is this the type of husbandry by which farmers have been able to feed the world? Of course not. Nor are farmers unaware of the nature of this revolution. Apart from anything else, it will greatly reduce the value of land as well as of chemical companies. More cost will be contained in the correct seed, correctly engineered, than in anything else. It is possible that seed might amount to more than half the cost of growing the crop. It is also possible that many crops will acquire the characteristic of today's soybean husbandry. This does not permit much benefit from any effort that the farmer may put into growing the crop. There is little the farmer can do to influence soybean yield. It may well be, in a generation, that this applies to nearly all crops. It is not a prospect that the average farmer welcomes.[40]

It is not unfashionable to discuss and deplore genetic possibilities in the animal kingdom the potential for creating horror that has attracted public attention to the future of genetic engineering. The nature of the positive potential is much easier to see among the flora than in the fauna. The great value of genetic engineering in crop husbandry is that the technology is absolutely transferable. At the moment, the Green Revolution depends upon First World seed, First World fertilizers, pest control, and machines for their application. Farmers have to be trained to apply nitrogen and other fertilizers at the right time, to spray with fungicide and weed killers at the right moment, to look after all the machinery involved, and to learn to care as much as a yeoman farmer in western Europe with centuries of husbandry behind him. This is not easy to instill.[41] But if the rice grower in Indonesia or the Philippines or Burma can be told to dispense with all that husbandry and just plant the seed at so many kilograms per hectare, then leave it, is this not transferable technology at its finest? Is this not a gift from the First to the Third World that will solve nearly all the possibilities of hunger, starvation, and famine? Even the *teff* of the obstinate, attractive Ethiopians could be engineered to survive the damage done by past generations.[42] The maize grown in Africa can be tailored to the requirements of the individual microclimate, as can the wheat in India, the sorghum in Pakistan, the rice in Indochina, and the barley in Iraq. The potential ability of the world to feed itself does not appear to have been so bright at any time before the present. With technology to avoid famine and most diseases under control, what is to prevent mankind from doubling in population before 2035? The real killer, to which the world should now turn its urgent attention, is pollution. Disease control and food supply are at a stage unimaginable 100, let alone 500, years ago, and can surely only advance further. What does this mean for Malthus's theory? Are we right to share the nineteenth century's optimism in the nearly always beneficence of science?

For the cold-blooded demographer writing at any time since the 1960s, there has always been a fairly simple proposition. At no time in history has population increase been known to survive beyond "sustainable levels." Always in the past, war, with its disruptive potential, or disease has solved the problem, or sheer numbers have exceeded food supplies. In other words, warfare, which directly and on its own has never killed very many, would be joined by its inevitable allies, disease and famine. These two could alternatively perform their role in peacetime once again as they have so often in the past. These associates, disease and famine, are much closer allies than war with either, and have been close friends for centuries, enjoying a special relationship.

The world now has a new condition. Warfare between major powers is so dangerous because of nuclear capability that total war cannot be entertained as a solution to demographic problems. Disease is so much perceived as an "enemy" that public opinion in those countries capable of medical technology would not countenance the slackening of "life-saving" efforts. Global food supplies are no longer a problem if mankind is sensible and applies effort in the right direction.[43] So what will happen? All previous population restraints have been swept away. The world will have to learn to live with these conditions.[44]

Forty years ago, world population was "only" about three billion. Today, it is more than double. Thirty years ago, few had heard of three globally important effects of overpopulation. These are the direct result of too many people consuming too many goods. Consumption makes it quite possible that pollution in peacetime will replace pollution by nuclear warfare as a real killer. These three effects of pollution are the greenhouse effect, acid rain, and ozone layer depletion. Thirty years ago these phenomena did not even have names. Today they are familiar problems to every concerned person.

Since the 1960s, world population has doubled. The per capita income of the people in the world has also doubled. The use of fossil fuels has more than quadrupled, intermittent crises notwithstanding. Although arable farmland itself is not fully utilized in the world, except in Europe (88 percent) and Asia (83 percent), it has proved to be cheaper to intensify than to make virgin land suitable for arable into production. This means the use of more fuel in one form or another. The burning of fossil fuels has now reached between 15 and 16 billion tons of coal equivalent per annum. This releases so much carbon dioxide (more than 6 billion tons a year) that it threatens to raise the temperature of the earth by the "greenhouse effect."

The cost to agriculture of adapting to the new climates in which rainfall and temperature are unlike anything in the past could well exceed the benefits of the overuse of fossil fuels. No one knows how much carbon the world can burn without danger. The figure is certainly below the present level. It could be as little as 8 billion tons a year of fossil fuel. This is about half the present "burn." Evidently, such a reduction could not be achieved without a massive increase in the use of nuclear energy. Yet the very people who now campaign most against nuclear energy are the same people who ought to be concerned about the much greater dangers of fossil fuel. There is a great irony in the shortsighted "ecology" of the anti-nuclear brigade. There is no merit of any kind in their intellectual blindness.[45]

Fossil fuels do not only create the greenhouse effect; they usually produce acid rain. Americans are very satisfied with the favorable results produced by checking automobile emissions. This effort, which costs several billion dollars a year, is nothing compared with the costs involved in eliminating acid rain. The use of "scrubbers" in power station chimneys needs, in some systems, a ton of limestone for every ton of coal or oil burnt, and another ton hauled away and dumped elsewhere. There are other systems, somewhat less demanding in the bulk involved. To check and reverse acid rainfall would probably require the reduction of the fossil burn to six billion tons and a clean exhaust campaign. This means that the world would have to plan to use an average of half of its present carbon of all kinds. At the same time, it would be necessary to agree that the whole world would become a smokeless zone. The world would have to be more than smoke- free; it would have to be acid-free as well.

Such an extreme program would take a dozen years to put into effect, but time is running out. Acid rain is destroying far more forest in Europe than man is using. Lakes are being turned from a neutral base into acid water that will not support life. It is not impossible that some seas will follow the lakes. Once again, the chattering classes have not comprehended the problem. There is a great movement against the use of tropical hardwood in domestic situations in the First World. Wholly admirable. But far more important than window frames, paneled doors, or toilet seats in suburbia are acid rains in Europe that have already affected half of West Germany's forest. Acid rain, however, is less of a giggle for the trendies. The cure is also more painful.[46]

Nor is the third evident new problem in the toilet-seat class. It is the destruction of the ozone layer in the Arctic and Antarctic. Chlorofluorocarbons (CFCs) are released into the atmosphere all over the high-consuming world every time a refrigerator leaks or an aerosol is used. At the time of its invention, CFC was seen as stable, not toxic, and not likely to decompose in the lower atmosphere and cause trouble where released. Instead, the compounds rise and reach the stratosphere. In most of the world, CFCs are dispersed by ultraviolet light over 22 km above the earth (above 14 miles up). The chemical compound breaks down into harmless chlorine that reacts with nitrogen oxides and water and becomes locked up as chlorine nitrate and hydrogen chloride, both harmless. Over the Poles, the chlorine reaction does not take place, and in turn the CFC compounds can destroy the ozone layer. This appears to affect only the stratospheric layer at the two Poles, but a more worrying question is whether or not the total amount of ozone in the world is finite. If so, the use of aerosols, mostly for vain and wholly frivolous purposes, and the use of CFCs in refrigeration are likely to damage life on earth as badly as acid rain or the greenhouse effect, but there is an even greater worry.

These three great threats to our environment were hardly in evidence thirty years ago. As noted, they were unknown fifty years ago. Acid rain only appeared as an issue at the end of the 1970s. Hard evidence for the predicted warm-up due to the greenhouse effect did not convince any skeptic until the early 1980s. The ozone layer depletion at the South Pole is quite clearly dated at 1984 as far as firm statistical evidence is concerned. There are three great consequences of this timetable.

First there is the "threshold" argument. Suddenly, this argument runs, something tips a problem over center and it becomes insoluble. The greenhouse effect took everyone by surprise, as did acid rain, noted by German foresters in the 1980s in areas that had been carefully managed for centuries. There was a more complete shock about the effect of CFCs upon the ozone layer.[47] These three problems have crept up upon scientists and tipped over into insolubility within a few years. What other horrors are likely to surprise the world, and will not reveal themselves until too late?

Second, since the evidence for the damage has only been forthcoming in the last few years, how old are the actions whose side effects are now being witnessed? It is logical to assume that the effects of CFCs are now being felt, belatedly, in respect to what was used in the past. The same with "greenhouse" CO_2 and acid rain. But how long in the past? Could these three problems be yet more legacies from the 1960s? If so, if all corrections were applied at once, when would the situation beneficially reverse itself? Not before the middle of the century, obviously. 2050? Too soon. 2060? Too optimistic. 2080? Perhaps.

Two massive disasters took place inside a month in August 1988. Both could have been predicted; neither was unprecedented; both were aggravated by careless, selfish, unthinking management of land and water resources over the medium term, and by political troubles over the short. They both occurred in areas of large increases in population.

Sudan is a country whose population has more than doubled since independence in 1956. The nature of political tension between the Muslim north and the Christian (or Animist) south, however, has meant near-civil war division in a country that is much poorer than it was under colonial rule. The plains around Khartoum are of impervious clay and nearly flat, and an excessive rainfall (as in 1946) has devastating results. Since 1946 the floodplain around Khartoum itself has increased in population by five times, against a national average of rather more than twice. The drift to the city had been caused by the usual Third World causes: underinvestment in agriculture, the best brains leaving the countryside, and the government cheating rural workers of the fruits of their labor. Khartoum itself has become largely a shantytown, like many others, bloated in numbers and ruled by leaders long on promises but short on delivery. On this insecure, undrained, physically unstructured area fell two disasters. One was the effect of about 200 mm (8 in) of rain on a sunbaked day. The second was the flooding of the Blue Nile.

In both Sudan and Ethiopia, the search for fuel and animal food has meant more and more trees, shrubs, and bushes cut down every year to cook human food and to keep domestic animals alive. It is not only mature forests that are destroyed in this manner, but in some areas almost every living plant is removed. If this deforestation and defoliation on tropical hillsides is followed by excessive rainfall, then runoff is accelerated, erosion is multiplied many times, and the rivers raise the level of their beds, automatically breaking their banks or flooding low-lying land. The results are far worse in the case of the Blue Nile that rises in the highlands of Ethiopia. In the case of the White Nile, which also flows through Khartoum, any rise in flow is buffered by the huge swamp, bigger than Wales, called the Sudd, which lies between the highlands and Khartoum.

The second disaster was in Bangladesh. This country, once "East Pakistan," was "created" largely by India, not from any noble reasons, but to weaken West Pakistan. More than half of Bangladesh is just above high spring tide level, by a margin that rarely exceeds 10 meters (32 feet). Equally, half the country is only 3–12 meters (10–39 feet) above the beds of the rivers whose normal area forms more than a quarter of the country's total surface. A heavy monsoon used to be of great benefit. Water was retained hundreds of miles upstream in Nepal, Bhutan, Northern India, and even China. It gradually seeped out from wooded mountain valleys and became the irrigation needed to grow three crops of rice a year in a country with the highest density of poor agricultural people on earth.

Every square meter of the surface of Bangladesh that it is possible to cultivate has been irrigated and is needed. Bangladesh has nearly 1200 people per square kilometer of arable land, more than 11 people per hectare, nearly 5 people per acre. This is more serious than India's population problem of 500 people per hectare of arable land, rather more in China proper, and should be compared with 800 people per hectare of arable land in the Netherlands, the last in a country where only 10 percent, at most, live by the land. In Bangladesh the proportion is nearly reversed. Eighty percent of the population is dependent upon the land and its products for their livelihood. Bangladesh has damaged herself in a classic Third World way. Population was 29 million in 1900 and 40 million in 1948 at the end of the Empire. It is more than 100 million today.

The rest of the damage has been done by bad water management upstream on the Ganges and Bramaputra Rivers; unmanaged runoff from monsoon rain is guaranteed to cause disaster in a low-lying country. To make possible the kind of water management enjoyed by the Netherlands requires the investment of between $50 and $100 billion over a ten-year period. It would also require proper forest management upstream, alternative fuel for hill country peasants, and food for hill country animals. None of this is likely to happen. The Netherlands has increased its population from 1.5 million in 1600 to 15 million today, and during those centuries there has been heavy and continuous investment in water management in a country as low-lying as Bangladesh. The Netherlands is fortunate, too, that it is not liable to tropical rainfall. Its upstream neighbors, Germany, Switzerland, France, Luxembourg, and Belgium, try to manage their forests properly and do not contain numbers of starving peasants who have to cut down trees to live. The moral is clear, implementation apparently impossible, solutions beyond reason.[48]

Critically, there is the problem of what else is going to be discovered. Without becoming hysterical, can anyone properly quantify the effects of new potential problems? Some can be identified already, but they have not yet reached the point at which the public is prepared to countenance their solution. These "new" problems are also closely connected with old problems. The basic enigma is the combination of high population increase in the Third World plus the desire of all First World people for "growth." It is "growth" that produces the greenhouse effect and acid rain and a depleted ozone layer. It is the relationship between personal consumption in the First World and the destruction of the rain forest that must be adjusted. It is the ratio between "development" and fossil fuel use in the First World that must be reassessed.[49] It is the production of sludge and sewage in the First World that threatens the oceans. It is the nitrate use of the past forty years that pollutes drinking water supplies.[50] It is the unthinking emission of all sorts of chemicals that threatens natural chemical cycles.[51]

In an ideal world, there would be only a sustainable agriculture. There would be "growth" supported only by natural ecosystems. There would not be any waste extruded into the atmosphere unless the effects were known. A worldwide effort to replace dead and dying forests would become a major campaign. Urban waste would be recycled to benefit agriculture and reduce the amount of inorganic fertilizer manufactured and applied. New advances in biological engineering would produce grains and grasses, bred for today's conditions, and trees would be developed that could survive acidity. The monitoring of naturally developing mutations, such as the algae that suddenly appeared in the Baltic in 1988, would be considered a priority. Perhaps most important of all, the safety of nuclear power must be made so much more credible that the burning of fossil fuel could be substantially reduced. Mankind does not live in an ideal world.

There are certain optimistic portents. The use of modern control systems has made possible more elegant fuel efficiency in industry. The breeding potential in genetic engineering leads to a belief in the possibility of a more sustainable agriculture. Energy efficiency has been significantly improved in cars, electrical appliances, process industry, and sustainable agriculture. Opportunities exist to cycle more efficiently and less destructively the six most important chemical elements: carbon, nitrogen, oxygen, hydrogen, phosphorus, and sulphur—these six making up 95 percent of all living matter. Ultimately, the hope is that fusion replaces fission, and nuclear power becomes demonstrably safe and clean.[52]

It is much more difficult to establish the attitude of mind necessary to produce a future less stark than appears likely. Profits, markets, and freedom to speculate and fail are all necessary to commercial and industrial efficiency. For the Third World, overburdened by excessive population, overcrowded medical and sanitary facilities, congested land, filthy cities, and food derived from droughty and dusty fields, the problems of the First World appear to be a small price to pay for enough to eat, a job, a house, and some education for the future. The doctrinal problems of the modern Russian Empire are akin to those of sixteenth-century Spain. Unlike Renaissance Spain, the Russian Empire is a prime polluter of the environment. It is to be hoped for the sake of the world that these problems can be solved without decay or explosion.[53] The First World inhabitant prefers to see no connection between "affluence" and the destruction of rain forests that recycle carbon safely and surely.

Nor are First World consumers impressed by calls to reduce consumption, greedy as they are both for rising standards of "life" and for the immeasurable virtues of clean air, beautiful countryside, fresh water, and a decent environment. The future has to include higher efficiencies in generation and use of agricultural systems and in stabilizing chemical cycles. Technological management must increase efficiencies by more than the rise in population or consumption patterns.[54] This must continue for a very long time, at least until total world population levels off; after that point, all increases in consumption must come from increased efficiencies.

Policies advocated by the hair-shirt brigade will fail for many reasons. One is that the degree of guilt required to implement them cannot be retained long enough to provide sustained motivation. Nor can self-denial achieve acceptance amongst the influential. Nor is self-denial the best policy. There is so much room for improvement in almost every process in everyday life that no one needs look further. Such a policy is essential to prevent the kind of breakdown that unbridled abuse of the environment will otherwise assuredly bring.[55]

During World War II the political idea of One World was launched. Predictably, it failed. We now live on only one Earth whose natural ecosystem is overstrained and beginning to revolt. "One World" was a political idea, a kite of the 1940s that failed to fly. "Only One Earth" has to be the paramount ecological idea of the present. Without it, the future will be destroyed by pollution.

It would be an absurd end for mankind if, having defeated the restraints of disease, having apparently solved the food supply problem, and having avoided nuclear war, the species should fall victim to pollution, to drown in its own ordure. Malthus, apparently defeated, would be laughing in his grave.

* * * * *

A New Year encourages prophecy; the beginning of a decade provides a pretext for prognoses; obviously, and more rarely, a new millennium offers a valid excuse for those inclined to prediction. Whichever way time is chopped, there is often an urge to foretell the future. Eminent astronomers are well placed to operate in this area. The British Astronomer-Royal, Sir Martin Rees, claims for his profession a special perspective (of time) because of the elongated scale on which astronomers work—the whole of history, say 10,000 years, is a mere interval in cosmology. Rees's book, *Our Final Hour*, is gloomy; he calculates that mankind has only a 50 percent chance of reaching 2100. In some ways, it is the old story. Innovation is developing too fast for mankind's managerial competence (or goodwill). Biotechnology in the hands of terrorists, for example, is a dire contemporary threat. Clever humanists, unbelievers in any afterlife, find it difficult to defeat less sophisticated men who are unafraid to die. Such "Simple Men" learned to fly planes into skyscrapers; they might weaponize germs or plant "dirty" nuclear devices in First World cities.

Without any evil intent, there are hazards. In Europe, natives are failing to maintain numbers. Immigrants, overwhelmingly Muslims, are said to be needed to do the cruder jobs that natives no longer exist in sufficient numbers to perform. In the United States there seems to be no effective thought about the Chinese (and Indian) industrial challenge. There is the problem of what happens when oil and natural gas are seriously, not politically, depleted. On the way, our material civilization would be hard-pressed to survive oil at $100 a barrel—without the benefit of nuclear power, thanks to Greens. Spectacular events in Nature tend to happen abruptly; witness the extinction of cod on the Grand Banks. If global warming is valid, then disaster could occur in the next generation.

What is obvious is that if the World's Population were a third of what it is today, as it was in 1900, no projection would be as difficult as it is. Nor would Africa, surely the most miserable of human failures, be as fraught as it is if the population of that unhappy continent were at the 1900 level—less than one-sixth of what it is today.

To return to the Astronomer-Royal. He optimistically believes that it is possible to help the World survive if environmental and biomedical issues were higher on the public agenda, but this assumes that the public cares enough on a daily basis to treat some of these consequences as more than a sensational horror show. Many people would surely prefer to return to the daily struggle or slump in front of the TV.

If the population of the World were much smaller and not increasing, greater optimism might be justified. There is the terrible contradiction of the Third World—at least half the people on Earth. Either they remain in a poverty comparatively far worse than any ever experienced in Europe or the neo-Europes in the past 500 years or they industrialize, adding massively to the depletion and pollution we have felt since 1970. Witness China since 1990.

It is easy to believe in Pandora's Box, which contained all knowledge, good and evil. It is plainly impossible for the well intentioned, well informed, and well governed (even if they coincide) to control everything that has escaped from her box. It is clear, however, that the more that escapes from the box, the better the human governments must be. Perhaps a real pessimism derives from the low quality—intellectual and ethical—of most of the political organizations in the world. Of these, their people are not now the only victims.

Notes

1 It is almost certain that a woman in New Mexico died of undiagnosed bubonic plague in 1987. A new theory about mutation in the basic bacterium was developed at the University of Umea, Sweden, in 1987–88. This was disputed by Professor Gillett of the London School of Hygiene and Tropical Medicine in August 1988.

2 If a disease killed more of the animal host than it did of humans, it would very quickly reduce itself, the disease, to impotence. Or, more properly, the disease would never have become a threat of any kind, let alone a pandemic or epidemic.

3 The nursery rhyme "Ring-a-ring-a-roses" refers to the string of lesions round the waist found in people with bubonic-type plague. "Atish-oo, atish-oo, we all fall down" relates to the pneumonic method of spreading the disease by droplet exchange.

4 India, 1907–25; Manchuria, 1920; Egypt and East Africa, 1930s; China, 1945.

5 Millennialism was named after hysterical feelings current in AD 1000 that Christ would return to earth 1000 years after his birth. This apocalyptic faith is commoner in the Jewish and some other Eastern faiths, but it was the anti-papal party in the Middle Ages along with German and Swiss reformers who later encouraged a belief that the end of the world was nigh. It was not difficult to find converts at the time of the Black Death. Superstition overcame belief; skepticism replaced curiosity; some people refused to think or feel at all about the future, living only for the present. The same choice was presented in times of trouble in Rome: Drink deep, be merry, for tomorrow we die. Or become a stoic, albeit perhaps a Christian stoic, and survive.

6 The Paston Letters present a picture of life in Norfolk in the years 1422–1509. The Paston family rose socially from being prosperous peasants, cultivating about 40 hectares (nearly 100 acres), to the Earldom of Yarmouth. They rose by marriage, education, the Law, fast footwork during the Wars of the Roses from 1455 to 1485, and sheer ability during several generations. The important point here is the effect of the plague upon their lives, even as late as the late fifteenth century.

7 France, 1789; most of Germany, 1808; Austria, 1811; Hungary, 1813; Russia, 1861.

8 William H. McNeill, who first identified the effects of disease in history in his brilliant book *Plagues and Peoples* (1977), also attaches great importance to the factors that, by their epidemiological effects, have an important new causative significance when the factor is abandoned. McNeill (among others) has drawn attention to the problems arising from the absence of dirt, also known as cleanliness, that gave rise to poliomyelitis; the use of fast steamships, instead of slower sailing vessels, that did not allow time for the incubation of certain diseases; and cultivation of waste ground as populations increased, destroying the habitat not only of rodent hosts of bubonic plague, but also of malarial mosquitoes. McNeill's book does not suggest that any control system operates among disease, food supply, and population growth. In addition, there is a vast literature of an anthropological nature about the link between demography and disease, but numbers

are often lacking in these papers. McNeill's illustrations of the disease factor and of weaponry were (*The Pursuit of Power*), he said, to make good the deficiencies in his magnum opus, *The Rise of the West*. He is one of the few historians who have written one great work, then two more as "footnotes," to use his own phrase. These amplifications to an already major effort place him on the shortest of shortlists of historians.

9 It is worth noting that Mamelukes recruited their successors each year from the steppes. The Mamelukes, most of whom were castrated, replaced themselves by buying blue-eyed, blond boys from Circassia. This occurred from 1382 until Napoleon brought the system to an end in 1798. Egypt became the place worst affected by the plague in the Mediterranean after 1382. A side effect of the plague was that Egyptian decadence, assisted by the Mamelukes' lack of commitment to the future, rendered Egypt a soft target. The true rulers of Egypt remained population growth and a nearly fixed food supply provided by the Nile flood, just as it always had been, with the ratio of the two modified by the plague. It was plague that kept the Egyptian population from exceeding the ancient total of three to five million before 1800. This ancient total was always within the ability of the marvelous Nile to afford a decent standard of life and, as in Roman times, to produce rations for another one million or two.

After Napoleon (and Nelson) cut the plague-producing umbilical cord between Circassia and Cairo in 1798, matters changed. Plague modified itself in Egypt and ceased to be chronic; the next serious outbreak was in 1844 by which time the population had increased from 3.5 million to 5 million. By 1900, it was 10 million; by 1950, 20 million; and today it is nearly 80 million. Cairo, capital of this country heading for unbridled population-induced poverty, has a population of well over 20 million. Most Cairenes are very poor, living in shantytowns, alive only because of a healthy climate that makes many diseases "unsuccessful."

10 More than a third of all cardinals, bishops, and archdeacons died between May 1348 and March 1350 in Western Europe.

11 In 1988–90 the English suffered the same phenomenon. There was the substitution of the community charge for the rates (a property tax). There were cries of "Poll Tax" and shades of 1381, when Wat Tyler's march on London led to a general rising against lawyers, serfdom, and the right to rent land for low cash payment instead of services rendered. In fact, the grievances of the peasantry were general; it was the occasion of the change in the tax base that triggered the revolt. The same phenomenon occurred in France, Germany, and other countries. It probably happened because the taxpaying classes are temporarily united with the poor in resisting a change for the worse in their circumstances.

12 Wolves became bolder, taking animals and young children in daylight; the habit of huddling in villages and abandoning isolated houses became necessary in many Continental countries.

13 In 1340 most of the population was directly engaged in agriculture. If in 1340, 90 percent of the population in any area lived in villages of less than 250 people, then in 1400 that proportion would have been reduced to about 75 percent. See note 22, this chapter.

14 Most European forests thus date from 1350 or later.

15 In England huge numbers of foxes reverse-commute today into towns to feed at night. Others live in waste areas and in parks in towns. Perhaps 50 percent of the fox population in modern England is urban, but not for the same reason as in the fifteenth century.

16 Post-plague returns for seed sown/seed harvested rose in Western Europe as follows:

wheat, from 4.1 to 5.5; barley, 3.7 to 4.8; oats, 2.5 to nearly 4. In some marginal areas pre-plague ratios were below 2:1. After the plague, few marginal areas were not cultivated.

17 East Germany and parts of Poland became comparable to the Midwest of the United States in the late nineteenth century: a granary for Western Europe.

18 It was herring that gave the Dutch a first chance to lift themselves. Herring were an analogue to wool in England and of the same kind of relative value to a country—Holland—of one-third of the English population.

19 People can use an abacus even if they cannot count properly; the modern comparison is with checkout devices for the innumerate.

20 The volume of paper production is generally unknown, but other evidence suggests that by the time that printing came along, paper was available and plentiful in almost any market town. Certainly this was true in England when Caxton set up his press in Tothill Street, Westminster, in 1477. Printing could never have become popular without the previous development of paper.

21 Clocks at Wells or Salisbury had not been reduced in any way to make them portable. Early mariners still used a sandglass marking off thirty-minute intervals. Water glasses were also available, more accurate since water is more fluid than sand, less accurate if not temperature compensated. Thirty-minute glasses were calibrated against known accurate clocks. Columbus set his by the cathedral clock at Cádiz before crossing the Atlantic. Someone then turned it over every half-hour until he returned the next year. That was the theory. Medieval clocks were authentic and long-lived; that of Dover Castle, made in the plague year of 1348, was exhibited in accurate action at a Scientific Exhibition in 1876.

22 The village ethos in the pre-plague Middle Ages can be savored today in a Third World country. The collective decision is all-important; consensus is promoted without the rigor of debate of an intellectual nature; there is normally only one answer to most questions. Present-day Europe has, in the end, the plague to thank for its freedom of choice.

23 Geoffrey Chaucer, 1345–1400. Son of a tavern-keeper and wine merchant of the City of London; page in the service of the Duke of Clarence, 1357 or 1358; in the King's service in France, 1359. The King granted him a pension in 1367, and he was on the royal service abroad in 1370, 1372–73, 1376, 1377, and 1378. Much of his subject matter was derived from Boccaccio (see below), but Chaucer's output, in English, was probably greater. The first great English poet, Chaucer left his most important work till the prime of life, starting it in 1387 when he was forty-two. The Canterbury Tales was never finished, but remains the greatest work of the greatest English poet before Shakespeare, who lived two centuries later.

Giovanni Boccaccio, 1313–75. Unlike Chaucer, Boccaccio was an adult throughout the Plague. Until 1350 he was a successful courtier, storyteller, scholar, and the romantic lover of the lady Fiammetta. After 1350 he became a diplomat and an early Renaissance scholar. This worthy existence did not prevent him from writing his most famous work, The Decameron. In this (not always bawdy) compilation, ten days are spent in escaping the Plague. Ten people (hence Decameron)—seven women and three men—tell ten tales each, one hundred in all. The effect of this great collection of romantic and classical folktales that had wandered round Mediterranean civilizations for five hundred years was considerable. Among the English, Shakespeare, Sidney, Marston, and Fletcher, as well as Chaucer, borrowed from The Decameron; so did French, Italian, Dutch, Spanish, and German writers; do did Dryden, Keats, Tennyson, Longfellow, Swinburne, and George

Eliot. *The Decameron* is still being used as a sourcebook on television, almost daily. There is now never any acknowledgement, of course.

24 William Langland, 1322–1400. Author of *Piers Plowman*, he wrote: "So we need an antidote strong enough to reform these prelates who should pray for peace but are hindered by their possessions. Then take their land from them, you nobles, and let them live on their tithes. For surely, if property is a deadly poison that corrupts them, it would be good for Holy Church's sake to relieve them of it and purge them of this poison before it grows more dangerous...." Penguin ed., pp. 194–195.

25 The dominating theory of disease was the humoral, which has always subconsciously influenced thinkers on the subject. In this doctrine, the body contains four humours: blood, phlegm, yellow bile, and black bile. Health is dependent upon the correct proportion and mixture. This passed into the psyche of ordinary, non-medical people from the time of Hippocrates (?460–377 or 359 BC). More lasting was the Hippocratic oath, which stated that service to the patient was of the highest importance and declared the importance of the healing power of nature. It is vital to remember that in the Middle Ages there were few doctors of medicine in Western Europe, fewer still after the plague.

26 John Wyclif, 1329–84. Scholar and teacher at Oxford University and Master of Balliol in 1360. In 1374 he became Rector of Lutterworth, Leicestershire, and in the same year was sent by the government on a mission to Bruges about Papal abuses. Wyclif believed that the temporal power should be paramount, that the secular power should control the clergy. The Pope became an enemy who addressed bulls to the King, the Bishops, and the University of Oxford. His allies were the common clergy, the merchants, and some of the nobility. Wyclif started to translate the Bible; denied priestly absolution, confessions, and penances; and anticipated many of the Protestant objections to papal misuse of power that Luther identified in 1517–22. Like Luther, Wyclif died in bed, but his bones were dug up in 1428, burned, and cast into the river. His followers, the Lollards, survived till the Reformation, and his works influenced others such as Hus (see below).

John Hus, 1369–1415, son of a peasant in Bohemia; educated at Prague University; became Rector, 1402. Highly critical of senior clergy, he followed Wyclif's Lollard views, partly religious, partly social. From 1410, Hus preached courageously against his spiritual enemies and worked and wrote energetically until driven from Prague by the Church Establishment. Even King Wenceslaus could not save him. Seized, thrown into prison, tried at Constance in May 1415, he was burned at the stake 8 July 1415. His death was followed by an uprising of the enraged Czechs against the Holy Roman Emperor, Sigismund, in the so-called "Hussite Wars."

27 The logic runs as follows. A parasite, to be successful, must multiply like any other species. It must not be so successful that it destroys its own host. (See note 2, this chapter.) It is therefore essential that the host of the parasite should survive, or that some hosts should survive. An ideal proportion has to be more than half—this is in the verdant country that harbors both logic and pure mathematics.

Both smallpox and measles could well have transferred from animals, in which they were less than successful. This was true of the transfer of myxomatosis (a relative of smallpox) from the guinea pigs of South America. Myxomatosis passed through the Brazilian rabbit (which is not really a rabbit) into the European rabbit in the neo-European country of Australia. Both transfers were effected by men moving infected animals. This transfer has happened under the eyes of pathologists from every country. Among guinea pigs, the disease was relatively harmless, as it was in the other Latin American rodent, the Brazilian rabbit. In the European rabbit, on the other hand, the death rate was at least 98 percent at first, and over 95 percent in every succeeding pandemic. The breeding abilities of rabbits, however, are great enough to combat these huge losses; there have been over 300 generations since the first introduction of myxomatosis into Europe in the summer of 1952, and there are still many rabbits about. The rabbits, however, have changed their habits. Survivors largely live aboveground, perhaps because folk memory suggests that a flea-spread disease is best avoided by abandoning underground homes. The nature of European rabbits since 1953, their habits, and their social organization have all changed, just as disease changes the lifestyle of humans. Social scientists should be busy among the bunnies.

28 The first person in the world to be injected with live cowpox "matter" was eight-year-old James Phipps. That was in 1796 in the village of Berkeley in Gloucestershire.

29 The Chinese, as always, had previously had a different method, which was for the patient to breathe live smallpox "matter" into his nostrils through a straw. This procedure had a death rate of about one-fifth. It was fashionable amongst the richer, most sophisticated Europeans before Jenner, and among Muslims. Lady Mary Wortley Montague (1689–1762), wife of the then British ambassador to the Porte in Constantinople in 1716, had brought this method back to England in 1721. It became general in Russia in the 1770s and in France because of Louis XV's death from smallpox (1774). Frederick the Great of Germany introduced inoculation into the court at Potsdam in the 1770s, and George Washington inoculated a large proportion of the Revolutionary Army after Bunker Hill in 1776. It was notable that "conscientious objectors" did not long survive.

30 These figures come from the *Imperial Encyclopedia*, compiled in 1726, which repeats a great deal of the work of the scholar Ssu-ma Kuang of the Sung Dynasty (960–1279). See William H. McNeill: *Plagues and Peoples*.

31 English judges still carry these posies in official processions, though prisoners are no longer lousy, or constitutionally smelly.

32 There is, of course, always a danger that a new strain of disease will prove lethal, or will emulate chicken pox and encourage a relative into the human body. Chicken pox, now relatively harmless, permits the ingress of the parasite that causes shingles many years later. Shingles is painful, quite unlike chicken pox.

33 Death from disease was often considered a kinder fate than public execution.

34 Japan only became obviously lousy and began carrying any kind of typhus in the summer of 1945; it is possible that the pathogen was brought over from Korea or China and that the national breakdown at the end of World War II made it too difficult to contain the disease by hygiene.

35 All Negroes are black. All blacks are not necessarily Negroes. In this book, a Negro is one who has sickle-cell anemia and, therefore, an antidote to malaria in the blood genes. The importance of this recessive factor is explained at length in the Quinine chapter of *Seeds of Change* by Henry Hobhouse.

36 The four pre-Renaissance slave routes were from Timbuktu to what is now modern Algeria, from Lake Chad to what is modern Tripoli, from East Africa down the Nile, and from Ethiopia and East Africa to Oman. Only the slaves gathered to walk north via Timbuktu would have come from a place where malaria was endemic, and the disease would not survive the desert.

37 The connection between stagnant, dirty water and the yellow fever mosquito raises the

question of how the disease ever started in a world in which humans were not densely packed enough to produce dirt and stagnant water. There has to be a satisfactory philosophic explanation.

38 There are numerous cases of female cooks, bakers, and dairymaids acting as carriers over many years. The longest known case was for fifty-two years, during which the woman showed no signs of the disease. How many men did she infect?

39 Unlike typhoid, dysentery was not alleviated by Florence Nightingale and her nurses in 1855.

40 In some armies, anti-typhoid vaccines were in use as early as World War I.

41 The antiseptic virtues of alcohol provided a fashionable excuse for the ingestion of hard liquor. Earlier, it was the reason for using wine and water mixtures, and for "small beer," a very weak brew that was, however, safe to drink. Hot drinks were also safer than water, hence the historical importance of tea and coffee.

42 Pilgrimages have always been great disease distributors. In India, it was the confluence of Hindus at the holy city of Benares that spread cholera throughout Hindustan; in Europe, it was pilgrims returning from Jerusalem who were responsible for bringing back one kind of tuberculosis. Pilgrims to Mecca exchanged and encouraged smallpox; pilgrims to Canterbury or Rome spread disease on both outward and return trips. The Pilgrim Fathers, to make a point, brought smallpox, measles, and influenza to the Amerindians of Massachusetts, even though it is known that some sort of killer disease had already spread from the French in Nova Scotia in 1616–18. The point is made. Pilgrims who, in the Middle Ages, may have out-traveled soldiers or sailors spread disease wherever they went, as did every other traveler.

43 Sir Almroth Wright, 1861–1947, was responsible for training innumerable fellow doctors in the pathology of parasites. In World War I, he successfully introduced anti-typhoid inoculation into the British Army. He was present as a young student at the early lectures by people like Robert Koch whose work on septicemia (1880) led to his identification of the TB bacillus in 1882, and of cholera in 1883. Wright, in turn, gave Alexander Fleming (1881–1955) the impulse to develop penicillin with Howard Florey (1898–1965) and Ernest Chain (1906–79). Since Robert Koch had sat at the feet of both Lister (1827–1912) and Pasteur (1822–95), there is a fine, almost apostolic succession through the work of Almroth Wright.

44 By the 1960s, it was predicted that "most" disease would be eliminated. One has been officially "abolished"—smallpox. If it ever returned, the carnage would be at a level comparable to the Black Death since inoculation was also "abolished." Measles, chicken pox, German measles, whooping cough, and some other childhood diseases have been controlled by prophylactic inoculation or vaccination. Malaria, once optimistically put into the "to-be-abolished" column has, in fact, become much more serious, perhaps now affecting 10 percent of the human race.

45 The non-Columbian explanation involves yaws, a spirochetes-infective disease that resembles leprosy in its worst effects; it shares with syphilis only its transmission by spirochetes. Syphilis is venereally transferred. Yaws is spread by a spirochete, very like that of syphilis, but entering the body through non-venereal contact. Yaws was probably classed as "leprosy" in the Middle Ages, if it had not then died out. After Columbus, syphilis broke out virulently in Europe, traveling everywhere by venereal means. Yet the yaws' spirochete and that of syphilis are hard to tell apart. The only explanation, if

the non-Columbian history is correct, is that the spirochete abandoned one method of transferring itself from host to host and changed the paths of infection that would be essential in view of the different methods of entry into the human system. This is not impossible but, as has already been said in the text, unconvincing.

46 Apart from syphilis, the only other notable Amerindian diseases were Carrion's disease and Chaga's. Neither of them survived a journey across the Atlantic. See Manson's *Tropical Diseases*, Baltimore, Williams and Wilkins, 1972.

47 Such a community might have been the descendants of those survivors from the mutineers in HMS *Bounty*, but by now, the inhabitants of Pitcairn Island have been disturbed too much to be a suitable case for investigation. By 1858 only a few families were willing to remain on the island. By 1900 the survivors were showing "a deterioration of morals, intellect, and energy." Are these not the symptoms also shown by some Amerindians, but not others?

48 In societies in danger of collapse through inbreeding, this hospitality may have offered the tribe a genetic pathway to survival. In other words, it could have been a strong instinct.

49 Historically, plebs have always sought to acquire more power or equality or social justice. Patrician resistance to this process required overt acts of wisely deployed strength. A minor weakening of the patrician resolve would result in some loss of power, however small.

50 The BBC produced an extraordinary mini-series on TV about the Borgias. Replete with Renaissance cruelty and lust, and wonderfully caparisoned, it provoked one critic to complain that there was too much sex, a lot of it incestuous. The tone of the series was explained, said the TV critic of the *Financial Times*, if you realized that the following exchange took place: Cesare Borgia to his sister, Lucrezia: "You're better in bed than Mum." To which Lucrezia replied: "That's what Dad says."

51 In 1319, two centuries before European syphilis, one fine at Avignon for indulgences was as follows: "A nun who has abandoned herself to several men in succession, either in or outside her convent, and wants to rise to the rank of abbess, should pay 131 pounds." This was quite a lot of money—about £500,000 in today's coin—but it would not have saved anyone from the scourge of syphilis.

52 Some countries are using blood tests to control the entry of long-term visitors suspected of carrying either HIV (Human Immunodeficiency Virus) or (subsequent) AIDS. It appears positive that HIV must precede AIDS by a gap of at least six months and not more than six years. HIV has been traced in tears, saliva, and urine, but it is still believed (in the United States) that no evidence exists that HIV may be transmitted through an exchange of these fluids. People in Africa are not so sure. A new cause of death has crept into the literature, AIDS-Related Complex (ARC). It appears likely that infected people can proceed from HIV to ARC without AIDS itself being diagnosed. Perhaps it should be stated at this point that the effect of HIV, AIDS, or ARC on human conduct is multiplied many times by the horror of the form of death and the prominence of homosexual or promiscuous media people who figure as victims. If a million people actually die of the syndrome, it is a fair calculation that ten or twenty times as many will avoid the disease by modifying lifestyles. This happened with syphilis since many early victims were aristocrats whose example was, in those days, followed.

53 The Archbishop of Canterbury, no less, has declared that there is no danger in the use of the communion cup. This may prove to be optimistic, at least in the tropics.

54 The word *elegant* in this connection is wholly scientific, as is its use on page 53.

55 This thesis, that disease has now "learned" to attack the immune system instead of the microparasites that resist disease and that the immune system calls into being, is also Darwinian. It could arise if diseases behave like other organisms and, if defeated, are then replaced by more vigorous, if similar, examples of the same sort of living matter. This metamorphosis already applies to animals and vegetables. There is no philosophic reason why it should not apply to pathogens. It certainly does apply to some fungi. If it applies to diseases, then it renders negative the optimistic view of the medical competence of mankind.

On the other hand, it would restore the perfect elegance of the automatic system that existed in 1347 at the beginning of this chapter. Nature usually does not like to be denied a working system because of interference, even if it be by the best educated group of biologists the world has ever known, giving rise to the antibiotic-defeating mutations of germs, "new" fungi, and animal disease. This theory—that diseases that destroy the immune system will take over from diseases that destroy antibodies—has not yet surfaced publicly. Perhaps it is too alarming

CHAPTER TWO

1 Verse is easier to remember, to declaim, and to use as a verbal teaching base. Even in 1492, there were not many books about, and not many who could read properly. Few farmers in Virgil's time could have used these lines usefully if they had not been in verse, easily remembered, competent to jog the memory. The first universally appreciated English manual of husbandry was that of Thomas Tusser, 1562. It was still being recommended for use in schools by Lord Molesworth, a great educator of the time as late as 1723.

2 The process of partial domestication is easily understood. Men succeeded by degrees in controlling the movements of herds and flocks; they would keep them stationary at night, then gather them and move them to a preferred area. Little by little, this relationship would allow for women to milk the cattle or sheep, and the pastoral system was born. This might take less than a whole human generation, and the effects were rather great. A herd of cattle can support several times as many human beings as pastoralists, as it could when wandering freely and hunted for meat.

3 A modern alternative to plowing is to spray the field with a weed killer and drill the seed directly into sod or stubble. This is a contemporary answer to the age-old problem of how to save power. One ancient answer was to scratch-plow in riverine soils with minimum cultivation. Another was to use flood irrigation as a preparation, as in the Nile, Tigris, Euphrates, Indus, Ganges, Mekong, and Chinese river basins. It is no accident that early civilizations often found cultivation easier in alluvial soils. Not only was power requirement lower, but returns were usually greater. They still are.

4 This myth may have been based on the fact that, after the Normans arrived, plowmen were usually too well educated for their jobs. Displaced native farmers might have become serfs or slaves, grumbling away, plowing for most of the winter regardless of weather.

5 Two, four, or eight oxen would be needed in the heavy clay. One man guided the plow; the other "called" the reluctant animals forward. It was debatable which was harder work. One had to exhaust his wrists trying to turn the sod, the other to walk backward talking all the time in a threatening or encouraging way. The "caller" was known as "Hywell" in Celtic, and cajoled not only with the voice, but with a long stick carried to

encourage the beasts in a more physical way. All this was expensive in manpower. There is another point against much heavy-land grain culture by Anglo-Saxons. No purely German quern, or hand-operated grain mill, has ever been found. Anglo-Saxons learned the art of bread-making from Celts or Romans.

6 It is not likely that straw was regarded as a desirable by-product of grain before the Anglo-Saxons. It was the need to keep cattle productive in winter during inclement conditions that made straw desirable as bedding. Romans and Celts did not nurture cattle for milk, and draft oxen usually wintered outdoors.

7 To make risen bread successfully requires a degree of skill in the grinding. Battered grain, to coin a phrase, will not make any better-risen bread than burnt grain.

8 Pliny, *Natural History*. This work is a wealth of information on early agricultural technology.

9 As a result of this property, modern wheat has been selected and bred for its gluten content. A high-gluten wheat is called "strong." The strongest wheats in the world are grown in the Northern United States and Canada, far "stronger" than the average European wheat.

10 Lenin made a personal effort to change Russian consumption from rye bread to wheat bread. It was a disastrous decision. Raising wheat is much more demanding of personal skill, and communal farms made wheat growing more risky than rye culture. The 1913 production of 28 million tons of wheat and 25 million tons of rye (total 53 million tons) became 32 million of tons of wheat and 21 million tons of rye (total 53 million tons) in 1940. This was from an area increased by 25 percent.

11 In difficult years, some wheats, but more obviously some grasses and rye, grow a fungus called ergot that poisons animals or humans who eat the grain. Curiously enough, goats grazed with other stock on ergot-infested grassland remove the ergot fungus without harm and save other stock from its effects. Ergot was derived from fungoid rye and used ethnically to encourage childbirth at least as late as 1940. It was widely used illegally in rural areas as a means of procuring abortion, but the abortionist had to use it with care. Low-level ingestion of ergot leads to hallucination; in wet harvest years, medieval people inevitably ate large quantities of ergot and suffered from generalized poisoning, the body undergoing gangrene as the blood supply diminished, and suffered nervous spasms. In either case, death was general. The last widespread case of chronic poisoning or ergotism was in the hungry year, 1816, in Lorraine and Burgundy, France. But the problem must have been serious in the Middle Ages and likely to act as an appreciable population control in times of wet weather when ergot fungus growth could cause abortion and death.

12 Barley, grown in Ancient Egypt 5000 years ago, was less valued than wheat in the esteem of Egyptian beer makers. Bread requires high protein, high gluten, beer the reverse. Ancient Egyptian wheat may have been of a low-protein, high-starch nature because of genetics, climate, or Nile husbandry.

13 The famous quotation is "A grain which in England is generally given to horses, but in Scotland supports the people." Dr. Johnson 1755.

14 Curiously enough, this Bengali method, Europeanized as "Patna Rice," was apparently unknown to both the Chinese and Japanese. Although they regarded it as of great importance that their soldiers could carry up to five days' supply of an undemanding food that required only boiling, both Chinese and Japanese High Commands knew by 1900 that

their soldiery would suffer from beriberi or thiamine deficiency. Ordinary polished rice was even carried by Japanese soldiers in World War II.

15 Ancient Ethiopia, a distinct culture in 2000 BC, was known for both wheat and sorghum excellence to travelers from Ancient Egypt. This makes the teff mystery even more extraordinary.

16 Besoms (or brooms) made of sorghum straw were sold as late as 1939 in Europe. Where Benjamin Franklin's came from is not known.

17 In 1905, Russian peasants who were, at most, two generations from serfdom were marched toward the railhead in order to fight the Japanese. They were wide-eyed with wonder. They passed the estate of their neighbor, then the next place, of which they had heard little, and then the next. The railhead was still far away, to be succeeded by 7000 miles' travel by train. "Where are the Japanese," they asked, "in the next estate or the one after?" This replicated what must have been true throughout Western Europe in medieval times.

18 In modern terms, the flow of a river in weight of water can be multiplied by the fall of the river in vertical distance and the product used to calculate kg/m to produce the theoretical horsepower available, less, of course, inefficiencies.

19 From this millstream, especially to drive the mill, it is a small intellectual step to a pipe leading to a more efficient turbine. This had to wait for the right materials. This took nearly 1850 years after Vitruvius, but preceded the generation of electricity. Low-efficiency turbines were built in 1828 in France, based on calculations made by Archimedes who died in 212 BC.

20 Pappus of Alexandria (Greek mathematician, early fourth century AD) perceived the classical weakness: "The mechanicians of Hero's school say that mechanics can be divided into a theoretical and a manual part; the theoretical part is composed of geometry, arithmetic, astronomy, and physics; the manual work in metals, architecture, carpentry, and the art of painting and the manual execution of these things. As it is not possible for the same man to excel in so many academic studies and at the same time to learn the aforesaid crafts, advise one who wishes to undertake 'mechanical work' to use such crafts as he already possesses in the task to be performed in each particular case." (Pappus, Book VIII, I.) The exchange between science and technology was one of the most positive, if unknown, factors in the Renaissance. Leonardo and Michelangelo made all kinds of inartistic devices to perform various tasks, an activity unbelievable in ancient times.

21 Econuts who wish to replace power stations with massive windmill farms should imagine the noise, discomfort, and danger caused by such developments. The idea of having to replace, repair, or renew windmills while another is cycling next door should deter all but the most enthusiastic doctrinaire. The other point is the high ratio of capital input to horsepower output. The windmill was often equivalent to a quarter of the investment on a prairie farm, apart from the cost of land itself.

22 The waste of power of all kinds has to be calculated to be believed. Even as late as 1952, 70 percent of all power "income" from carbon fuels, water power, or animal or human energy was wasted in process, transmission, and poor control. In 2004, after three energy crises, the 70 percent lost had only been reduced, at best, to 50 percent efficiency.

23 The actual order adopted for these improvements was published in the *Encyclopedia Britannica* of 1790, printed in Edinburgh. These eight factors were in all of the six or eight

"books of husbandry" printed in the eighteenth century. The *Britannica*, Third Edition, represents a consensus.

24 A great deal of very pleasant research is required to establish just how many metal-bashing establishments were started in the United Kingdom in the eighteenth and early nineteenth centuries. During the French Wars from 1792 to 1815, a huge number were involved in the supply of hardware to the army, the navy, and the thriving export trade. All of them derived, intellectually at least, from blacksmiths. They were the contractors and sub-contractors to many industries, including the leaders of the time, wool and cotton, coal and iron.

25 More properly, the horse blacksmith is a farrier, but a farrier was once not only a shoer of horses, but the precursor to modern veterinary surgeons. Horseshoes were unknown in Roman Europe and were introduced to England by William the Conqueror. The farrier, practicing farriery, was an important craftsman-expert who ministered to the health of the horses of the nobility and chivalry, with a particular knowledge of horse anatomy. At least as late as 1914, university graduates who became horse vets described themselves as "farriers."

26 In 600 BC what is now modern Greece probably had a population density of only about 15 people per square km. Modern densities are still only about 70 per square km, not much by Western European standards, but still forcing many people to live in remote areas, too steep and inhospitable for railways, too far for edibles to reach them before the internal combustion motor.

27 In the days before "artificial" fertilizers, which can increase the fertility of a farm at the tenant's expense, all fertilizers had to be "made" at home. To remove the stored-up fertility in animal residues from the lord's land and credit one's own with such wealth was a form of theft.

28 Daniel Defoe, *A Tour Through the Whole Island of Great Britain*, 1724.

29 The physical value of a soil is very much conditioned by the population of earthworms and, therefore, its lime status. Earthworms mix organic matter with the soil and prevent the formation of a mat in grassland and litter in arable conditions. They improve the soil by promoting aeration and drainage and the power of any soil to absorb and benefit from rain or irrigation. Earthworms also increase the "workability" of a soil, making it kinder for the cultivator, and there is a distinct advantage of several days in any soil with plenty of earthworms compared with the same soil without many.

30 Clover is a leguminous plant that lives in symbiosis with an appropriate strain of the nodule organism Rhizobium. The clover produces the carbohydrate and the organism synthesizes the nitrogen (from the air) required by the partnership. The nitrogen is used for the growth of the clover, and some may become available for the accompanying grass in the pasture. Grasses also benefit from the breakdown of the residues of the clover—leaves, roots, and the annual crop of nodules. In the days before synthetic nitrogen, clover was almost essential for the successful growth of nitrogen-demanding plants in the rest of the rotation.

31 In Ireland such outcrops were known as "elkpits."

32 Remission of rent was a powerful persuader in the hands of the landlord. In times of great change, it was often employed to make sure that tenants moved with the times.

33 It is worth noting that great British entrepreneurs, knowing something that the locals did not, scoured the battlefields of Europe for the bones of the fallen and the marl made

by the action of time and weather upon those bones. These were exported to England, either to make bone china or paper or to make bonemeal for manure. The marl, heavier, was sold locally. No one, before the romantic Victorians, thought such behavior reprehensible or sacrilegious.

34 Arthur Young, *Annals of Agriculture.*

35 One of the major effects of technology is to make land increasingly possible to cultivate, less "marginal." No one can do anything about the climate or weather, but soils can be made less acid, and more difficult conditions are susceptible to better implements. The horse proved to be much more flexible than the ox; careful breeding of livestock showed that they were more suitable for new conditions than had been the case in earlier times.

36 Nor was there any need at the time. Between 1750 and 1850, England had the largest increase in population ever measured up to then; the increase was even greater than in Ireland—a special case. This kind of increase was unknown in any other area of the world with the English limitations of land per person. In 1850, England, not Britain, had a density of population such that each individual enjoyed the produce of about 0.7 hectare. The next densest area in Europe (and probably in the world) was the Low Countries where each person was fed by about 1.2 hectares of farmland in 1850. See also Sir James Caird, *English Agriculture in 1850–51.*

37 These estimates of horse numbers have been worked out without any great confidence that some worthy will not query them. Railways increased, not reduced, horse numbers. There were more non-agricultural horses per million urban population than in rural areas. Horses were an index of prosperity, trade, and wealth. In both 1750 and 1850, England probably had a higher horse/people ration than any other European country, probably higher than any country except what is now the United States. Horse statistics given in *European Historical Statistics* are agricultural and very incomplete, non-existent in most countries before the late nineteenth century.

38 Illuminated Psalters are a good resource for medieval information, with reservations. (Psalters originated as plain collections of the Psalms of David.) The Luttrell Psalter (1338) is a great, illustrated tome, attractive to anyone interested in the period. It is in the British Museum, London. There is a caveat to be entered. All the processes described and illustrated were performed at a time of excessive and abundant labor. The procedures one hundred years later were quite different. The Windmill Psalter (illuminated in Canterbury in 1270) has the earliest extant illustration of a Western-type windmill, but it is known that windmills were in use in Normandy nearly a century earlier. Many Psalters have as illustrations the process of plowing, but there are no surviving illuminations of eight-ox teams although it is known that eight-ox teams were essential in many places. On the other hand, there are several illustrations of one-way plows that allow the furrows to fall all to one side by swinging the body over at the end of each bout. Yet a swing-plow, or one-way plow, was difficult to build in terms of medieval technology. They were too difficult for most Victorian plow builders, as were wheeled plows. There were probably more wheeled plows in Psalters than on the ground. Anyone who has plowed knows that a wheel can be a positive disadvantage in stony soils like chalk or oolite or "cornbrash," which constituted nearly three-quarters of the plowland of medieval England. It is difficult to avoid believing that Psalters illustrated what the aspirational patron wanted illustrating, so they should be used with pleasure tinged with caution.

39 Lapus lazuli probably came farther than any other raw art material that Europeans ever used. Marco Polo visited the mines in 1271. They were in modern Afghanistan, on the banks of the River Kokcha. The stone made a brilliant blue "enamel" and, ground up, a pigment to produce the true ultramarine or azure blue, a sky blue color and a greenish tinge. It is probable that no one in England knew it came from several thousand miles east of the Eastern Mediterranean, where it was probably purchased in Levantine markets.

40 After years of efforts, the manufacturing classes, led by cotton manufacturers Richard Cobden and John Bright, joined with radicals and free traders to persuade the Prime Minister, Sir Robert Peel (1788–1850), to repeal the Corn Laws in 1846. The laws, which covered the import and export of wheat from England, were originally introduced to try to keep the price of bread stable. They became unpopular when Britain began to import much of her grain supplies, resulting in high bread prices at a time of economic depression. The pretext for the repeal was the Irish Potato Famine in 1845, but the free traders were more interested in the principle than the circumstance.

41 Neo-Europeans were initially not necessarily interested in European food supplies. It was population pressure in Western Europe that outgrew home-produced grain, then "Baltic" grain, then made men look to the United States from the 1780s; every neo-Europe would not be in place as an exporter for another hundred years.

42 This is detailed in the Potato chapter of *Seeds of Change*, by the author, and it is not intended to repeat the narrative or arguments.

43 L. Quinctus Cincinnatus (c. 519–438 BC) Consul; dictator in 458 BC; found plowing by the messengers summoning him to office. He rescued Consul Minucius, who had been defeated and surrounded by the Aequi. He retired to his farm after sixteen days' dictatorship. A year before his death at the age of eighty, he became dictator once more to deal with a rising of the plebs. He is admired because he is supposed to have preferred work on the land to high office and because he gave up being a dictator voluntarily—an uncommon attribute.

44 As with Ireland, the whole contemporary view of Malthus in 1845–50 is reviewed in the Potato chapter of *Seeds of Change*, by the author, and it is appropriate for further reading.

CHAPTER THREE

1 Quoted in *Ecological Imperialism: The Biological Expansion of Europe*, Alfred W. Crosby Jr, Cambridge, 1986.

2 At that date, Madeira could probably feed itself. Today's capability is probably not much higher than in 1850 since the land is difficult to mechanize. Large areas still must be cultivated by hand, which is economically acceptable for wine, less acceptable for wheat.

3 The fisheries of Madeira are neither as productive as those of the Canaries nor as those of the Azores.

4 Finches, *Fringillidae*, are an adaptable, widely disseminated race of small songbirds with hard bills, often parasites on mankind, and capable of changing their habits with man-induced changes in the environment. The finches of the Canaries are the songbirds called "canaries," more properly *Serinus canarius*. They are native to the Azores and to Madeira, but not to the mainland of Africa near the Canaries. The native stock is olive green, darker above and mottled below. The yellow color is produced by selective

breeding in captivity. The native stock, though, differs greatly on each group of islands. See Charles Darwin, *Animals and Plants Under Domestication*, London, 1868.

5 Lanzarote, named after a Genoese, Lanzaroto Marocello, who discovered it in 1325, has become yet another tourist paradise since jet travel has made for easy access.

6 Dogs in Tahiti were fed meat by white sailors for the first time during the late eighteenth century, at the time of the first European visits, by Bougainville, Cook, and Bligh. Previously, the dogs had been vegetarian and were eaten by the indigenous natives. The same metamorphosis probably occurred in the Canaries.

7 The total land area of the Madeiran Islands is less than 80,000 hectares (200,000 acres).

8 The relationship today is that 1 kilo (2.5 lb) of gold is worth the same as 70 tons of sugar.

9 Carthaginian coins have been found on the island of Corvo.

10 Favorable Northeast tradewinds make possible the westward voyage of a crude sailing or sailing and rowing ship. There was not enough room on board to feed the crew of a pure (rowing) galley so that any return to Europe would require the ship to discover the Eastward winds north of the Azores, which, incidentally, Columbus knew about and used for his return to Europe in 1493. The Carthaginians, as far as is known, did not return. Perhaps they did not want to.

11 *Acor* means "hawk" in Portuguese.

12 The Azores have joined Bermuda, Shannon and Goose Bay in Labrador, and Gander, Newfoundland, as once-important refueling stops. These were all vital for years during and after World War II. Today, most people would not know of their onetime fame.

13 In 1950, people of African descent (all Negro) in the Americas numbered as follows: Unites States, 20 million–plus; Caribbean-washed countries, 20 million–plus; non-Caribbean Iberian America, at least 30 million—total 70 million–plus. In Africa the numbers were: from Senegal to Nigeria inclusive, excluding non-Negroes, 45 million– plus; from the Cameroons to Angola, excluding non-Negroes, 20 million–minus, probably no more than 18 million—total 63–65 million. Since 1950, West African population censuses have been very suspect for a number of political, not demographic, reasons. See R. M. Protheroe, *Geographical Magazine*, London 1974.

14 The words "cassava," "tapioca," and "manioc" all come from three different Amerindian languages describing the same plant. The botanical name is *Matlihot esculenta*, and Europeans found it cultivated between 25° N around Southern Florida, and as far as 25° S in Southern Brazil.

15 According to one Jesuit in about 1550, "natives" who knew neither leavened bread nor wine could not be Christians by nature, and were, therefore, logically not able to be pagans either. Such a doctrine, widely adopted, might have saved much misery.

16 Mexican mines reached their pre-Independence peak about 1810, just before the successful revolutions. The revolutions cut the gold supply, causing a slump. The production of the Mexican mines alone had been five to six times all the silver mined in the Americas in, say, 1550. It is a fair comment that if the Spanish Crown had had access to all the silver that was annually exported in the early 1800s, financial management would not have been developed enough to have dealt with the wealth. In other words, management was the problem, not precious metals. See Braudel, *The Mediterranean in the Age of Philip II: American Silver*. Fontana/Collins, London, 1975.

17 These seven cultivars are:

Pod maize: A primitive form of the corn, not commercial, turns up as a freak; was sometimes preserved by Amerindians who attributed to it magical virtues.

Popcorn: Grains small, with hard outside and small, soft, starchy center. On heating, steam generated inside the grain causes it to pop or explode.

Flint: Northern type, used by Pilgrim Fathers in 1619. Predominant ecotype in Europe, Asia, some parts of the Americas, and tropical Africa. Early maturing.

Dent: Southern type. Principal natural hybrid of Corn Belt in United States and of Mexico. Origin of most grain improvement in twentieth century. Late maturing.

Flour maize: Dryland grain type. Easily chewed when uncooked. Used to make Amerindian beer *Chicha* and mealie beer in South Africa. Easily ground. Used by primitive Amerindian tribes.

Sweet corn: Recessive prevents conversion of some sugar into starch. Used sometimes in conjunction with flour maize to make *Chicha.* Internationally used, cooked on the cob.

Waxy maize: Has different starch composition from other cultivars. Found mainly nowadays in Eastern Asia, particularly Japan. Useful as a source of industrial starch.

These are ecotypes, or cultivars, not botanical varieties. Maize has never been found growing in a wild state, and much work has been done by one man to uncover the origin of maize in historic terms. Maize going back to 3600 BC (carbon-dating) was found in the so-called Bat Cave in New Mexico in 1948–50. Further excavations in La Perry Cave, Northeast Mexico (1949), and the nearby Swallow Cave (1954) are to be compared with the Bat Cave discoveries. In 1954 maize pollen was discovered in a drill core 70 meters (300 feet) below Mexico City. This was carbon-dated to 80,000 BC. This was before mankind reached America and proves that it is an American plant unknown elsewhere. The work has been best described in *Corn: Its Origin, Evolution and Improvement,* P. C. Mangelsdorf, Cambridge, 1974. There are many technical papers by Mangelsdorf, MacNeish, Galinat, Kelley, and Lister. Maize is a fast-growing crop that requires a frost-free period of at least 120 days; the grain yield is very variable. In Israel and New Zealand, crops of over 6000 kg/ha (5340 lb/a) have been recorded; average, in New Zealand, over 4000 kg/ha (3560 lb/a). In peasant Africa, the yield is of the order on about 500 kg/ha (445 lb/a), one-twelfth of what has been achieved in Israel or New Zealand, and one-eighth the New Zealand average. The average in the United States is about 3 tons per hectare. This, in some places, fell to less than 1000 kg/ha (890 lb/a) in drought years like 1988.

18 Changes in the meaning of crop names are plentiful in the early post-Columbian period.

19 Elephant, lion, leopard, giraffe, hyena, buffalo, many kinds of antelope and gazelle, and innumerable monkeys. In the rivers there were rhinoceros, hippopotamus, and crocodile. There were more varieties of birds larger than pigeons than exist in Europe. These were the animals reported within 50 miles of the coast of the Bight of Ben before 1500. How could maize survive such predators? No wonder immune cassava caught on.

20 The three methods were first to interplant beans, which produced enough vitamin B4 to provide against pellagra; second, the Amerindians used ashes, lime or naturally occurring soda, or mollusk shells to process the grain by boiling for one hour, then washing, drying, and grinding the corn. This breaks down the cell walls, making the main storage protein, *zein,* less available to the human body. This in turn increases the availability of lysine by 2.8 times and of tryptophan by 1.3 times and releases B4.

Other tribes allowed the corncob to rot under mud for two to three months. This has the same effect as adding beans, or boiling with ashes, lime, etc. None of these three techniques were taken by Europeans to Europe. As a result, pellagra (*rough skin* in Italian) became a common complaint in the Mediterranean. Pellagra is a deficiency disease of poverty, caused by an absence of alternative foods, common in winter when homegrown vegetables are scarce. Ironically, the disease retreated during the Depression in the Deep South when unprofitable cotton gave way to subsistence vegetables that provided balance to the staple of maize.

21 The *Solanaceae* include tomato, potato, aubergine, capsicum, the tree tomato, Cape gooseberry, tobacco, belladonna, thorn apple, henbane, and mandrake; only belladonna, henbane, and mandrake are native to Europe. The rest come from the Americas, although there is some suggestion that thorn apple is indigenous, in some forms, in tropical Africa as well as America.

22 Apart from cannibalism, the Incas had almost every attribute of which modern liberal Democrats disapprove. It was a dictatorship, illiterate but highly numerate, with a statistical obsession expressed in knots of a decimal nature and akin to a crude computer. The central records were called "Quipu." The people below the Royal Incas by birth were all equal, all servile, and all working for the greater glory of the rulers. There was no money, no written record except statistics, no slavery in the European sense, and no form of exchange except through state barter. Marriages were controlled by the state; social security was from the cradle to the grave; famines were abolished by great storehouses of several seasons' food. The central government controlled the amount of land allotted to each person and denied all any real private ownership, except perhaps the peasant's house in some places.

23 The full story is told in the Potato chapter of *Seeds of Change*, by the author.

24 See E. C. Large, *The Advance of the Fungi*, Jonathan Cape, 1940.

25 German potato production increased from 7 million tons in 1846 to just below 50 million tons in the years immediately before 1914. In the same period, the population increased from 30 million to nearly 70 million. As recently as 1935–50 in what used to be Imperial Germany, a greater tonnage (by dry matter) was grown of potatoes than of wheat or rye.

26 The only other plant common to New Zealand and the Americas is the cotton plant, *Gossypium*, several varieties of which have been floated in seawater for up to two years while the seeds remained viable. It is possible that cottons, coconuts, and the sweet potato floated from the Americas to the South Pacific.

27 *Travels in France*, 1794.

28 Fatty liver is the human condition, usually attributed to living too well. There is, however, a cottage industry in inducing the same condition in geese through forcible feeding without choice. A goose liver in epicurean condition may weigh as much as one-fifth of the entire plucked and clean carcass. This condition of the liver was encouraged as early as the time of Justinian in Constantinople sixth century AD. But maize made the job much easier. More digestible than any Old World animal food, maize permits a very rapid over-fattening of the goose, usually by force-feeding.

29 Starving Irish peasants were given uncooked, whole maize without being told how to deal with it. Not surprisingly, they continued to starve. This cruel folly was first committed during the Famine of 1845–46, but repeated at later moments of shortage.

30 Scurvy was an annual familiar in pre-Columbian Europe during the late winter and spring, before the fresh vegetables first appeared.

31 The population of Pomerania and East Prussia, where the peasants came from in the nineteenth century, remained fairly static, while that of the Rhineland and Westphalia increased by more than any other part of Germany in the fifty years before 1914, with the sole exception of Berlin, the capital. *European Historical Statistics 1750–1975*, Macmillan, 1981.

32 The alkaloid, *piperine*, creates its own demand in the system. Demand is inelastic. When supply was a problem in the years immediately after World War II, the world price rose by over sixteen times, and attempts were made to naturalize the plant in the United States. See *Journal of Economic Botany, 1955*.

33 S. E. Morison, London, *Christopher Columbus Mariner*, 1956.

34 One effect is that, in secondhand aircraft of the so-called Curry Airlines, an appreciable sum has to be discounted for refurbishment. It may cost nearly a million dollars to tear out the curry-infested furnishings and replace them with new. Curry Airlines therefore has to depreciate aircraft at a higher rate than other airlines. There is no means of ventilation that can cope with the olfactory burden.

35 Caribou have been tamed in more recent times.

36 Certain very vulnerable animals survived, like the passenger pigeon.

37 There may or may not have been domestic poultry.

38 See page 96.

39 George Ordish, *The Great Wine Blight*, Sidgwick & Jackson, 1987.

40 See description, Quinine chapter in *Seeds of Change*, by the author.

41 Certain fish oils and olive oil, uniquely amongst edible oils, actually reduce cholesterol in the human bloodstream. Animal fats, of course, increase the level.

42 Charles Darwin noticed one such phenomenon in 1833. By 1870, this had become an important industry. The orange groves of Paraguay produced millions of cases for export before 1914, and millions of tons of *floating* oranges and lemons, and crosses, were netted from the rivers downstream and fed to pigs and beef cattle, and the carcasses exported. As far as is known, there were thousands of acres of citrus fruits before the white man arrived in force in Paraguay in 1620; none of the early citrus orchards were planted by humans.

43 A French engineer named Frezier (no pun; the French for strawberry is *fraise*) was in Chile in the early eighteenth century. He brought back the large-berried native Chilean strawberry. It was crossed with the *fraise du bois* in about 1720, and modern strawberry culture began. The South American cultivar had the size; the European, the taste.

44 The loganberry is named after its breeder (or discoverer), Judge Logan; this Californian is said by some to have bred the cross between a raspberry and blackberry. That was in 1881, and dispute still rages as to whether the hybrid was a natural "sport" or developed with judicial cunning.

45 There cannot have been many wild dogs or wolves, or the sheep refused to panic. Almost any European breed of domesticated sheep today refuses to stand up to dogs when attacked.

46 Ironically, however good merino wool may have been in the sixteenth century, it can never have been of the same quality as fiber from the Andean ungulates—alpaca, llama,

vicuna, and guanaco. Alpaca wool is supreme in the world for length, sometimes stretching to 304 mm (12 in). Vicuna is soft, fine, and very supple. In fact, none of this wool could find its proper market until Titus Salt (1803–76) invented a method of machine weaving, using a cotton warp and an ungulate weft. From the date of this invention in 1836, imports into England from Peru and Chile rose from $50,000 a year to an average of more than $1.25 million a year in the last ten years of the nineteenth century. In 1853 Salt also built a model manufacturing town, on the River Aire, named Saltaire, inspiration for Cadbury, Hershey, and Lever company towns built later in the nineteenth century.

47 How quickly can wild pigs multiply? How long is a piece of string? De Soto, in Florida in 1539, brought ashore thirteen pigs, sex unspecified, and killed them with careful restraint only when very hungry; three years later, there were seven hundred. Hodges & Lewis, *Spanish Explorers in the Southern United States,* Scribner, New York, 1907.

48 There have been innumerable instances of horses warning their riders of hostile humans, dangerous snakes like rattlers, or bad paths ahead. The wise rider makes use of this information.

49 Within a few years of the English arrival in Virginia, the plantain was known by Indians as "The Englishman's Foot." It was meant to grow only where an Englishman had trod. A hundred years later it had reached the Mississippi, long before more than a few Englishmen, if any.

CHAPTER FOUR

1 Review of *Seeds of Change* in *Smithsonian Magazine,* 1986.

2 t should not be forgotten that the United States, acknowledged by the world in 1783, was followed into nationhood by Iberian America within forty years. This time, the British encouraged those who believed in independence.

3 This was almost a deliberate policy, that overseers and managers should be half-breeds. There was a feeling that they could act as intermediaries between the black slaves (or Amerindians) and the white owners.

4 Many consider the potato to have arrived indirectly from Spain, but it was important in Ireland by 1620. Tobacco was widespread in Europe by the same date.

5 There was a very early comparison between the climatic difficulties for European manual labor in Virginia and the same sort of work on the same sorts of farms in New England. In fact, summer temperatures are often very similar. The slave trade to Virginia can be seen as a cultural matter. It was a very different problem when cotton came along in the nineteenth century, in an important way.

6 George Vancouver was a captain, RN, who accompanied Captain James Cook on the second and third voyages from 1772–1780. After the Treaty of Versailles of 1783, which gave the United States true independence, Vancouver was sent as commander of an expedition to the northwest coast of America, north of the Spanish settlements in California, and south of the Russian settlements in Alaska. The impulse was as much anti-Spanish and anti-Russian as anti-American. A *Voyage of Discovery to the North Pacific and Round the World in 1790-95,* London, 1798. Incidentally, George Vancouver was one of John Kerry's ancestors, but no relation to Charles Vancouver, U.S. agriculturalist

7 This perception was of great importance in building Puritan morale.

8 "The Indians," wrote William Bradford of Plymouth, "fell down so generally of this disease as they were in the end not able to help one another, no, not to make a fire, nor fetch a little water to drink, nor any to bury the dead." *Of Plymouth Plantations*, ed. S. E. Morison, New York, 1952.

9 There was an interesting selection process at work. Settled Indians were hit harder than hunter-gatherers. Did smallpox over, say, two centuries induce Indians to cease being settled, as did the horse? By extension, have diseases, deep in history, inhibited or retarded early settlement of land and the establishment of agriculture? Have diseases dependent upon density been responsible for mankind's rather short period as a farmer?

10 The Common Law is shared with every English neo-Europe except South Africa, which has its own complicated system. The ex-colonies, starting with the United States, have produced judicial decisions that have then become part of the laws of England. Seven once-Spanish Western states in the United States also have specific, non-English laws, such as communal property.

11 The chief long-term permanent effect of the now forgotten Swedish colony was to make Nordic construction for houses, now known as log cabins, fashionable throughout the American colonies. The English timber method of the time was "clapboard."

12 The "fall line" was the point on a river on the Eastern Seaboard where ships met the first serious waterfall or set of rapids. This was farther inland on the Hudson than on the Connecticut River, but the fall line existed on every river as far south as South Carolina. The extent of navigation possible below the fall line often dictated the rapidity of development of the colony, the Chesapeake Bay area being outstandingly well placed.

13 This problem of "poor" land, impoverished by settlers, was an issue within a generation of arrival in every colony, especially where the exhausting crop tobacco was grown.

14 Average size of ship, as measured in those days, under 100 tons. This was smaller than all but the smallest individual ship crossing the Atlantic other than Spanish ships whose minimum in 1587 was raised to 300 tons. It was not a question of safety so much as the relationship between crew and cargo that was much more favorable on large ships than on small ones. However, English and American sailors were free men, did not favor over-manning, and were often largely employed on "shares," like ancient and modern fishermen. Small ships also gained favor after 1650 because developments in guns made the small ship much closer to the large in a fair fight.

15 The great Mississippi Valley offered a southbound waterway from a few miles west of the Appalachians in Western Pennsylvania and Virginia, and the Great Lakes were connected to the Hudson by the Erie Canal in 1825. A network followed, connecting Lake Erie with the Ohio and Wabash Rivers, Lake Michigan at Chicago with the Illinois River at La Salle, and two other canals that crossed the Appalachians. These were mostly in place before the slump years 1837–44. The Chicago–La Salle canal was not finished until 1845 and was exceptional in that it carried sewage and that it fell from Lake Michigan to the Mississippi River. Most of the canals were state funded. Eight Western and Southern states defaulted by 1840, confirming the view that risk was best taken by private investors.

16 Chicago was made by the railroads. Before 1830, it took three weeks to reach New York; in 1860, two days; in 1890, one day; in 1910, sixteen hours. Before 1840, wagons would stream across the surrounding plain to deliver grain for the waterborne trade at Chicago. By 1870 there were twelve railroads meeting at Chicago; by 1900, more than twenty, after which date there was some amalgamation and rationalization. The population has

followed the railroad into the great city: in 1830, less than 100 people; in 1840, 4479, after which the city grew at 8.6 percent compound per year until 1900, when its population was over 1.6 million. The great fire of 1871 caused hardly a dent in this material progress, which was celebrated at the World's Columbian Exposition in 1892–93.

17 The rate of growth of the white American population before 1846 reached annual increases of 3 percent—not so many died in childhood as did in Europe. Population increases among black slaves were sometimes at a higher rate. Both impressed Malthus with the extraordinary reproductive capacity of human beings in a favorable situation. It was Ireland, of course, not America, that proved Malthus's gloomy predictions right, but the Irish surplus turned up in America in any case. Or the more fortunate did.

18 No one should be impressed by the anachronistic sentiments that are current about the early white settlers in Australia, mostly convicts. They were extremely lucky, most of them, as many realized when they looked back in prosperous old age, at their progress since being reprieved from the gallows. To claim, as some have done, that they should not have been transported is to use today's attitudes to criticize actions two hundred years old.

19 In the Finnish famine of 1697, 35 percent of the population died. In the most recent famine, that of 1867, 8 percent still died, but huge numbers went to the United States.

20 Average for Iowa in 1900–05.

21 Clarence Darrow, the great liberal lawyer, after the Pullman strike, 1894.

22 The critical problem is not frost, but snow. Frosted land can be plowed; to plow snow into the ground is difficult and creates trouble for future cultivation.

23 The gold-equivalent cost today would be $12.50 and would buy a good deal of simple food, steak, potatoes, bread, vegetables, coffee, eggs, bacon, or corn flour.

24 Australia was at times a great source of supply of horses, often as army "remounts" exported to British possessions in the East, in South Africa, and even to Egypt. There were great stories about Australians and horses; see *Breaker Moran*, 1902.

25 American wagons, unlike those in Europe, carried grain in bulk, not sacks, from at least as early as 1840 during the canal era and before railroads were widely spread. These wagons were "tippers" long before those in Europe. All this to save labor.

26 Yield tended to fall, on average, after the first few seasons.

27 One searcher after artifacts found a hundred-year-old plow in a creek near Waterloo, Iowa, in 1976, just in time for the bicentennial.

28 The continuous cheapening of the "factory" chicken has proved to be both virtuous and vicious. Ostensibly, poultry meat is now available for far less in real terms than in 1910, but the means to this end are unpleasant for the birds, and the process offensive to many consumers. Dietary value is also suspect.

29 Mendel never affected plant breeders or geneticists consciously until the years after World War I, and Mendel was not wholly accepted until 1930 at the earliest. There was a contemporary saying that a cross between black and white would produce one white, one black, and two khaki. This was the extent of understanding of Mendel in about 1910. It was on a par with Disraeli, who, when asked in the 1870s with reference to Darwin whether he thought mankind was descended from apes or angels, replied, "On the whole, I am on the side of the angels." This saying has since been much misunderstood and misused.

30 Successful farmers ceased to be primary producers and became converters of (often imported) feeding stuffs, tailoring the product—milk, eggs, meat—to the demands of the market. Business acumen became more important than husbandry, even more important than technical skills. Survivors amongst farmers became people who could survive at any job.

31 Chemical expertise in Germany was essential to its expansion before 1914 and to its wartime efforts afterward. This was in every area of life as well as farming, but agriculture benefited then as now. Western Germany is now home to three of the world's largest agrochemical companies.

32 See George Ordish, *The Great Wine Blight*, Sidgwick and Jackson, London, 1987.

33 To *empolder* land, the first step is to surround the area with high, raised "quays" of soil to keep out the external water and to control that within. The next stage is to pump out the water within the polder. This may take two years by windmill and is a continuous process, since the new polder must be drained for all time. Water pumping by windmill became cost-effective about 1560; after 1850 steam was sometimes substituted. Much of the Netherlands is now below sea level and is provided with drainage pumps that need 12 hp (now electrical) for every 1000 hectares (2471 acres) that are one meter (three feet) below sea level, but more or less elsewhere. In most of the Zuider Zee, empoldered in this century, this means about 1 hp per 100 hectares (247 acres). The drainage channels, which are higher than the new polder, are used for navigation and irrigation canals. The reclaimed soil may take ten years to become fully desalinated.

34 Mussolini's Fascist regime was not a great economic success, leaving aside the incompetence and cruelty associated with bully-boys and castor oil. He was praised in some circles in the 1920s and 1930s because "he made the trains run on time." Despite this, plus cleaning up the drains of Venice and removing malaria from the Pontine Marshes and some of the Po Valley, there was nothing consistent or competent about Fascist "planning." The weakness of Fascism was the same as that of Nazism or Communism. No economy can operate efficiently in a climate that does not permit plural political or economic opinion, namely choice. This is what has saved democracy throughout the world. Modern examples may include Russia, Poland, and Ukraine.

35 Since Roman times, white bread has been a status symbol. Until 1870 modern white bread was impossible to make. White bread flour needs steel rollers that are easy to adjust and maintain and use one-fifth the power of stone rollers. Steel-ground flour is far easier to sieve since the particle size is far more uniform. Steel rollers that came from Austria-Hungary, one of that Empire's few contributions to technology, and fine sieves had, by 1890, rendered the bread of the poor little more than energy, of little greater value than white sugar.

White bread of a hundred years ago contained no vitamin A or D and little vitamin B1. Iron and Niacin (vitamin B4) were nearly halved by the exclusion of the fibrous portion of the flour. In London in 1890–1900, the lack of fiber plus the low level of value in the white bread led to malnutrition among the poor, who ate little else besides tea, margarine, and condensed milk. At that date, none of these products were fortified with vitamins. (See *The Englishman's Food*, London, 1957.)

Army officers were horrified by the poor physical state of recruits during the South African War of 1899–1902. Compared with soldiers from the neo-Europes, the British had 5 cm (2 in) less height, thinner bones, less muscle, and far less chest expansion; their teeth were also of poor quality. This military horror seeped through into the national consciousness and conscience, but it would be forty years before action was taken to protect the poor by the reinforcement of bread and margarine, by raising the extraction rate of flour to 85 percent, by encouraging consumption of fresh vegetables and milk, and by increasing the awareness of food values. During 1940–53, food became a weapon of the Welfare State fairly distributed to all, largely rationed. After the War itself, "fair Shares" became a social and political policy that bred unwanted and uncovenanted side effects.

36 Some grain is grown in Sweden, even north of Stockholm, and in small quantities in Iceland and Eastern Siberia, for "strategic" reasons.

37 Any serious student should consult an atlas with good climatic charts.

38 Ratio of people to soil remains considerably more favorable than the same ratio in the United States, less favorable than in Canada.

39 The fierce Russian reaction to Muslim nomads from the days of Ivan the Terrible (d. 1584) was supported by peasants and nobles alike; presumably this was a folk memory of the slaving sweeps from the south and east. The capture and sale of Christian boys to become the Mamelukes of Egypt did not stop until 1798, but by that date this largely affected the hinterland of the Crimea.

40 It is worth noting, perhaps, that the plague still raged in Central Asia. Russian railways were built to avoid ancient cities and plague itself.

41 Russian peasants moving south and east took with them their own microorganisms. These diseases acted like white man's diseases in the Americas, and the biological experience of the natives in the new settlements in Siberia was similar to that of the Amerindian.

42 "The *mir* was not a collective; farming in it was carried out privately, by households." *Russia under the Old Regime*, Richard Pipes, London 1974.

43 A primitive man, achieving a small increase of seed garnered over seed sown (in 1900 this might be only on the order of 6 or 7:1 against an increase in England of 20:1), might well decide to try a different piece of land or a different farm. In the absence of soil analysis, cultural expertise, fertilizers, and proper implements, what better alternative was there? The Soviet Union ought to have solved the problem between 1917 and 1990.

44 Sisyphus, father of Odysseus, cheated death for a time and was punished by being forced to roll a stone up a hill; each time the stone neared the top, it rolled down again. This was considered a just punishment for a crafty, deceitful politician, which Sisyphus was. The labors of Sisyphus are commonly experienced in the development of ideas before their time, or in ideas beyond the audience, or in any good idea badly managed.

45 Professor Nordman, *Peace Problems*, London 1920.

46 Statistic used derived from *European Historical Statistics, 1750-1970*, B. R. Mitchell, London 1975. Caution should be exercised in this area. There are Stalinized statistics still at large.

47 Trade had been carried on between Japan, Korea, and China from about AD 700, and Chinese navigators knew of the extent of the Japanese political empire. Some of this information may have reached Europe upon Marco Polo's return to Venice in 1295. For the next two hundred years, scanty information about Japan was blown up into mythological wonderland territory.

48 It also remains a mystery as to how long Columbus went on thinking that those few islands in the Caribbean that he *did* discover in 1492–93 were part of Asia.

49 Jesuits then and ever since have found it economical of manpower to convert Top People and let example, authority, or fashion operate upon Top People's followers.

50 The pre-Spanish population of the Philippines was on the order of half a million, against today's 50 million. The total land area is almost exactly the same as that of the whole of the British Isles. The native Filipinos were ignored by their neighbors until 1570 when they found themselves to be the bone of contention between Spanish soldiers from Mexico and Muslim *Moros* from Borneo. The Spanish won without a great deal of difficulty.

It was no accident that the Philippines was colonized from Mexico. It thus became the most westward of the Spanish Dominions, although it should, under the Treaty of Saragossa in 1529, have been the most eastward of the Portuguese. The Spanish, of course, cheated, and to make their deceit legitimate they continued to approach the Philippines from Acapulco. This had two results. The first was that the Philippines became the Asian port of entry for all American cultivars: tobacco, cocoa, pineapple, capsicum, tomatoes, maize, potato, and so forth. Maize reached China before it reached India; tobacco reached Japan before it reached Persia; capsicum reached Hungary from the Philippines and became paprika. Second, antagonism between Spanish and Portuguese Far Eastern traders informed their behavior in Japan, even after the nominal unity between Portugal and Spain under the Spanish Crown from 1580 to 1640. The Japanese always distinguished between the two nations as far as traders were concerned.

51 Translated by Captain Frank Brinkley, RN, *The Times* correspondent in Japan, and historian, 1906.

52 Connoisseurs of Sir Walter Scott will not forget the Muslim sword, given by Saladin to Richard the Lionheart, that would cleave a cushion, a feat then impossible for any Western sword. Japanese swords were even better, able to cleave the traditional human hair. Sir Walter Scott, *The Talisman*, 1825.

53 There were from 5 to 7 percent of noble samurai and their families in the population. It is difficult to believe that there was more than half of 1 percent of skilled sword-makers.

54 There was, of course, the fabled meeting of the French and English Royal Guards at the battle of Fontenoy in 1745. The two lines met face-to-face, and an English officer ran forward and asked the French to fire first. The French refused, whereupon the English fired, and nearly 1000 French Guards officers and men fell at the volley. Such niceties of conduct were uncommon in Europe, nor did this case help the English, who, with their German and Dutch allies, lost this particular battle.

55 In 2000, as in 1980, 99 percent of Japanese were "functionally literate" against 80 percent of Americans, and this with a much more difficult language than English. Japanese IQ is the highest in the world, seven points above that of Japan in 1938, and ten points above the United States or Western Europe. Two percent of Western Europeans' and Americans' IQs are above 130, 10 percent of Japanese. Yet Japan spends a lower proportion of GNP on teaching than any other advanced country. Classes of seventy are common; but there are no dropouts, no streaming, no underachievers. There is a national consensus that education is an absolute necessity for nation and individual alike, not a battleground, or a privilege, or a pressure group. Nor is there much abstract love of knowledge. The whole Japanese success for forty years after World War II was due to the relationship of the intelligence of the nation to conceptual skills. It is a function of attitude, not money.

56 Buddhist attitudes to fish and game are not the same as feelings for other animals, otherwise Japanese intelligence would not be as high as it is.

57 Chinese intervention in 1950 prevented the United Nations from defeating the Communist North Koreans after the latter had invaded the South.

58 This is a comparative term. Constructing a "basket" of the world's ten least successful economies reveals that such an index against the yen has declined by over 300 times since 1950. Burma, which is far poorer than it was in 1922, has declined in relative prosperity since the Greater Asian Co-Prosperity Sphere came to an end in Japan's defeat in 1945, by 1000 times, compared with Japan forty years on.

59 Watchman, Walkman, RAM, world's newest rail system, magnetic levitation, low temperature physics, compact COs, etc.

60 The magnificence of the Edo period, of almost complete isolation, was made plain to the West in *The Great Japan* Exhibition, London, 1981–82. What was not obvious was that the unique nature of the civilization was due to the response of the Japanese to the Forces of Change. No other people responded in exactly the same way to its own space challenge. Their problems in the last ten years do not deny their virtues, but emphasize their limitations.

CHAPTER FIVE

1 A simple progression—64–41–26. Years, in each case, for the population to double.

2 It is important to remember that medical improvements have to follow previous improvements in microscopes. Magnifications of about 20 were possible in 1800, 100 in 1900. No germs are visible with the naked eye; without microscopes, pathologists would be blind. At 250, not only is the flea that carries the Bubonic Plague, *Xenopsylla cheopsis*, visible, but the flea's own parasite can also be seen. Doubtless at 2000 the parasite of the parasite of the flea can be seen. The electron microscope has increasingly superseded the optical instrument since about 1960.

3 Robert Koch (1843–1910) discovered the bacillus of TB in 1882, of cholera in 1883–84, and the phthisis bacillus in 1890. In 1891 he was Director of the new Berlin Institute for Infectious Diseases. In 1896 and 1906 he worked on rinderpest and other African cattle disease. Nobel Prize, 1905.

4 Quinine chapter of *Seeds of Change*, by the author.

5 The new disease threats, MRSA and HIV 1 and 2, are detailed in this chapter.

6 Barbitone was discovered by Nebelthau and christened "Veronal" by his friend von Mering, since the latter considered Verona to be the most restful city in the world.

7 Sarah Gamp, a character in *Martin Chuzzlewit*, 1843–44, was unwashed, selfish, opinionated, and, in terms of the infectious patients whom she nursed, a killer; she was not deliberately evil, just ignorant and careless, knowing and suspecting nothing about microbes. For a time, her typically English umbrella became known as a "Gamp." She was apparently representative of the period before Florence Nightingale, despite Dickens's record as a propagandist in other matters.

8 What is "the natural term"? is a difficult question. It is obviously far beyond the ability to reproduce, which is the natural term of most other animals.

9 There are alternatives: Witness the imaginative and productive use of the superior tactile sense of the blind in Japan; in some industries, the blind perform very high-tech tasks.

10 According to *Scientific American* in 1976, *unused* potential arable land was as follows in each
of these areas: Europe, 12 percent; Asia, 17 percent; USSR, 36 percent; North America,
49 percent; Africa, 78 percent; South America, 89 percent; and Oceania, 90 percent.
Shortage of suitable land is not, therefore, a problem in America, Africa, or Australasia.
Population changes since 1976 have modified these figures, but not by very much, except
in Africa.

11 The drift into the shantytowns in Africa is a function of rural underinvestment. Ironically, it may be less difficult to fund rural areas than towns.

12 Ethiopia, an area in a repeated war-famine-disease syndrome since 1979, has always had
a surplus population problem. In 2000 BC, Ethiopian slaves were on offer in the markets
of Egypt, some of them voluntarily. It is probable that slaves also reached what is now
Iraq at the same time.

13 Medieval rations for workers in Cairo were lower than 1500 calories a day; at the time
of the Christian slaves who built the Citadel after Saladin's victories over the Crusaders,
there was a special ration for the "Franks," who were large men, larger than most native
Muslims. This was in 1187–90. Smaller rations are appropriate in warmer climates for
obvious reasons.

14 Disease was greatly reduced in East Africa. As a result, the population has increased
by nearly five times since 1900, and by nearly three times since 1950. Forests have been
destroyed, erosion increased, agricultural potential reduced, and intertribal warfare and
horrors beyond imagination have become commonplace outside Kenya, which, despite
its near 4 percent annual population increase, is managed relatively well. Not so elsewhere, where deforestation threatens more than East African livelihoods. In addition
to massive tribal killings in both Uganda and Rwanda-Burundi, there has been serious
deforestation that has threatened to affect the Nile flow. In 1988 the region was made
miserable not only by savage acts of mankind, but also by excessive rainfall in some
places and serious drought in others.

    Much was expected of Tanzania in 1960, but it has become a notorious socialist
slum, not far behind Burma in human-induced misery. However, economic failure
has at least kept down the population increase; Tanzania increased its population by
94 percent between 1950 and 1975, Kenya by 126 percent, Uganda by 140 percent, and
Rwanda-Burundi by 100 percent. The misery induced by population increase is plain for
all to see. In East Africa most of the increase was due to reduced disease unmatched by
agricultural husbandry.

    The original edition of this book was written before 1989. Since that date HIV/AIDS
has ravaged parts of sub-Saharan Africa. The proportion of babies born with HIV/AIDS
in their bloodstreams varies from 10 percent to over 60 percent in places. Abstinence and
sexual fidelity are seen to be more effective than condoms whose successful use requires
a kind of domestic hygiene not always present.

    Malaria has made a great comeback, the protozoa having mutated faster than the
antibiotic drugs. The comparison with MRSA and antibiotics is apt.

15 The Pill is relatively expensive and can cause thrombosis; the coil is dangerous; the
rhythm method is often ineffective if desire overcomes arithmetic. A successful birth
control program involves a degree of literacy and numeracy, as well as an effective medical infrastructure.

16 During the Nigerian Civil War in the late 1960s, dried milk was sent as a relief measure for Biafran babies. Much to the surprise of the milk providers, many Biafran babies

died when given milk to drink. Milk, to be properly digested, requires an enzyme in the stomach, lactase. This enzyme is peculiar to the milk of each species. Most babies either have the enzyme necessary to digest their own mother's milk or receive the enzyme in the mother's milk. With the exception of Western Europeans and neo-Europeans, most humans in the world do not have the enzyme or the ability to digest the milk of cows, sheep, or horses. In most of the world, domesticated animal milk has to be turned into cheese or yogurt to make it available to humans. Countries that have the highest level of lactase in human stomachs are those with a long tradition of drinking raw milk: Sweden, Switzerland, and some states in the United States. None of this was discovered before 1970.

17 The number of Canadian farm horses impressed the young A. G. Street, who spent a year or two in Canada before World War I. There were two million farm horses in Canada, as many as in the United Kingdom. He was also impressed by the practice in the prairie provinces of letting horses fend for themselves during the winter. They apparently returned to work in the spring as fat as butter, despite sub-zero temperatures for more than 100 days.

18 With a similar input of machinery, hand labor, fertilizers, pest control, etc., maximum output *per acre* has often returned many crops to the country of origin. Some countries have been able to increase levels of certain inputs: New Zealand leads the world for maize production, Holland for potatoes, France for tobacco.

19 This direct import of the dung beetle was an example of lateral thinking of a high order. There were no major herb-eating species in Australia until the whites imported them in the late eighteenth century. By the time the bicentennial was within sight, the more productive pastures of Eastern Australia held 150 years of unrecycled dung, impossible to manage without physical removal or plowing the pasture. Ergo, introduce a dung-cycling insect. The best available was the African scarab, considered an almost holy creature in Ancient Egypt for the same reason.

20 Large numbers of Aborigines were killed by the parasites brought in by the First Fleet and every succeeding immigrant ship. *The History of Smallpox in Australia, 1788–1900,* Australian Quarantine Service, 1914. Some Aborigines thought that the British deliberately brought the disease with them to kill the natives. The British, at the time, did not make the imaginative leap necessary to realize what they were doing.

21 Research at the Copenhagen Zoo in the 1950s produced a good Landrace look-alike from one pair of wild boar after twenty generations of selection. The genetic bank in a pair of pigs is almost as rich as that in a pair of humans.

22 The European rat, unconsciously introduced by every ship landing in the New World or Australia, often threatened the very lives of the human immigrants with whom they had crossed the oceans. Rats grew in size, aggression, and numbers in the neo-Europes, multiplying far faster than humans. In the early days of colonies in America and Australia, rats also multiplied faster than human food crops; it was the humans who suffered, not the rats.

23 Sir Edmund Hillary, born 1919. First man, with Sherpa Tenzing, to stand indubitably on the summit of Everest, 29 May 1953. First man to cross the South Pole overland, 1958–59. The "Conquest of Everest" occurred just before the Coronation of Queen Elizabeth II, and for a time encompassed the Coronation Year with rosy expectations of new Elizabethan glory, adventure, exploration, and success.

24 A "unit" of nitrogen is one kg per hectare (one lb per acre), and the problem with a grass-clover sward is that in cold springs, drought, or very wet summers, production may be so uneven as to be unmanageable. Better potential management makes the use of nitrogen much more attractive to the farmer. In New Zealand, on the other hand, clover is worth much more, probably three to four times its European value. This is by reason of climate. It is worth mentioning here for the sake of those who protest at the use of Nitrogen because of its effects upon nitrate in drainage water, there is no drainage difference between organic and inorganic Nitrogen. Clover nodules, broken down in the winter, produce as much nitrate as inorganic nitrogen from the chemical works. The latter, of course, has to be converted to organic Nitrogen largely in the soil before it can do its work in any case. See *Bulletin* 48, Commonwealth Agricultural Bureaux, Farnham, England, 1970.

25 Australia and New Zealand are in many respects geologically similar.

26 "Kiwifruit" is the Chinese Gooseberry, not much thought of in China, grown wild, a creeper, never domesticated, "discovered" by a British botanist in 1900, and named *Actinidia chinensis.* Naturalized in New Zealand and first harvested in 1906, it became fashionable only with *nouvelle cuisine* in the 1960s. Planted in Southern Europe and California before 1970. To the delight of anyone who knows its history, it appears in wooden boxes in England marked "Genuine Italian Kiwi Fruit." Rich in vitamin C, the fruit keeps for several months in cold store, as do apples.

One astonishing Darwinian transformation has been that of the New Zealanders into neo-Europeans. Tied to the British market until the 1970s, and in deep economic trouble after the United Kingdom joined the EEC in 1974, New Zealanders consciously became Thatcherites by the 1990s. One example of their success is wine. New Zealand wines were unknown in Europe or in commerce in 1985. Twenty years later they sell for a higher unit price than other New World wines and threaten all but the best European alternatives, even in France. Enough said, but there is a great deal besides wine in the transformation.

27 The importance of an independent judiciary has always been understood in terms of human rights. A similar and perhaps equal importance attaches to a fraud-free, fair, unbribable system of commercial justice. No successful economy has existed over a period of time without such a benefice. In some Latin American countries it has been impossible to enforce the law of contract without bribery, as has been the case for many years in certain Asian countries.

28 Brazil, with about 150 million people, is much the most populous Iberian country, but it is hardly a neo-Europe, being largely in the tropics. Argentina, with more than 30 million, is indubitably "the most populous Southern Hemisphere neo-Europe."

29 Hong Kong, with a population of 10,000 when ceded to Britain in 1842, now has a population of over five million; nearly all the massive growth has been in this century. It is a one-off city that defies analysis.

30 Cash crops by definition have to yield better than subsistence crops in a free society. In some landholding systems, the occupier has been compelled to grow an unprofitable cash crop. Not so in India, ever.

31 The way that farmers exchange information over methodology is in contrast to their discretion about actual markets. There is as much pride in showing neighbors the production process as there is discrete satisfaction about achieving a good price in the sale of produce.

32 There was apparently a time in the 1930s when steam locomotives in Brazil were fuelled with coffee that could not be sold. The smell was said to be unforgettable.

33 Most historians agree that the Soviets killed more people than the Nazis.

34 By 1965, twenty years after World War II, there was probably not a crop of any significance anywhere in the world that could not be protected from its associated weeds.

35 DDT, dieldrin, and aldrin, in many ways the most effective, have given way to less persistent insecticides. Insecticides, in any case, are more persistent than weed killers, since by definition weed killers have to metamorphose to do their work. In reverse of the intellectual chemistry of the late 1940s, any country with capacity to make pest control products could now turn to the making of chemical weapons. This is suspected in several cases. In the 1960s both East Germany and Czechoslovakia made use of the same capacity to make LSD to help Western youth destroy itself. This kind of potential is the worst side effect of such a capability, now in the hands of perhaps forty to fifty nation-states.

36 Gregor Mendel, 1822–84; Charles Darwin, 1809–82. As far as is known, they did not meet or correspond, although one of Darwin's later works came close to Mendelism: *The Effects of Cross- and Self-Fertilisation in the Vegetable Kingdom* was published in 1876. No published work on Mendelism until W. Bateson, *Mendel's Principles of Heredity*, Cambridge, 1902, also Royal Society *Reports*, 1902–06.

37 Pigs known a generation ago are now forgotten: Large Black, Tamworth, Gloucester Old Spot. A human generation is potentially the same length as sixty porcine pregnancies and births; in human terms, 1500 years.

38 There are useful sheep crosses, half-breeds between Cheviot and the Border Leicester, that do not breed true and must be "renewed" in each generation; hybridizing sheep is another matter altogether and more recent.

39 Two scientists at Cambridge University, James Watson and Francis Crick, discovered that DNA was a double helix with two strands intertwined. Each strand has four different chemical bases—A, C, G, T. The bases may be arranged in any order, but links can only be made between successive pairs: A to T, G to C. In 1960–61 Crick and others postulated that DNA was mathematically organized so that "codes" actually specified the selection and assembly of amino acids that make up DNA. By 1970 this was proved. The codes were found to be in groups of three called "codons." A series of codons formed the sequence of orders to make a protein; each series of codons was, in effect, a gene.

Genetic engineers, who have now come out of the closet and are often hypercommercial, can be found in all sorts of places, usually linked to universities. By AD 2000 many claimed that a good geneticist could take a gene from almost any living tissue and insert it into almost any other living thing. There is the problem of rejection, which it is anticipated, will be overcome.

The most important factor in the improvement of crop yields and human food supplies since World War II is, in large part, attributable to genetic improvement as a result of selective breeding. Since fertilizer usage and pest control chemicals may have reached their limit, why not let genetics take the strain? It is entirely possible that geneticists could engineer a 1.5–2 percent compound improvement in crop yields without increasing chemical inputs. That is the good news. The bad news is the possibility of deformed animals—horrors like a man with a pig's brain, a pig with a tiger's motives, or a rat the size of an elephant. Fortunately, this kind of horror-breeding is more difficult than breeding new lettuces. See *The Double Helix*, Cambridge, 1968.

40 Soy is a crop that had to wait for technology. It needs special machinery for successful husbandry: harvesting is difficult, and drying was an insurmountable problem on a field basis before this century; the seeds require sophisticated extraction techniques or else too much of the original oil (typically 20 percent) is left in the meal or flour. Over 10,000 cultivars can be used in various latitudes, and the crop is grown from the Argentine to Ontario and from Indonesia to Manchuria. Seed is not produced with any success in Europe or Africa. The protein is very digestible, even by infants. As a garden crop, soy was, and is, the raw material of both *soy sauce* and *tofu*; each was, and is, made with the aid of a different benign fungus. Today there is a huge trade in beans, meal, and oil, amounting to over 80 million tons in all; world production of the primary bean is nearly 100 million tons. The crop is also grown for forage, hay, and silage; the beans remain the world's best hope for increased vegetable protein, and the crop as a whole is a soil improver and an excellent "entry" for maize. Yet in 1942 only 1 million tons of beans were harvested for the market, in the whole world.

41 Transferable technology does not include husbandry, which is an instinct, not an art, let alone a science.

42 But the Ethiopians have also reduced their forest area in this century from 50 percent of the country to 8 percent, with dire results. For all of the ninety years of this century, except six, Ethiopia has been ruled by Ethiopians, so it is not easy to blame Imperialism. The real cause is population increase.

43 Given goodwill, even transferable technique is not a problem. Provided the Third World accepts the gifts, the first is only too willing to give the poor nations transferable technology since it is so much cheaper than giving food, tractors, oil supplies, or whatever hardware is needed today.

44 There is no respectable demographer who can honestly produce a leveling off at less than 10–12 billion, twice today's population, with most of the increase in the Third World.

45 In private, Friends of the Earth admits that they campaign against nuclear energy because it is more emotive than the greenhouse effect. Someone ought to have the courage to be logical.

46 To clean up acid emission from Britain alone would cost a capital sum equal to one-half of one year's national income. Similar differing proportions exist throughout the industrialized world.

47 The use of CFCs is now diminishing; alternatives are in fashion.

48 The reason why men of goodwill are gloomy about the future of the Third World is a matter of arithmetic. It is entirely possible to construct a future carrying out the necessary capital works, dams, hydroelectric schemes, and so forth, that could turn Bangladesh into a stable entity with a sustainable future. It could cost up to $100 billion, or $1000 a head—not all that much money. To apply the same kind of treatment to every overcrowded Third World country, however, would cost several times the savings ratio of the entire First World for at least a decade. That kind of altruism is unlikely. On the other hand, if nothing is done except to keep people alive, the future is repetitious with the countries involved treading delicately from one disaster to another. There is another point. Years before any white man reached the Amazon highlands, the mouth of that river spewed chocolate- or coffee-colored water into the Atlantic. Perhaps erosion also existed elsewhere without any excessive population.

49 In addition to direct damage from increasing effluents, indirect damage is done by forest depletion. Seventy-nine percent of world forest area that existed in 1900 has been destroyed. Hence one reason for increased carbon.

50 No estimate has ever been made, but it is unlikely to be less than ten billion tons in this century, not properly recycled. More nitrate is wasted in Europe than used in Africa.

51 The virtue of the market economy, if it is allowed to function properly, is that it does not permit waste. In sulphur emissions, the moral is quite clear. In kilograms of sulphur emitted per $1000 of GNP, Japan is the lowest, at 1 kg, followed by Sweden (4), France and West Germany (5), the United States and the United Kingdom (7), and the "planned" economies: USSR (19), Romania (28), Hungary (31), East Germany (35), and Czechoslovakia (40). On the other hand, California air pollution is notorious and the United Kingdom dumps nearly a third of its man-made sewage (raw) into the sea, the highest proportion of any industrial country.

52 This much-to-be-desired future benefice will retreat if the anti-nuclear lobby combines with temporarily cheaper fossil fuels to discourage development.

53 Much more difficult than *glasnost* or *perestroika* is the cleaning up of Russian and Comecon rubbish; these are probably at several times Western European levels per unit of GNP. The difficulty is compounded by the fact that the Eastern peoples will have to be promised more food, more hardware, and more attractive consumer goods to keep them happy. This will make the task of Comecon industry, already the world's dirtiest, all the more difficult.

54 No one reading (or, indeed, writing) these words could fail to remember the awful unforeseen effects of trying to increase efficiency. Truly, "efficiency" has to be examined in the whole. For example, 95 percent–plus of all fuel used throughout history has been wasted. Less than 5 percent has produced heat, light, or power. Yet without the wasteful use of fuel, no culture could have lifted itself out of the hunter-gatherer stage. The future is a race between what is known and what is done.

55 Earth-friendly policies do not necessarily mean triumphalism of the hair shirt, rather the reverse. Properly managed tropical rain forests (less than 5 percent of the whole) produce from five to ten times as much desirable timber as that available from badly treated tracts. *Sustainable* forest management of any sort is a bonus for everyone—logging companies, the local community, and the world at large. Most "mining" methods also destroy the ability of the forest to recycle carbon dioxide (CO_2) and accelerate the *greenhouse effect*.

The cure is in the hands of the First World, not the Third. Countries that manage their forests properly—Australia, Malaysia, Belize—do not need help in financial terms. Countries that need bank assistance, coincidentally or otherwise, do not manage their forests at all well. Putting the two factors together would return an enormous yield for the First World in terms of reduced CO_2. How long will it take to put such an obvious policy into effect?

Bibliography

Many of the books cited here are in the author's possession; therefore the edition or the place of latest printing may not be that of the books as identified.

Acland, J. D., *East African Crops*, London, 1971

Albion, R. G., *Forests and Sea Power*, Cambridge, Mass., 1926

Alngren, B., *The Vikings*, London, 1968

Altschul, Siri von Reis, "Exploring the Herbarium," *Scientific American*, May 1977

Alvord, C. W., *The Mississippi Valley in British Politics*, Cleveland, 1917

Anderson, A., *An Historical and Chronological Deduction of the Origin of Commerce*, rev. ed., 4 vols., London, 1787–89

Anderson, Edgar, *Plants, Man and Life*, London, 1954

Anderson, R. C., *The Rigging of Ships in the Days of the Spritsail Topmast, 1600–1720*, Salem, 1927

Anderson, S., *The Sailing Ship*, New York, 1947

Andrews, C. M., *The Colonial Period of American History*, 4 vols., New Haven, 1938

Anstey, Roger, *The Atlantic Slave Trade and British Abolition 1760–1810*, London, 1975

Arnold, Edward, *Rural Economy and Country Life in the Medieval West*, London, 1965

Arnold, Sir Thomas, and Guillaume, Alfred, *The Legacy of Islam*, London, 1931

Atkinson, William C., *A History of Spain and Portugal*, London, 1960

Babcock, W. H., "Legendary Islands of the Atlantic: A Study in Medieval Geography," *American Geographical Research*, New York, 1922

Baker, J. N. L., *A History of Geographical Discovery and Exploration*, London, 1931

Barbour, Violet, *Capitalism in Amsterdam in the 17th Century*, Ann Arbor, 1963

Barrett, W., *The History and Antiquities of the City of Bristol*, Bristol, 1789

Bastin, J., *The British in West Sumatra 1685–1825*, Kuala Lumpur, 1965

Bearce, G. D., *British Attitudes Towards India 1784–1858*, Oxford, 1961

Beazley, C. R., "Prince Henry of Portugal and the African Crusade of the Fifteenth Century," *American Historical Review*, New York, 1910

Berlin, Isaiah, *Four Essays on Liberty*, London, 1969

Berlin, Isaiah, *Historical Inevitability*, London, 1953

Biddulph, J., *The Pirates of Malabar*, London, 1907

Birmingham, D., "The Regiment of Mina," *Transactions of the Historical Society of Ghana*, Lagos, 1971

Blegen, T. C., *The Kensington Rune Stone: New Light on an Old Riddle*, Minnesota Historical Society, 1968

Bloch, Marc, *Feudal Society*, London, 1961

Boswell, James, *The Life of Samuel Johnson*, 6 vols., ed. Augustine Birrell, London, 1904

Bougainville, L. A. de, *Voyage Autour du Monde*, Paris, 1771

Bourguignon d' Anville, J. B., *Nouvel Atlas de la Chine*, Amsterdam, 1737

Boxer, C. R., *The Dutch Seaborne Empire*, London, 1965

Bradford, E., *Christopher Columbus*, New York, 1973

Braudel, F., *The Mediterranean and the Mediterranean World in the Age of Philip II*, 2 vols., London, 1972–73

Brebner, J. B., *The Explorers of North America*, London, 1933

Broglie, Duc de, *The King's Secret: Being the Secret Correspondence of Louis XV with His Diplomatic Agents*, 2 vols., London, 1879

Broughan, Henry Peter, *An Inquiry into the Colonial Policy of the European Powers*, Edinburgh, 1803; New York, 1969

Bruce, J., *Annals of the East India Company*, London, 1810

Burke, Edmund, *Works*, 12 vols., London, 1808–13

Butzer, Karl W., *Early Hydraulic Civilisation in Egypt*, Chicago, 1976
Cambridge Economic History, Cambridge History of England

Campbell, John, *The Spanish Empire in America, by an English Merchant*, London, 1747

Campbell, W., *Formosa Under the Dutch*, London, 1903; New York, 1970

Caraci, G., "La Vinland Map," *Studi Medievali*, Spoleto, 1966

Carus Wilson, E. M., *The Merchant Adventurers of Bristol in the 15th Century*, Bristol, 1962

Carus Wilson, E. M., *Medieval Merchant Venturers*, London, 1954

Chambers, J. D., and Murgay, G. E., *The Agricultural Revolution*, London, 1966

Champion, Richard, *Considerations on the Present Situation of Great Britain and the United States*, London, 1784

Chang, Kwang-Chih, *The Archaeology of Ancient China*, New Haven, 1978

Childe, V. Gordon, *The Dawn of European Civilisation*, 6th ed., revised, London, 1973

Chittenden, F. J., *The Royal Horticultural Society Dictionary of Gardening*, 4 vols., Oxford, 1956

Cipolla, Carlo M. ed., *Fontana Economic History of Europe*, London, 1978

Cipolla, Carlo M., *Before the Industrial Revolution*, New York, 1976

Cipolla, Carlo M., *The Economic History of World Population*, London, 1976

Cipolla, Carlo M., *Public Health in the Medical Profession in the Renaissance*, Cambridge, 1976

Clapham, Sir John, *The Economic Development of France and Germany 1815–1914*, 4th ed., Cambridge, 1966

Clark, Colin, *Population Growth and Land Use*, London, 1967

Cohn, Norman, *The Pursuit of the Millennium*, Oxford, 1957

Cook, James, *Journals*, 3 vols., ed. J. C. Beaglehole, Cambridge, 1966

Cooke, Alistair, *America*, New York, 1973

Cox, Tench, *A View of the United States of America*, Philadelphia, 1794

Crane, Eva, *The Archaeology of Beekeeping*, London, 1983

Crosby, Alfred, *The Columbian Exchange*, Westport, 1972

Curtin, Philip D., *The Atlantic Slave Trade*, Madison, 1969

Dalrymple, A., *An Historical Collection of the Several Voyages and Discoveries in the South Pacific Ocean*, 2 vols., London, 1770–71; New York, 1967

Dampier, William, *A New Voyage Round the World*, 3 vols., London, 1697; New York, 1968

Dantzig, B., and Pridds, A. V., *A Short History of the Ports and Castles of Ghana*, 1971

Darlington, C. D., and Wylie, A. P., *Chromosome Atlas of Flowering Plants*, 2nd ed., London, 1955

Davis, David Brion, *The Problem of Slavery in Western Culture*, Ithaca, 1966

Davis, Ralph, *The Rise of the English Shipping Industry in the Seventeenth and Eighteenth Centuries*, London, 1962; New York, 1963

Deanc, Phyllis, and Cole, W. A., *British Economic Growth 1688–1959*, Cambridge, 1967

Deerr, N., *The History of Sugar*, Oxford, 1950

Defoe, Daniel, *Two Great Questions Considered*, London, 1700

Dickey, I. M., *Christopher Columbus and His Monument Columbia, Being a Concordance of Choice Tributes to the Great Genoese*, Chicago and New York, 1891

Dodge, Ernest S., *New England and the South Seas*, Cambridge, Mass., 1965

Dols, Michael, *The Black Death in the Middle East*, Princeton, 1977

Dow, A., *The History of Hindostan*, 3 vols., London, 1768–72

Drummond, J. C., *The Englishman's Food*, London, 1957

Duby, Georges, *The Age of the Cathedrals: Art and Society, 980–1420*, Chicago, 1980

Dufferin, Lord, *Letters from High Latitudes*, London, 1857

Dunn, William Edward, *Spanish and French Rivalry in the Gulf Region of the United States, 1678–1702*, Austin, Texas, 1917

Edwards, Bryan, *History of the West Indies*, 3 vols., London, 1794

Encyclopaedia Britannica (editions since the 3rd of 1797–1801), London

Enterline, J. R., *Viking America*, New York, 1972

Ephson, J. S., *Ancient Forts and Castles of the Gold Coast*, Accra, 1970

Ernle, Lord (Rowland Prothero), *English Farming, Past and Present*, 4th ed., London, 1927

Fanfani, A., *The Vinland Map and the New Controversy over the Discovery of America*, New York, 1965

Fernandez Armesto, F., *Columbus and the Conquest of the Impossible*, London, 1974

Ferwerda, F. P., and Wit, F., eds., *Outlines of Perennial Crop Breeding in the Tropics*, Wageningen, 1969

Fisher, H. A. L., *A History of Europe*, London, 1936

Fortescue, J. W., *History of the British Army*, 13 vols., London, 1899–1930; New York, 1970

Frankel, O. H., and Hawkes, J. G., eds., *Crop Genetic Resources for Today and Tomorrow*, Cambridge, 1975

Franklin, Benjamin, *Writings*, 10 vols., ed. A. N. Smyth, New York, 1907

Free, J. B., *Insect Pollination of Crops*, London, 1970

Freyre, Gilberto, *The Masters and the Slaves*, New York, 1970

Freyre, Gilberto, *The Portuguese and the Tropics*, Lisbon, 1961

Furnivall, J. S., *Netherlands India: A Study of Plural Economy*, Cambridge, 1944

Furnivall, J. S., *An Introduction to the History of Netherlands India*, London, 1934

Galbraith, V. H., *Domesday Book—Its Place in Administrative History*, Oxford, 1974

Gibbon, Edward, *The History of the Decline and Fall of the Roman Empire*, London, 1969

Gierset, K., *History of Iceland*, New York, 1924

Gillespie, Leonard, *Observations on the Diseases Which Prevailed on Board a Part of His Majesty's Squadron off the Leeward Island Station Between November 1794 and April 1796*, London, 1800

Gipson, L. H., *The British Empire Before the American Revolution*, vol. X, *The Triumphant Empire: Thunder-clouds Gather in the West, 1763–1768*, New York, 1961

Gipson, L. H., *The Coming of the Revolution, 1763–1775*, New York, 1954

Gipson, L. H., *The Great War for the Empire; vol. VII, The Victorious Years, 1758–1780*, New York, 1949

Glamann, K., *Dutch Asiatic Trade 1620–1740*, Copenhagen, 1958

Glass, D. V., and Eversley, D. E. C., eds., *Population in History: Essays in Historical Demography*, London, 1965

Goodrich, A., *A History of the Character and Achievements of the So-Called Christopher Columbus*, New York, 1874

Gottfried, Robert S., *The Black Death, Natural and Human Disaster in Medieval Europe*, London, 1983

Grant, Charles, *Observations on the State of Society Among the Asiatic Subjects of Great Britain . . .*, London, 1797

Gray, L. C., *The History of Agriculture in the Southern States to 1860*, Washington, DC, 1933

Greenberg, M., *British Trade and the Opening of China*, Cambridge, 1951

Greene, L., *The Negro in Colonial New England 1620–1776*, New York, 1942

Hakluyt, R., *The English Voyages 1494–1600*, London, 1964

Hall, D. G. E., *History of South-East Asia*, London, 1964

Hamilton, E. J., *Money, Prices and Wages in Valencia, Aragon and Navarra 1351–1500*, Cambridge, Mass., 1936

Hamilton, E. J., *American Treasure and Price Revolution in Spain*, Cambridge, Mass., 1934

Hardey, Dorothy, *Made in England*, London, 1987

Hardey, W., *A Checklist of Economic Plants in Australia*, Canberra, 1979

Hardiman, J., *History of Galway*, Galway, 1926

Harlan, J. R., de Wet, J. M. J., and Stemler, A. B. L., eds., *Origins of African Plant Domestication*, The Hague, 1976

Harler, *The Culture and Marketing of Tea*, Oxford, 1955

Harlow, V. T., *The Founding of the Second British Empire*, 2 vols., London, 1952; New York, 1964

Harper, L. A., *The English Navigation Laws*, New York, 1939

Harrison, Gordon, *Mosquitoes, Malaria and War: A History of the Hostilities Since 1880*, New York, 1976

Harrisse, H., *The Discovery of North America*, Paris and London, 1882

Harvard Bibliography of American History

Haskins, C. H., *The Normans in European History*, Boston and New York, 1915

Hawkesworth, J., *Voyages in the Southern Hemisphere*, 3 vols., London, 1773

Herklots, G. A. C., *Vegetables in South-East Asia*, Hong Kong, 1972

Hermannsson, H., *The Northmen in America*, New York, 1909

Hilton, R. H., *The Decline of Serfdom in Medieval England*, London, 1969

Historical Statistics of the US, Washington, DC, 1960

Hobsbawm, E. J., *Industry and Empire*, London and New York, 1968

Holand, H. R., *Explorations in America Before Columbus*, New York, 1956

Hollingsworth, T. H., *Historical Demography*, London, 1969

Holroyd, John Baker, 1st Earl of Sheffield, *Observations on the Commerce of the American States*, London, 1783

Hourani, G. F., *Arab Seafaring in the Indian Ocean in Ancient and Early Medieval Times*, Princeton, 1951

Howard, E., *Genoa: History and Art in an Old Seaport*, Genoa, 1971

Howard, Michael, "Power at Sea," *Adelphi Papers*, no. 124, London, 1976

Howard, Michael, *War in European History*, Oxford, 1975

Huffnagel, H. P., *Agriculture in Ethiopia*, Rome, 1961

Huntington, Ellsworth, *Civilisation and Climate*, New Haven, 1924

Hutchinson, Sir Joseph, ed., *Evolutionary Studies in World Crops*, Cambridge, 1974

Irvine, F. R., *West African Agriculture*, vol. 2, *West African Crops*, 3rd ed., London, 1969

Irving, W., *A History of the Life and Voyages of Christopher Columbus*, London, 1828

Jackson, Melvin H., *Salt, Sugar and Slaves: The Dutch in the Caribbean*, James Ford Bell Lectures, no. 2, 1965

Jacob, A., and Von Uexkull, H., *Fertiliser Use: Nutrition and Manuring of Tropical Crops*, 3rd ed., Hanover, 1963

Jenks, Leland, *Our Cuban Colony: A Study in Sugar*, New York, 1928

Johnson, W., *Genoa the Superb: The City of Columbus*, London, 1892

Jones, G., *A History of the Vikings*, New York, 1968

Keary, C. F., *The Vikings in Western Christendom*, London, 1891

Kershaw, Ian, "The Great Famine and Agrarian Crisis in England," in *Peasants, Knights and Heretics*, ed. R. H. Milton, Cambridge, 1976

Klerck, E. S. de, *History of the Netherlands East Indies*, 2 vols., Rotterdam, 1938

Knott, J. E., and Deanon, J. R., *Vegetable Production in South-East Asia*, Laguna, 1967

Labaree, L. W., *Royal Government in America: A Study of the British Colonial System Before 1783*, New Haven, 1930

Lacour-Gayet, Robert, *A Concise History of Australia*, London, 1976

Lambert, S. M., *The Depopulation of the Pacific Races*, Honolulu, 1934

Las Casas, Bartolomé, *Historia de las Indias*, Madrid, 1875

Lawrence, A. W., *Fortified Trade-Posts*, London, 1969

Leakey, C. L. A., and Wills, J. B., eds., *Food Crops of the Lowland Tropics*, Oxford, 1977

Lee, J., *Colonial Government and Good Government: A Study of the Ideas Expressed by the British Official Classes in Planning Decolonisation, 1939–1964*, Oxford, 1967

Ligon, R., *A True and Exact History of the Island of Barbados*, London, 1657; New York, 1970

Lloyd, C., and Coulter, J. S. L., *Medicine and the Navy*, 4 vols., London, 1961

Lynch, J., *Spanish Colonial Administration: The Intendant System in the Rio de la Plata*, London, 1958

Lynch, John, *The Spanish American Revolutions*, London, 1973

MacNutt, W. S., *The Atlantic Provinces: The Emergence of Colonial Society*, Oxford, 1965

McEvedy, Colin, and Jones, Richard, *Atlas of World Population History*, London, 1985

Madariaga, S. de, *Christopher Columbus*, London and New York, 1940

Maheshwari, P., and Singh, U., *Dictionary of Economic Plants in India*, New Delhi, 1965

Major, H. R., *The Life of Prince Henry of Portugal, Surnamed the Navigator, and Its Results*, London, 1868

Markham, C. R., *Life of Columbus*, London, 1892

Marwick, Arthur, *Britain in the Century of Total War*, London, 1968

Masefield, John, ed., *Dampier's Voyages*, London, 1906

Massal, R., and Barrau, J., *Food Plants of the South Sea Islands*, New Caledonia, South Pacific Commission, 1956

Matheson, J. K., and Bovill, E. W., *East African Agriculture*, London, 1950

Medawar, P. B., *The Hope of Progress*, London, 1974

Merrill, E. D., *Plant Life in the Pacific World*, New York, 1945

Milburn, W., *Oriental Commerce: Containing a Geographical Description of the Principal Places in the East Indies . . . with Their Produce, Manufactures and Trade . . .* , 2 vols., London, 1813

Mitchell, B. R., *International Historical Statistics: Asia and Africa*, Cambridge, 1982

Mitchell, B. R., *European Historical Statistics 1750–1970*, London, 1975

Mitchell, B. R., with Deane, Phyllis, *Abstract of British Historical Statistics*, Cambridge, 1962

Morison, Samuel Eliot, *The European Discovery of America: The Northern Voyages*, New York, 1971

Morison, Samuel Eliot, *Christopher Columbus, Mariner*, London, 1956; Boston, 1955

Morison, Samuel Eliot, *Admiral of the Ocean Sea: A Life of Christopher Columbus*, Boston, 1949

Morse, H. B., *The Chronicles of the East India Company Trading in China, 1635–1834*, Oxford, 1926; New York, 1965

Musmano, M. A., *Columbus Was First*, New York, 1968

Namier, Sir Lewis, *Crossroads of Power*, London, 1962

Nicolson, Harold, *The Congress of Vienna*, London, 1946

Norwood, Richard, *The Seaman's Practice, Containing a Fundamental Problem in Navigation, Experimentally Verified, viz: Touching the Compass of the Earth and Sea, and the Quantity of a Degree in our English Measure, Also to Keep a Reckoning at Sea for All Sailing, etc. etc.*, London, 1637

Nunn, G. E., *The Geographical Conceptions of Columbus*, New York, 1834

Ochee, J. J., Soule, M. J., Dijkman, M. J., and Wehlburg, C., *Tropical and Subtropical Agriculture*, New York, 1961

Oleson, T. J., *Early Voyages and Northern Approaches*, Toronto, 1964

Oman, Sir C., *A History of the Art of War in the Middle Ages*, London, 1924

Origo, Iris, *The Merchant of Prato*, London, 1957

Orwin, C. S., *The Open Fields*, Oxford, 1967

Oxford History of Technology

Parry, J. H., *The Discovery of South America*, New York, 1979

Parry, J. H., *Trade and Dominion*, London, 1971

Parry, J. H., *The Spanish Seaborne Empire*, London, 1966

Parry, J. H., *The Age of Reconnaissance*, London, 1963

Parry, J. H., *Spices: Their Morphology, Histology and Chemistry*, New York, 1962

Pendle, George, *A History of Latin America*, London, 1983

Philips, C. H., *The East India Company 1784–1834*, Manchester, 1940

Plato, *The Republic*

Plumb, J. H., *Man Versus Society in Eighteenth Century England*, London, 1969

Pohl, F. J., *Atlantic Crossing Before Columbus*, New York, 1919

Pole, J. R., *Political Representation in England and the Origins of the American Republic*, London, 1966

Postlethwayt, Malachy, *The Universal Dictionary of Trade*, London, 1751

Price, A. Grenfell, *The Western Invasion of the Pacific and Its Continents*, Oxford, 1963

Purseglove, J. W., *Tropical Crops: Monocotyledons*, London, 1972

Purseglove, J. W., *Tropical Crops: Dicotyledons*, London, 1968

Purseglove, J. W., Brown, E. G., Green, C. L., and Robbins, S. R. J., *Spices*, 2 vols., London, 1981

Read, Herbert, *Anarchy and Order: Essays in Politics*, London, 1954

Rostow, Walt, ed., *The Economics of "Take Off" into Self-Sustained Growth*, Washington, DC, 1963

Rousseau, Jean-Jacques, *A Discourse on the Origin of Inequality*, London, 1952

Russell, E. John, *The World of the Soil*, London, 1961

Sadler, D. H., "Introduction", *Man Is Not Lost: A Record of 200 Years of Astronomical Navigation with the Nautical Almanac, 1767–1967*, London, 1968

Salaman, R., *The History and Social Influence of the Potato*, Cambridge, 1949

Sauer, C. O., *Agricultural Origins and Dispersals*, New York, 1952

Sauvy, Alfred, *General Theory of Population*, London, 1969

Sawyer, P. A., *The Age of Vikings*, London, 1962

Schery, R. W., *Plants and Man*, 2nd ed., Englewood Cliffs, 1972

Scientific American: Food and Agriculture, September, 1976

Sherborne, J. W., *The Port of Bristol in the Middle Ages*, London, 1965

Shetelig, H., *The Viking Ships*, Oslo, 1951

Simpson, J., *Everyday Life in the Viking Age*, New York, 1967

Sinclair, Keith, *A History of New Zealand*, London, 1969

Smith, Adam, *Wealth of Nations*, ed. E. Cannan, London, 1904

Steel, David, *Elements and Practice of Naval Architecture*, 2 vols., London, 1805

Steel, David, *Elements and Practice of Rigging and Seamanship*, 2 vols., London, 1794

Stefansson, V., *Ultima Tule*, London and New York, 1940

Tacitus, *Histories*, trans. Kenneth Wellesley, London, 1964

Tawney, R. H., *Religion and the Rise of Capitalism*, London, 1969

Thacher, J. B., *Christopher Columbus: His Life, His Work, His Remains*, New York, 1903

Thomas, Hugh, *An Unfinished History of the World*, London, 1979

Thomas, Keith, *Man and the Natural World*, New York, 1983

Thompson, E. A., *The Early Germans*, Oxford, 1965

Thompson, E. P., *The Making of the English Working Class*, London, 1965

Thordarson, M., *The Vinland Voyages*, New York, 1930

Thorndike, L., *A History of Magic and Experimental Science*, New York, 1934

Thrupp, Sylvia L., *The Merchant Class of Medieval London*, Chicago, 1948

Tornoe, J. K., *Norsemen Before Columbus*, London, 1695

Trevelyan, G. M., *English Social History*, London, 1942

Tucker, Josiah, *The True Interest of Britain, Set Forth in Regard to the Colonies: And the Only Means of Living in Peace and Harmony with Them*, London, 1774

Tucker, Josiah, *The Case of Going to War for the Sake of Procuring, Enlarging or Securing of Trade*, London, 1763

United Nations, Department of Economics and Social Affairs, Statistical Office, *Demographic Yearbook*, London, annually since 1949

Verger, Pierre, *Flux et Reflux de la Traite des Nègres Entre le Golfe de Benin et Bahia de Todos os Santos*, Paris, 1968

Villiers, Alan, *Captain Cook, the Seaman's Seaman*, London, 1967; New York, 1970

Wadia, R. A., *The Bombay Dockyard and the Wadia Master-Builders*, Bombay, 1957

Walpole, Horace, *Memoirs of the Reign of King George the Third*, London, 1845

Walter, R., *A Voyage Round the World*, London, 1748

Washington, George, *Writings*, 39 vols., ed. John C. Fitzpatrick, Washington, DC, 1931–44

Weber, Max, *The Protestant Ethic and the Spirit of Capitalism*, London, 1930

Weckman, L., "The Alexandrine Bulls of 1493: Pseudo-Asiatic Documents," in F. Chiappelli, *First Images of America*, Los Angeles, 1976

Westropp, T. J., "Brazil and the Legendary Islands of the Atlantic," *Proceedings of the Royal Irish Academy*, Dublin, 1912

White, Lynn, Jr., *Medieval Technology and Social Change*, Oxford, 1962

Williams, E. T., *A Short History of China*, New York, 1928

Williams, Glyndwr, *The British Search for the Northwest Passage in the Eighteenth Century*, London, 1962; New York, 1967

Woot-Tsuen, W. L., and Flores, M., "Food Composition Table for Use in Latin America," Bethesda: INCAP-INNND, 1961

World Bank (International Bank for Reconstruction and Development), *World Bank Atlas*, annually since 1966, London

Worldwatch Institute, *State of the World, 1984, 1985, 1986, 1987*, New York and London

Index

Printed in the United States
by Baker & Taylor Publisher Services